A DISTANT HEART

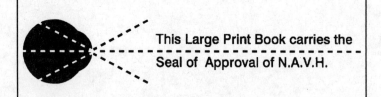

This Large Print Book carries the
Seal of Approval of N.A.V.H.

A DISTANT HEART

SONALI DEV

THORNDIKE PRESS
A part of Gale, a Cengage Company

Farmington Hills, Mich • San Francisco • New York • Waterville, Maine
Meriden, Conn • Mason, Ohio • Chicago

Copyright © 2018 by Sonali Dev.
Thorndike Press, a part of Gale, a Cengage Company.

Thorndike Press® Large Print Core.
The text of this Large Print edition is unabridged.
Other aspects of the book may vary from the original edition.
Set in 16 pt. Plantin.

LIBRARY OF CONGRESS CIP DATA ON FILE.
CATALOGUING IN PUBLICATION FOR THIS BOOK
IS AVAILABLE FROM THE LIBRARY OF CONGRESS

ISBN-13: 978-1-4328-5013-5 (hardcover)

Published in 2018 by arrangement with Kensington Books, an imprint of Kensington Publishing Corp.

Printed in the United States of America
1 2 3 4 5 6 7 22 21 20 19 18

*For Rupali, because friendship
is the schoolhouse of love.
And you are my entire education.*

ACKNOWLEDGMENTS

Kimi and Rahul's story was an utter joy to write. From the moment they sprang up in my mind, these two knew exactly who they were and what they wanted to do (a bit like my children, so at least I knew how to handle them), and I feel fortunate to have been allowed along for the ride (also how I sometimes feel about my children).

This story is set in India, in Mumbai's suburb of Bandra, where I spent a large part of my own childhood. Bandra carries within its endlessly open heart a microcosm of the spirit of the rest of the country — from barely functional slums to wildly ostentatious mansions, from the oldest traditions to progressive new ideologies and everything in between. Bandra was where I made my first friendships and dreamed my first dreams, and I am eternally grateful to its shaded lanes and rocky beaches for affording me such a vibrant canvas first for my life and now for my story.

I am also eternally grateful to my always generous editor, Martin Biro, for the gift of his excitement when I told him that this one would not be set in America. And to my agent, Claudia Cross; my publicist, Vida Engstrand; and everyone at Kensington Publishing for their boundless enthusiasm. Embarrassing though it is to admit, my own enthusiasm often needs theirs to rely on and they never fail me.

As always, writing this story was only possible because of the veritable caravan of guiding stars who are my critique partners and beta readers. Without them, this story would only make sense in my head and not on the page. So, thank you, Tamar Bihari, Robin Kuss, Joanna Shupe, Heather Marshall, Clara Kensie, India Powers, Savannah Reynard, Nishaad Navkal, and Kalpana Thatte.

Thanks also to Rutvika, my gorgeous and brilliant niece, and Sr. Inspector Ravindra Bhide for jointly helping me stay in the vicinity of authenticity in terms of the Mumbai police force. And to my dear friend Pallavi Divekar for helping me hunt down the various legal nuances of organ donation in India.

Lastly, to the people who do not get to

shut the book and walk away when the story ends — Manoj, Mihir, Annika, Mamma, Papa, and Aie — thank you for keeping me grounded and for letting me fly. And to you, dear readers, thank you for flying off with me on another adventure.

1

Rahul
Present day
Kimi had summoned Rahul to The Mansion and naturally he had come, because relationships, like people, were creatures of habit. He stood at one end of the massive gilded room and watched Kimi pace the silk-carpet-covered marble. The glow of the huge crystal chandelier picked out every nuance of her restlessness. If he didn't know better he'd say she looked like an imprisoned princess. But she wasn't. Not anymore.

Earlier that morning she had sent him a text message saying: *We need to talk.*

Those four words had never in the history of humankind ever led to anything good. Nonetheless, it had been two months since Kimi had shut him out after that bastard gangster, Asif Khan, attacked her in broad daylight on the streets of Mumbai, a city

Rahul was tasked with keeping safe. So roughly half an hour after her text had arrived, here he was.

The Mansion's main living room never failed to make him feel like he had wandered up to the forbidden first-class deck on the *Titanic*. For all the time Kimi and he had spent in her home, they had barely ever been together in this royal-court-like living room. But today, Kimi had greeted him with nothing more than an uncharacteristically curt nod, led him here, and then wordlessly proceeded to pace. Watching her struggle with what she wanted to say made an all-too-familiar heaviness drag at Rahul's limbs, the kind that made him restless to move while also digging him into place. Not being able to form words out of feelings was his special gift, not hers.

Kimi and Rahul had been friends since he was sixteen years old — a friendship that had spanned fourteen years. For most of those years their friendship had been cloistered within these walls, where all that they shared had been safe, where they had been only who they were to each other. Over the past two years, their friendship had been let out into the world where it had never stood a chance.

Suddenly, she stopped and spun around

to face him. Her ever-present ponytail whipped around her neck and spilled across her shoulder. With a flip of her head she flung it all back in place. Her face was, as always, all eyes. He had missed her eyes. Missed all she was able to say with them. Now, every golden-brown fleck trapped her struggle to get the words out.

"Just tell me what the bastard did to you, Kimi," he pushed, finally abandoning the subtlety that had earned him his reputation for having some of the best interrogation skills in the Mumbai police force. His legendary patience was also suddenly nowhere in sight. The Asif Khan case had consumed him for two years, and he hated that the gangster had somehow found a way to drag Kimi into his cesspool of crime. The man's evil wasn't just inexhaustible but downright immortal in its power.

Two months ago, Rahul had finally caught up with the bastard and emptied five bullets into him. But instead of dying, the gangster had slipped into a coma with all the answers Rahul needed trapped inside his seemingly indestructible brain, leaving Rahul, and all the people Khan had wreaked havoc on, holding their breath until he woke up.

"Good is strong," his father had loved to say. But ten years in this job and Rahul knew evil possessed all the real strength. Good just had to keep on faking it to stay in the fight.

"Is the case all you care about?" she asked, and the sadness in her tone multiplied the weight dragging at Rahul's limbs many times over. "Never mind," she said before he could answer, letting him off the hook and reaching for the anger she had embraced so determinedly these past few months.

Over the years, Rahul had marveled at how Kimi kept herself from anger. From real anger. Because whether she was throwing her playful bluster at him to push his boundaries, or trying to hide from him all the frustration of wanting impossible things, she never let the anger consume her. Not the way he did.

Even now when she had every reason to be furious with him, it was taking her some effort — her shoulders squared, her jaw tight, the deliberate effort reminding him of the way she had once tried to walk in heels too high — and that made him feel at once too big and too small.

The crystalline brown of her eyes darkened with the words she was about to say and Rahul braced himself. "I'm going to give you what you want. I'll tell you what happened with Asif Khan. But after that you have to promise that you'll leave me alone." She took a breath, steadied her voice. "Forever. I never want to see you again, Rahul."

It was the ninth time in the span of their friendship that Kimi had said those words to him.

Yes, he kept count. He kept count of everything.

Four surgeries, one hundred and eight hospitalizations, twenty-six transfusions, seven times that the doctors had asked her family to say their good-byes. And nine "I never want to see you agains."

He gave her his disbelieving look. Because he couldn't let her see how much he hated when she said those words. When he believed them for those first few seconds.

"I mean it this time, Rahul," she said with her jaw set, but then the impact of her declaration gathered in a sheen across her eyes. He was about to reach for her, but she caught the hesitation in his fingers and he stopped.

The rush of longing in her gaze lasted the barest second before she turned it back into a glare. Her anger regained steam as she squeezed her eyes shut and stemmed the tears before they fell. She backed away from him without waiting for him to respond. She knew him too well for that.

"Let's do this in Papa's office. He's waiting for us." She headed up the dramatically sweeping marble staircase that still felt alien beneath Rahul's feet even though he'd stopped using the servants' stairs years ago. "I want Papa to be there for this."

Kirit Patil greeted them without leaving his deep wing chair in his dark-paneled, high-ceilinged library office. The wall of windows behind him framed an orange morning sky over a blue-gray ocean. A backdrop befitting the longest serving home minister of Maharashtra state, and one of Bollywood's greatest erstwhile superstars. But Rahul's mentor no longer looked anything like the larger-than-life hero who had saved Rahul from every roadblock and land mine life had thrown in his path. He looked defeated. After all these years, they were just two men equalized by their inability to protect the girl who tied them together.

Kimi walked to the windows and stared out at the ocean across the building-covered hill that The Mansion was perched on top of. Rahul tried not to think about how a reckless trip down to that very strip of beach with her had changed the course of his life. Tried not to think of how well she wore the

16

calm she'd always known how to pull on for the benefit of everyone around her. More than anything else, he had wanted her to learn how to pull it on for her own benefit. And now here it was.

She rubbed the transplant scar that ran down her chest under the intricately embroidered silk of her *kurta* and threw him a glance that caught the flash of all they had shared in his eyes before he looked away.

Kirit pointed to the chair next to him, but Rahul couldn't sit. It had nothing to do with the fact that he never sat in the minister's presence. He was too wound up to sit down.

"This won't take long," Kimi said, her entire focus back on the ocean. "Two months ago, I was working on a story and waiting outside Mithibai College to speak with students about a starlet's private pictures that her jerk boyfriend had leaked. I noticed the SUV that had been following me around for a few days." She threw Rahul a warning glance and he swallowed his interruption. "Papa already had two bodyguards tailing me everywhere."

She didn't bring up the fact that she had come to Rahul and begged him to convince Kirit to call off the bodyguards and Rahul had refused to get involved.

Kirit opened his mouth to say something,

but then he too thought the better of it and slumped back in his chair.

Kimi hesitated, then squared her shoulders. "I walked right up to the SUV to ask why they were following me."

Rahul groaned. "What the hell, Kimi?"

"I know it was stupid!" she snapped. "I shouldn't have done it. I know that. But I had bodyguards with me. I thought I was safe." Her voice went quiet again. "I just wanted to scare them off. They were making me feel trapped."

He shut up after that and let her finish.

"When I saw Asif Khan . . ." She swallowed and Rahul felt all her sickness at saying that name turn into rage right in the pit of his stomach. "I knew I had made a mistake. I tried to get away, but he reached out of the SUV window and grabbed my shirt. Before I knew what was happening one of his men had a gun to my side." An eon passed before she spoke again, her voice dipping to a whisper. "He ripped open my blouse."

Rahul didn't move. If he moved, he'd break something. And this was hard enough for her without him losing it.

She cleared her throat and strengthened her voice. "He wanted to look at my scar." She touched her chest, tracing her scar, and finally met Rahul's eyes again. "He knew about my transplant. He wanted to know where my heart had come from."

That was the last thing Rahul had expected her to say. Why on earth would Asif know about her transplant?

Before he could ask, she turned to her father, then back to Rahul. "Papa won't tell me who my donor was. Do you know anything about it?"

Kirit stood, cutting her off from view for a second before she stepped around him. "You have to stop this nonsense, Kimi *beta*, please. The man is a sociopath. He messes around with people's heads. It was a confidential donor. We signed papers agreeing to let the donor be anonymous. It's wrong to break that confidence, not to mention illegal. You're letting a madman get inside your head."

How had Rahul never asked about Kimi's donor? How had he never wanted to know who had given her the ultimate gift?

Maybe because when you found out that your best friend had a new lease on life, yanking apart the jaws of the gift horse to stare into its mouth wasn't your first instinct. Apparently not his tenth or twentieth instinct either. Plus, she was right, the bloody case had completely consumed him.

Even now, two years after her surgery, when Kimi had refused to speak with him for weeks, he had been too absorbed in the case, and he had convinced himself that her silence was an extension of the deep freeze their friendship had descended into since her transplant.

Kimi looked so disappointed with her father, Rahul didn't know how he stood it. "It's not just my head the madman has messed with, Papa. He tracked me down in broad daylight. He's killed hundreds of people including Rahul's friend Jen Joshi."

Rahul didn't like the way she made the word *friend* sound like an accusation, but then there was nothing about this conversation that he did like. "Can you come into the station and make a statement?" Of all the things he wanted to say to her, of course he said the least important one. And the one that would make her the angriest.

She looked up at the ceiling and shook her head. "I should have known DCP 'Stonewall' Savant would only act so interested because the precious love of his life is involved here."

"Jen was not the love of my life." Could they step back from this bull for one moment? When the hell had Kimi learned to derail every single conversation he tried to have with her? No matter what happened between them, they had always been able to talk to each other.

Her eyes dimmed with hurt but her stance remained combative, hand on hip, jaw raised. "I was talking about your job, not about Jen. But thank you for that."

He threw a glance at Kirit. His eyes were squeezed shut in defeat. Rahul hated doing this in front of her father.

His silence only made the anger in her eyes heat up, but then she pulled on that calm once again as though reminding herself that she was wasting her time. "Listen, Rahul, I've already told you all I know. After that the bastard pushed me into the ground and drove away. That's all the statement I can give you. And no, I didn't call you here to ask for your help. I didn't want any loose ends." She gave her father a quick hug. "Bye, Papa." Then swept past Rahul and out of the room.

Rahul followed her into the empty corridor, pulling the door shut behind him. "Kimi."

She was about to take the stairs, but she turned around and faced him. "Don't make this harder, Rahul. You have Asif in a coma. You have the answers you wanted from me. We're done. I know you didn't believe me

21

before, but this isn't like all the other times. I'm not that girl anymore. This time I mean it."

Once again she turned away, tried to walk away. But then she was looking at him again, every familiar brown fleck in those too-brave eyes of hers focused on him. "This was what you wanted." He did. "And you were right, we don't work." They didn't. Not the way she wanted them to. "I need this. I need to get away from you, from everything. Just let me go."

There were so many things he wanted to say, but there was no expectation in her words. This wasn't her riling him up for a reaction. This was her leaving.

She ran down the stairs without a backward glance, yanked the door open, and then she was gone from sight. The ornately carved door slid shut behind her, the subtle click loud in the silent house. Rahul couldn't remember the last time the caged-animal feeling had been so crazed inside him. It had been the bane of his teenage years and now it squeezed outward against his rib cage.

"Let her go, son," Kirit said behind him.

That's exactly what he intended to do. But not while that monster was still alive and his men were running around Mumbai where they could hurt her.

2

Kimi
Present day

Freedom was a beautiful thing! Mumbai in all its grimy, gray, pre-monsoon glory flew past Kimi as her auto-rickshaw sped between cars and pedestrians with the zeal of a bastard child born of a Diwali rocket and an immortal god. She almost asked the driver to slow down, but with the wind whipping her ponytail and the driver's mop of curls in a joint symphony she felt as recklessly brave as the whirring vehicle racing along on its three wheels.

Emblazoned across the dashboard of the rickshaw was the goddess Durga dancing on the corpse of a demon like the evil-hunting badass she was. Bowing to her was Bollywood's favorite superhero, Krish, with his muscles bulging like fat rubber balls and his hair coiffed high. In a perfect background score to her life's drama, the techno-beat-laden remix of an old Bollywood number drowned out the cacophony of horns the driver left in his wake.

The combination was delicious and exactly worthy of what she had just done. What she was about to do.

Freedom!

You know who else was badass? Kimaya Kirit Patil, that's who.

There had been one hundred and twelve instances over twelve years when each breath had been a fight and her limbs had turned to mist. She had fought. Not like a warrior, because that would involve the use of said limbs, but like someone drowning, where all you could do is keep the water out of your nose, so it wouldn't keep the air from your lungs. Breathe out. Breathe out. She had followed those breaths. Grabbed on to those thin wisps of air like lifelines and made herself live one grip at a time.

Then the cure she had waited twelve years for in a sterile room had come. A heart had become available. Surely that meant something. Someone had died, after all, so she might live. Someone with the exact kind of blood and plasma that would let a foreign heart beat within her chest with the confidence of an indigene. Surely that meant she could now have what she never thought she would — all that she had gazed upon from the windows of her room, sealed tight with every technology known to man, so no germ, no pathogen would dare venture into her world, let alone an entire human being. Except Rahul — he had ventured. And then gone on venturing until he was all the way inside.

He'd helped her understand calculus and the nuanced stories of Premchand. He had known how atoms split, why Europe went to war twice within half a century, and the why and when of each invention that transformed the history of civilization. He had touched her, despite promises he'd made. Because it was exactly what she had needed. His gloved hand in hers. He had given her anything she had asked for when everyone else had been too afraid. And she had known that if she lived, if her parents got what they had sealed her in a room twelve years for — a daughter who lived — she would spend the rest of that life taking care of him. The way he had taken care of her.

Except she hadn't considered the most important part of her plan: him. She had returned from Hong Kong with her new heart and he had looked at her with those dark-tar eyes turned even darker by all that emotion when she ran to him. "You're running," he had said, as usual choosing the least words to say the most.

"Yes," she had said, knowing exactly why every single hard-won breath had been worth it. But then she had told him her grand plan: the two of them living happily ever after.

As always she had asked him for what she wanted. What she hadn't for one moment considered that he didn't also want.

He had thanked her for the offer to love him forever, and passed on it.

The person who had kept her from being alone when she was locked up in a room had finally shown her what loneliness was when he walked away from her, leaving her alone in the crowded world she had craved for so long.

No one had the right to 'that kind of power.

She leaned back into the overstuffed vinyl seat of the speeding auto-rickshaw feeling awfully light.

It only made sense that losing a part of yourself would bring lightness.

No. She wasn't doing that. She was not going all morose and doing the Tragic Princess shit anymore. That wasn't her. No matter how people saw her, that was not her. Not anymore.

Actually, it had never been her. Why the hell was she letting herself go down that path now?

She was past the Rahul-induced sadness. Done with it. He'd made his intentions clear. They were no longer — well, they just weren't anymore. Nothing, anything, they just weren't.

Plato would ask if the fact that they weren't anymore meant they had never been. Or was it Aristotle? You know who would know? The one person who she could not, would not, call for a fact check. This wasn't a Tragic Princess thought, but here it was anyway: She had to stop thinking of life in terms of thoughts she saved up for Rahul like seashells collected on a walk along the beach.

To cut herself some slack, it wasn't easy. For ten years (fourteen, really, but that made her sound *really* pathetic, and she was cutting the slack so she allowed herself some delusion) . . . for ten years she had collected everything that happened in her head in neat little lists to share with her best friend. Her only friend, as he loved to remind her, the way only he could, without a whit of pride.

Once you're out in the world, everyone's going to want to be your friend, Kimi.

28

Who said those things to you if they didn't love you? Who?

Who said those things to you and then acted like they didn't mean anything?

Rahul Surajrao Savant. That's who.

But that wasn't true either. Or at least not the whole truth. Which was life, wasn't it? An endless braid of half-truths.

Rahul loved her.

She knew that. He knew that.

It had flashed in his eyes when he had wordlessly begged her to wait until Papa wasn't in the room before discussing their issues. It had flashed in his eyes when he'd heard what Asif Khan had done to her. Her belly cramped when she thought about the bastard. Her transplanted heart would take a while to react to the terror the bastard made her feel. Kimi had recently read in an autobiography by a heart transplant recipient that transplanted hearts had no direct connection to your nervous system. You could sew up the tubes and tissue, but not the nerves. So her brain couldn't send her heart direct messages and her heartbeat responded to things at its own pace depending on how adrenaline rushed around her body.

Reading that had explained what she had felt since the transplant, what no doctor had warned her about. It was all a bit like a disconnected little dance between her brain and her heart. Like two partners who, try as they might, could not get their rhythms and steps to match up. And there it was, her heartbeat racing moments after she had actually thought about Asif Khan. Or maybe it had to do with her thinking about how Rahul's love flashed in his eyes every single time he looked at her.

She hated it now. Hated it, because how dare he? She made the effort to check her feelings from oozing out of her so she didn't embarrass him with them anymore. The least he could do was make an effort to stop those damn eyes from flashing his half-truths at her. He managed the whole stiffness-and-distance thing with the rest of his body; surely he could rein in his eyes.

No matter what stupid aphorisms movies and books came up with, there was no difference between "I love you" and "I'm in love with you." It was a bullshit distinction. Romantic love was no different from love. Romantic love was just a social definition of what you could do with your love, how intense you could let it become. It was a scale thing, so civilization and society could go on around all the love we felt for one another without messing up their rules.

If you loved someone, you loved them. To back away from that and hide behind the *ins* and *not ins* of love was a coward's way out. She ignored the gut-kick of disloyalty she felt at thinking of Rahul as a coward. Because he wasn't. He was the bravest person she knew.

You're the bravest boy I know.

How many times had she said that to him?

Great, here she was again, going around and around in circles.

This was why she'd had to walk away, make a clean break. At least for a short while to begin with, then she'd work the rest of it out.

How did you work out how to stop carrying around a friendship that was all of you? All your innocence and hope, every happy memory you owned. The brave thing to do would be to let it go forever. To start from scratch, because more happy memories would come, more friendships would come. They had to. But she wasn't brave enough to think about that right now. Her bravery was engaged elsewhere, thank you very much.

Courage wasn't only fighting your circumstances; sometimes making peace with your circumstances required more courage. It was one of Mamma's more hypocritical

31

aphorisms. Another gut-kick of guilt hit her for thinking that way about Mamma.

It was time Rahul realized that he had to let her go. Completely. She couldn't do this half-assed thing because he needed to believe that he wasn't *in* love with her.

He was right about one thing. The fact that she loved him had more to do with her than him. She *could* love like that. Therefore, she *would* love like that. If not him, then someone else. There was a lot of living to be done — twelve years' worth of it — and as she discovered life and herself, she would discover love again with the right person this time. A person who was *in* love with her too. Enough that he wanted to admit it.

The first step was this. This break. This decision to finally claim her freedom. For all the years that Rahul and she had waited for the cure that would set her free — they had called it The Great Escape (after a movie they had watched an embarrassing number of times. Okay, eight times. They'd watched that movie eight times.) In the end her transplant had turned out to be The Great Escape, but instead of setting her free it had tied them up in other ways.

Now this would be the real Great Escape: spending two weeks without The Usual

Suspects who had defined her life and lived it for her. Finding out what that bastard Asif Khan had meant when he ripped the buttons of her shirt on a crowded street and traced her scar with his crusty fingers and bloodshot eyes, and asked where her heart had come from.

Why don't you ask your daddy? he had said when she hadn't had an answer.

Papa had no intention of telling her the truth, and Rahul had no intention of helping her find the truth. The only truth those two understood was protecting her. If she understood anything at all, she understood that she had to live without their protection now that she had a choice. And she could not live with herself without tracing her gift back to the person who had lost it to her. Not after Asif Khan's knowing gaze had told her more truth than anyone in her life ever had.

Maybe she was on the wrong track. Maybe she was heading to the wrong place. She leaned into the rickshaw driver, who seemed entirely lost in the trance of the music and his war on the road. Maybe where she needed to go instead was to see Asif Khan. Yes, he was in a coma, but she understood illness and how the world around you influenced what you were able to make your body do, even as you had no control over it. Maybe all Asif Khan needed to wake up from his coma was her going to see him and giving him a reason to wake up.

It wasn't like she could just walk up to the creep. The entire Mumbai police force was probably holding hands and standing around his bed with Rahul inspecting their interlaced hands at regular intervals.

This case had changed Rahul. If she were stupid enough to blame external causes for things, she would have blamed Asif Khan and Jennifer Joshi for losing Rahul. Asif had killed Dr. Jennifer Joshi because she had been digging around his racket of killing people for their organs and illegally selling them overseas. The doctor had been trying to stop a heinous crime, trying to help Rahul, so blaming her made Kimi feel like the worst kind of human being.

Even so, she refused to let herself feel admiration for the woman. She refused to feel like a terrible person for how she felt every time she thought about that day when she had walked in on Rahul with her.

Jen was not the love of my life.

How dare he say those words to her?

How. Dare. He.

And how dare she let it hurt so much.

It felt like hot embers in her chest. It felt

34

like they'd removed her heart again and put burning pieces of coal in its place. That's how it had felt when she had first heard him talk about Jen. But she had ignored it as silliness. She had lectured herself about learning to deal with sharing him with the world once The Great Escape happened.

She needed to stop calling it that.

She needed to stop using all the terms Rahul came up with. But what would that leave her with? No language to reference anything.

That ball of panic filling her belly wasn't real. It was no longer real. He was no longer her window to the world. She was now inside her own world, and she intended for it to stay that way.

She had already made up her mind where she wanted to go. Her entire life, all she'd done was change her plans because of things outside of her control. Nothing was changing her mind this time. Waiting for Asif Khan to wake up and answer her questions was a coward's way out. She was going to track her donor down on her own.

Settling back into her seat, she watched the world jerk and flash by as the auto-rickshaw tore through the traffic-clogged streets as though it were invincible — a perfect metaphor for how she was going to live her life now that death no longer loomed at every corner.

3

Rahul
A long time ago
Rahul understood death. He felt a kinship with it even. It had settled inside him when he was fourteen years old, when his father lay bleeding on his lap. Blood mixed with warm, undefinable things leaked from Baba's perforated body and collected in the indentations his weight pressed into Rahul's thighs. Death tremors tapped indelible beats into his muscles, leaving a tattoo of pressure rhythms against his skin, leaving the forever wetness of blood on his palms as he tried to plug the bullet holes and failed.

He should have known then that death was seeping into him, pushing out half of him, merging into him like a ghost image that disappeared with corrective lenses, leaving behind crisper edges. He should have known then that the sensations of death would burrow like flesh-eating worms under his skin as soon as they pulled Baba off. But all he knew was that time had been trapped inside him after the gunshots had shut down his ears.

It took two officers to lift Baba, his limbs heavier in death, magnetic in their stubbornness for wanting to fall back into Rahul's lap.

It struck him with some incredulity that death gave men weight, turned them into a sack of mud caked inside skin.

Baba had been mud, even before they had put him on that stretcher.

He will be okay. Keep courage.

Courage.

That's what they kept calling it.

This thing they wanted him to keep.

But how did you keep something you did not own? Did not know? Could not find in the hungry panic inside you? Where everything was swallowed whole by your mother's face, by your younger siblings' faces, waiting at home with their noses pressed to the slats of the balcony railing, waiting for you to come home with their father, because the permanence of a parent was their entire reality.

"Can I keep terror instead?" he wanted to ask as the holes in Baba's chest refused to stop oozing blood in too many springs for his two hands to constrain.

Can I keep terror instead?

Because that's all he could find.

Why had he laughed with Baba when he had made fun of Aie for wanting him not to go?

"It's money, woman of mine. How will you get to show off a new sari on Diwali if I don't report to duty when I'm called? It's election season. Once it's gone, I'll stay home and worship you every weekend." Baba in his brand-new assistant-sub-inspector, Mumbai Police uniform had been a sight to behold.

"I don't want a new sari for Diwali if it means your children don't know the face of their father," Rahul's *aie* had said, flushed with anger because her perfect Sunday had decided to rebel out of her control.

"They know your face, beautiful one, you're their *aie*. It's a more beautiful face anyway. Who would choose my ugly *thobda* over that?"

It had calmed her. Rahul never thought of his *aie* as vain, but Baba could always get her to calm down with a little bit of flattery. His secret weapon.

Baba was right too. Aie was beautiful. He'd heard all the aunts in the compound taunt her about it. Half envy, half joy that someone who looked like her — with that glossy skin and hip-length hair and eyes darker than melted tar — had to wait in line at the water tap just like they did.

He'd heard Baba shout about it on Fridays when he came home tipsy.

"I'll kill any bastard who looks at you. You're not a Bollywood heroine. This show is mine. Mine! Move along, suckers." Baba would sweep his hand, shooing away the imaginary mob of men.

Aie would laugh her shy laugh into her sari and watch Baba hand out the Cadbury chocolate eclairs he always remembered to bring the children, no matter how hard it was for him to stand up straight.

"Come help me maintain my dignity," he'd say to Rahul. And Rahul, who'd been as tall as Baba at ten, would shoulder him to the bathroom, help him out of his clothes, and then help him to the mattress on the floor that Aie and Baba shared in the inside room.

"You know what the best thing about your *aie* is? Don't let me fool you. It's not that she looks like a goddess. It's that she gave me you and your brother and sister," Baba had said to Rahul once, leaning unabashedly on him. "All a man wants is a strapping son to take care of him in his old age.

I'm giving you practice, what, Rahul?"

Now here he was, watching as they lifted Baba into the ambulance, stumbling after them, leaving red handprints on the white ambulance door.

"You can't go in there, *beta,*" one of the constables said, holding Rahul back, his arms gentle but firm.

"He can," an authoritative voice said. It belonged to the politician Baba had jumped in front of when the madman had started shooting, the man who should have been on the stretcher instead of Baba. He nodded at the constable. Just one nod from him was enough to get the man to back away. "That's the child's father. Put him in the ambulance."

The constable lifted Rahul into the ambulance and the politician followed.

"Sir, we can follow the ambulance in your car," someone said behind them, but the politician didn't stop. He squeezed himself in next to Rahul.

Rahul shifted as far away from him as he could in the cramped space that smelled like blood and sweat and the alcohol doctors swiped on your arm before giving you an injection. He wanted to push the man into the stretcher bed, switch him out with Baba.

41

"Let's go. What are you waiting for?" the man shouted at the driver and they started moving. "I'm Kirit Patil," he said, turning to Rahul. "I'm going to do everything I can to make things all right."

Two lies in one sentence from a man whose bullets sat inside his father's bleeding body. Anger bloated inside Rahul, dulling the terror for a few seconds.

"I've seen you in movies," Rahul said, although it had been a while since he had seen the man in one.

"Yes, I used to be called Karan Kumar when I acted in movies, but that's not my real name."

"Why would anyone change their name?" It seemed like a horribly dishonest thing to do.

"The world is a very complicated place. And our name is not as simple as two words."

Rahul shrugged. Baba's hand in his was getting colder and heavier and Rahul shook it as though that would change things.

"What is your name?"

"Rahul Surajrao." Baba's name stuck in Rahul's throat and he had to push around it. "Savant."

He didn't want to speak to the man. He wanted him to go away.

But he didn't. Not once they got to the hospital and not when a doctor came out of the operation theater and told Rahul what he already knew: that Baba was gone. That the skin on Rahul's thighs that had pressed down under Baba's weight would stay that way forever. That Aie and Mohit and Mona were still waiting at home for their usual Sunday dinner of fried fish, Baba's favorite food in all the world. That Rahul would never again be able to eat fish without throwing up.

The minister stayed there through it all. And for some reason as long as he was being watched by the skinny, tall film star or politician or whoever the man was with his mop of hair as black and thick as Baba's, Rahul could not cry.

To his horror, the man came home with Rahul. He, along with a crew of officers and constables from Baba's *chowki* post, drove Rahul to the *chawl* compound where he had lived all his life. But as they stomped across the caked earth of the playground, edged on three sides by three long, squat buildings that made up the community that was his home, everything felt foreign, as though he were visiting for the very first time.

Neighbors — their *chawl* family Baba called them — stared down from the front verandas that ran the length of the buildings. The viewing gallery had been as permanent a fixture in Rahul's life as the fact that he had two parents. It seemed to freeze as their procession crossed the ground. Everyone seemed to know. A few of Rahul's friends who were kicking around a ball called out to him, but the uniform-clad sentry surrounding him kept anyone from actually approaching him.

They trudged up two flights of stairs. The red betel leaf and tobacco juice sprayed into the grimy walls of the stairwell made Rahul's stomach push acid up his throat. By the time they made their way down the veranda that connected the homes on their floor, he could hear the sound of his own breath ricocheting against the perpetually open front doors with their peeling blue and green paint. In all his life, Rahul had never walked down this path in silence, never without queries about his grades from the grandpa who sat in his easy chair all day and all night. Never without being stopped by the retired uncle who never let Rahul go until he had helped with the crossword. Never without the grandma next door shoving her latest sweet confection into his mouth.

Finally, they stood outside Block Number

Fifty-Five, where nothing more than a green door separated them from their *chawl* family. As always, the door was unlocked. Just last week Baba had bought the only cell phone in their family. They had never owned a landline. No one inside his home knew what he brought with him today. But the wall of uniform-clad officers behind him was almost as loud of a signal as his blood-stained shirt would have been if the politician hadn't procured a clean shirt for him from somewhere.

Even before Rahul said a word, Aie's face went white. They said that in books — *the blood drained from her face* — but he could not have imagined his mother's dusky skin turning Hollywood-actress white. Even her eyes faded. The black losing all its gloss. She fell back against the kitchen door, the latch rattling behind her. Mohit clung to her sari with both hands. Mona ran to Rahul, excited that he had brought home so many guests. She jumped up in his arms and his stiff body worked from memory and pulled her close.

Her skinny legs wrapped around his waist, her sticky-sweet Mona smell filling his lungs and sitting on top of the hot, metallic tang of blood as she whispered a wet whisper into his ear. "Is Aie angry because Baba

45

brought home too many people for dinner again?"

Then she stiffened. Ever so slightly at first and then more and more as her body registered that there was a person missing from the crowd. A feeling Rahul would never lose. As though someone who should be here wasn't, but only because he wasn't looking hard enough.

She stretched her neck to search. "Where's Baba?" she said in an uncharacteristically scared voice.

And Aie started to sob.

For weeks, an endless stream of uncles and aunts flooded the house, the *kakas* and *kakus* bringing with them an even more endless stream of questions and opinions.

Has Rahul cried yet?

Someone needs to get that child to cry. It's unhealthy.

Has anyone talked to Rahul about what he saw?

No on all counts.

Rahul hadn't gone back to school yet either. His friends from the *chawl* compound had come over a few times and tried to talk to him, no doubt coerced by their mothers, who didn't understand that social duty and fourteen-year-old boys didn't go

46

together. There had been shuffling feet and no words. Finally Mukesh, who could barely speak a sentence off the football field but turned into a dynamo of words (mostly of the swearing variety) on the field, dragged Rahul down to the playground.

But his friends were worthless adversaries. The harder he played, the more accommodating they became, and that made him get more and more aggressive until the older boys playing on the other side of the field noticed and beckoned him over. "*Oy*, show-off, come show us what you've got."

He did, and they sent him home with bruised ribs and a bloody nose. It felt good. Standing around with the older boys as they smoked and leered at passing girls also felt good. Nothing was expected of him there. In their shadow he was invisible.

"How old are you?" one of the older boys asked, a cigarette hanging from his lips.

"Almost fifteen."

"You look like a fighter. You interested in the fight club? I can put in a good word with Azaad *bhai*."

Azaad *bhai* was the local gang lord. Aie would break Rahul's legs if he even said that name in their home. Rahul walked away without answering. But fighting with his fists and getting paid for it sounded so good it made him hungry for it.

4

Kimi
A long time ago

Mamma was worried. Which was like saying the bitter gourd was bitter. It was, to use one of Mamma's own phrases, stating the obvious, and to throw in one of Papa's phrases, just her natural state. Mamma always worried.

Kimi had come home from school and sneezed. Three times. Usually, one sneeze was bad enough, but sneezing three times around Mamma was inviting the Big Box.

Mamma's father had been a *raj-vaidya,* a grand master of ayurvedic medicine. Kimi had never met her grandfather. He had died just after Mamma had become pregnant with Kimi. It was a story Mamma could never tell without needing to dab her nose and eyes with her embroidered handkerchief. But then the story of Kimi's birth was one no one ever seemed capable of telling without tears. The part of the story Kimi had not been able to piece together (because stories like this did not come with a question-answer section) was what her birth had to do with her grandfather's death. All Kimi knew was that the two things were related.

The Big Box was her grandfather's legacy to Mamma. The servants weren't allowed to touch the leather-bound trunk with its two shiny brass latches. Iron locks hung by the latches, and the keys always hung by Mamma's waist along with the cluster of keys she tucked into her sari with a large silver key hook. The hook with its bells and embossed statue of Saraswati the goddess of knowledge had been in Mamma's family for centuries, mothers passing it down to daughters from generation to generation. According to Mamma this was the rarest of things, because most family treasures were passed down from father to son or mother to daughter-in-law.

Kimi loved to run her fingers over the timeworn silver when she hugged Mamma. No matter how hot it got, the key hook remained cool to the touch. When Mamma moved through the house, the tinkling sound of the bells mixed with the muted jangle of the keys. It was possibly Kimi's favorite sound in all the world.

Inside the Big Box were all the herbs and remedies her grandfather had mixed into potions that could cure everything from a common cold to broken bones. Kimi loved to hear the stories of her grandfather's miraculous potions. He had once saved the prime minister from an attempt to poison him by identifying and delivering an antidote after one look in the minister's eyes. He had healed the warts on a grand maestro's vocal cords and given him back his singing voice. Mamma had told Kimi that she could walk into any of the maestro's concerts anywhere in the world and tell him whose granddaughter she was and she would be invited into the concert for free.

He was legendary, her grandfather. But he wasn't a miracle worker, as Mamma made sure Kimi knew. He was a scientist. He could identify a plant not just by sight or touch alone but also by smell, even if the plant had been plucked years ago. He was said to have had a hundred thousand vials in his storerooms before his dispensary in Ahmednagar had been burned down during one of the communal riots. Fortunately, her grandfather had been traveling to Pune with the Big Box at the time to treat the dean of the Film Institute. It was the only reason his most precious remedies, or at least remnants of the most vital ones, had survived. Her grandfather had left the box to Mamma along with guidelines for formulations and their usage.

Three sneezes meant Kimi's grandfather's genius was in order and out came the Big Box. The first question Mamma asked Sarika *tai*, Kimi's nanny, was if any of the servants had been sick recently.

Apparently, *mali kaka* had shown some signs of sniffling. Not that the gardener ever came inside the house. Kimi wasn't about to tell Mamma that she had helped *mali kaka* pluck the flowers for Mamma's evening prayers yesterday.

Mamma leaned over the open trunk, extracted one measure of gray powder from a jar with a silver spoon, and placed it in the glass Sarika was holding out. "Twenty milliliters of water and three drops of coconut oil," she said, and then to Kimi, "up to bed."

Kimi groaned. Not that anyone heard it. Kimi made sure no one ever heard her groaning. But she had an entire dictionary of inner groans tucked away. First, she hated coconut oil. It made her gag. But Mamma seemed to believe it was the cure for all evil. She had Sarika *tai* massage coconut oil into

Kimi's hair every Sunday and then wash her hair out with scalding-hot water. Anyone who saw Kimi and her hip-length hair seemed to remark upon it, so Kimi knew that Mamma's remedies were not entirely without merit. Still, her grandfather's potions were so vile tasting it wasn't a miracle that the germs all died. They must choke to death from the taste alone.

Mamma stood and Kimi wrapped her arms around her. Her mother smelled as beautiful as she looked, like the tuberoses *mali kaka* planted in endless rows along the front wall of the garden.

"Were you careful in school?" she asked, stroking Kimi's hair. "Have you been using your disinfectant gel?"

Kimi nodded. She was feeling a little achy in the head, so having Mamma stroke her head felt really good.

"Do you want me to come up and tuck you in?" But she was leading Kimi up the stairs even before she responded.

"Papa had promised to pick me up from school, but he never came. Did he have to leave town again?" Kimi asked as her mother tucked her quilt tightly around her. She really badly wanted to sneeze again, but she willed herself not to.

Mamma's face paled. She had been a little

53

distracted all afternoon. Kimi had thought it was because of her sneezes. Apparently, it wasn't. Usually, Mamma's face brightened at the mention of Papa. Sarika *tai* had once slipped up and told Kimi about Mamma and Papa's grand love story that all of India had been envious of. This was discomforting, because, eww! But still, Mamma never looked like this when Papa was mentioned.

"He'll be home soon. You rest up. He'll need us to cheer him up when he comes home today. He's had a horrid day." Mamma closed her own eyes, indicating that Kimi should close her eyes too.

Sometimes Kimi wished Mamma would treat her like she was almost twelve and not five. She had a million questions. What did that even mean? What was a horrid day for Papa? From what Sarika *tai* told her, Papa got to be a king at his job. From what Papa told Kimi, he was a servant of the people. When she had asked him how he could be both those things, he had laughed and said, "In a democracy the public is the king, and the rulers the servants."

Mamma said that meant he was a good man.

Despite the fact that Mamma's head massages were always so comforting that Kimi's eyes closed of their own will, she could not fall asleep. Not when she knew that something was wrong with Papa. Not when Mamma looked this worried. Not when her worry wasn't about Kimi this time, but about Papa.

When she was convinced Kimi was asleep, Mamma dropped a kiss on Kimi's forehead and left the room. There was no spring in her step, no bounce in her bobbed hair.

Why hadn't Kimi tried harder not to sneeze? She knew this wasn't about her, but it might have helped. She was used to the worry being focused on her. She knew how to handle that, had learned to work around it. Because Papa always said we had to know how to clean up our own messes. And her parents' worry was entirely a mess of Kimi's making.

Even her name was a reminder of it. Kimi was short for Kimaya, which means "miracle" in Sanskrit. She was her parents' miracle, born after twelve years of penance. Prayers, fasting, denial, donation, every possible plea to every possible god. There was a corner outside the Babulnath temple named after Kimi — The Surviving Patil Baby Corner — where the homeless gathered every Thursday knowing there would be food. Her parents begging for blessings from the city's beggars.

How many times had Kimi heard it? The saga of her parents' pilgrimages around the world — from being blessed by the Pope, to being kissed by the Dalai Lama, to touching the holy wall of Babylon, to having laid their foreheads at Harmandir Sahib, the Golden Temple in Amritsar, to having hiked barefoot up to Vaishno Devi, and having stood through raging storms surrounded by the churning ocean at Haji Ali. In their desperation, her parents had found the ideal of the secularism those public service announcements kept preaching on TV. Any god. All religions. As long as they got what they wanted.

Maybe they had struck upon something, because it worked. Mamma became pregnant again. Kimi had heard Sarika *tai* call it her mother's seven months of hell. A pregnancy spent waiting, barely moving, with a literal stitch sewed into her to keep Kimi inside until it was safe for her to be born.

"Your mother lost seven babies before you were born," Papa had told her the first time she had thrown a tantrum because Mamma had refused to let her out of the house for a week after she coughed a few times. "You're her miracle, so she wants to take care of you enough for all your brothers and sisters who are gone."

It was the last time Kimi had ever thrown a tantrum.

Kimi didn't move until she heard the car pull through the gates.

Usually, when Papa came home the house buzzed with anticipation before the doorbell rang. He would burst into the house and even before taking off his shoes he would bellow for Kimi and she'd fly down the stairs and into his arms.

She waited for the buzz of energy, the clang of the bell, the bellow of, "Where's my princess?"

Nothing.

She slipped out her door and down the corridor.

Papa was sitting on the bottom step of the staircase by himself. None of the servants had dared to come anywhere near him. Mamma was nowhere to be seen either. Kimi tiptoed down the stairs and sank down next to him.

His quick intake of breath before he wiped his face on his sleeve was the only reason she knew that he had been crying. She sidled into him and he wrapped an arm around her. Until that day, Kimi had never seen her father cry. Unfortunately, it would not be the last time she would see him wet eyed with despair. All the fear she saw in his eyes that day when he pulled her close would appear there over and over again. But neither of them knew that then.

"I don't think I could ever bear to lose you," he said in a voice she had never before heard from him.

The only meaning the words *lose you* held for her then was her wandering off at the Mount Mary fair. Which could never happen because her mother never let her get out of the car when they drove past the rides and the stalls and went straight to the church where the parish priest led them right into the chapel through a back entrance so they could light their candles during the holy fair week. Kimi only ever saw the crowds from the car.

"I'll be careful never to get lost, Papa," she said, and he laughed through those tears and it was the scariest thing Kimi had ever seen.

"Sometimes it's not in our hands," he said and then went quiet for many minutes.

"Are you not feeling well?" she asked because the silence was starting to terrify her.

"I was just at the cremation of a policeman who did a very brave thing," he said in that same unrecognizable voice.

Kimi squeezed in tighter.

"If not for his bravery, I may not have come home today."

Kimi felt tears start to creep up her throat. Papa had to come home. What would Mamma and she do if he didn't?

"The man has three children," Papa said, as though he couldn't believe that he was saying those words. There was a dull tremor in his voice, as though he had to force the words out, as though in telling her this he had just learned it himself.

"Who will take care of them?" The horror of losing Papa suddenly felt too real and Kimi wrapped her arms around him.

Papa seemed to feel her distress because he pulled away and met her gaze. He opened his mouth, straightened up, but he, who always took care of everything, couldn't seem to form a response. He wiped his eyes on his shoulder again.

"You have to," she said, feeling some sort of wild urgency. "You have to take care of them, Papa."

The way he was looking at her changed. She had always seen delight in her father's eyes; this was the first time she saw something she'd never seen before. It would be years before she knew that it was respect. He looked at her as though she had somehow saved him.

Years later, that look would become practically the only way he looked at her. Every time she fought for her life and won she would remember that this had been the first time.

Mamma hated when people ate or drank anywhere in the house except for the dining areas, but she brought Papa a cup of tea and sat down next to him on the stairs.

He took a sip. "Kimi thinks I should take care of the Savant kids."

Mamma studied Papa, and one of those looks passed between them, the kind they passed around anytime she said or did anything that amused them, or made them proud, or worried them. Kimi thought of it as their parent code language. Usually, it involved Papa trying to convince Mamma to let Kimi do something. She wasn't entirely sure this wasn't one of those times.

Mamma then turned her gaze on Kimi, reaching across Papa to wipe her cheek. "And how do you expect him to do that?"

Kimi looked away from her mother and into her father's eyes, because she knew he was listening, really listening, and she had a sense that he was asking for her help. "You have to do everything for them that you do for me. Everything their papa would have done. You have to."

He plucked the handkerchief Mamma was holding out to him and dried his eyes again, then he dabbed Kimi's cheeks. "You are my pride and joy," he said, and she knew that he would do everything he could for that policeman's children.

5

Rahul
Present day
The minister stood in the doorway of his office studying Rahul. When had Kirit turned into an old man? Rahul barely recognized him anymore, with his skin sallow and his still-thick hair almost all silver. This past year seemed to have wrung every remaining bit of youth from Kirit, sucking him dry when he finally had what he'd spent years fighting for — Kimi's life.

"Do you know who Kimi's donor was, sir?" Rahul asked.

Kirit swayed on his feet and sagged against the door frame. Rahul went to him, and taking his arm led him back to his chair.

"Do you want me to call a doctor? Where's ma'am?"

"I'm fine. Rupa is on one of her pilgrimages, making sure we all stay in her beloved Krishna's good graces." Kirit pointed to a bottle on his desk and Rahul extracted one white pill from it and handed it to the minister.

Kirit placed the medication carefully under his tongue and leaned back. "Kimi was on a waiting list for heart recipients in Hong Kong and as soon as they brought in a brain-dead patient who was a match we flew her out. The donor wanted complete anonymity. That's all there is to it."

That had been two years ago. It had been the best and worst time. Kimi finding life and Jen losing her life. And Rahul hadn't been able to help either one of them.

At least he had Jen's killer in custody, even if he was hooked up to machines and no bloody use to anyone. All Rahul wanted to do right now was storm into the bastard's hospital room and pull the plug. But that would leave too many questions unanswered. Who had protected Asif when he was killing all those people? Why had he come after Kimi? Her transplant surgery had taken place in Hong Kong. What possible interest did Asif have in it?

Kimi might have done the right thing in walking away from him, but that look in her eyes when she walked out that door meant Rahul could not rest until she had her answers.

"I'm going to lay down for a bit," Kirit said, dismissing Rahul.

Rahul didn't move. "Where did she go, sir?"

If Kirit was surprised that Rahul did not immediately comply with his wishes the way he usually did, he hid it well. "She made me promise not to tell you."

Rahul's heartbeat sped up. Over the past month Rahul's team had dismantled most of Khan's gang, but a part of it was still at large. Not keeping an eye on Kimi was not an option. "I won't tell her you told me."

"You know blood is thicker than water, right, son? She was serious this time. I think your involvement with the Jennifer Joshi case might have done your friendship with Kimi more damage than you know. I kept trying to tell you to back off, to not let your emotions get involved, but you didn't listen." With nothing more than that Kirit turned and left the room, dragging his feet in a way Rahul had never seen him do before.

Two people had walked out on him today, and it wasn't even eight a.m. Not the most promising omen for his next task. Visiting Asif Khan and his doctors was always as much fun as having your fingernails plucked out. The doctors kept assuring Rahul that

Asif was on the verge of waking up, that his body was healed and it was just a matter of his brain catching up. If they were right, Rahul had to figure out exactly where Kimi was headed.

He let himself out of The Mansion and took the marble steps that led down from the pillared porch. Bougainvillea spilled over the sandstone compound wall that was two heads taller than Rahul, who was only about an inch under six feet. The wrought-iron-trussed wooden gates were even higher so passersby could barely see any more than the sloping roof when they came around to look at it as part of the "Homes of Bollywood Stars" tour.

Tina, his Enfield Bullet and "other best friend," as Kimi liked to call his motorbike, stood in wait. He took her off the stand and straddled her before noticing a folded piece of paper tucked into the seat. He picked it up and stared at his name scrawled across it. No one else wrote his name the way Kimi did. "Rahul" with the tail of the R too long and the back of the H too high, as though it were her signature, not his.

He unfolded the paper.

This time I mean it.

He knew that. It had been a long time coming. From that moment when he had told her he didn't feel the same way she did or want the same things, he had known that he would have to let her go. Eventually.

If Asif had attacked her for a reason, then his men were still a threat to her. And if there was any chance she was in danger, he was going to make sure she stayed safe. She'd have to wait a little longer to leave him. That's all there was to it. As soon as he kick-started his bike, his phone buzzed and he pulled it to his ear.

"Boss, are you close to Lilavati Hospital?" Maney, the best damn assistant in the world, said with enough desperation that Rahul knew what it was even before Maney finished.

"Did the bastard wake up?"

"Yes."

Maney speaking in monosyllables was not a good thing. They didn't call him Maney-Loose-Bowels for nothing. Generally, the man suffered verbal diarrhea and you had to cork him up.

Rahul popped in his Bluetooth earpiece and sped down the hill, automatically avoiding every pothole and putting all his focus on not hitting the crisscrossing pedestrians. Maney was breathing heavily on the phone. As though he had just run a mile. "Please tell me I'm going to find him at the hospital when I get there."

Silence.

"Maney?"

"It happened too fast, boss. Two men held the children's ward hostage. Khan walked out of there with another three men holding three doctors at gunpoint."

"Fuck! The children?"

"No casualties in the children's ward."

That meant there were casualties elsewhere.

"They got Pandey and two constables. And one of the nurses got a bullet in her shoulder. But we got four of his men."

"I want the entire department on this. Right now!"

"Every single *chowki* in the city is on alert, boss. Code Red. We have roadblocks everywhere. He's not getting far. We'll find him."

"Where was he last sighted?"

"Koliwada. Abandoned Mahindra Jeep. I'm already here."

"I'm almost there."

Bloody fucking hell. Koliwada was a study in high-density housing. Shanty hutments and plastered brick-and-mortar buildings all piled on top of one another at the edge of the ocean. It was going to be damn near impossible to find the rat bastard. He could be camped out in any one of the half-million

67

homes. No civilian in their right mind would hand a gangster with Asif Khan's reputation over without the fear of losing every single member of their extended family.

His men had the immediate area surrounded. But Mumbai was a seamless mass of humanity with every neighborhood and suburb bleeding into the next. Within hours Asif could be anywhere in the city.

Kimi.

He dialed her number and got a message telling him her number had been switched off. Fantastic. He sent her a text message. But it went undelivered.

Next he dialed Nikhil's number. Asif Khan had attacked Jen's husband, Nikhil Joshi, and his girlfriend, Nikki, two months ago, and Rahul had pumped Asif full of bullets and put him in a coma. The bastard was like a bloody earthworm; you could chop off parts of him and he kept regenerating back to life.

Rahul hadn't expected to become such good friends with Nic and Nikki, but it must be true what they say about surviving near-death experiences together — it did create an instant bond.

Neither of them was answering their phones. They were set to leave for America this week, which meant they were out and about doing whatever it is people did before they traveled. Which meant they were exposed targets. Rahul dispatched men to Nikki's flat and left messages on both their phones that made him sound as panicked as he felt. So much for Stonewall Savant. He hated that stupid nickname of Kimi's.

Rahul wasn't in uniform but Maney and the rest of the team were. Rahul felt a flash of pride, spotting the Mumbai Police badges shining on epaulets as they combed the crowded lanes. Civilians scattered in panic as they passed. Windows and shopfront shutters slammed around him as the public sensed danger.

He found Maney at the mouth of a narrow lane, about to lead three sub-inspectors into the alley, gun drawn. Rahul caught his eye and nodded, pulled his own pistol from his holster, unlocked the safety, and turned Tina around and into the parallel lane. "I'll meet you on the other side," he said into the earpiece.

"We just spotted three targets," Maney responded. "One black kurta, two white, over jeans."

"No civilian casualties. Draw them into the open toward the beach."

Rahul pulled into the unpaved lane, raising dust around him, and hopped off Tina, as three gunshots went off and the three hunted men ran across the lane. He ran toward the beach across the road where he knew they were headed, his gun drawn, shouting at the crowds to get out of the way. "Get down!" The caked earth pounded beneath his shoes. Something good had come out of the monsoon playing hide-and-seek with Mumbai: Dry earth was so much better for running.

The fuckers wove through the quickly thinning crowd, exchanging fire with Maney and his men, who led them straight into Rahul's path. He had them. His sight shifted like clockwork between the three as Maney and the others boxed them in and kept them from scattering again.

They flew across the road and hit the beach, horns shrieking around them, screams rising from the crowd. The cold metal recoiled in Rahul's hands. The familiar flash of warmth kissed his palm as the impact of the bullet leaving the muzzle shoved his arm muscles up as if he were pushing snug sleeves up his elbows.

Boom. Boom. Boom. Three shots.

He spun the pistol around his trigger finger and shoved it back in his holster. The bastards were out cold. All three of them.

He sauntered over to the bodies sprawled across the dry sand. They hadn't even made it to the wet part of the beach. No point hurrying; the bastards weren't going anywhere good. Hopefully, they were already burning in the special hell there'd better be for fuckers who held children at gunpoint.

Avoiding the bloodstains that spread around the bodies in imperfect circles, he leaned over the first body and shoved two fingers at the pulse that didn't even stutter. Just the way the cop had done to Baba when he lay bleeding on Rahul's lap. He didn't bother to push away the memory and withdrew the hand he found rubbing the spot on his thigh where the imprint of Baba's head would never stop burning.

Every single time he put one of these bastards down, he relived that day when the constable had shoved a finger into Baba's neck. The memory was inevitable. He'd given up fighting it years ago. He let it slash through his mind and pass. It was easier that way. Less messy than struggling with it, because it always won.

"Gone, boss?" Maney said, running up behind Rahul.

Rahul straightened without answering. Of course he was gone. If they cut him open, they'd find Rahul's bullet exactly in the center of his heart.

"We got one more down that way." Maney ran the finger check on the other two bodies. "Perfect shots, boss, as always." He waved to his team, which was already cordoning off the scene. "*Oy,* boys, over here, come see, Savant-sir's handiwork."

Now that the danger seemed to have passed, a crowd was gathering again. The resilience of Mumbai's citizens never ceased to amaze Rahul. It was almost as if they were so numb to danger and violence that they didn't even internalize it before moving past it.

But the danger was alive and well. Asif wasn't among the dead.

"I think we got all of them from the hospital, boss!" Maney said, but one look at Rahul's scowl and his cockiness dissipated. "Except Asif, of course."

Rahul turned away from the bodies and headed back to Tina.

Maney fell in step beside him. "He can't keep running. We've dwindled his gang down to almost nothing. We'll get him. It's just a matter of time."

Time. The starkest truth of life — either you didn't have enough or then it went on and on. And bastards like Asif used every moment of their endless lives to make it purgatory for the rest of the sods who trudged along trying to get by. It was about damn time someone ended his time here.

Leaving Maney to deploy search teams, Rahul headed back up the hill to The Mansion. The sun was almost all the way up in the sky and blazing with that pre-monsoon intensity that parched every inch of the city and made it beg for the rains like a starving child.

6

Kimi
Present day

Kimi's office cubicle was chock-full of pictures. Mostly story ideas (what she wanted to do) and events she had covered (what she did do). Getting hired as a celebrity reporter for the Indian operation of the world's largest Internet media company hadn't been hard. There wasn't a celebrity who wouldn't give Kirit Patil's daughter an interview. Consequently, there wasn't a media outlet that wouldn't give her a job. And there wasn't one that would give her a job reporting on anything other than celebrities, given that "dangerous work" wasn't what Papa wanted her to do.

She hit "send" on the piece that was due today: "Yummy Mummies: How Star Wives Rock Pregnancy." She stuck a finger in her mouth and made a gagging sound. It was such cutesy, syrupy drivel, she thought she was going to make herself sick. But she had no one but herself to blame. After refusing to do an exposé on star marriages ("Rocky Marriages That Fake Being Rocking Marriages"), her boss had asked her, with enough syrupiness to rival her piece, what kind of "non-damaging" pieces she'd be okay with doing, and she'd had to come up with stupidass ideas such as this one.

Pregnant women were adorable and all, but seriously, just the photo shoot had been enough to induce failure on her poor secondhand heart. Imagine five pregnant women in couture trying to look thin and cute and complaining the entire time about being in pain. Because, hello! Those heels alone would give even an Olympic athlete aches and pains. Finally, airbrushing had saved the day. Whatever the magazine was paying Rumi, her photographer partner, it was not bloody enough.

She peeked into Rumi's cubicle, but it was too early for anyone to be at work. "It's media, darling," Rumi loved to say. "Nothing of interest happens in the mornings."

She scrawled Rumi a note, trying not to think about another note she had scrawled. She could imagine the smile on Rumi's face when he got it. He thought it was so cute that she left notes.

The note she had left Rahul? Nope, he would not be thinking there was anything cute about that.

She plucked a picture off her cubicle wall and slipped it into her bag. Taking the picture with her was another stupidass idea, but she did it anyway. Then she threw a quick glance around the office and made sure no one was around in the sea of cubicles before running her hand over the red fabric-draped wall. "I love you," she whispered to her cubicle and then quickly to her computer and her chair and to Rambo, her fern. "I'm going to miss you."

Her job might not be the dark-underbelly journalism Kimi had dreamed of, but much as she hated that it wasn't, and much as the work she did sometimes annoyed her, she also loved it. Having something as normal as a job was a dream she had been too afraid to dream even in her most reckless moments, and she loved it. The cubicles, the offices of the bigwigs that sat in the center where everyone could covet them, even the bathrooms with the psychedelically painted stalls and mirrors stenciled with inspirational quotes. All of it, she loved all of it.

Rolling her suitcase across the office, she attempted a minor lecture to herself. *You're going to be gone for just two weeks. All of this will still be here after two weeks. You will still be here.* Yes, she would. She would still be here. She passed a mounted poster of the National Award for Media Excellence. A collage of earthquake-ravaged slums, the prime minister with his hands folded in a namaste, and the parliament houses, death and suffering juxtaposed over power. She had to still be here, for a long, long time. There was so much she had to do.

All those times when she'd had this thought and everything had slipped from her grip like sand turning to air swept through her in a disorienting wave and she almost stumbled. But she caught herself. She refused to stumble. She might want to report on hopelessly depressing and infuriating things, but she would not allow herself to become those things. Those were the exact things she had sworn never to become when The Great Escape happened. Hopelessness and anger were exactly the things she hated about people who took themselves too seriously. People who took themselves too seriously were her pet peeve.

Except Rahul. He was so good at taking himself too seriously that it felt almost as if he was too serious despite himself. He carried it like armor that got so heavy you wanted to take it off him so he could breathe.

Or that's how she had felt most of her life.

Not anymore.

Now she saw Rahul for what he was. Someone she had idolized and put on a pedestal for too long. Far too long. And he had let her. That made her angry again. How dare he? She had to think of something positive. All this anger was corrosive and not at all good for her heart.

Raja the doorman jumped up from his wood stool when he saw her. "Going on trip, madam?" he asked in that wonderfully friendly yet shy way of his that cheered her up instantly. "Travel safely."

She beamed at him. Ah, forget it. She let go of the suitcase she was dragging and took his hand in both of hers and shook it with all her heart. "Thank you, Mr. Raja! I'll see you when I get back!"

He blinked, then blushed, then stuttered, and she felt a bit awful for making him so uncomfortable. But the smile that ultimately settled in his eyes made everything okay.

Her superhero auto-rickshaw was waiting in the parking lot. She had asked the driver to wait, since she didn't want to be stuck with going out and finding another one to take her to the airport. The Bandra-Kurla complex was notorious for it being impossible to find rickshaws and taxis when you wanted them.

The driver was dozing across the passenger seat in the back, and she cleared her throat to wake him. He jumped awake and swaggered to the driver's seat. Kimi settled back against the sticky vinyl seat.

Finally, she was on her way to the airport. She had the mad urge to stick her face out of the rickshaw and laugh. How on earth had Papa let her go? He didn't know where she was going, of course. She wasn't stupid enough to tell him. Plus, she was seeking freedom here, and telling the people you were seeking freedom from how exactly you were seeking it was missing the point a bit, now, wasn't it?

She could barely believe it. Why had it taken her so long to ask? It's not like Papa had ever denied her anything she wanted. Well, *wanted* was a complicated term. He definitely hadn't denied her anything she had asked for. To call him an indulgent father was to shortchange him. She was alive today because he never took no for an answer.

Now his part was done. It was her turn to make sure he hadn't done all he had for nothing by not just being alive but by living. It would be two weeks before Papa would expect her to come back home. Rahul wouldn't care one way or the other. At least she hoped he wouldn't care. Actually, it didn't matter, not what Rahul wanted, not what Papa wanted, not what Mamma wanted.

Although Mamma was the least of her worries. She was in Dharamsala chanting with the Dalai Lama's monks. After all these years of praying for Kimi, it was now time to say her thank-yous and to go on praying for Kimi to keep her health. It was yet another awfully ungrateful thought, and Kimi shook it off along with all the other misguided thinking that had defined her life. The life she was defining for herself from now on had no place in it for negativity. Only happy thoughts and forward motion.

All that mattered now was what Kimi wanted.

And Kimi wanted to live. Not breathe and exist, but live.

She was going to climb mountains, swim seas, go to the Galápagos Islands and Antarctica. She was going to photograph the migrating caribou traversing Alaska on their way to the Arctic.

There, she was happy now, all set to traipse off across the world (or at least across a small part of Asia) armed with a smile and a bounce in her step! As if on cue, the auto-rickshaw jerked to a stop outside Chatrapati Shivaji Airport departures. She got out, staring fondly at the musclebound Krish and the gleeful-with-victory Durga and getting a narrow-eyed look from the driver. *Are you a little off?* that look said.

No matter. She often wondered that herself.

"I love your rickshaw!" she said, reaching across to touch the vibrant transfer-sticker art she couldn't seem to look away from.

The driver sat up a little straighter and dropped his gaze to her breasts. "I'll wait if you want more return journey?" he said as though there were some sort of hidden meaning to his words and threw a look at the backseat.

Discomfort prickled along her skin.

"Thank you. I don't need a return journey," she said, taking a step back and kicking herself for having done something wrong, although she couldn't exactly identify what it was.

The man licked his lips and his hand lingered a second too long on her fingers as she paid him. She yanked her hand away, her skin crawling, and tried not to think about Rahul lecturing her about being careful whom she trusted. All she had done was compliment the man's auto-rickshaw. How was that being careless? Even so, the driver leered at her as she turned away.

"Come on, princess, I'll show you how to love my rickshaw," he said behind her, and she almost turned around and told him to buzz off. But there was something so sick about the look in his eyes, as though he knew how uncomfortable his leering made her and that somehow excited him, and she couldn't make herself look at him again.

Instead, she ignored the sound of him revving his rickshaw behind her and walked through the high-pillared canopy toward the terminal entrance. She didn't need any more trouble than she was already seeking out.

The world is an ugly place, Rahul had once told her. *At least in here there is no ugliness.*

He had apologized almost instantly for saying it, for being so insensitive. That was the thing about Rahul: He always knew when things hurt her, even when no one else did. Although he might have misunderstood why she had been hurt by those words of his. There was something so inherently ugly about sickness, especially sickness that seemed insurmountable and constant, that it had made her wonder about his life. What kind of life did he have that he could see her life as desirable, even for a moment?

To her, everything about him had always seemed beautiful. From that very first time she'd seen him, there had been this wildly beautiful thing inside him. He had felt like a tornado, all that freedom, all that energy. Someone who could go anywhere untethered. Someone who could jump rocks until he reached the farthest one before the ocean churned away from it to travel halfway across the earth. That moment when she had held his hand to balance herself against the whipping surf and wind was what she had held on to for all those years. The tangible form the intangible, out-of-reach idea of freedom had taken in her mind. Now here it was. Finally in her hands and entirely different from how she had expected it to be. Freedom.

For years Kimi had tried to forget what Rahul had said about the ugliness. She tried not to see it in the eyes of bastards like Asif Khan, in the leer of the rickshaw driver. Being determined to see only beauty was a hard job, and Kimi had tried not to think about that word on Rahul's lips every time one of those things happened. But it was like a Post-it note being slapped across her vision: Ugly Place. The world is an Ugly Place.

The queue to get into the airport was ridiculously long. Something had to be wrong given how thoroughly they were checking everyone before letting them through the metal detectors and into the terminal. Kimi joined the line and tried not to think about Asif Khan. The psychopath had taken elementary school children hostage on their school playground last month. That's when Rahul had pumped him full of bullets, rescued the children, and put Asif Khan in a coma. She drew in a long breath. Thinking about Rahul usually did strange things to her, but she especially hated when she got these awful bouts of discomfort in the pit of her stomach, as though something deep inside her seemed to sense that he was in danger.

She tried to talk herself out of doing it, but she couldn't stop herself from turning on her cell phone even though she had sworn not to do it. This made her certifiably stupid given that the reason she had switched it off in the first place was to make sure that Rahul or Papa did not find a way to derail her escape.

Please call me. It's important.

Before she could push it away, a jubilant

blast of hope popped inside her at the sight of those words. She seriously needed to have her head examined. She squeezed her eyes shut and, within the span of a moment, the hope was replaced with a blast of anger just as violent. Why couldn't he leave her alone? She could practically taste her freedom. Why couldn't he let her claim it?

She pulled up his number and glared at the picture of him in those Ray-Ban aviators she had bought him — the only present he had ever accepted from her. They obscured his eyes but left his wide, too-soft-for-that-jaw mouth to express all his amusement at her wanting to take a picture of him in his uniform.

No, she wasn't thinking about him in uniform. And no, she wasn't calling him. Puppy-dog Kimi in all her worshipful glory doing as Rahul asked her to do had left the building. And she was about to leave the country.

Turning off the phone again, she stepped forward as, wonder of wonders, the crawling line moved. She wasn't letting anything ruin this — not his stupid text, not that stupid discomfort in her belly. That part of her life when she would have done anything to make sure he was happy was behind her.

85

7

Rahul
A long time ago
It was hard enough coming home with a split lip and bleeding knees when it was just Aie, Mohit, and Mona. But when Rahul walked through the front door of their housing block and saw his *aie* serving the minister tea, he wanted nothing more than to turn around and go back to the playground. Then Aie caught sight of his face and the cup shook in her hand and Rahul stopped in his tracks.

Aie wasn't like other mothers in the *chawl.* She never raised her voice, never used the cane or the broom to teach her children right from wrong. But she had never let Rahul get away with anything without a firm tongue-lashing that induced enough guilt to rival any caning. These days, however, she treated Rahul as though he were breakable. She tiptoed around him.

Through the doorway across the outside room he could see his own face in the mirrored metal cupboard in the inside room. His jaw was streaked with mud, his lip bloody. Usually, Aie would have asked him a million questions, maybe even threatened to go down to the playground and speak to the boys who had done this to him, threatened to complain to their mothers. Now she looked at Rahul and the cup in her hand barely trembled enough to cause a stutter on the saucer.

Handing Kirit the tea, she withdrew into the kitchen and retrieved a water-soaked piece of cloth. It was a piece of her old cotton sari that she sewed and quilted into napkins and bandages for Rahul's constantly scraped knees and elbows. She pushed him into a chair, and wiped his bleeding nose and dabbed his bruised jaw. But she would not berate him for being a ruffian, not when the man who was alive because his father was dead sat on the divan next to them, and with two aunts from their floor and his grandfather from Pune looking on for good measure.

Kirit had been like an ant infestation these past few weeks. Rahul couldn't seem to shake him off. He kept coming over and trying to strike up conversations with Rahul. But Rahul had a hard enough time talking to Aie and Mona and Mohit, so talking to a man he hated with such ferocity was out of the question.

Finally, when the silence became too heavy to breathe around, Kirit spoke. "Your mother tells me that you and your brother and sister have not yet returned to school."

Rahul had been thinking about that. While he hungered to go somewhere where his mind would have something to do other than what it did now — play memories in an endless loop all day — the idea of being stuck for hours in a place where everyone knew him and therefore expected him to act the way he had before was out of the question. The only thing worse would be if they didn't expect him to be the same person.

In either case, what he and his brother and sister did was not the politician's concern. Why couldn't the man stop coming around and rubbing in their faces the fact that he was alive and kicking?

When Rahul didn't respond, his mother said, "Patil-*saheb* wants you and Mona and Mohit to go to St. Mary's — that English school across the tracks by the bay."

Rahul pushed his mother's hand away. His nose wasn't the only thing throbbing. His entire body vibrated with anger. "No."

Everyone in the room looked at one another as though he, not they, had lost his mind. Didn't they see that Baba would still be here if not for this man?

But those looks held another truth. Suddenly, these decisions lay on his shoulders.

Sometimes Aie used to ask him what he'd like for dinner. She usually gave him a say in what she packed in his tiffin box for lunch. But other than that both Baba and she had expected the children to do as they were told. Rahul hadn't realized what a gift that had been.

Now all those eyes stared at him, as though things of this magnitude suddenly were his to decide. Their gazes reminded him of the impact of the bullets that had vibrated through the air before exploding Baba's chest. And like the bullets, the looks changed everything irreversibly.

Over his mother's head he saw his baby sister hiding behind the curtain that separated the outside room from the inside room. Aie had sewn it from an old bedsheet last year to provide Rahul some privacy when he did his homework in the inside room. Mona clung to the curtain the way she had taken to clinging to Rahul, not letting him go even as she slept fitfully, her open mouth drooling, her nose sniffling at intervals as though in sleep she registered her suddenly scary world in beats.

Her eyes watched him and he gave her the barest nod, answering the question in her beautiful eyes, indicating that yes, she could come to him. She jogged across the room self-consciously and snuggled up next to him on Baba's wicker easy chair with its long arms.

"It's the best education money can buy in this city," the minister said, watching them with his always calculating eyes.

"We don't have money of that kind," Rahul said, not recognizing the adult voice coming from his mouth. Not recognizing anything anymore. All the comfort and familiarity his home had been steeped in had disappeared, gone with such finality it might as well never have existed.

"You don't have to pay for it." Kirit's gaze fell somewhere between respect and a challenge. So this was how adults talked to each other, with their eyes and their tone filling in the gaps children could never quite fill in. Kirit waited to make sure Rahul understood, then filled that gap for him anyway. "I'll take care of everything."

Blood money.

Baba had used that phrase to describe the

money the gangster Azaad *bhai* paid every month to the family who lived in the block right below them. Their oldest son had died in an encounter with the police. Died for Azaad *bhai,* apparently.

"We can't take your money. We won't." Not when his bullets had melted with Baba's ashes.

Baba would never have wanted that.

Or would he?

"We can think about it, right, Rahul?" his mother said gently, that deference in her voice like barbed wire around his wrists.

Kirit got up and walked to him. Rahul had the urge to rise, to meet him halfway, to somehow not be dwarfed by him. He stayed in the chair, his sister tucked into his side, his mother leaning on the chair back, his baby brother fast asleep on a quilt on the floor. Kirit sank to his haunches and spoke directly to Mona. "What do you want to be when you grow up?"

"A doctor," Mona said without hesitation. Baba had bought her a toy doctor set on his last payday. Ever since then, she had been pushing that stethoscope into the chest of anyone who would get within arm's distance of her. Suddenly, Rahul was grateful she hadn't been in that hospital that day. Her dream remained untainted. For that one thing, at least, Rahul didn't feel like such a failure.

Kirit smiled as though Mona had impressed him deeply. "My wife wants our little girl to be a doctor too, like her grandfather," Kirit said, and for one moment he looked just like Baba had looked when he talked about them. "You know you have to study very hard to be a doctor. Almost hundred percent on all your exams."

"She's only six years old," Rahul cut in, and Kirit turned his focus on him.

"You know that medical college, engineering college, any college, in fact, is all in English in our country, correct?"

Rahul refused to flinch. "Our school teaches English." He switched to English. "Mona can speak English." He sounded like he was reading a sentence out of Mona's textbook: *This is Mona. Mona can speak English.*

"I speak English. I write English." Mona recited next to him, and he dropped a kiss on her head.

Kirit patted her cheek and turned to Rahul again. "I've looked at your report cards. Your marks are impressive. Near one hundred percent on everything. You could be whatever you choose to be. English as a second language will only hold you back."

And my father had to die in your place for me to get that? It wasn't an option. Rahul would take his chances with what Baba had provided.

Kirit stood. "There's no hurry. This is a lot to think about. Talk to your mother before you make up your mind. I'll come back tomorrow."

Aie wasn't speaking to him. She placed the steel plate with his favorite okra with dal and rice on the cement floor in front of him, with a little more force than necessary. Mona raised startled eyes at Aie and then looked at Rahul for an explanation. He gave her a nod. *Eat, don't worry.* He wanted her not to worry. He wanted to wipe that look from her eyes forever. The constant fear of someone walking on a shaky bridge over deep water when they didn't know how to swim. A look too old for her beloved face.

Mohit, on the other hand, hadn't registered that their lives had altered in any way. Every evening when the sun sank down to the edge of the sky, which was usually the time Baba came home, he ran to the railing that edged the veranda connecting the blocks on their floor and pressed his face between the timber spindles. His eyes brightened as other fathers returning home

93

from work walked across the courtyard playground, then deflated each time he realized they weren't Baba. When Rahul could't take it anymore, he would pick up Mohit, grab his plastic cricket bat and ball, and take him down to play. Just that easily Mohit would forget. Until dinnertime when he'd ask again. "Dada, when will Baba come home?"

Aie's eyes would fill and Rahul would try again to distract his three-year-old mind with cricket or a story.

Aie mixed a bowl of rice and dal and placed it, a little more gently, in front of Mohit. He stuffed his mouth until his cheeks puffed out. As soon as he started to chew, the excess rice squeezed out between his lips. Without even thinking about it, Aie swiped it off his mouth with her fingers and glared at Rahul.

"Do you realize how selfish you are being?" She popped the excess rice back into Mohit's mouth.

"You want to take money from the man responsible for Baba's death?" Rahul still couldn't believe he could use that tone with Aie when just weeks ago she would have slapped him upside the head for it.

"Don't talk like a mad person, *beta*. I've stayed silent so far because I know what

you've been through. You've been so brave."
Her eyes softened. "But it was your *baba*'s
job to protect the minister and he did his
job like the brave, upstanding man he was.
Like an officer." Her voice wobbled before
cracking again. Baba had worked his way
up the ranks from constable to *naik* to *hawaldar,* and then studied hard to take the
exams that let him jump to the position of
assistant sub-inspector. "You are insulting
his memory by blaming the minister for his
death."

Mona started spilling tears into her food,
and Rahul pushed away his plate, stood, and
lifted her onto his hip. He carried her out
and sat down on Baba's easy chair. His
hands were clean. He hadn't touched his
food.

"Did that minister man really kill Baba?"
Mona asked as he wiped her chubby, light-
skinned cheeks. Little Foreigner they called
her in their *chawl.* She was the only one of
the three kids who had not only taken their
paternal grandmother's light coloring and
pale eyes but also inherited their mother's
flawless features. He carried her to the sink
in the corridor and wiped up her nose,
which had been running as much as her
eyes.

"I'm sorry I said that. It's not true."

She wiped her face on his shirtsleeve. "Then why don't you want us to go to the big English school?"

Before he could answer, his *aie* stuck her head out of the kitchen door, Mohit on her hip, his face and hands smeared with rice and dal. He must've gotten into the food when Aie looked away. "Very soon the minister is going to stop coming around and making that offer," she said.

Rahul put Mona down. "Go wash Mohit up. Then tell him a story and put him down to sleep."

"Yes, Dada." Mona took Mohit from Aie and carried him through the back door to the back corridor that connected the communal bathrooms they shared with their neighbors.

Aie continued to glare at Rahul, but she grabbed his arm and dragged him back to his *paath* — the low wooden stools they sat on to eat. "At least eat your dinner. All that stubbornness must be burning up so much energy." She smiled weakly, and he sat down cross-legged in front of his plate and ate.

"Did you know that your *baba*'s father always told him that he was stupid for working so hard to become an officer when he was already a *hawaldar*? He thought it was wrong for someone to be unsatisfied with their station in life. 'You were born a *hawaldar*'s son. It's your destiny. Why can't that be enough for you?' he always asked. But your *baba* believed we make our own destiny. He believed that, in this country, in this city of ours, if someone works hard, there are no limits. Your grandfather believed that breaking caste lines was a sin. But your *baba* believed that if you didn't take the opportunities God offered you, that was a sin. He would want you to take this opportunity and make the best of it. If something good comes out of something bad, who are we to turn it away?"

But Rahul couldn't. He didn't know why, but he could not take money for Baba's death. He wiped up the last of the dal and rice from his plate and poured water over his hands to rinse off the food. Then he rose and carried his plate to the drain in the corner of the kitchen. Some of the other blocks in their *chawl* building had installed standing sinks in their kitchens. Baba had promised to have one put in for Aie when he received his first promotion. Now it fell to Rahul to make sure Aie didn't spend the rest of her life washing dishes squatted over a drain.

"Baba's pension and provident fund insurance will pay for books. Many children from our school become doctors and engineers," he said.

"Really? Like who? The Kulkarnis' son was the first one in our *chawl* to do it. He's been at JJ Medical College for only a year, and his mother tells me he has been struggling so much he's become as thin as a broomstick." She picked up the *paath* stools off the floor and stacked them up in a corner. "And what provident fund? We'll have to bribe everyone up and down the chain to see any of Baba's fund and insurance money. By the time we see one paisa, you'll only be able to use it for your children's education. If we're lucky, that is. His pension barely covers food. My sewing and catering orders and the money your *baba* saved up can only go so far."

The way her lips were pursed together told him she wasn't going to let this go.

"I'll go to the police station tomorrow and talk to someone about Baba's provident fund."

But he would not take money from that man.

The only reason Rahul showed up at the police station so early was that he hadn't been able to sleep one wink all night. One problem with being good with numbers was that once he started making calculations in his head he couldn't stop until he had a solution. Frustrated by his ability to race through the problems they gave him, a few years ago his teachers had let him take math with the upper classes. Those classes were harder, but until now he had never been faced with a problem he couldn't find a solution for.

Try as he might he hadn't been able to come up with a way to stretch Baba's pension check and the interest from the savings to pay for rent, school, and food. Not even if Aie's sewing and cooking orders magically doubled. Let alone put money away so they would have enough for his college. Once he got a job he knew he would be able to take care of everything, but until then their money kept feeling like their sheets, not sufficient to cover the feet and the shoulders at the same time.

Baba always said that the only time a police *chowki* didn't feel like the chaos outside a sold-out movie theater showing a super-hit movie was before ten in the morning. Apparently, criminals liked to sleep in. Maybe eight a.m. was far too early, because the criminals weren't the only ones asleep at this hour. The constable folded over the reception desk was drooling onto its metal surface and snoring loud enough to scare away anyone looking for justice. Rahul was about to knock on the desk to wake the sleeping constable, but a sub-inspector came out of the bathroom and Rahul caught his eye.

"*Kay re?* What for you're here?" he asked, looking Rahul up and down while zipping up his fly.

"I'm *Hawaldar . . .* I mean . . . Assistant Sub-Inspector Savant's son. I need to speak with Shinde *kaka.*" Inspector Shinde was Baba's boss. He had only recently been transferred to this *chowki,* but Rahul had met him a few times and then in the hospital and at the cremation. He had asked Rahul to come to him if he needed anything.

The man looked around as if to check who else was listening. "Oh, you're that Savant's boy. Sorry about what happened." But he didn't look sorry at all, and Rahul's defenses rose. "Shinde-sir is off duty today. Out for family wedding. You come." He scratched his crotch and beckoned to Rahul to follow him into his office.

Rahul joined his palms. "I can come back when Shinde *kaka* is here." But the officer didn't stop so he followed him into the office.

The man sank into a chair behind a desk

and narrowed his eyes at Rahul. "What's so special about your Shinde *kaka*? Tell me what you need and maybe I can help you."

Perhaps the man wasn't as creepy as he looked. "I wanted to talk about Baba's provident fund."

The man looked over Rahul's shoulder. "Shut the door behind you, boy."

Rahul had nothing private to talk about, and the request struck him as odd. But beggars can't be choosers, as his *aie* loved to say. So he did as he was told.

"You look more like your mother, ha?" the sub-inspector said needlessly. Matching you up with your parents seemed to be the favorite pastime of adults who met you for the first time, and Rahul nodded. "Very beautiful woman, that one is."

Rahul had heard it a million times, but coming from this man it sounded somehow offensive. But he didn't know what to do about it, so he said, "Where would I find out about Baba's provident fund?"

"I'm in charge of that paperwork. Did you know that?"

"Good, so I'm in the right place then."

The man laughed, an unnecessarily loud guffaw, and walked around the desk and pulled out a chair for Rahul. "Sit."

Rahul didn't move. "I can stand."

"Did you not hear me? I'm responsible for the paperwork. That means if I don't file it, you don't get the money. Do you know how much of a backlog we currently have? Most people have to wait for a few years."

"A few years? But Baba died on duty."

He laughed that sick laugh again and patted the chair. "Put your bum here and I'll explain. I said it could take a few years. I didn't say you would have to wait a few years."

Rahul had this thing inside that he always thought of as a barometer. He could gauge when things were wrong or right. And he knew something was wrong here. Something was very wrong with this man. He knew sitting down was a bad idea, but he knew he had to get Baba's money. So he sat.

"I can tell you're a smart boy," the sub-inspector said and licked his lips and scratched his crotch again. Did he have some sort of infection down there? Because he kept touching himself far more than was decent. "So your *baba* was a *hawaldar* until last month?"

Rahul nodded. Baba had studied late every night to pass his exams to go from being a *hawaldar* to an officer. Rahul had stayed up with him, quizzed him, and even explained some of the math on the test to him.

"That means you really need this money, ha? Your father didn't get a chance to stash bribes away for a rainy day. Why didn't your mother come? Why did she send you, a mere boy?"

"I was only trying to help my *aie*. I can come back with her if you want an adult to take care of it. I just need to know what the procedure is."

The man gave Rahul another narrow-eyed look. "You're one of those boys who thinks he is too smart, aren't you?"

Another question that had absolutely no good answer, so Rahul said, "What paper-work do I need to fill out to get Baba's money?"

The man rested his hip on the table. "So impatient. Okay, I'll come to the point. But first I want you to understand that I am the only person in charge of these papers. No one else. You do as I say and you'll have the money in your bank next week. Otherwise, who knows . . ." He looked at his watch, then counted something on his fingers. "With our backlog, maybe a year, year and a half."

So this was how the corruption adults kept talking about worked. The man wanted a bribe. Rahul relaxed a little. "If I had money to give you, would I be here?" Maybe the man wanted some of Baba's fund money, but Rahul was damned if he would offer that up without a fight.

The man leaned forward, treating Rahul to the nastiest mix of tobacco and chai on his breath. "Not all needs are satisfied by money. Some are satisfied rather more easily."

The barometer inside Rahul went mad, sending discomfort crawling across his skin. "What do you want?"

He shouldn't have asked, because the man answered by reaching out and stroking Rahul's cheek.

Rahul swatted his hand away and tried to get up. "What are you doing?"

The man held the chair in place. "You're a smart boy. I think you know what I'm doing." He grabbed Rahul's hand.

Rahul struggled to snatch it away, but the man's grip was stronger than Rahul had expected, and before he knew what was happening, he pushed Rahul's hand into his crotch, his possibly infected crotch. He was horribly hard and his engorged penis twitched under the fabric of his pants.

Rahul put all his strength into pushing away, his grunt of effort getting trapped in his throat. The man let him go and watched calmly as Rahul jumped out of the chair and scampered back, nausea churning in his belly like spoiled milk.

"The first time you touch it is the hardest. It gets easier," he said almost kindly, a sick mixture of amusement and cruelty making his eyes strangely bright. He took another step closer and Rahul stumbled back again.

He kept stepping closer, and Rahul kept stepping away until his back was pressed against a wall.

"Not so tough anymore, are we, little boy?" he said, although Rahul was almost as tall as him. He leaned into Rahul's ear, making that spoiled-milk sickness creep up into his mouth and causing him to gag. "Another man would have asked you to send your mother. You're lucky you'll do just fine for me. Come to my house this evening and I'll take care of the paperwork." With that he almost pulled away, but then he leaned in again. "Oh, and don't even think about telling anyone. No one will believe you, and the ones who do believe you will see you as a faggot forever. Now stop staring at me and get out before I put your hands and mouth to good use."

The waves soaking Rahul's clothes were

warm, the sun beating down on him hot enough to burn off his skin, and yet he couldn't stop shaking from the cold inside him. He had no idea how long he'd been sitting on the rock with the ocean crashing around him, but the salty spray splashing him at intervals was so steady and rhythmic it almost soothed him.

Part of him wanted to storm back to the police *chowki* and turn the man's gun on him. Part of him felt so tired he wanted to slip into the ocean until Baba's dead weight eased off his lap, until the sick turgidity burning the palm of his hand washed off, until the corrosive guilt of those two sensations living inside him at once drowned.

"*Oy,* you! Are you blind? Can't you see the tide rising? Get back here before you drown," someone shouted to him from the beach.

He slipped off the rock and into the water that had risen all the way to his thighs. A wave rolled up to him. He let the surface of the water slap his palm as he skimmed the glassy surface, surfing the wave with his hand before submerging it in the powerful gush. He stood there like that, wave after wave washing his hand, knowing he had to get it clean before he touched his life again, knowing the events of today were something he had to leave behind in this ocean, because he could not carry them into his home.

He spun around and faced the palm trees lining Carter Road as it ran along the Arabian Sea. Across the curving road, Pali Hill rose in a gentle pincushion of buildings. Faceless garden-filled terraces and balconies witnessing the endless churning of the ocean edged by a beach, half rocks–half sand, and him, Rahul Surajrao Savant, a nameless speck looking up at a world where payment was demanded of children to claim the legacy of their dead fathers.

Up at the top of the hill overlooking the ocean was Kirit Patil's house. Aie thought he was being stupidly proud by refusing the politician's guilt money. She was right. When you had nothing else, pride left you with unwanted things in your hands. Someday he'd earn his pride. But to get there he'd have to let someone help him first. It might as well be the man who got other people to take his bullets for him.

8

Kimi
A long time ago

It had been eight days since Mamma had let Kimi out of the house, and she was so bored she was climbing the walls. Like, literally. She had climbed over the stone wall that ran around their backyard, jumped into the neighboring building's back lawn, and then walked over to the play area and parked herself on a bench to watch the children play. It wasn't the first time either. Every time she had the sniffles, Mamma acted as though she was going to catch some sort of fatal infection and die. It was most annoying.

The joke in her school was that she spent more time out of school than in school. They called her *"Kum Aya"* instead of Kimaya, a sorry wordplay on how little she "visited" school. She couldn't believe her classmates were jealous of her. As if being locked up in the house any time you so much as sneezed was something anyone would enjoy.

Add to that the fact that she was never allowed to go to the playground (too many other children had touched the equipment with their germy hands). Papa had put a jungle gym in their backyard when she had complained, so she had stopped complaining about anything else, because who wanted to play by themselves on swings and slides? Well, she had to now that Papa had done that for her. She was never allowed to go to her friends' homes (who knows how sanitary their parents kept their homes?). Her friends never came over because who wanted to explain to them why the servants kept asking them to wash their hands?

Okay, so strictly speaking, Kimi had no friends. For all of these reasons. The only reason that she was even allowed to go to school at all was because she promised Mamma that she cleaned her hands with alcohol disinfectant every fifteen minutes, and that she wiped her desk with Lysol, and that she did not let anyone bring their face too close to hers when they talked. She poured out half a travel-sized bottle of alcohol gel into the school commode every day so Mamma thought she actually used it.

Now, she was fully aware of what a big waste that was. Just because she lived in a big house and had to be careful not to say she liked something to stop her parents from promptly buying it for her, it wasn't as if she didn't know how lucky she was. When you stayed home every time you caught a cold, and when you had no friends, you read a lot of books and you watched a lot of TV. And TV was basically filled with how wretched the world was. Unless you watched the soap operas where the world was filled with very large families that wore a lot of makeup and fancy clothes and conspired to ruin one another. It gave her a headache. So she watched the news instead where, come to think of it, reporters wore too much makeup and fancy clothes and talked about people conspiring to ruin one another.

How she envied those journalists. The fact that they got to travel to all corners of the world and share their experiences with people who never left their homes was amazing to her. The world was such a huge place, and the only people who truly seemed to comprehend its magnitude were the journalists. It was all she had ever wanted to be. Which was hilarious, because even to just sit on a bench in the building adjoining her house she had to arrange pillows on her bed and pull the covers over them so she could slip out her balcony and climb over a wall.

Her watch beeped. She had set an alarm for forty minutes, because her nanny would check in with sugarcane juice to hydrate her every hour and she had to be back in her room before her next round. She had precisely ten minutes to make it back. Circling the building, she went to the front gate. She picked late afternoon for her outings because it was when Bhola, their security guard, went inside to get his chai and chatted too long with the kitchen staff. Just enough time for Kimi to jump over the wall and get back inside. She climbed the embankment around the huge banyan tree outside the stone wall between the building and her house, then pulled herself onto the wall, and then landed on their gatehouse roof.

She was about to jump off the gatehouse and onto the high retaining walls around the bushes when she noticed Bhola standing right there talking to a boy who looked like he had just walked through a tropical storm. Except it was April and the monsoon wasn't due for three months. He was trying

111

to convince Bhola to let him come in and see Papa.

"Patil-saheb knows who I am," the boy said, his proud stance completely at odds with his wretched, damp state. "If you tell him Assistant Sub-Inspector Surajrao Savant's son is here to see him, he'll see me."

He had to lean back and look up at Bhola, who was the tallest human being Kimi had ever seen in her life. But even staring up at gigantic Bhola, the boy's demeanor was confident, almost confrontational.

Kimi folded herself into a crouch. If Bhola saw her, these little adventures would be over. Some of the servants she could convince to lie for her, but Bhola was too loyal to Papa and too obsessed with security to let her get away with it. Plus, he'd lose his job if she forced him to lie and he got caught. Her only hope was that if she stayed very still they wouldn't see her.

"Patil-saheb isn't expecting you, and no one can just walk in off the street and see him." Bhola tried to make his tone kind but firm in his Bhola way.

The stormy boy looked up, ready to present his case again, and met Kimi's eyes. *Yipes!*

She pressed a finger to her lips and joined

112

her palms, pleading for him to stay quiet. But she was an idiot. Why would he? He didn't even know her.

Bhola must have noticed the quizzical frown that folded between the boy's brows because he was about to turn around when the boy pushed both palms into his face and started to cry. Really loudly. Bhola spun back to him.

"You know Patil-saheb was shot at during that election rally, don't you?" he said through remarkably realistic sobs that even she would have believed if they hadn't come on so fast. "My father was the policeman who took the bullets for him."

Kimi pressed a hand to her mouth. How terrible! Was he really the son of the man who had saved Papa's life?

The boy continued to fake-sob. At least she thought the sobs were fake. "Patil-saheb said I should come and see him if I needed something, and now here I am and you won't even tell him I'm here."

"*Arrey, beta,* don't cry. I had no idea who you were. Wait while I call him." He pulled his stool out of the gatehouse and placed it next to the boy, whose sobs had magically cleared. "Here, sit for a bit. Did you walk here?"

He sat. "Thank you. Are you calling him

then?" he asked, and Bhola went into the gatehouse to use the intercom.

The boy narrowed his eyes at her as she crouched there staring at him. He flicked his chin and she realized that he was telling her to move. She jumped onto the retaining wall.

Bhola was about to emerge from the gatehouse. "I'm so sorry. Saheb wants me to take you inside. Come, come."

She froze, and the boy threw himself on Bhola, hugging him and pushing him back into the gatehouse. "Thank you, thank you," he said. "I really don't know how to thank you."

"*Oy*, mention not, mention not." Bhola sounded so confused she had to press her hand into her mouth to keep from bursting into giggles as she ran across the side yard, slipped into the side door, and took the stairs to her room just in time for her juice delivery.

Sarika *tai* found her giggling when she came in with the tray.

"Baby must be feeling better." She touched Kimi's forehead. "The color is back in your cheeks."

Kimi's heart was beating fast and she had the craziest urge to jump up and down. All her life she had wanted to have an adventure. Today she'd had a real-life one. She started giggling again.

"Did Baby read a joke or something?"

She thought about Bhola's face when Storm Boy had burst into sobs. "Yes, Sarika *tai,* it was so funny."

"Silly girl." Sarika smiled and handed Kimi her glass of juice, which thanks to being out in the sun for an hour was exactly what she needed.

She gulped it down, relishing the bite of ginger and the tartness of lemon mixed in with the stark sweetness of the sugarcane. "I feel amazing. Do you think I can walk around the house for a bit?"

"Mamma said to rest," Sarika said. "But you do look better, so I suppose a little bit of walking around wouldn't hurt anyone."

As soon as Sarika left, Kimi raced down the stairs to her mother's office, which happened to be right next to her father's study. Fortunately, Mamma wasn't home. Kimi pressed her ear to the door connecting the two rooms.

"Mona can go," Storm Boy said in that too-grown-up voice. "Mohit doesn't start school for two more years."

Papa's voice was nothing like his usual voice. He used neither the tone he used with her and Mamma, nor the tone he used with the staff, but rather something between those two. "The condition is that all three of you go. I'll pay for everything. The uniforms, books, lunches, transportation. But you have to go as well. My offer is only valid if you go as well."

The boy didn't respond, and Kimi pressed the door open a crack because she had to see his face. He looked so angry. But it wasn't how anger usually looked. His eyes reminded her of those people they interviewed on TV after disasters. So much anger but also so much restlessness because there was no one and nothing that could ease them, as though their situation was so absolute that their anger seemed like a waste to even themselves.

If she ever lost Papa, it's exactly how she would feel.

Papa took a step close to the boy, and he stepped back. For a moment his anger and confidence collapsed around him as though Papa were someone to fear. Papa stepped away and the boy straightened again, puffing his chest out with salvaged pride.

"Listen, *beta.*" Papa's tone was suddenly gentle, almost helpless. "I know you blame me for what happened. And I am to blame. Those bullets were meant for me. I know. I can't bring your *baba* back. I wish I could.

116

But I don't have that power. No human being does. What I can give you is any life you choose. You dream it up and I can make it happen. That power I do have. Let me use it. Whatever you want to be. I'll make it happen."

"Can you fire a sub-inspector?" he said, his eyes shining with anger again.

That threw Papa off and he didn't respond.

"Fire him without asking questions?" the boy pushed.

When Papa still didn't answer, he smiled. "See, no one can make *anything* happen."

Papa opened his mouth, then closed it again. They studied each other. Papa and this Storm Boy, who retained no hint of the person who had pretend-sobbed to help her escape into her own home.

No one ever stood up to Papa. He was a gentle man, but everyone always did as he said. Except maybe Mamma. He was also six feet tall and he could stare anyone into submission.

Except the boy didn't seem to see it that way.

Papa flicked his hand and his assistant left the room. "Give me the bastard's name." His voice was angry enough to match the boy's.

117

Instead of being happy at getting his way the boy deflated again. As though what Papa had said was the last thing he had expected.

"I won't ask questions. I promise."

"You can really have him fired? Just like that?" Suddenly, all the storm was gone from him.

"Not just like that. It will take some work, but yes, I can have it done. Because it seems like it will convince you to trust me and take my help."

Another silence passed between them and Kimi held her breath.

"Okay," the boy said at last.

"Okay, you'll give me the name?"

"No. I'll think about going to St. Mary's and letting you help me."

"And the sub-inspector?"

"I don't want you to mention him again."

"Fine. How much time do you need to think about it?"

He shrugged and Papa's phone rang. "Sorry, I need to take this. I'll check back in a few days. I hope you'll make the right decision. Rafiq will show you out." With that, Papa left the room, and his assistant, Rafiq *kaka,* came in and led the boy away.

Kimi ran down the stairs and through the empty guest suite and pushed open the French doors that led to the terrace. She jumped over the railing and circled the house to the main entrance just as Rafiq *kaka* and the boy left the front porch and headed toward the gate.

She had no idea what she was doing. All she knew was that she had to talk to the boy.

"Rafiq *kaka*," she called before she changed her mind and ran back inside.

They turned to her. Storm Boy's eyes almost popped out of his head. He hadn't been this surprised to see her on the gatehouse roof.

"Yes, Kimi-baby?" her father's assistant asked and she desperately racked her brain for an answer.

"Kimi-baby, are you feeling all right? Do you need something?" Rafiq sounded so worried the boy frowned.

"No, no. I just wanted to tell you that Papa is looking for you. It sounded urgent. Very urgent."

Rafiq's brows drew together in confusion. He turned to the house. Kimi quickly waved at the boy. He looked behind him to make sure she was waving at him before waving back. Then he looked at his hand as though he wasn't quite sure why he had just done that.

Rafiq turned back to her. "I'll show Rahul

out and go see what Patil-sir needs. Thank you. I'm glad you're feeling better."

"It looked very urgent," she said. "I think Papa needs something right now. Don't worry, I can show him out." She grabbed Rafiq *kaka*'s hand and pushed him toward the front door. Thankfully, Rafiq *kaka* always found great amusement in everything she did and he laughed and disappeared into the house, shaking his head fondly.

The boy was staring at her as though she had a few screws loose. Right now she totally agreed with him.

"Are you sick?" he asked her in English that sounded the way her papa spoke it, as though it was being spoken in Marathi first and then translated. And really, why was that the only question anyone ever asked her?

"I'm fine," she snapped, when all she'd really wanted to do was thank him.

"Then why was Patil-saheb's PA acting like you're sick? And if you're sick, why were you sitting on top of the gatehouse?" Suddenly, he seemed to register that she might be crazy. He took a step back from her and looked around to see if anyone would help him if she lost it.

She considered scaring him by making crazy faces, but these things were only funny if they were spontaneous and she usually thought about everything before she did it and that ruined it. "I wasn't sitting on top of the gatehouse."

He narrowed his eyes and studied her. "It was definitely you."

She rolled her eyes. "Of course it was me, silly. But I wasn't sitting there, I was trying to get back in the house."

Once again, he looked around to check if someone was nearby in case he needed help. "You ran away?" He gawked at the house. "From this mansion?"

She shrugged. "Every afternoon. It's the only way I get to leave home by myself."

Now he looked scared.

"I'm not crazy, okay? My parents think I'll get sick if I leave the house. It's complicated. Anyway, I just wanted to thank you for helping me earlier. Thank you. The gate is that way." She pointed to the gate and turned away, oddly disappointed. She had no idea what she had expected.

"Wait," he said behind her. "Where do you go when you run away?"

She spun around, all her excitement rushing back. "To the next building."

That made him laugh. Like flat-out laugh at her as though she were a comic strip in the newspaper.

And it made her very angry. "What? You know a better place to run away to?"

"Of course I do," he said so smugly, she found herself walking past him. Bhola wasn't at the gatehouse. He must have gone to get some chai. Papa and Rafiq were probably really trying to solve some emergency, and Mamma would not return from the temple until it was time to turn on the lamps, which was hours away.

"Come on," she said and broke into a run.

"What are you doing?" But he ran after her.

"You're going to show me your better place."

"No, I'm not." But she was already on the retaining wall and jumping onto the gatehouse.

"Stop," he said, but he followed her.

They were both a little winded when they jumped into the compound of the neighboring building behind the big banyan tree.

"Are you mental?" he asked her.

Instead of answering his stupid question she grabbed his hand. "I want to see where you go when you run away."

9

Rahul
Present day

Rahul hopped off Tina and jogged back through the gates of The Mansion and up the porch steps and through the giant front doors that the doorman held open. Having been a servant in the house for so long meant he knew every inch of it well. Having been Kimi's best friend meant not a single servant would stop him from going wherever the hell he wanted to go.

Kirit's peon rushed up to Rahul and led him to Kirit's office. Kirit was on the phone looking like he had popped all the blood vessels in his face at once. His hand shook as he wiped the sweat beaded across his forehead.

"If you come anywhere near her, I will kill you, I swear." He threw the phone across the couch and noticed Rahul. "Rahul! What the hell? Who the hell is doing your job?

How did Khan get away?"

Was that Asif Khan on the phone? Had he been talking about Kimi? It was clear from the minister's face that Kimi was in danger. The pressure of his anger built so fast, his chest felt like it was going to split open.

"He took the children's ward hostage. We got another four of his men. Why did he call you? How does he even have your number?"

"You're interrogating *me* right now? When that bastard is running around town when he should be in custody?" Kirit was inches from Rahul's face. For a moment Rahul thought Kirit was going to shake him. Rahul was pretty certain he was about to shake Kirit too. But then Kirit stepped away.

"He's threatened to go after Kimi," he said almost to himself, then glared at Rahul again, rage alive in his eyes. "You've put Kimi in danger and you call her your friend?"

For two years Rahul had tried to get Kirit to back his investigation of the organ black market that Asif had been running. Kirit had repeatedly shut him down. Now Kimi was at risk and the minister wanted to blame Rahul?

"You have to tell me where she is, sir." For the first time in years, the term of respect felt sour on his tongue.

Kirit's face was sweating. Now was not the time to have a heart attack. Kirit called for his shoes and one of the servants ran in and started helping him into them. "She asked for two weeks." His voice fell to a whisper and he cleared his throat. "She asked for two weeks of freedom. On her own. She said she couldn't breathe. Said she wanted to live. That's why she called you here this morning, to tell you."

"How could you let her go? Now?" After all these years of controlling Kimi's every breath, Kirit had decided to ease off now? With a psychopath who had attacked her still breathing?

Rahul had felt rage at Kirit once, the kind he had never allowed himself to feel again. He reminded himself of how unwarranted that rage had been. This rage was unwarranted too. Kirit wasn't the only one at fault here. Rahul was just as much to blame for driving her away.

Kirit pulled a monogrammed handkerchief out of his pocket and dabbed his face. When he looked up, his anger seemed to have disappeared into the pathos of that gesture. Suddenly, he was nothing more than a father with a child in danger.

"She's been locked up for twelve years. I

locked her up for twelve years. I had her watched every minute for the past two years. I didn't think Asif would wake up. You put five bullets in him. I thought she could live now. I thought it was time to give her that. You have to find her. And you have to keep her safe. No one else can."

"I intend to." He had never meant anything more. He touched the piece of paper in his shirt pocket. She was gone because of him. Because he'd broken her heart over and over again when all she'd ever done was patch his up. From the first time she'd befriended him, she had taken him in — utterly lost as he was, alone in ways that left him with no one to turn to. She had always understood him in ways he didn't understand himself. Now she was gone. And a psycho was on her tail. And no one seemed to know why.

He met Kirit's eyes, channeling all his rage into purpose. "We need the entire force hunting that bastard down."

"Anything, everything. You have full control. Do what you must. Shoot at sight. And shoot to kill. You understand me? No more damage from that bastard."

Those were not instructions Rahul needed. Asif Khan would not leave his sight alive again. "I need details of what he said, sir, and why he called you."

This time Kirit's face remained unflinching. "It's because of your damn obsession with the Jennifer Joshi case. He threatened me last year to get you off the case. He threatened to go after Kimi. But you wouldn't listen to me. He went after Kimi because you went after him. You wouldn't let the case go, and now Kimi's the one who's paying the price."

That's why Kirit hadn't supported his investigation? Why hadn't he just told Rahul?

Kirit's gaze went sharp again. Not a trace of the withered old man. "Would you have dropped the case if I had told you Kimi was in danger?"

Rahul didn't have time for twenty questions right now, but the guilt in his gut was a live thing. He would never let her pay the price for his actions. That much he knew. "I'll make sure he doesn't get anywhere near her."

Kirit didn't respond, but Rahul didn't expect him to. Rahul had never kept a single promise he had made to Kirit about Kimi. That was all going to change now. "I need her location, sir. And please don't deny you're tracking her every move."

The airport was teeming with people. It was as though every human being in Mumbai was trying to get away, like those disaster movies Kimi and he used to love so much, with names like *When the Time Ran Out* — with a volcano erupting, or a tornado eating everything in its path, or a ship sinking while the doomed passengers tried to head to safety in its upturned hull.

Kimi was standing in a queue that snaked almost all the way around the terminal building. Rahul didn't know if it was a good thing or a bad thing that she didn't know that the first-class line was on the other side. In a sick sort of way, the crowds made it safer.

He stepped up behind her and the smell of tuberoses under expensive perfume cut through all the acrid smells of Mumbai. "Hi, Kimi," he said, trying not to fill his lungs with the relief of her scent.

She turned to him, her eyes brightening for an instant before disappointment took over. Then anger followed. She looked away, not even bothering to acknowledge him.

He reached for her suitcase. It wasn't easy. The damn thing was bright purple. A purple so bright, in fact, that he was grateful to be wearing his sunglasses. Still, he tried to take it from her. They had to get going because they were an open target here. Her grip tightened around the handle of the purple monstrosity, even as she refused to look at him.

Leaning closer, he spoke to the back of her head. "Please, Kimi, you have to come with me. It's not safe here."

Instead of responding she took a step away from him. The old lady standing behind them threw him a look fierce with warning, which naturally Kimi caught and it instantly cheered her up. One look at the grandma who seemed to think he was somehow assaulting Kimi, and Kimi grinned at her with such sweetness that Rahul wondered if he had imagined the intensity of her anger just now. But of course he hadn't.

Instead of telling the lady she knew him, she shared a long commiserating look with her. Grandma took that as an invitation to glare at Rahul some more. He had no doubt Kimi was memorizing that glare to use on him later, all the while continuing to play suitcase tug-of-war with him. He knew she wasn't going to let the bag go, so he did. Then he swept the area one more time, moving his body to cover hers so bullets from the most crowded parts wouldn't reach her while he tried to find a way to do this without scaring her any more than he had to.

"What are you doing?" she asked, finally catching on that something was wrong.

He tried not to notice the exact moment when she registered that this getaway she wanted so badly was about to be ruined. Her eyes did that thing where they struggled between fighting and accepting, and her lips pouted with how much she hated that struggle.

"This is not how I wanted to tell you." He placed a hand on her shoulder, then withdrew it too quickly when the touch zinged against his palm.

She grew even more annoyed.

He had to stop being such an idiot about touching her. She was his best friend, for shit's sake. These fireworks that his body threw out when he got near her had to stop. Especially now. He needed to stay sharp.

A scuffle of some sort erupted down the line, and he moved around her again to cover that side. Two of the other officers rushed at the arguing passengers.

"What the hell is going on, Rahul?" she hissed behind him.

So much for trying to do this without

scaring her.

This time when he turned around he braced himself before taking her arm and leaning close to her ear. "Asif Khan woke up and escaped from the hospital."

He felt every nuance of the tremor that went through her at those words.

"Let's go," she said. But before she followed him, she turned to the old lady who had come to her aid.

"He only looks scary," she said with a grateful smile. "Nothing to worry about. Enjoy your trip." Then she gave her a quick hug, this complete stranger, who in turn grabbed her face with wrinkled hands and kissed her forehead before waving good-bye as though they were in some sort of melodramatic climactic scene of a Bollywood film.

As they made their way through the crowd, a formation of officers surrounded them. They were all in plainclothes and no one would've known who they were or what they were doing. Not Kimi, though. She didn't miss a thing.

"Maybe if all these cops had been at the hospital watching Khan instead of gallivanting about town, we wouldn't need to scurry around like this," she snapped, and he had the insane urge to smile.

The feeling didn't last long.

He focused on his surroundings again as they made the long walk to the back of the terminal and approached the restricted area where he had left his Jeep. The crowd thinned out until it was just them and the officers with the terminal building behind them and the parking lot beyond. A spark of awareness tugged at Rahul's senses, a horrible feeling that he was missing something. His Jeep was parked by the curb in the restricted area, which was completely isolated. Someone should have been watching the Jeep. One of the constables approached it, and Rahul shouted for him to get away. "Stop, Rao! Get back!"

In the time that it took the constable to turn and break into a run, a deafening blast ripped through the air. The constable's body flew forward.

Rahul spun Kimi around, wrapping his body around hers.

For a few endless seconds everything froze in place — the officers around him caught in the middle of twisting away from the explosion, the constable suspended spread-eagled in the air, Kimi's face pressed into his chest, her hands fisted in his shirt.

Then everything started to move at once.

The scraps of metal flung from the jeep

fell to the ground with dull thunks and broke through the buzzing silence. The constable's body slammed into the pavement. Kimi pushed away from Rahul, her hands shaking as they examined him for damage, her terrified eyes flooding with relief when she found him unhurt. Screams rose around them in fits and starts and then exploded into a din.

"This way, boss." Maney ran up to them. "You have to get her out of here."

The other officers ran at the destroyed Jeep and to the fallen constable, who sat up looking disoriented. Breath flooded back into Rahul's lungs.

"Take my car," Maney said before grabbing Kimi's bag and breaking into a jog.

Rahul followed him, his arm still around Kimi. They crossed the restricted area, the smell of smoke and carbon filling the afternoon air.

Maney led them to a white Santro on the other side of the lot. "It's the missus's car. I tried to tell her that a Swift was a better idea. So much more value for money. I mean yes, the Santro is a little cheaper, but —" Maney stopped when Rahul cleared his throat as they reached the white Santro.

He handed Rahul the keys. "It should be safe. No one knows it's mine, so no one will know you're in it. I'll get a ride from one of the boys. Murli wants to show me his car, but he lives all the way on the other side of town. Hassan lives just —"

This time Kimi cleared her throat to stop him. Bless her.

Rahul unlocked the car. Panic was spreading through the crowd and scattering people in all directions. They had to get out of here before every car in the parking lot tried to leave at the exact same time.

"Thanks," he said to Maney. "Keep me posted about Rao." But the constable who had been approaching Rahul's Jeep had been far enough away from it that he would be fine.

"Based on the size of the blast, it looks like a homemade pipe device, boss," Maney said, echoing what Rahul was thinking. "Rao will be fine. Definitely traumatized, maybe even bruised, but nothing more serious, I'm sure."

"Get him to the hospital and let me know what the doctor says."

Maney whipped a little salute, slammed Kimi's door shut, and ran back into the chaos as Rahul pulled away.

Kimi buckled herself in without a single word. There was the slightest tremble in her fingers, but she wasn't shaking anymore.

She hadn't screamed or panicked. There had been no histrionics. She was the most exuberant person he knew in all the world. The slightest little thing made her explode with excitement, but he had never seen her lose control of herself in fear, and she hadn't today.

He wanted to turn to her, wanted to take her hands in his and soothe her in some way. Instead, he shifted gears with more force than necessary and maneuvered the car up the entrance ramp to exit the parking lot, flashing his ID at the attendant who ran at him. The approach road to the airport had already been cordoned off and he was able to use it to get out of the mess that was fast turning into a full-blown disaster even as his men tried their best to contain it. If Kimi hadn't been her stubborn self, if she had listened to him and left with him immediately the way he had asked her to when he found her standing in line, they would have reached the police jeep sooner. They would have been inside the jeep when the bomb went off. She would have been sitting in the passenger seat. Which is where the bomb had been planted. There was no longer any doubt about what Asif Khan wanted or who his target was.

10

Kimi's ears were still ringing. But she didn't know if it was from the bomb that could have taken her butt right off her body or from the anger that someone had done that. To her, to Rahul, to that poor man who could have been killed if Rahul didn't possess that super-cop DNA that had made him sense danger and shout for the man to get away from the car.

Rahul! Just the thought of him was not doing good things for her anger levels. Rahul, who thought it was okay to lie to her, to turn away from her, to refuse to help her, and now somehow thought it was okay to throw himself in the path of bullets for her! As if that were in any way a thing she could ever live with! Every time she thought she couldn't be angrier with him, he proved her wrong.

And now, after acting like her human armor and sweeping her away from a bloody (she couldn't believe she was even thinking the word) *bomb!*, he sat there in stony silence taking her to God knows where. Well, he wasn't the only one who could do silence.

She wrapped her arms around herself. But she hated having to go inside herself, hated that old feeling of not having any control over anything but her mind.

"Don't do that," he said, deciding to break his silence just when she had decided that she didn't need him to, and knowing exactly what she was feeling. The man made her so very tired. "I found you. You're safe now. I won't let him touch you again."

She glared at him. "You're the one who let him escape." He was also the one who had taken away her first chance at freedom. "Don't try and be a hero about this."

He was about to respond, but of course his phone buzzed, and he held up a finger and spoke into the Bluetooth device sticking out of his ear. "Nikhil. Where are you and Nikki? Where's Joy? Sorry about the voice messages."

He listened. Apparently, Rahul had left this person messages about Asif Khan's escape too. She thought about the message he had left her.

Please call me. It's important.

Yeah, this wasn't quite what she had been expecting that to be about.

"Okay, stay in a public place. Yes, the food court is good. I'll send someone to take you home, and I'll see you there in half an hour."

More silence.

"Yes. She's with me. I'll fill you in when I get there."

He disconnected the phone, then made a call to send someone over to the mall to take the people he had been speaking with home.

Then he turned to her. "Do you mind going to Andheri first? I need to take care of this."

She shrugged. "Why am I here, Rahul? And don't say, 'Because Asif escaped.' I want the real reason."

He opened his mouth, then closed it. "Because he threatened to come after you. And I'm going to kill him before he gets anywhere near you."

"Why?"

He gave her a look from behind those aviators that she was glad she couldn't see.

"Don't flatter yourself, I'm not trying to get you to profess your love for me." Doing it once was stupid enough. "You've made it

138

abundantly clear how you feel. What I meant was: Why is Asif coming after me? I've only seen the man once in my life. Why is he so interested in me?"

"I don't know."

"I don't believe you." Had he always lied to her about everything so easily? Or was it that everyone lied out in the world and it was just another thing she needed to learn to navigate? "Does it have anything to do with Papa?"

His hands tightened on the steering wheel, making the thick muscles in his forearms jump to life under his folded-up shirtsleeves. "I only just found out about this. But Kirit-sir told me that last year Asif Khan started blackmailing him to get him to drop our organ-black-market investigation."

"The one you were involved in with . . . with that doctor?" Kimi tried not to think about that day when she'd seen them together. Possibly the worst day of her life.

"Jen was a really good friend, Kimi, that's all," he said with far too much gentleness, as though she were a jealous puppy who needed a head pat.

"I thought I was your only friend, Rahul." Another lie he had told her over and over again. But saying it made her feel like that jealous puppy again, one that was fast developing a pathetic whine. "It doesn't matter. So, the fact that Khan came after me has to do with your investigation with Jen Joshi?"

He changed gears and turned toward the overpass. He was avoiding smaller, more crowded streets. "Jen was running the medical clinic in Dharavi and trying to set up an organ donor registry. People on the registry started to disappear. That's when she came to me. But we couldn't find bodies, and these were undocumented slum dwellers so we had no case. She couldn't let it go. She kept digging. Finally we found out that someone was stealing organs from people on the registry and killing them off. And Asif was the man running the operation."

"I know. This was all in the newspapers. Asif Khan is a bastard. But why is he coming after me now? When you already have the evidence to put him away and he should be fleeing the country to save himself? What do I have to do with any of this?"

"I'm not entirely sure. My best guess is that he has some sort of vendetta against Kirit-sir for not stopping the investigation. Irony is, Kirit-sir did try to stop me."

"Papa tried to stop you from investigating an organ-theft ring?" That sounded entirely unlike her father.

"He believed the ring was already dismantled."

"Then why didn't you stop?"

"Because he was wrong. It wasn't dismantled. It was worse than ever. Asif apparently
had the backing of someone very powerful."

"And you don't know who that is?"

He shook his head. "Whoever it was is a
ruthless bastard. I was just speaking to
Nikhil Joshi, that's Jen's husband. We're
headed to see Nikhil and his girlfriend,
Nikki Sinha. The bastard who was protecting Asif Khan blackmailed Nikki and sent
her after Nikhil to steal the evidence Jen
had collected and hidden."

It sounded like the plot of a crime thriller
gone wrong. "So, Nikki's the woman who
was sent to steal the evidence from Nikhil
and now she's his girlfriend?"

"Yes, they're together. It's strange. It's like
they have this connection. They're such a
family, you know."

She knew. Inexplicable connection she understood.

Rahul's gaze lingered on her for a second
too long and she had to look away, because
sometimes an inexplicable connection
wasn't enough. "How did you know to find
me at the airport?"

He withdrew behind so many walls so fast

he might as well have disappeared from her sight.

Had he always been this good at shutting her out? Had she really been naïve enough not to notice? "If you're planning to lie, I'd rather you didn't answer," she said, affecting enough aloofness to give him a run for his money.

They pulled into the parking lot of a cluster of gray low-rise buildings with clothes flapping on clotheslines strung across balconies like cheery flags determined to not notice the dreariness.

"Give me your phone." He held out his hand.

Fat chance. He was delusional if he thought her puppy-dog-ness was this complete.

He sighed and deigned to offer an explanation. "It can be traced." He removed his own phone from his pocket, it was in two pieces. "I've disconnected mine too. The one I'm using is a ghost phone. Completely untraceable. We can't let anyone know where we are. Not until Khan is in the morgue."

She handed him her phone and watched as he pulled it apart, removing the SIM card and battery, and placed all three pieces in a high-tech metallic plastic bag that he pulled

142

from his pocket, along with the pieces of his own phone. Then he placed it all in the glove box.

"You were tracking my phone?"

Without answering, he swept a gaze across the surroundings and pulled out his gun. Sliding the magazine out, he checked it, then clicked it back in place with strong, sure hands. It was the first time she'd seen him handle his gun. It was the scariest thing she'd ever laid eyes on, but also hot as hell. Those damn aviators still covered his eyes, but she knew the exact moment when he caught her following his movements.

She would not allow warmth to suffuse her cheeks. She would be cool and sophisticated and focus on the fact that he had tracked her phone!

"It wasn't me," he said before getting out of the car and then jogging around the front to let her out. "I wasn't the one who was tracking you."

11

Kirit
Present day

Somehow Kirit Patil had always known the worth of fate. Fate wasn't destiny. Destiny was the assorted pieces of ourselves tied up in a cloth pouch that we hung on a stick and slung over our shoulder like a hobo. Fate was what we did with those pieces when we unpacked that pouch and chose which pieces we reached for and which ones we hid away.

His pouch had come with dead parents, a legacy of land that bore gold, and his million-rupee face. At eighteen he'd learned that his face would be where his fate and destiny met. His uncle's movie producer friend had seen him at a party and decided he was perfect for the magnum opus he'd been waiting to make for years. One look at Kirit and his search had ended. He'd found his humble prince who would fall in love with the daughter of the man trying to overthrow his father. India's answer to Romeo and Juliet, complete with costumes and war scenes to rival Mankiewicz's *Cleopatra*. Only because it was India, instead of Liz Taylor, the star had to be a man with a god's face and a saint's eyes.

Back then, the body wasn't treated like the ticket it was now. Not that it would have changed anything. If they'd needed a six-pack, Kirit would have given them the best six-pack a human being could sculpt. But in his day, muscles were the realm of villains. Physical strength was for those not capable of intellect and charm. An ideology Kirit couldn't help but subscribe to.

Mehra-sir's vision had taken five years to make, but by the age of twenty-three Kirit had a new name and the title of superstar that would stick for the next two decades. But he hadn't let it go to his head. He had watched from afar as his colleagues in the film fraternity fucked everything that moved. They spent all their time high or high-handed. Kirit didn't do that, because he didn't come from the gutter. His family had been growing sugarcane and supplying their great country with sugar even before the British turned their sweet bamboo into a printing press for their coffers.

He had no memory of his parents, and his uncle had only developed an interest in him after he had become a star and the Patil coffers had needed some debt correction. Kirit had corrected the debt, taken over the lands, and made gold there the way he had mined it on the silver screen.

In other words, when life gave him sand, he ground it down to silt and planted a forest in it. And yes, he was proud of all he'd done. The only sin he'd ever been guilty of was a little bit of hubris. A fact that, ironically enough, he was also proud of.

"Does your daughter have any idea what a bastard you are?" Asif Khan said over the phone. He had the kind of guttural twang that made Kirit's skin crawl. It wasn't snobbery. It was an appreciation of the finer things in life and being deeply disturbed by filth. And Asif Khan was toxic filth.

"You're making a huge error bringing my daughter into this. She has nothing to do with this." Being an actor and a politician meant he could make his voice do just about anything. Now he made it at once blasé and menacing.

"You're right. You know how your police force clears out the area when you're going to carry out one of your 'encounters' where you butcher my men under the guise of

146

police duty? You know why they clear out the public, don't you? It's because bullets don't know the difference between enemies and friends. Between guilty and innocent. You're the one who deserves to die. Your daughter's the innocent bystander who's going to get shot."

"You won't touch her."

Asif laughed. "Oh, I already did. She's all soft like a *rasgulla*. You know how no one can eat just one *rasgulla,* right? I can't wait for another taste. I will touch her in so many places, you won't recognize her body when I'm done."

The bastard was pressing his buttons, much like Kirit was pressing his. Kirit's tone stayed as calm as his heartbeat. "This is the last time I'm offering you this, Asif. I will look the other way if you get on the next plane to Dubai, or Pakistan, or wherever the hell you want to go and hide out. As long as it's for the rest of your life."

Asif grunted in that horribly uncouth way. "You smug bastard. I'm going to enjoy ripping your life into shreds."

"You'll never find her." Because Rahul would die before he let Kimi come to harm. That much Kirit had made sure of.

"You hadn't thought I'd find out about your grand scheme to get the evidence from

Jennifer Joshi's husband either. But I did, didn't I? Even for you that was fucked-up beyond words."

Asif was right about collateral damage. Kirit hadn't meant to hurt Nikhil Joshi. "I'm not the one who handed the evidence to the cops, Khan. Why don't you go after the person who did?"

Asif laughed so hard he went into a coughing fit, the ugly medley of sounds making Kirit sick. "Still trying to save your little princess and throw an innocent woman over the cliff in her place?"

"She's hardly innocent." Nikita Sinha had ruined everything. If she hadn't become involved with Nikhil Joshi, they would not all be under threat from this bastard again. The human condition was a pain in the arse sometimes.

"Well, your machinations aren't going to work. I know that Nikhil Joshi and his shiny new family are leaving the country today. If I hadn't wanted to let them leave they'd be dead. But they're not the ones who deserve to die. You're the one who double-crossed me. And I had promised you that your daughter would pay for it if you did."

"I've already made you an offer. Take it or leave it. But we will find you, and this time the bullets will do their job." In the mean-

148

time, he had to make sure Kimi didn't try something stupid.

Asif's cool tone matched his own. "You don't go into my line of business if you're afraid of death, *chutiye*. You better say goodbye to your princess. I'm not leaving this earth without her by my side."

12

Rahul
A long time ago
It was another two years before Rahul saw
the girl with those strangely large eyes that
reminded him of the baby doe he had seen
on a school visit to the Jijamata Zoo —
slightly lost, wildly playful, and unabashedly
curious. But over those two years he had
thought about her on that gatehouse roof
and smiled more times than he could count.
Dirty as Rahul had felt when he walked to
the Patil mansion that day, he couldn't seem
to forget how he had felt coming home. The
day had completely flipped on its axis after
she had dragged him to his rock, their
bizarre adventure painting over everything
else.

When he thought about that day, what he
remembered was the strange sense he had
experienced when he had seen her crouched
on top of the gatehouse. Like unexpectedly

spotting your reflection while passing a window. She had looked as fragile on the outside as he had felt on the inside, standing there talking to the hulking guard. He'd experienced that same feeling again when she had magically shown up on the front porch of The Mansion looking as though her life had taken an entirely unexpected turn.

Between Kirit Patil giving him the power to know that he had choices and the girl giving him a chance to be fourteen again, he'd found himself on steady ground for the first time since losing Baba. How had he been stupid enough to turn away the opportunities Kirit had offered?

If he never wanted to be helpless again, he needed power. To have power you needed money and for someone like him, education was the only way to get it. Turning away opportunity wasn't a mistake he ever planned to repeat. What had happened that day was dead and buried, he would never touch it again. Those other memories of that day that had changed his life were so much safer. And his favorite one was of the girl with the baby-doe eyes on his rock.

When he was trying to convince Rahul to go to St. Mary's, Kirit Patil had told him that his own child went there too. For a long

151

time after Rahul started at his new school, he kept an eye out for her during assemblies and when he passed the lower classes. But if he hadn't seen her in two years it probably meant that she wasn't at the same school.

In any case, Rahul had no direct contact with Kirit and he intended to keep it that way. At least until he could pay the man back for all his generosity. Rahul wouldn't lie. He had grown to love his new school. He hadn't realized how bored he had been at his old school. Here if he found something easy, they moved him to a class where there was material that challenged him.

Kirit Patil had kept his word and provided Mona and him with brand-new uniforms and shoes and backpacks and books and no one at school knew that they lived in a *chawl* on the other side of the tracks. Patil-sir had also tried to arrange for one of the English teachers to make sure that the fact that Rahul's medium of education had been Marathi until now did not interfere with his education. But Rahul had refused. He could read English well enough, but speaking was different. His mind tended to make sentences in Marathi, but recently his internal translator had become faster and faster, and now sometimes when Aie asked him something he answered in English without even thinking about it.

It usually made her giggle into her sari, but some days she would tear up and dab at her eyes with it instead.

The school had a huge cathedral-ceilinged library that they opened up to students every lunch hour. This had solved the only two problems Rahul had with the school — one, he didn't have to socialize with his classmates, who all spoke English as though they had been born in a whole different country, and two, after reading through almost the entire contents of the library, his English improved enough that he could converse with his classmates with only minimal embarrassment when he mispronounced something.

Mona had taken to the school and to English like a little *memsaab.* She loved their new school even more than he did, and when he took her home on the bus with him every afternoon she prattled on in English about all her teachers and classmates. Last year she had become something of a celebrity in her grade after winning the state science championship. Aie had made *laddoos* and sent him with a steel-box-full to the Patil mansion. But the family seemed to not be home and he had left the box with the guard, Bhola.

Today on the number four bus going home, Mona was barely talking.

"What happened, chatterbox?" he asked her, and she laid her head on his shoulder and told him that she was tired. By the time they got home she was dragging her feet, and when Aie touched her cheek to see why she was behaving the way she was, the worry that creased Aie's forehead made Rahul put his cup of chai down and go to her.

"She's burning up," Aie said to him in that way where she expected him to do something about it.

Sometimes the speed with which things happened seemed so fast your memories couldn't quite keep up and you forgot the sequence of events. For years to come, Rahul would carry with him every instant of those forty-eight hours in the starkest detail.

The fact that he tucked Mona in bed and ran down to the chemist for some Crocin while Aie placed cool cloths on her burning forehead. How Mona had tried to grip his hand when he told her he'd be right back and he'd registered the lack of strength and pushed away the trickle of panic. The speed with which Aie's frown had gone from worried to panicked. Until that day, Aie had never worried when they got sick, but for

154

years after, if Mohit ever so much as sniffled she would practically collapse where she stood. Rahul would never again tell his mother when he felt sick, because he could not put her through that.

The fact that the medicine had done nothing to reduce the fever — the cool cloths had warmed on Mona's forehead but not taken away the heat that burned her skin. The doctor's face when she told Rahul that they had to take Mona to the hospital immediately. And not the municipal hospital either.

The fact that the doctor at the private hospital had refused to start treatment until he was paid a deposit. Taking a rickshaw in the middle of the night to the Patil mansion while Aie sat in the hospital waiting room with Mona in her lap. Riding back to the hospital in a Mercedes with the leather seats cold against his sweating back, with Kirit Patil sitting next to him with a briefcase full of cash and not saying anything the entire ride.

And the futility of it all.

Meningitis progresses really fast.

There's nothing we can do.

It's too late.

Words.

And no Mona.

■ ■ ■ ■

The two times in his life when Rahul's life altered unrecognizably had nothing in common. Who would have thought devastation could have such varied means? The first time with Baba had been like a knife wound. Slow and sluggish, with his mind still registering pain and working around it to go on. Each day had been the sink and sweep of a needle and thread sewing together torn flesh, followed by the slow effort of standing up and walking again.

And then with Mona. That second time had been a bullet wound exploding everything into darkness forever after. A slamming scab armoring his being in one fell swoop. A black coating of no hope, ever. The taste of food, the meaning of words, all of it gone only for a flash and then slammed back in place so fast the grief couldn't linger. Nothing could linger. Not after a child too small wrapped in sheets too white was laid on a pyre too bright that burned out too fast.

Rahul had walked home from the cremation ground. Alone. Then gone out to play football. For hours, running after the ball, using his skill, his brain. No slamming into anyone, no relief of split knees, torn elbows, bruised ribs, just the ball and the goal and him. Then he'd come home and washed and worked, lifting the urns of water and moving them around. Moving the dinner *paath* stools. Moving his mother's grain. Shifting things and cleaning under them the way Aie usually had to nag him for days to do. Aie silent somewhere in the house. Everyone silent. This time there were no mourners. Some tragedies couldn't be mourned.

Mohit followed him around with a cricket bat. But Rahul couldn't do it. He couldn't pick up Mohit, his sixteen-year-old arms with their grown man's strength couldn't pick up his little brother or his plastic bat or his plastic ball. He couldn't do any more than leave Mohit calling softly behind him. "Dada, you want to play cricket with me?"

He had walked again across those lanes and roads, his blue slippers splattering the wet mud across the backs of his legs as they carried him to the other side of Bandra where up on a hill overlooking the ocean a mansion sat. There was no girl on the gatehouse, which seemed odd without her. But there seemed to be a hole in the air where she had folded in a crouch, making that terrible day well again. He wondered where she was, the girl with the baby-doe eyes.

Bhola let him in. Patting his shoulder with sad eyes Rahul could not acknowledge. Because he would not mourn.

"I want to pay you back for the hospital fees," he said to the man he had once hated but now couldn't remember why.

Kirit didn't tell him it was impossible for a boy with empty hands to pay a briefcase full of money back to a man who didn't need it. He simply nodded. "What can you do, son?"

"Work. I can work it off. I'll cut your grass. Trim your trees. I can clean your floors. Your toilets. Whatever you need done."

He could not mourn her, but he would pay for every bit of effort that had gone into saving her and getting to hold her as she went. And he wanted the payment to hurt, so he could feel at least that and remember it.

That's how three times every week Rahul left his fancy school and walked to The Mansion and climbed up on a ladder and cleaned bird droppings that splattered in thick, amorphous patterns across the ocean-facing windows of The Mansion. He scrubbed and scraped the glass, the frames. And when that was done he washed the cars and dug up the weeds. For almost six months he did not see the girl with the baby-doe eyes.

And then she returned.

13

Kimi
A long time ago
Kimi rarely thought about Storm Boy. But today for some reason she kept thinking about him helping her keep her balance on the rock in the middle of the ocean. Well, she knew it wasn't the actual middle. But it had felt like that and that's what mattered.

It had been two years since she had seen him. She'd spent most of that time in London. Unfortunately, not in that glamorous, "Oh, I spent two years in London, darling!" la-di-da way. She'd barely seen anything more than the inside of the clinic and the place they called Rehab. Most of that time she'd spent struggling to breathe. It was funny that after Mamma and Papa had spent so much time trying to protect her from the outside world, she'd carried the problem inside her.

She'd apparently been born with a rare

condition where her body did not make enough antibodies and platelets to let her body fight infections. So it turned out Mamma had been right to protect the heck out of her, because if Mamma had not done that Kimi would have joined her dead siblings in the roster of Those Lost years ago.

Amazingly enough, Kimi had come home from her trip to the beach with Storm Boy ecstatic and soaked to the bone (she had tampered with the evidence rather cleverly by leaving her clothes on the bathroom floor and then letting a tap "leak"). The next day she had woken up with a bronchial infection and a fever that would not go away. That's how the doctors had discovered the immune deficiency problem.

Fortunately, the problem could be temporarily solved by regular blood transfusions, which she could only get in London, until Papa worked with the hospital in India to bring the technology to them. The bigger problem was to keep out infection between the blood transfusions that happened once every two months. She had stayed at the clinic in London where the laminar airflow room kept her cut off from pathogens in the air. This naturally was much harder to do in India, and so she hadn't come back until

Papa had imported all the filtration equipment from America and then had an extension put on the house and turned her room into a laminar airflow room. The good news was that this meant she could live in her own home and not in some hospital thousands of miles away. The bad news was that she could never leave her room unless it was to go to some hospital.

In truth, it sounded more pathetic an existence than it actually was. If she only thought about it as one day, each day, it became much easier. One of the social workers at the London clinic had told her that — *think about what you're going to do today when you wake up in the morning, and don't worry about tomorrow* — and amazingly enough it had worked.

Most days.

Today was not one of those days. It was always harder a few weeks after she had finished with a transfusion, after those first few weeks when she felt mostly sleepy, she felt suddenly energetic. Her brain seemed to go crazy with the blast of oxygen. But she wasn't supposed to move around much to get everything to settle. She had read through all her lessons. She still didn't understand her algebra at all, and Shakespeare was driving her batty because, seriously, who talked like that? She usually did her lessons with her tutors in London over videoconferencing equipment that Papa had procured even though it was still in the prototype stage, and her exams weren't for another six months; she'd probably take them when she went back for the next set of transfusions.

She was rarely bored out of her mind, but today she was. Mamma was probably in the temple room doing her prayers, which she had become more and more obsessive about over the past two years. Sometimes Kimi felt like she never saw Mamma anymore. She could hear the clinking of bells every so often. Although she was probably imagining it from her days in London where Mamma did her prayers in the next room and not on the other side of the house. Given that she would be chanting all the *sahasranaams* for all the gods and incarnations, she would be gone all afternoon. How or why each god had a thousand names Kimi didn't know, and chanting each one of them over and over seemed like an awful waste of time when you could use that time actually doing things. But what did she know?

Mamma had told her not to get out of bed today and Papa had asked her to listen to Mamma. All the equipment in the new

163

room was still new, and they weren't sure how it would all work out in the KAKA program. That's what Kimi had named the joint goal of her parents and her doctors: Keep Ailing Kimi Alive. If Mamma had her way, they would have stayed on in London (*it's so much cleaner*) but that meant not seeing Papa unless he visited and that wasn't possible to do often enough for Papa (*our life is here*). Thank God her father had a way of moving the universe so it did as he wanted. The fact that Kimi was thirteen years old with this disease and still alive was testament to this fact (as she'd heard one of the doctors in London say).

Ah, forget it. Much as she was all for KAKA succeeding, she could not stay in bed and read *Moby-Dick* for another second longer.

She sat up and let the dizziness clear. No, it wasn't that she was sick. She could tell the difference between sick-dizziness and well-dizziness, thank you very much. Well-dizziness just meant that her body was getting used to going from prolonged horizontalness to verticalness.

She walked to the window and pressed a button to retract the shades. She had arrived after dark the day before yesterday, and the drugs they'd given her had knocked her out, so really, this was the first time she'd seen the view out of her window. It was quite lovely, in that way that everything here was lovely. Because it felt like it was hers. It fit around her perfectly. The way Mamma's food tasted or the way Papa smelled. There was no wait between experiencing it and recognizing it. With everything in London there had been that wait. Just that fraction of a second after she tasted a scone when this entire conversation passed between her taste buds and her brain.

Taste Buds: Hmm, what is this?

Brain: It tastes like cake with the texture of a *nankhatai* biscuit but with a pasty aftertaste something like a *laddoo.*

The length of the conversation reduced the more she ate scones but still, when she popped a *laddoo* made by Cook into her mouth (after it was processed through the nuking machine to kill any germs, of course), there was no conversation. Her brain knew all its little details seamlessly.

This view from her window was like that. All the roofs of the buildings between the ocean and their home were something her eyes didn't even see, they were part of that thing labeled HOME in her head, and her eyes went straight to the ocean, her favorite thing in the whole world.

The tide was rising, making the waves churn in that particular way, where they seemed torn between which direction to go in, and then they just crashed into the rocks, coming faster and faster until one by one they ate up the rocks and the water was all the way to the thin strip of sand. She reached out and touched the glass, trying to stroke the waves. And jumped, because someone was perched on a ladder and wiping away at the window a few feet away from her.

It wasn't one of the regular staff. Had Papa hired someone new? The splatters of gull droppings on the windows made Papa really crazy. Her window was gleaming; none of the amoebic white and gray shapes she was so used to. The person on the ladder moved and something about him was so familiar it was like one of those shocks you got when you touched something that had collected too much static electricity. Then he turned.

It was Storm Boy!

At least she thought it was. She had to look at him a bit longer to make sure that it really was Storm Boy. Because Storm Boy had changed.

She waved, but he wasn't looking at her. His entire focus was on the gunk that the seagulls managed to acrobatically splatter against the windows every day. It had been one of her favorite things to do as a child: watch white projectile gull poop splatter into starburst patterns on her window. When he didn't look at her, she tapped a fingernail on her window. But he still didn't turn, so she made a fist and rapped the glass harder with her knuckles.

He startled and his foot slid off the ladder, but instead of falling back he made some sort of trapeze artist maneuver and, despite missing a few rungs, he grabbed on and hung there for a second before finding his footing again.

He glared at her, then suddenly his expression registered recognition and he looked excited and waved back. Because apparently through all his tumbling she was still waving. She remembered the expression on his face when she had waved at him from the front porch and he had looked behind him to check if it really was him she was waving at. The memory made her laugh and she beckoned him over.

He did it again. Looked over his shoulder as though someone might be floating midair behind him. But when it made her laugh and beckon more vigorously, he jumped off the ladder, grabbed a pipe running alongside her balcony, and climbed it. Before she knew it, he had jumped over the railing and was standing across the glass from her, and she was so excited it was as though they were long-lost friends. But she had only met him once. Even though it had been the best day of her life.

He was wearing a *ganji* inner shirt and jean shorts and he was covered in sweat. It must be hot outside. The sun was beating down so harshly it was making him squint. Her room was so overly air-conditioned she was wearing a long-sleeved thermal shirt, with thumbs cut into the cuffs, over sweats. His hair was also wet with sweat and sticking to his forehead over his thick, dark brows, and he was still carrying the rag he had been using to scrape away her favorite animal excretion.

He followed her eyes to the rag and self-consciously made circular motions with it. "I was cleaning the windows."

Oh! She could hear him! The windows were sealed, but she could hear him. It made her ecstatic.

"But why?" she asked.

He beamed, also realizing that they could hear each other.

"Why are you cleaning our windows?" she asked again.

He pretended to give it grave thought. "Because they're dirty." He shrugged, one brow raised, one hand on his hip. Then he grinned at his own cleverness.

In the years to come, whenever she tried to put a finger on when exactly she had fallen in love with him, she would always think of this moment when he had given her that entirely unexpected cocky grin.

"Are you on a mission to clean the city then?" she asked, mirroring his nonchalance.

"Only Pali Hill mansions. I'm not very ambitious."

She laughed. As in wrapped her arms around her tummy and laughed until it hurt. "No, I mean, why isn't one of the servants doing it?"

"He is," he said more seriously. "Where have you been? I haven't seen you around for months."

"I was in London."

"Wow, I thought your parents didn't let you leave the house!" he said, as though he'd caught her in a lie.

She thought about that day when they had jumped the wall and he had taken her to that rock. A longing to do it again tingled all the way to the very tips of her toes. She curled her toes and dug them into the soft

169

soles of her slippers. With all her heart she wanted to climb a wall, run down a sloping, curving road, cross a street with zipping cars, and run across sand in her bare feet, her sandals gripped in her hand. She tried to remember what the social worker had taught her. Think only about what you're going to do today.

He had thought it was strange for her to be locked up in the house back then. What would he think now if he knew she couldn't leave her room?

"Is it really hot outside?" she asked, but the sudden change of topic seemed to upset him.

"No, I usually sweat like a pig for no reason." He didn't look like a pig at all, and she wanted nothing more than to step outside and sweat like that.

"Pigs don't really sweat much," she said unnecessarily. "That expression comes from this form of iron called pig iron that sweats when it's being smelted from iron ore."

That made him laugh. His entire face crinkled when he laughed, and she found herself laughing too as though his laughter were an infection. And she was good at catching those.

"Why don't you come outside and see for yourself how hot it is?" He studied her with suddenly curious eyes that seemed to get gentler the more they studied her.

"I can't."

"Why?"

"Because if I breathe air that isn't treated to get rid of all the pathogens in it I'll catch an infection and end up dead."

"For real?"

"Can you end up dead for pretend?"

He smiled and then looked sad and then smiled again.

She often did this herself when something made her happy and then she thought of everything that was wrong and then she decided not to think about that part of it and she was happy again.

"So why were you really in London?"

"Because my parents thought the doctors there could make me well. But all they can do is try and prevent infections until some-one else finds a way to make me well."

"And until then you can't leave your room?"

She nodded.

"That's terrible."

"It's not so bad."

He watched her and she frowned at him. "Okay, it's pretty awful. But the social worker in London told me that if I can train my brain to only think about the present

171

moment, then it would be easier to get through."

He looked thoughtful. "She's right."

"How do you know?"

"Because it makes sense. How long do you have to be inside?"

"Until they come up with a cure for my condition."

"That makes sense too. What do you do in there?" He pointed his rag at the room behind her.

"I go to school via videoconferencing. Do my lessons, watch TV, play video games, and read a whole lot. And don't say that makes sense because you sound like a broken record."

He pursed his lips as though he was trying to stop himself from smiling. "Well, you have to be ready for life outside when they let you out, now, don't you?"

She made a face. Because, ugh, it made sense. And that made her want to giggle again.

"School via videoconferencing? That sounds very science fiction. And fantastic."

"It's really not. Especially not algebra."

"Why?"

"I hate algebra."

"It's my favorite subject."

"Are you mad? How can xs and ys be

172

anyone's favorite subject?"

"Because they're not just xs and ys. They could basically be anyone or anything." He grinned that cocky grin again, totally thrilled with his own cleverness.

Come to think of it, it was pretty clever. "Will you teach me?"

"From across a window?"

Well, that was a problem. She could ask him to come inside, but she knew Mamma and Papa would never, ever allow it.

He was grinning again and she frowned at him. "What's funny?"

"You think really loudly. I can almost hear it. So, no one can come inside your room?"

"You can come inside one part of it, but you have to wear a mask and gloves and whatnot."

He looked down at himself. "And wearing bird shit the way I am wouldn't work, huh? Let's try to do it like this. You want to show me your problems through the window?"

She grabbed her homework off the desk and came back to the French doors. "Can you do quadratic equations?"

His eyes actually lit up.

14

Kimi had brought Rahul a chocolate bar once from one of her stays in Switzerland. It was smooth chocolate wrapped around this sticky hard toffee filled with silky mousse. All these layers of melting softness folded in with toughness that almost took out his teeth. He'd teased her that it reminded him of her. She'd countered that it was all still sweet and that's what mattered.

She was such a mix of soft and tough that Rahul never knew where she was going to fall on any given day. Okay, so he was lying, he always knew. Ever since her surgery he had tried to convince himself that she only fell on the side of tough, but that wasn't true. She was just protecting herself after he had hurt her.

He wasn't proud of it. But when she had come to him with all her feelings in her eyes, with her metaphorical heart in her hands when the new physical one in her chest had barely decided if it wanted to stay, he hadn't been able to lead her on. She was his best friend, his only friend. But that's all he could ever feel for her. That was all they could ever be.

He watched her watch Nikhil and Nikki pack up the last of their bags with eyes he could only describe as hungry. She looked like Mohit when Aie told him not to touch the sweet wheat *laddoos* she had made because they were on order for a customer. Nikhil was trailing Nikki, anticipating her actions and trying to calm her. The bastard seemed to have no trouble putting how he felt about Nikki; about his first wife, Jen; about the whole bloody world right out there where everybody could see it. It didn't even seem to strike him that he was exposing himself.

Rahul had witnessed firsthand the mess Nikhil had been after Jen's death. How the man could be like this again, after he had lost it all once, Rahul would never know. The discomfort in Rahul's belly had decided it was recklessness and wouldn't let him acknowledge that it might very well be something else entirely. Nikki seemed much more comfortable with Nikhil's single-minded brand of attention than she had been when Rahul had first become friends with them just months ago.

After that incident when he had shot Asif and put him in a coma, Rahul had spent a lot of time interrogating both Nic and Nikki and also trying to get answers for them. Somehow it had been easy to become friends with them, and to hang out in Nikki's flat. It had been a long time since he had felt so at home around someone. How the hell did Khan know how to pick on the people Rahul cared most about?

Thank God, Nikhil and Nikki were headed to Chicago today to visit Nikhil's family and attend his niece's naming ceremony. A police escort was going to take them to the airport and, hopefully, once they got on that plane, Asif would not be able to reach them. He wished he could take them to the airport himself, but taking Kimi back there was out of the question, and leaving her alone wasn't happening either.

"We're going to get a doggie when we come back," Nikki's little boy, Joy, said to Rahul in that way kids had of throwing out random thoughts that were weighing on their minds. "Right, Dr. Nic?"

"That's the plan," Nikhil said, snapping one of the suitcases shut as Joy ran circles around him.

"What kind of doggie?" Kimi asked Joy.

"A golden retriever!" Nikhil and Joy both said together.

Kimi frowned. "A golden retriever is too big and hairy for an apartment this size," she said in her Kimi-the-Know-It-All voice.

Joy and Nikhil matched Kimi's frown.

Nikki smiled at Kimi. "Thank you!"

"Are you a doggie expert, then?" Joy was clearly not thrilled with Kimi the Know-It-All. He was usually completely thrilled with everyone.

Kimi looked undaunted by the disappointment on Joy's face.

"No, but I did an interview with an expert last month and I did a lot of research." She did love her research. "I can help you find a dog who will be happy and healthy in a flat."

The disappointment on Joy's face lifted a little. Nikhil winked at him. "Ah, an expert! I don't think Mamma can say no if an expert picks out the dog."

Nikki narrowed her eyes at Nikhil, but Joy ran up to Kimi, picking up on Nikhil's cue like a pro. "Can it be brown? I want a brown doggie."

Kimi pulled out a little notepad from her humongous, also very purple, handbag and started taking notes. "I think that can be managed. Other requirements?"

"Cute."

"Doable."

Before she had finished jotting down his list, which included things like "can bark really loud," Joy was perched on Kimi's lap and pouring out his considerable excitement about traveling to America to her.

"Maybe we should cancel our trip," Nikki said to Rahul, keeping her voice low enough that Joy wouldn't hear. "It feels wrong to take off like this. What if you need us?"

"What's he going to need us for?" Nikhil asked. "You're not sticking around where that psychopath can find you." He pulled her into his lap. "Stop worrying. Rahul's got this."

She pushed Nic's hair off his forehead, the gesture so intimate Rahul looked away. He caught Kimi across the room throw her head back and laugh at something Joy said. Her usually perfect ponytail had slid a little askance on her head. Trying to run from a bomb would do that to you.

"Nikhil's right. I think you're safer out of the country," Rahul said. It would be three fewer people to worry about.

Across the room, Joy asked Kimi if she had ever been to America.

She threw a quick look at Rahul, turning

away when she caught him watching her, and started telling Joy about her Almost American College Experience. Rahul tried not to feel that familiar kick of anger in his gut. How could she talk with such ease about all the things she had missed out on and lost? But she could and she proved it by filling Joy in on all the details with a smile on her face, and then went on to describe all the fun things he could do in Chicago. There was that research again.

So, yes, the sight of her chatting away with Joy on her lap with her too-wide smile reaching her too-wide eyes messed with Rahul's theory about her having turned hard. Truth was she still fell squarely on the side of soft, much less these days than she used to, thank God, but still far too much for his liking. Sometimes it made him want to throw himself between her and the world and shield her somehow, made him want to tell her to hide her feelings away and build some armor. But he had sworn to help her live on her own terms, with complete freedom. He had let her go. Except, here they were with her in need of protection again and hating him for it.

He hated himself for it too.

"How long have you been in love with her?" Nikhil asked looking very amused

179

with himself. At least he had the good sense to lower his voice.

Rahul had liked Nikhil much more when he was grumpy as shit and Rahul could barely get a word out of him.

"She's a friend, Nikhil." That's all he was going to say. Because people loved to invoke the theory of overprotestation.

"Right," Nikhil said with no more than a smirk and turned to more important matters. "So we go off to Chicago today, and then what?"

"Then you stay there until that bastard is inside a hole in the earth."

This was the difference between men and women. Nikhil knew Rahul didn't want to talk about something and he let it go. If Nikki or Aie or, God forbid, Kimi, asked him a question to which she thought she already knew the answer, they'd be going around and around in circles about it all day.

Nikki looked like she might pick it up again, but Kimi walked over to them. She had just shown Joy an encyclopedia of dog breeds on his new laptop, and he seemed to have forgotten how to blink.

Nikki smiled at her. "Thanks," she said and threw Joy a look that reminded Rahul of his *aie.* "You know we're going to have

180

to get him a dog now."

"Sorry," Kimi's smile was wide enough that those crooked canines made an appearance. He hadn't realized how much he had missed them.

"Sure you are," Nikhil said, smiling in a way Rahul wished he could still smile at her. "It was only a matter of time anyway. And he's not going to look up from that thing on the entire plane ride, so thanks, seriously."

Nikki threw Rahul a tentative look. "Once Asif is gone, much as I want him dead, we'll never find out who was behind everything we went through." She got off Nikhil's lap and sat down next to him. "We'll never find the man who blackmailed me and sent me after Nikhil."

"Is Asif the only person who has that answer?" Kimi asked. "No suspects or clues as to who the person might be?"

"I've never seen the man's face," Nikki said through barely clenched teeth. She wasn't one for displays of emotion, but between her tightly controlled anger and Nikhil's wide-open rage, the atmosphere in the room visibly darkened. "All his interactions with me were over the phone. Then after Asif got shot, the man all but disappeared."

"And he hasn't called you again since Asif escaped?" Kimi laid a soothing hand on Nikki's arm.

The gesture seemed to melt through all of Nikki's stoicism, and for a moment her eyes seemed to fill before she squeezed Kimi's hand and got a hold of herself. "No he hasn't."

Rahul went to Nikki and squatted in front of her. "He knows that you have no idea who he is. He also knows that you gave the evidence to the police and there was nothing to implicate him in the evidence but enough to put Asif away. If he's as smart as we think he is, he isn't going to contact you again. Asif on the other hand is a loose cannon who's entirely unpredictable. So, I'm glad you're leaving."

Nikhil moved in closer next to her. "Our flight leaves in a few hours. Everything's going to be all right."

"So after all he's done, he's going to get away with it. With protecting Asif Khan's organ-stealing operation and allowing hundreds of people to die."

Kimi put her arm around Nikki as though she'd known her all her life. Her eyes shone with fierceness. "I have a feeling we're going to find out who the man is. Rahul put five bullets in Khan and he's still alive. I think everything happens for a reason. We have to believe that Khan survived for a reason. You will find out who did that to you. Rahul will make sure of it."

And for all her anger at him, her voice held not a shred of doubt.

15

Kimi
Present day
Bidding farewell to Joy, Nic, and Nikki was
the strangest experience. It had been all of
a couple of hours since Kimi had first met
them and still she felt this quiet sense of
loss. Meeting them had sparked something
inside her, something she could only describe as potential, this little beat of joy at
the possibility of a new friendship, and now
she had to put it away until she saw them
again.

For some reason Kimi had always believed
that she would have a hard time sharing Rahul with the world. But she had completely
misunderstood her own isolation and
bought into everyone else's opinion of her
life. Being isolated didn't mean that your
world revolved around you. Isolation was
characterized by craving, by the insatiable
need for contact and an almost constant

reminder of your own insufficiency. Contrary to what people believed about her, she didn't believe that she was the center of her universe. She was in fact someone whose entire existence focused on wanting a universe she could be part of.

Maybe that's why she had let Rahul become her entire universe, and wanted nothing more than to be a satellite and revolve around him. What an idiot she had been. No wonder he didn't want her. She wouldn't want someone that needy and parasitic either.

But as Dr. Girija, who had been Kimi's doctor for as long as she could remember, loved to say, Kimi was proof that every mistake could be fixed. Her doctor never seemed to address the fact that each fix had come with yet another mistake, but that wasn't the point now, was it?

Maybe she had finally succeeded in her quest to disconnect from Rahul, because she had expected to feel lost, even jealous, seeing Rahul with his friends. Instead it had given her an entirely unexpected sense of wholeness. Was this how the world worked and stayed together? Where one person connected with another and those connections intertwined and snapped more and more people into place? There was something beautiful about the idea: this circular, interlaced fabric of the world, which until now she had been left out of. And today three people who loved one another and who obviously loved Rahul had taken her in and made her part of that tapestry.

The good-bye had teared Rahul up. Not on the outside, naturally. He was Rahul, after all. His tears always stayed on the inside. It was something Kimi had seen him do countless number of times with her but never with anyone else. Until now. When Joy had body-hugged him, arms and legs and all, he had held Joy tight, and she had felt all his choking up in her own throat.

Nikhil and Nikki had both assured her everything was going to be okay. Nikhil had even tried to convince her that she and Rahul should go to Chicago with them. Asif Khan couldn't reach any of them in Chicago.

Even if getting an American visa hadn't been the long drawn-out process that made this impossible, running off to America would solve nothing. She would find no answers there. Her answers lay somewhere else entirely, and she needed them so she could start afresh and leave her old encumbered satellite self behind once and for all.

When she'd left home that morning she'd

had a goal, and a plan to achieve it. So, her plan had been derailed, as plans often are, so what? Her goal hadn't changed and now she had a new plan. Problem was she needed Rahul to go along with it. Thankfully, she had a plan for that too. That should be her middle name: Kimaya Has-a-Plan Patil.

She threw a quick look at him as he navigated Maney's wife's car through Mumbai's unfailingly choked up traffic. Looking at him for extended periods of time was too much of a throwback to her good old satellite days, and she would much rather not revert to those, thank you very much.

As usual, he looked deep in thought and tortured by something. Fair enough — there was currently much to be tortured about.

Even though it was a quick look, he caught her before she looked away. "Don't you want to know where we're going?" he said to her turned-away head, a blast of emotion slipping through all that restraint in his voice.

"How does it matter where we're going?" she wanted to say. But she couldn't say it without sounding like a pathetic little bird that had been caught in a net moments before its first flight. So she mirrored him and stayed silent.

"We're going to a police safe house in Co-laba," he said more evenly. Then he took one of those deep calming breaths and threw her a conciliatory look. "You should be, you know, safe there." Was that the hint of a smile in his voice? Was Stonewall Savant attempting to resuscitate his long dead humor?

Was he crazy? She might have moved on, but she wasn't far enough away from all those stupid dreams she had dreamed for attempts at banter. There would be no sliding into playfulness, not when she needed to stay away from all the slippery slopes that led straight to where he had no interest in going. Not when she knew the pain of being kicked to the curb by him. Once was quite enough, thank you very much.

Plus, the idea of heading to a safe house needed a little more time inside her head before it would feel, you know, safe there.

Fortunately, his phone buzzed, and they were saved from any more asinine attempts at making this ridiculous situation seem in any way normal.

"Yes, Maney," he barked and then followed it up with a furious, "What the fuck?" and a quick "Sorry" thrown in her direction.

She waved it away.

He emitted some sub-human-decibel growls into the phone. Maney must know him very well, because he seemed to understand the growled code.

"Okay. Great job. Thank you," he said before hanging up, and she hung on to his kind, albeit gruff, tone to keep from being terrified of what was going to come out of his mouth next.

"The safe house location has been compromised," he snapped, sounding like such a cop.

What did that even mean?

Before she could ask, he went on. "Maney has intel that someone leaked the location of the safe house. We can no longer use it. And we still don't have any leads on where Asif is. Whatever is left of Asif's gang, they're lying low. We can't find a single bastard anywhere."

Fantastic. "So where do we go to be safe now that there's no safe house to be safe in?" She was proud of how breezy she sounded in the face of his neat little recap that essentially meant that a psychopath might drive up any minute and empty some bullets into her.

He looked over her shoulder at the window she'd pictured being shattered by bullets just as a pedestrian ran across the street in front of the car. Rahul slammed on the brake, reaching out with one hand to hold her back as she jerked forward against the seat belt. For once she was glad her heart didn't know when to speed up because, hello! his hand was splayed across her chest!

He pulled it away with super-cop speed, apologized, and then clasped the steering so tight his knuckles looked like they might pop their sockets. Then just as fast he gained his calm again and eased the car back into motion. Well, "motion" was pushing it, because this was Mumbai, and traffic and movement didn't often meet.

She knew his silences and this one meant the gray matter was in overdrive. DCP Savant was in case-cracking mode.

"We can't go to The Mansion," he said finally, in the tone he had used when they solved the *Times* crossword puzzle together. He always called her home that. Never "your home." Always "The Mansion."

"Why can't we go to *The Mansion*?" Yes, she stressed the words, because sometimes being juvenile actually made you feel better.

"Because Asif Khan called Kirit-sir and threatened to come after you. The Mansion is out."

"How about your office, then?" she asked, falling into their puzzle-solving two-step.

"Too many people there who could leak our location."

He meant her location, naturally. She was the hunted, after all, not him. And it was really pissing her off.

"Listen, Rahul," she said, knowing it was a bit silly to say that when she knew he was already listening, rather intently at that. "I thought you needed to find Asif Khan."

His thick brows furrowed as though he knew he wasn't going to like where this conversation was about to go. "Um, yes, except I need to focus on making sure you're safe first. The rest of the force is hunting Khan down. We'll find him."

She turned in her seat and looked at his hands on the wheel. At some point she was going to have to stop avoiding his eyes. "Why are you the one charged with being my bodyguard?"

He didn't answer, but his pursed lips told her exactly what he thought of the question.

"Did Papa force you?"

"He didn't have to force me, Kimi."

She squeezed her hands in her lap. "Right." The Great United Front of KAKA. How could she forget? "What if I refuse? What if I don't want you protecting me? What if I asked for a different officer to be my bodyguard?"

"It wouldn't matter. I'm the one who's doing it."

Of course. "So I don't get a say?"

He had the gall to sound apologetic, and she wanted to shake him. "Not in this. No."

She laughed and it tasted bitter in her mouth. "Yes, it's a truly unique situation, isn't it? Papa and you making all the decisions."

The traffic light turned red, but they hadn't moved for a while. This felt remarkably like the conversation they were having. He did another very cop-like sweep of the traffic before trying to catch her eye again. But she couldn't bring herself to look away from that red light. "I should have killed the bastard. If I had done my job right, we wouldn't be in this situation. But until we find him, this is how it has to be. I'm sorry."

Finally, she met his eyes, and an explosion of horns went off all around them as the light turned green.

"Isn't 'detective' part of your job description?" she bit out. "Shouldn't you be trying to find out why he's after me? Why he came after me in the first place?"

"I told you it has to do with Kirit-sir not being able to end the investigation and save the bastard's arse. It has to do with the case becoming too important to me."

Of course, it was all about his guilt. Always his damn guilt. Rahul in all his heroic glory wanting to take on all the blame, and missing the point.

"I don't think it's that simple." Despite her resolve to stay detached, her tone rolled up all her bitterness.

He made everything worse by looking past her anger at what she was trying to say. "What do you mean?"

Okay, here went nothing. Or everything. "Whatever he's after me for has to do with my heart, not with the fact that Papa couldn't stop your investigation."

Yet again the crawling traffic came to a standstill, and he turned all the focus in those eyes on her. "Your heart?"

His tone made her want to squeeze her eyes shut. But she kept them wide open. "Yes, I need to track down where my heart came from. That is what will tell us what Asif is hiding."

"Dammit, Kimi." He glared at her, as though he had suddenly figured out some sort of nefarious scheme. "This is about finding your donor again? Come on! Kirit-sir has already told you the donation was anonymous."

"What kind of cop are you that you believe anything can actually be anonymous?"

Another cacophony of horns rose around them, but he didn't move and she didn't look away. The traffic was packed tight around them like leeches on a wound. There was really nowhere to go. "I have to go to Hong Kong and trace my heart back to its donor." All on its own, her hand rubbed her chest. His eyes picked out the action that had become such a habit she usually didn't even notice it.

Naturally, she noticed now, because he noticed. She stilled her hand. "If you have any intention of convincing me to let you guard me with this psycho on the loose, you're going to have to do this my way and help me."

Miraculously, the cars in front of them started moving and he looked back at the road, his dark-tar eyes so intense, she knew exactly how this was going to go.

"Help you how, exactly?"

"You found me at the airport." He had to have wondered where she was headed. "Go with me to Hong Kong and help me trace the donor."

"You know that's not possible, Kimi. I can't do that."

"Why?" She wanted to tell him that she couldn't move forward with her life, really move forward, until she put this to rest. But it felt too much like groveling, too much like exposing her heart again. "I'll postpone my ticket to tomorrow, but I am going. You can't protect me once I leave. If you go with me, you're doing your duty and keeping me safe and moving forward with your investigation, because — and you have to trust me on this — this will lead us to the bottom of Asif's plan."

He threw her another one of those gauging looks and she knew exactly what was going through his head. It had always made her feel powerful, reading him this way. Now it made her awfully sad.

"Do you have any proof at all?" he asked, flicking away her sadness and filling her with hundred-proof anger.

"Hold on, let me think about that." She stared off into the distance and did a slow blink. "Oh yes, the man held a gun to my belly and told me to find out where my heart came from." Her glare told him exactly how long he'd have to wait for any more proof than that. "You don't think that's proof enough?"

"He's a sociopath. He messes with people's heads." But he knew she had a point. She could see it in the tightening of his jaw. "Even if I wanted to I'd never get authorization. Kirit-sir has already refused. I'll lose my job. And don't say you'll get your papa to take care of it."

"I would never say that!"

He narrowed his eyes at the road.

Unbelievable! He was bringing that little piece of their history up? "That's not what I had meant. I still can't believe you would accuse me of saying that. I know this job is yours because you've earned every bit of it. I know how much you deserve it, how good you are at it. How can you forget that I was the one who always knew?"

He looked at her again, but he wouldn't have that conversation. Not now, not ever. Good. No trips down memory lane for them. "Listen to your cop's intuition, Rahul. You know what I'm saying is correct."

"This is important to me," she almost added when he didn't respond. Instead she said, "This is vital to the case, don't you see?"

He still didn't respond. But he cut across four lanes of traffic and made a U-turn.

16

Rahul
A long time ago
Rahul landed on the balcony outside Kimi's room. It had been six months since he'd been helping her with her homework. At least it had started with him helping her, but then one day she had started arguing with him about the right way to solve polynomials and he had brought his backpack up to the balcony to show her something and then they had both sat there with their backs against the glass pane of the sealed French door, side-by-side, and started to do their homework together, and it had become a habit.

Today, however, she wasn't here. Usually, she stood on her side of the glass, bouncing on her heels, waiting for him to finish scrubbing the windows before he could join her. And she always looked so excited and impatient it made him work at warp speed.

Fortunately, at that time of the afternoon no one came out to check up on him. Her father was at the office or out of town, and her mother had her prayer meetings at the temple and it was off-duty time for all the other servants. Bhola would let him in, ask his usual questions about how he was doing in school, and then go back to napping in the gatehouse. Sarika would hand Rahul a list of things he had to get done and then go back to studying for her master's degree. The afternoon heat was no one's favorite thing. Except maybe his. He hated when it got cold. Something about the sun burning his skin made him feel like he was working hard. He loved the feeling.

The strange thing was that Kimi's shades were drawn, and something about that made the sun on his skin burn more harshly. Plus, he had finished *Moby-Dick* — despite being bored out of his mind when he'd started. And she was right; it caught on, once he gave it enough time to get to know the characters. His reasons for liking it would be different from hers though, and he had to find out what they were.

He hopped off her balcony and walked to the side of the house and into the kitchen. The cook always left a glass of milk and a snack out for him when he got here from school. He had tried to refuse the food when he first started, but Kirit had let him know that it was non-negotiable. Rahul had to eat when he got here and he had to keep his school grades up — that was the only way Kirit would let him work. And Rahul could consider it part of the debt he was paying off. Which was moot, because his debt was unpayable anyway.

Rahul walked across the kitchen and while washing his hands did something he never did, started peering into the house through the double doors.

"What do you need, Rahul *beta*?" the old cook asked, pouring him another glass of milk with her gnarly, workworn fingers. "Still hungry? There's a lot more *vadas*. Here, let me get you more."

He didn't really want more, but he nodded.

"Is the saheb home today?" he asked, watching her ladle the *vadas* and the *sambar* onto his plate, not quite sure what he would say if Kirit was at home.

"Yes, he's with Kimi-baby. She's sick. Been sick since yesterday." She touched the Ganesha locket hanging by a chain around her neck, closed her eyes, and chanted a little prayer. "Why Ganesha is putting our precious child through so much I don't know. What is His plan I don't know. Here, eat. It's not like anyone else will eat in this house until her fever reduces."

"Do you know what's wrong with her?"

"Only Ganesha knows. But they say her blood cannot fight germs." She waved around the kitchen as though the germs Kimi could not fight thickened the air. "So she gets sick all the time."

"Can I see Kirit-sir? I needed something," he lied. Kimi hadn't told him that she got sick often. She'd always implied that as long as she stayed inside her room, she would be fine. Or maybe he'd simply assumed that.

"Well, the saheb is very fond of you, only Ganesha knows why. So go, go on up and find him. But if it can wait I would wait. He has not left our baby's room since yesterday. He doesn't need any more tension." She grabbed her locket and started chanting another prayer, which Rahul took as a dismissal.

The house had an eerie silence about it. There was a distant chiming of prayer bells, almost a constant sound in The Mansion — it seemed Kimi's mother spent more time in the prayer room than anywhere else in the house. Aie only used her prayer bells on festival days and on the days when he or Mohit had exams. There were almost no servants around The Mansion today and the lights inside were dimmed.

He climbed up the servants' staircase that led up the side of the house and emerged into an endless corridor with no idea which way to turn when Kirit's personal assistant, Rafiq, came out of a door in his usual kurta and formal pants. He pulled off a surgical face mask he was wearing and gingerly shut the door behind him.

"*Arrey*, Rahul *beta*, what are you doing here. Do you need something?"

"I need something for school." Rahul hadn't meant to ask, but it was the only thing he could think of to convince the man to let him see Kirit.

The man looked thoughtful. "Sir is busy today. Is it urgent?"

The school was asking them to pay for computer classes, but they didn't need the money until next month. "Yes." He nodded.

The PA scratched the back of his neck, considering. "Well, Sir has said never to turn you away if you needed anything, and he could use the distraction." He beckoned to Rahul.

"Wait here. I'll go see what I can do."

"Rafiq-sir, wait. Can you tell me what's wrong?" He looked at the door Rafiq had come out of.

Rafiq pressed his fingers into his eyes. "It's our Kimi-baby. Sir's daughter. She does not keep well."

"Is she going to be all right?"

Rafiq raised both hands heavenward. "Only Allah knows. But she better be, because her parents won't let her go. Poor child. How long will the little mite fight?"

As soon as he had said it, his terribly sad eyes got wary. "I didn't mean that — you know that, right? I was just . . . Never mind all that. You wait here."

He put the mask back on and slipped into the room. As Rahul waited he took in the house. It looked nothing like it had that day when he had walked in here and argued with Kirit-sir about letting his siblings go to St. Mary's by themselves. He pushed away the familiar pain in his gut that always lingered beneath the surface and tried not to think about the second time he had walked in here in the middle of the night. But he couldn't block out the look on Kirit's face when he had driven Rahul back to the hospital in his car with a briefcase of cash that had not saved his baby sister.

The third time he had been inside The Mansion was when he had asked Kirit to let him work off those hospital fees. Was Kimi's condition the reason Kirit had been that understanding and compassionate? Could someone as chirpy and bright as Kimi really be that sick? No one else he knew would be so filled with life if they were stuck in a room endlessly. He himself needed the football field so badly, sometimes when practice was canceled at school he felt like he might explode.

All these months he'd been doing his lessons with her, and he had never thought about the fact that she was stuck indoors while he sat out there with the sun and the breeze in his hair. She had seemed so pristine and cozy in her air-conditioning, all bundled up in sweaters — like a princess in her tower — that he hadn't taken a moment to consider what it must be like.

Rafiq stepped out of the door again and waved Rahul toward a bathroom and pointed to the sink. "He'll see you. But get cleaned up a little and here, put this on." He handed him a mask. "Stay close to the door and don't touch anything."

Once he'd cleaned up, Rahul pushed the door open and went in and was instantly accosted by the strongest medicinal smell. The smell of a hospital multiplied a hundred times over. The room was pure white with white plastic furniture that looked like it belonged inside a spaceship. A few chairs were arranged around a coffee table and some medical-looking machinery. Kirit Patil sat amid all this whiteness, his clothes covered with a blue gown, gloves, and a blue shower cap. His eyes were sunken deep and dark rimmed. "Hello, *beta,* Rafiq *bhai* said you need something for school?"

Rahul looked behind him at a plastic curtain that separated him from another room with one of those hospital beds where Kimi lay with her eyes closed. An IV line ran into her arm and she was covered in bright pink sheets. Where her feet should have been two fuzzy yellow rabbit slippers stuck out.

He stepped back. "It doesn't matter. We can talk about it later. I'm sorry. I didn't mean to intrude."

"You're not intruding. This is my daughter, Kimaya. She's resting. I'm just sitting here in case she needs anything."

Rahul had never heard the ex-film star sound like this. He sounded defeated, and yet as though he would never, ever accept defeat. Rahul had also never seen Kirit so focused and still. He was a man who tended to exude energy and action. Today he seemed almost meditative.

"What's wrong with her?" Rahul asked for the third time that day.

"She's sick."

"Sick with what?"

"A few things. But basically her body has almost no immunity."

"No, I mean what is wrong with her right now? Does she have an infection?" It was strange to see Kimi lying down like that, and he very badly wanted her to open her eyes, because her eyes had a way of dancing. Her baby-doe eyes. How had he forgotten that's how he had thought of her when he'd seen her on the gatehouse?

"She has a fever. Usually that means an infection."

"So what happens when she has an infection?"

"We give her a transfusion and pump her body with antibodies and hope that the infection is very minor."

"How long will it take?"

Kirit shrugged. "It can go on for weeks — but the longer it goes, the harder it becomes to get rid of it." He scrubbed his face and looked up at Rahul as though he didn't know why he was asking all these questions. "How can I help you?"

Rahul couldn't get himself to ask for money for the computer lab. Not right now.

"Do you need time off? Is it exams? You know you don't have to work in the yard.

It's been a year. I think you've paid off the debt."

Rahul wanted to laugh. Kirit had never treated him like a child. Although to be fair, after Baba's death no one had. But even someone who was bad at math would know that washing windows and scrubbing garden furniture for one year did not earn you two lakh rupees, which is how much Kirit had paid the hospital that night.

"Would you like to do something else?"

"Is there something I can do inside the house, perhaps?" In here, where he would be able to check up on Kimi.

"The library."

Both Rahul and Kirit turned around because Kimi had spoken behind the curtain.

She coughed a little, and Kirit walked to the plastic curtain near the bed, placed his hands inside plastic gloves attached to the curtain, and handed her a glass of water. His shoulders were stiff with relief, which was an oxymoron but it made absolute sense.

Rahul's own relief at hearing her voice was almost violent, like a football hitting him in the stomach when someone had kicked it with all their force.

"Kimi *beta,* you're up. How are you feeling?" Kirit asked in a tone that Rahul could never have imagined coming from him.

"Your library needs to be cataloged, Papa. Remember?"

"Yes, it does. We'll take care of it. Are you feeling any pain? I'll call Sarika to take your temperature."

"I feel fine." She sounded anything but fine. "You've always wanted to get someone to catalog the library. Maybe he can do that."

"Who? Rahul?"

"Is that the boy's name?" she said and winked at Rahul behind her father's head.

He waved at her. If his relief had seemed extreme at the sound of her voice, seeing her eyes dance again made him want to dance. Naturally, he held himself utterly stiff. "Hi, I'm Rahul," he said. "How are you, babyji?"

She narrowed her eyes at him. "Hi, my name is Kimi. I'm fine. Thank you for asking."

Kirit looked from Kimi to Rahul, and Rahul had a sense that he was examining their conversation for something.

"I should go tell your mamma that you've woken up so she can stop harassing her Krishna for a little bit. Rahul, would you like to work in the library? I can get some-

207

one to explain cataloging to you."

"I did a project on the Dewey Decimal System," he said, sliding a glance at Kimi. "I'll be happy to take care of the cataloging."

"You can start that tomorrow then," Kirit said, holding the door open.

"Bye, Rahul," she said. Her voice was thin and seemed to take an effort, but her smile split all the way across her face. When she smiled wide enough, her two canines made an appearance, sticking out like playful versions of Count Dracula's fangs. And instead of being menacing they made her look like she couldn't stop laughter from bursting out of her.

She waved. Yup, her eyes were definitely dancing. Terribly tired yet dancing. He found himself smiling when he left The Mansion and walked home through the monsoon-muddy streets with his slippers splattering brown dots up the backs of his legs. He had told her about his library-cataloging project just the previous week.

17

Kimi
A long time ago
The word *breakthrough* was regarded with
the devotion of sacred texts in their home.
Papa regularly combed through every single
medical journal to keep up with advances
in immunology. Truth be told, ever since
they had installed an Internet line, Kimi
spent more time than she would admit
searching through any medical papers she
could find. The research was amazing and
totally fascinating. So much so that every
once in a while she found herself channeling her *vaidya* grandfather and wanting to
be a doctor so she could do the research
herself and fix herself.

Not that it was her time to decide what
she wanted to do with her life. She already
knew what she wanted to do. She was starting to worry a little bit about Rahul. It
sounded totally Romance Novel Hero, but

the boy — well, man, he had just turned nineteen — was so good at everything, he had no passion for anything. Seriously, sometimes she wanted to shake him until all his stoic equanimity flew from him. Then again, she loved that most about him.

"Why are you glaring at me instead of balancing your chemical equations?"

As he was aware, balancing equations was her least favorite thing to do. For all his effort and inherent genius (his words, not hers) Rahul hadn't been able to change her distaste for equations of any sort. Actually, to get into medical college you needed to be really good at chemistry, so there was yet another reason why carrying on her grandfather's legacy wasn't happening. If not for Rahul and his thirty tons of patience (and inherent genius, of course), she wouldn't even be doing advanced organic chemistry. Sometimes she hated him for pushing her into things.

"Why do you think I'm glaring? This stuff is evil," she said, sitting up on her wing chair and staring at him across the plastic curtain. She still couldn't believe that he was allowed to sit in the guest room outside her curtain and tutor her face-to-face — well, face-to-plastic-to-face, but still. All her scheming had worked. When he had first been tasked with cataloging Papa's library it had taken him a good week to sneak into her room. She had jumped on him. Figuratively, naturally. He'd have to be wrapped in plastic for her to jump on him for real.

"You took one week to come see me?" she had yelled. Again, figuratively, because yelling would mean he'd have been caught and that would defeat the purpose of yelling in the first place.

He'd done one of his the-best-response-is-no-reponse things. As though he had been struggling with whether to come and see her or not. For someone so smart with equations (that inherent-genius thing wasn't entirely untrue), he was such a thickhead when it came to some things.

"Why would I have suggested the library, which I am fully aware is down the corridor, by the way, if I did not want you to come see me?"

But she hadn't been that excited since the first time he'd landed on her balcony. Excited and furious. She had sat, ears peeled every single day, waiting for him to show up, and he'd taken his own sweet time.

"It took you an entire week to come see me, and now I am going to flunk my algebra unit test," she had hissed, loving how great it felt to be able to hiss at someone.

He had narrowed his eyes at her, a teeny-tiny bit, which meant he was really furious too. "You've got me working in the library. How am I supposed to get out on your balcony?"

For someone so smart. So. Thick.

"I got you into the house so we wouldn't have to study across the window, you goose. There's nobody in the house between four and six, and everyone thinks I'm resting. So you can come in here and we can do the lessons here."

His eyes did an "Ah!" then a "Hmm . . ." before he said, "But is it safe?"

"Are you a dangerous person, then?"

"Funny. I meant the infection thing. There's a reason for all this, right?" He'd indicated her room with his chin.

"There's a thirty-horsepower motor killing all the germs on this side of the curtain," she had said. "Just make sure you don't come running through the curtain in your excitement to see me." Although, today, she wanted nothing more than to ask him to do just that. God help her.

For two years he had been squishing all the cataloging work into an hour and a half so he could spend the rest of the time with her. Just one of the many, many reasons he was her best friend. Or, as he loved to remind her, her only friend. Which was a bit mean, if you asked her.

But she digressed. There were a few issues at hand. For one, there was The Breakthrough, but that meant she had to go away to the hospital for a while again. There had been a few over the past two years — five, actually — so Rahul wasn't entirely unused to it. The first few times he had been all prepared to be able to see her without the plastic when she returned. He hadn't learned to manage his expectations back then. But if Rahul was anything he was a quick study. He had learned to manage his hope so fast that instead of being relieved, Kimi had been almost disappointed.

Not that he had come anywhere near attaining her skill at managing hope. She could balance it like a juggler — let it soar and curb it and pass it from hand to hand. She could spin hope and spin herself through it. Forget mere juggling; she was a veritable trapeze artist with this hope thing.

His brand of managing hope, on the other hand, reminded her too much of Storm Boy. She wasn't a fan.

The difference this time was that she was going to a hospital thousands of miles away. It was the first time she was leaving the country since they'd become friends. She didn't know if Papa knew he'd been sneaking in. But after her last spate of infections, Papa himself had asked Rahul if he wanted to help her with lessons and he hadn't had to sneak in anymore. He'd also let him visit when Kimi was sick. Which was great, because she loved hearing his voice, even when she couldn't respond. For someone as quiet as him, he sure couldn't stop talking the moment she got sick and passed out. One part of her hoped that he would never find out that she could still hear people when she was too sick to talk or react.

He had asked her about it once, well, not flat-out asked, but done that typical Rahul-style thing where he slipped a question into a conversation so smoothly no one would know he'd asked. And she'd lied, well, not flat-out lied, but she'd slid past the truth and led him to believe that she was really passed out when she lay there too weak to respond. It's how she had found out how much he missed his *baba,* or how out of place he had felt at his school, or how mind-numbingly dull he found engineering college.

"I'm going to London," she blurted out, because he already knew she was only pretending to balance those vile equations.

He put down the book he was reading and

sat up in that alert way of his. "What have they found?"

"Possibly a drug to raise the platelet count."

"That would mean no plastic room?"

"Maybe. But it would definitely mean fewer infections."

He stood, energy bursting from him. "That's fantastic, Kimi."

She stood too. They were standing across the curtain the way they had done so many times. The way they did every second day. But today the urge to see him without any barriers, to part the curtain, was so strong it had her bouncing on her heels.

His gaze moved to the gloves falling limply out of the plastic curtain like the arms of a ghost who had fallen asleep. He had never put his hands in there. Never shown any interest in doing it. Never shown any interest in touching her. She was a sixteen year old girl, and he was the most handsome boy she had ever seen, not to mention the most brilliant. But also the most virtuous. He probably thought it was entirely inappropriate to put his hands there, so to speak.

"Why are you smiling?" he asked, and she shook her head.

He followed her gaze to the gloves again, and slipped his hands behind his back.

It felt like he had physically pushed her away, and for a moment she turned away from him. But there was this thing she always did every time she went to the hospital. She said bye to everything. Not just to the entire staff, but to her room, her bed, the view of the ocean, even the plastic curtain with its limp glove hands. All the things that were so intimately familiar. Because she had this sense that if it were the last time she was seeing these things that made up her life, she wanted to at least have said bye.

Until now she'd never had to say bye to Rahul. One, because usually, her hospitalizations came unexpectedly and he wasn't around, and two, because she didn't want to.

"Rahul," she said, and he looked up from the limp gloves.

"When will you be back?" he said, trying to distract her because he knew he wasn't going to like what she was about to say.

"They don't know how long it could take." And then, "Mamma and Papa do it, you know."

She didn't have to tell him what she was talking about. He knew.

"I'm not them. I'm not family. I'm a servant here, Kimi."

"You're not a servant. You're my best friend."

His look at that was so intensely sad, so intensely angry, she almost thought he would do it, reach through the curtain. But he kept his hands behind his back. "None of the servants are allowed to do it."

She hated when he called himself that. He knew that wasn't what he was. He knew Papa only let him work here because Rahul wouldn't let him help otherwise. She stuck her chin up. "If you're a servant, you have to listen to me because I'm your master. I want you to. So you have to."

He looked amused, and she felt a little less awful about what she had said. But he didn't move his hands. "Please, Rahul. Would you please? Just once. You may never see me again. Then you'll have to live with not having given me my dying wish."

He tried to roll his eyes and look amused again. "Shut up," he said and then in his Storm Boy voice, "I can't."

"Why?"

"I promised your father I'd never touch the curtain."

"Why would you make a promise like that?"

"It's the only way we could do this, Kimi. It's the only way I can be here. The only way he would know you were safe."

She grabbed the gloves and started flipping them inside out. She had never done this and her heart beat the way it did when she was running a high fever.

"What are you doing?"

"You can't touch the curtain. But I can. I never promised Papa anything."

His eyes were what she loved most about him. Tar-black and dark-lashed and deeply shadowed under his thick brows. And they spoke. All the words he couldn't say. They were so full of those words right now. His body looked like it was gathering energy, getting ready to step away. But he stayed where he was.

Her hands were inside the gloves. If she reached out, she could touch him.

He released his hands from behind his back and let them fall to his sides. And she did it. She reached for him. Trailing the back of his hands with her fingers. There was a wild zinging awareness, a warmth that flashed up her arm, a lighting up inside her, and she withdrew her hand quickly, her eyes meeting his. Had he felt it too? She couldn't tell. He swallowed and reached for her this time. Threading his fingers through hers.

"Are you scared?" he said so softly she almost wanted to ignore the question.

"Terrified," she answered as he pressed her fingers apart and let their palms join. "Just a little bit."

"How is one terrified just a little bit?" This close up, his lips were thick and sharply etched, as though someone had lined them in marker and then filled them in.

"I don't know. I just am." Sometimes breakthroughs worked. Sometimes they didn't. It was Dr. Girija's favorite thing to say. Kimi stubbornly refused to let herself unravel the entire meaning of those words.

He took the tiniest step closer. "I've never met anyone as brave as you, Kimi."

She felt a smile split her face even as a lump collected in her throat. "Really? You really think I'm brave?"

He shook his head in that amused way and smiled back at her but only with his eyes. "Why does that surprise you?"

"Because I think of bravery as something big and strong people possess. Like soldiers and commandos and policemen. Like you. You would be so good at something like that, something that requires bravery every day." Years later she'd curse herself for uttering those words.

His fingers tightened around hers and then let go. His face got all strained and awfully serious.

219

"What happened? What did I say?"

But he never answered anything the first time she asked him. At least nothing that was important. That's how she knew what was important to him and what wasn't. It was in how hard she had to push before he gave it out. "Tell me, Rahul." She reached for his hands again.

He squeezed hers and tried to pull away. But she hung on. "Rahul?"

"My father started out as a constable, just like his father before him. But then he worked his way up to becoming an officer. He always said if he became a police officer it would be that much easier for me to start out as an officer." He looked down at their joined hands and then looked up again. His eyes were a little lost, the way they always got when she forced him to do things he didn't want to.

"I can totally see you chasing down criminals and bringing them to justice," she said, seeing it so clearly now, him in a uniform, looking like a Bollywood hero. "You would be a fantastic police officer. You know what? You should take the Civil Services Exam! My mamma's uncle used to be DIG of police in Mumbai. When I was very little he used to always tell me how it was the hardest exam in the world and that he thought I should be an IAS officer when I grew up. He thought I'd be able to pass the exam. I wouldn't. But you know who is great at taking exams?"

Rahul frowned, those dark, thick brows drawing together until they met. "I'm already in engineering college, Kimi. I already know what I want to be."

"But you find engineering boring." Even without her sick-time spying, she knew how much he hated it.

"Everything isn't about excitement, Kimi. And I'm not ambitious enough to take the Civil Services Exam."

"Why not? Your baba wanted you to be a police officer, imagine how proud he would be if you were an IPS officer? You can be a civil servant, Rahul, a part of our country's most prestigious service!"

"Do you think you'll be rid of the plastic room this time?" And he was done with the conversation. Again he tried to tug his hands away. Again, she didn't let him go. If she had her way, she'd stand like this with him forever, palm-to-palm, face-to-face.

"I don't know. But if I am, you know what the first thing I will want to do is?"

"What?"

"Kiss a boy."

His dark-tar eyes darkened just that little

bit more. He made himself smile as he always did when he was trying to appear nonchalant. "And who is this boy you will kiss?"

"There is this one."

"Poor thing. Someone should warn him," he said, but his hands stroked hers when she glowered. "Do I know him?" He no longer sounded nonchalant, even though she knew he tried.

"Only a little. I think there is much about him you don't know. And I think the next time I see him he will have decided to take the Civil Services Exam."

18

Rahul
Present day

Kimi had this way of always getting him to do what she wanted. It almost made Rahul laugh how she had played him like one of her bloody video games. He should have known she had a plan when she'd been suspiciously undemanding after he picked her up at the airport. Even though her face had virtually collapsed in despair upon seeing him, not a word of protest had crossed her lips.

Rahul had assumed it was because Asif was at large, and she was going to do whatever she had to do to get through things. That was exactly what Rahul had expected. It was exactly what everyone always expected of her. For her to adjust what she wanted to meet what needed to be done. But with him, at least, she had always been able to protest.

All the way to Nikhil and Nikki's, however, she had sat there with her ill-fitting calm shell burying the storm he knew was swirling in her head. Then she had been her usual warm, wide-open self with Nikhil, Nikki, and Joy. There hadn't been a hint of bitterness about the fact that they were escaping while she was stuck with Rahul, whom she had done everything to avoid for the past year, and with a psycho bent on hunting her down.

One part of him wished she would go to Chicago with Nikhil and Nikki. He could prevent Asif Khan from leaving the country. The airports were the most realistically controllable public places. But he was incapable of letting her out of his sight right now.

Not to mention the fact that Kimi would not go. No matter what he did. She had this way of letting everyone around her take control while somehow holding on to enough that essentially she retained the heart of the thing. It's what she had been doing in all the time that she had let him drive her around today. She'd had a plan, and here he was unable to find a reason not to follow along, and feeling a bit rabid in his need to do something, anything, to make this easier on her.

Next to him she sat silent. She hadn't even asked him where he was taking her. It was almost as though she wasn't speaking to him again after demanding the impossible. Again. At least her silence wasn't the defeated silence that said, "I want this to be over so I can get away from you." Instead, her silence said, "I'm not speaking to you because I want to torture you into doing something I want." And what did it say about him that he preferred this option?

Saying no to her was a skill he had never quite mastered. Which was probably why the one time he had said it, he had made such a colossal mess of things. But every single time she pushed him to go along with what she wanted, something terrible happened. This was not the best thought to have right now, when he was on the verge of letting her turn all his plans upside down again.

To be fair, someone in his department leaking the safe house location is what had turned his plans upside down, not her. And she had a solution which for all its craziness made sense. How the hell did she manage to always put him in these situations, his back against a wall with no idea how not to want what she wanted? Her stupid mirror eyes and mirror face, reflecting all the best and worst of him, leaving him with no escape.

You would be a fantastic police officer!

Why couldn't he say no? Why couldn't he put things she said out of his mind? He wasn't nineteen years old anymore, he was thirty years old, for shit's sake. And when she snapped her fingers and said, "Sit," he had the instant and infuriatingly insistent urge to sink down at her feet, and kiss them for good measure. Figuratively, of course. He would never think about really kissing her feet. Because letting himself think about the time he had kissed them, kissed her all over, would mean he was certifiably insane.

He slid a gaze at her and she looked away. She was back to not wanting to meet his eyes, which only made his inability to keep his eyes off her that much more of a problem. He had to stop this. They were stuck together until she was safe again, and he needed to keep his focus.

He reminded himself that every single time he had let himself slip, let his control slip, disaster had followed.

Her mother had been right. He would do well to not forget her words.

He had only seen Rupa Patil outside her temple room a few times, but she had always put things in perspective for him.

226

Kimi had been fighting off another infection, and Rahul had arrived at her room door hoping it had passed. Fortunately, he had heard her parents' hushed voices before walking in on them.

"Something about that boy is cursed," Rupa Patil had said. *"No child loses a father and a sibling so randomly unless his stars are truly misaligned. I can see the anger in his eyes. He has bad energy. Every time he gets close to Kimi, something bad happens to her."*

"Calm down, darling. Something bad has been happening to our Kimi long before she met Rahul," Kirit Patil had told his wife, and despite his endearment there was a coldness in his voice that had surprised Rahul. *"She's blossomed since she's befriended him. She's smiling and laughing again. She's so much more than just her sickness. How can you not see that? She's come back to herself, and I will not take that away from her because you don't like his* energy."

Rupa Patil had been dead right in her judgment. Something terrible had happened to Kimi's health every time Rahul got carried away and did something he wasn't supposed to. The first time he had taken her to his rock on the beach, the second time he had put his hands through those gloves and touched her, and the third time — No, he

227

couldn't think about that. Not now, with her close enough to touch. Not now, when she could be hurt again.

He had known what he was doing was wrong all three times, but he'd let Kimi goad him into it. Even though he had promised Kirit he wouldn't do it, he'd done it. Even though deep inside he had known his curse, he'd done it. And the curse had never failed him.

After overhearing the conversation between her parents, Rahul had left without seeing Kimi, determined never to return. His determination had lasted two days. All he'd meant to do was peep into her room to make sure she was all right. He had even checked with Sarika first to make sure Kimi was asleep. He hadn't meant to let her see him.

She'd been livid when she caught him. She'd told him she hated him for not coming to see her when she was sick. It was the first time she'd asked him to go away and never speak to her again.

Instead of listening to her, he had gone back the next day, expecting her to throw him out again. But she had looked so relieved and acted so deliberately normal, it was the only way he had ever reacted to those words after that.

Except today. Today he knew she had meant it even without that note in his pocket. When he had shown up at the airport she had been anything but relieved.

They weren't children anymore. It was time to stop acting like they were. He'd sworn to act like an adult after The Great Escape. When you were an adult and someone told you to go away because they never wanted to see you again, you did it. You respected their wishes. You respected yourself.

This time he was only disregarding those words because she was in danger. The thought made him squeeze his hand around the pistol in his holster. He had put her in danger. The worst kind of bastard had been plaguing him for years, and somehow he had allowed Kimi to become caught up in the crossfire.

She believed she knew how to solve this mess. On one hand were her instincts — she was more perceptive than anyone he knew. On the other hand was the fact that letting her talk him into things always backfired.

Around them another monster traffic jam clogged the streets. Cars, rickshaws, bicycles, and motorbikes scrambled toward an opening in the dug-up road like ants on a carcass, no lanes, no rules, just hands on horns, spinning tires, and the stubborn multitude of hope that somehow the entire quagmire would clear by magic. It was times like this when he really missed Tina. Thinking about Tina brought alive the memory of Kimi's soft body pressed against his back with Tina purring under them and Rahul felt like the steering wheel would snap in his hands.

What was wrong with him?

Unable to navigate the car through the knot of traffic, he forced all his energy on navigating his mind through all the reasons why it was imperative that he stop fantasizing about Kimi on his bike. Because, what the hell?

They were stopped in the middle of traffic and all his focus had to be on keeping an eye on the crowds around them. A magazine seller climbed over the hood of a car next to him, and the driver stuck his head out of the window and let out a stream of expletives so virulent it couldn't have had anything to do with the fact that his car had just been violated. Tempers were starting to flare as high as the afternoon heat. They needed to be indoors. For a moment he regretted not having his siren in Maney's wife's car, but that would attract far too much attention and the point was to lie low.

Maybe Kimi was right. Leaving the country for a couple of days might be the only way to make sure a bastard with a gun didn't jump out from around a corner.

She was staring out of the window, her jaw set, her demeanor quietly confident. She knew he was going to come around to doing what she wanted.

Rahul caught the eye of a passing traffic cop and flashed his badge. The man ran over. It took another half hour and three more traffic constables to dismantle the deadlock and they were on their way.

The right thing to do would be to tell her they were going to the *chawl*. But he needed some time to adjust to the idea. Because the thought of Kimi in the *chawl* was so preposterous it made him want to change his mind and make another U-turn.

Instead, he turned into the narrow lane lined with open sewers that led to his home, and that ancient tug between shame and pride at where he came from twisted inside him. They drove across the muddy playground where preschoolers ran around playing ball in their underwear. The older children were in school. Once they came home, the little ones would have to make way for the big kids' cricket and football.

He thought of all the times he had gone home with a bloody knee after a particularly grueling game. He still played football on a league with some officers, but it wasn't anywhere near as satisfying as playing with the neighborhood boys had been. The healing force of teenagers trying to get their aggression out had no parallel in adulthood.

He pulled over in one corner of the muddy playground, raising a cloud of dust, and turned to Kimi, who still refused to ask where they were.

"This is where I live," he said.

That made her sit up and forget all her sullenness in her excitement. She studied the decrepit buildings edging the ground on three sides. The viewing gallery was out in full force today. The entire population of the *chawl* seemed to be leaning on the veranda railings and watching the car.

She looked down at herself. "I've never met your *aie*. Will she be there?" She chewed on a hangnail and patted her impeccably neat hair into place. She had retied it at Nikki's place after the bomb experience had messed it up.

"You look beautiful." That's what he wanted to say. But he had never said those words to her, even though she was the most beautiful girl he'd ever met. Baby-doe eyes and crooked teeth smile, and all.

"I wish you could stay in the car, but I can't leave you here. You're going to have to come up with me."

Her eyes widened with hurt, then they got all indifferent again. What had he said now?

"No one knows we're here. I can stay here if you don't want me to go inside with you."

Of course he didn't want her to go inside. Why would she want to? Not like there was a choice. He couldn't leave her in the car with a psycho at large. It wasn't going to be quick either. Getting tickets and coming up with a plan was going to take some time. But this was the safest place to be right now. No one he worked with knew that he still lived here and not in his government-issued police housing.

He did another sweep of the surroundings before opening the door for her. "I'll try to make this quick," he said and led her to the dingy timber stairway of Building Number Three. The tenants' association had put in new cement tiles on the lower-floor veranda last year, and he had thought it looked really nice, but not when you compared it to marble so white it was disconcerting to walk on.

She followed quietly, taking in every inch of the peeling paint on the walls, the ancient fading varnish on the wood railings. He rarely stopped to notice the dank, mildly dusty smell, but now it blasted his senses. Thankfully, the red betel leaf and tobacco juice sprayed into corners from his childhood had been cleaned and painted over. Not too many of the adults in the *chawl* chewed betel leaves and spat onto walls anymore. Progress was a beautiful thing.

They turned off on the second floor, her purple bag a beacon in his hands. And he was right — every one of their neighbors was out on the veranda studying them.

A chorus of "Hello, Rahul *beta*!" "What, at home in the afternoon today?" "Who's your friend?" engulfed them as they made their way to his housing block.

Kimi was wearing spotless white jeans that stopped at her calves and an embroidered *kurti* that looked like it cost his month's salary. Her thick, blond-highlighted ponytail cascaded down from the top of her head. Diamonds the size of peas shone in her ears. Her usually pristine appearance multiplied tenfold when surrounded by Ramu *kaka* in his yellowing *ganji*-tank and faded *lungi* and Shanta *kaku* and all the other *kakus* in their cotton saris, which God help him, were stained with spices. Just his luck that today was spice grinding day.

Twice a year all the *kakus* on their floor gathered to grind the mounds of red chilies and yellow turmeric pods that they had been drying for weeks along the veranda on white sheets. The huge brass mortar and tall wooden pestle they used to pound the spices into powder stood like proud sentries in their path.

Kimi studied the mortar and pestle as though she had never seen anything more fascinating. Rahul had loved pounding down on the spices as a child and having the fine turmeric and chili powder tickle at his nose. It scented the air and Kimi breathed it in, and it made her smile widen.

He looked around but didn't see Aie and wondered why she wasn't here. Everyone else was. And they studied Kimi with unabashedly curious eyes.

"Not going to help us today, Rahul?" Shanta *kaku* asked, wiping her spice stained hands on her sari.

He caught Kimi's eye and nodded in the direction of his block, urging her along. "Next time, Shanta *kaku*. Busy today."

"At least introduce us to your friend before you run off," one of the other *kakus* said.

"I'm Kimaya, how do you do?" Kimi said to the *kaku,* who smiled as if she hadn't expected an answer.

Shanta *kaku* pinched Rahul's arm and slapped a hand to her cheek. "*Arrey wah,* the girl speaks Marathi!"

Everyone nodded in appreciation.

"Of course I speak Marathi!" Kimi said indignantly, smiling her too-wide smile so those crooked canines made an appearance. "Is this turmeric?"

One of the grandmas picked up a piece of dried turmeric root and thrust it into Kimi's hand. "You rub it on your face for *facial!*" She said the word *facial* in English and rubbed her own cheek.

"And what do you know about facials, Aji?" a little girl Rahul had never seen before said through giggles, and everyone laughed, including Kimi.

"What does she need a facial for? She already looks like a Bollywood heroine, what, Rahul?"

His cheeks warmed as though he were fourteen again, and he grabbed Kimi's arm. "Let's go. Everyone needs to get back to work."

Kimi waved to everyone and burst into giggles when someone behind them exclaimed that her nails were painted blue!

He wanted to laugh. Really, he did. But this was his home, and the fact that she looked like a string of pearls that had fallen into a muddy puddle made him feel dirty himself, as though he were on his hands and knees trying to dig the pearls out of the mud but they kept slipping from his fingers. He needed to get her out of here and back where she belonged fast.

Kimi was still grinning and waving at the giggling gallery when he knocked on the door, which was locked. It was only ever locked when it was time for bed. The doors in the *chawl* tended to stay open and they were most certainly never locked.

The latch clattered and Aie pulled the door open a crack, then pressed her hand to her mouth when she saw him. She looked utterly horrified when her gaze landed on Kimi.

"Who's this?" she asked, and completely uncharacteristically, she didn't move out of the way and ask them to come inside.

"I'm Kimaya Patil," Kimi said and touched Aie's feet, keeping with the traditional gesture of respect even through the crack in the door.

Now Aie looked mortified. She patted Kimi on the head. "Bless you. May you live long. Wait, are you Patil-saheb's daughter?"

Kimi nodded.

Aie studied Kimi. "How is your health

237

now?" The door remained unopened.

"Very good, thank you," Kimi said as if they weren't still waiting out on the veranda.

Rahul shuffled his feet. He was about to ask Aie to let them in when she looked over his shoulder at the staring neighbors, and finally, with all the reluctance befitting a last resort, she ushered them inside.

19

Kimi
Present day
Kimi understood that Rahul was not used to his mother being less than enthusiastic in ushering him into his home. And yes, the distraught look on his mother's face together with the entire gaping-at-them-through-a-crack-in-the-door thing was a bit disconcerting. But the panic that flashed across Rahul's face when she finally let them in meant something was very wrong.

"Where's Mohit?" Rahul asked as soon as his mother shut the door behind them — rather hurriedly — and bolted it.

Without answering the question, she went into the kitchen and started pouring water into steel tumblers from a *matka*. The clay flask was unglazed and perfectly smooth. It reminded Kimi of the time last month when she had tried to convince her editor to let her do a story on the nomadic potters who traversed the country with their beautiful earthenware. Naturally, her editor had asked her to do a piece on "The Favorite Handicrafts of Celebrities" instead.

She took the tumbler of water she was offered with a thank-you. But Rahul, who was looking like he had swallowed a storm, took it away from her and then glared at her as though she was the one who had shoved the storm down his throat. She let the tumbler go without a fight. She was fully aware that she was only supposed to drink bottled water, thank you very much.

"We don't have a filtration system here in the block," he growled as though not installing filtration systems in your home, on the off chance that a sickly person might visit, were a cardinal sin.

He put his hand inside the bag that was hanging from her shoulder and fished out her bottled water and put it in her hand. Then he proceeded to empty the tumbler of water down his own throat.

His *aie* smacked her forehead. "Sorry," she said in English and then went on to add in Marathi how they were so lucky to get "bottle water" everywhere these days.

Kimi squeezed her arm. "Please don't apologize. It's just a precaution." She touched the terra-cotta *matka*. It was deep

240

red and glossy with use. "This is beautiful."

His *aie* smiled into her sari. "*Ish,* what 'beautiful'? It keeps the water cool. Rahul's *baba* bought it when I was pregnant with Rahul. We didn't buy a fridge until years later, but water from the fridge bothers my throat."

"Mine too," Kimi said. Her own mother had never let her drink anything other than water just this side of boiling as a child — generally with a few drops of one of her grandfather's germ-killing concoctions — and her throat now felt violated when the water was any colder than room temperature.

His *aie* smiled. It was the sweetest smile. She was . . . what was the word for it? Lovely. No, gorgeous. Yes, she was more gorgeous than anyone Kimi had ever seen. Which was something, given her current job of poking at the lives of the nation's most flawless faces.

"Are you hungry?" Aie asked, her face suddenly turning more somber and making her look even more like her son, those exact same dark-tar eyes and wide lips getting all serious in unison.

"A little," Kimi said just as Rahul said, "Not at all," and both women stared at him and then at the kitchen floor.

241

Rahul looked like they had jointly conspired to make his life a special kind of hell. Seriously, the man had no humor left in him.

Okay, that was a lie. It was more like his humor had to fight through six feet of earth to see the light. Like a live body stuck in a grave.

It was admittedly an awfully morbid analogy, but Kimi was suddenly feeling more than a little morbid. Not to mention hopelessly sad and angry, despite her vow to avoid those tiresome feelings at all costs.

"Kimi can eat. I have a few phone calls to make," said the cause of at least sixty percent of her hopeless sadness and anger. "We have to take a trip for a few days. I have to make arrangements."

Wait a minute. What?

He shrugged when she balked at him as if to say, "What? Weren't you the one who wanted to go to Hong Kong?"

She had the sudden urge to launch herself at him. She didn't. "Thank you," she said instead, in a tone that made his *aie* throw all sorts of questioning glances at him.

They were all saved from this storm of ocular smoke signals by a crash in the inner room.

Rahul went for his gun and pushed Kimi

behind him.

"Put that away. What is wrong with you?" his *aie* snapped — no question about where he had inherited his snapping from — and walked past him and into a back room.

He followed her, gun still drawn, Kimi still pushed behind him.

"I hope you're not planning to set that thing off," a very crumpled-looking man (more boy, really) said, sitting up on a bed. One of his eyes was swollen shut and alarmingly purple. "Gunshots are arse on a hangover."

Kimi hadn't meant to but she laughed, and the boy leaned sideways to throw her a glance over Rahul's shoulder. "Well, well, what do we have here? DCP Upright has brought home a girl. And a hottie at that!"

"Mohit, be quiet, *beta*. Does your tongue have no bone?" Rahul's *aie* said far too calmly for someone speaking to a son whose face looked like a gang of street fighters had gone freestyle on it.

So this was Mohit. The brother Rahul never talked about. Actually, he never talked about his family at all.

Rahul holstered his gun. His expression said that the gang-of-street-fighters thing was not as uncommon as one would think. This explained his *aie*'s reluctance to let

243

them into the house and Rahul's panic at her reluctance.

"What did you do this time?" Rahul asked.

"What? Are we pretending to care in front of your girlfriend?"

"Mohit!" their *aie* said with a little more heat.

"Are you okay?" Kimi said, elbowing her way out from behind Rahul. "That looks like it hurts!"

"You should see the other guy," this Mohit person said, and Kimi smiled. She liked this guy, clichés and smashed face and all.

She held out her hand. "I'm Kimi, Rahul's, umm, just friend."

"Mohit, Rahul's just-about brother."

Kimi's smile widened. "Same. I'm just-about his friend too," she said, and Mohit grinned.

Rahul slipped into full-on Storm Boy mode. "You're waking up *now*?" he said, pointing out the obvious as he often did when especially grumpy.

"Actually, I was trying not to wake up, but beer's shit on the bladder." And with that Mohit dragged himself out of bed and out a back door, leaving Rahul glowering in his wake.

"I'll get lunch ready," their *aie* said with

an exhausted sigh, and Rahul's face softened a little.

"I can help." Kimi followed her to the kitchen.

Or tried, because Rahul called her name and she turned around. "Did you want to, you know, freshen up or anything? It's been a crazy day."

More of that stating the obvious. He wasn't just grumpy, he was downright tortured, and she had the unbearable urge to go to him and tell him all would be well.

"Thank you," she said, hating that she hated seeing him this tortured.

Her gratitude made things worse. "Kimi, please," he said and took a step closer but then stopped and turned to a door. "The bathroom's there. It's . . ." Something at once too alien and far too familiar tinged his eyes. "It's the only room with a door. Or you could wait for Mohit to come back and then lock these two doors." He looked at the two doors on two sides of the room as though they were somehow offensive. And she knew that thing in his eyes was shame.

"The bathroom works fine," she said and left him before she told him he was being an idiot.

She splashed her face and wiped it with the hand towel that smelled of lemony detergent and sunshine. The bathroom was pure white, tiled from floor to ceiling and sparkling clean with an exposed metal water heater mounted on a wall, a stainless-steel bucket under a brass faucet, a commode, and a sink.

The shame that had darkened Rahul's eyes was something she had only seen there a few times, but she remembered each time clearly. His eyes were usually so proud, so self-confident, that the flashes were like acid burns she could never heal from.

She wanted to be angry with him, was angry. But she felt small in her anger now. Her anger flaring outward beyond him to a world that was so unbalanced, so utterly without reason in how it distributed privilege. Who Rahul was had nothing to do with this three-room block, this spartan white bathroom. And yet he seemed to think it had everything to do with it.

Why are all the billionaires in books and movies men? she had asked him after they had watched *Pretty Woman,* a film she found amazingly sexist and yet madly romantic.

Because men are supposed to provide. Our manliness rests either on the shoulders of our financial success or on our physical strength. It's the way the world is structured. There had been finality in his voice but also enough cynicism that she knew he didn't agree. He just bought in.

That's bogus, she had said. *So when a man shares his money with a woman, she's made a catch. But when a woman shares her money with a man, he's no longer man enough?*

No one said society's rules weren't bogus, Kimi. Just convenient.

Good thing she didn't rate convenience too highly. Rahul didn't either. But fat lot of good that was going to do either of them.

So they had been born into families that owned different amounts of wealth. She was entirely aware of how fortunate she was to be born where she had been born. For starters, she wouldn't be alive if not for that little piece of luck. She wished she could tell him to stop buying into this stupidass patriarchal way of thinking. They didn't live in a time when she would travel across villages in a bullock cart to join his family and be relegated to giving up her way of life if they married.

Not that she needed to worry about that, given his decided lack of interest in that particular option.

She dug into her bag looking for her antibacterial gel and her hand touched the picture she had plucked off her cubicle wall when escape had seemed so near. When freedom had seemed like such a simple solution. It was her favorite picture. Taken at the top of Kalsubai Peak from her first full-fledged hike. Admittedly, the peak was only sixteen hundred–odd meters and not a hard climb for seasoned mountaineers, but for her it had been the difference between knowing she could do something and fearing she couldn't.

Truth be told, it had been the moment that had changed her life, in so many ways. It had only been one year since her transplant, and the first few meters had been terrible. But once she learned how to listen to her body and stop and go in a way that kept her breathing constant and her pulse under one forty, everything had changed. The secret was monitoring herself with the same zeal that Mamma and Papa had monitored her during KAKA. Only, doing it herself was a little less frenetic, because she knew what she was feeling and knew when to push forth and when to pull back. As opposed to her parents, who had lived in perpetual pull-back mode.

She stroked a finger over the faces in the picture. There he was — Rahul — both her arms wrapped around him in complete possession. Rahul. Caught in a moment of joy, shaken out of his usual somber glory by this moment of triumph.

She shouldn't love the picture so much, shouldn't love how the giggling girl from a hiking troop who happened to have made the climb just then had captured Rahul and her exactly the way Kimi saw them in her mind. Leaning into each other, caught between laughter and disbelief at having made it up together. Burning bright with connection. The very essence of their selves laid bare.

Moments before he had broken her heart.

She had climbed up that mountain as one person and come down as another. Her plan had been to make the climb herself. She hadn't asked him to show up at four in the morning just as she was getting ready to leave. He had dismissed the driver, and taken the backpack from her and stashed it in Tina's carrier. And, no, when she had talked to him for months about making the hike, she hadn't been dropping hints for him to come along. The night before, they had been talking on the phone and he had asked who else was going with her. She had told him she was going by herself, and he'd gone all silent and then shown up at her door the next morning.

Maybe it had been wrong to puke out her

feelings for him up there where there was no graceful exit. She hadn't meant to do it. But all that adrenaline had mixed with all those feelings that filled her up, and it had messed with her head. Then there was the fact that she hadn't for a second considered that something so all-consuming could still not be enough.

I don't feel the same way about you, Kimi. I've only ever thought of you as a friend.

That . . . that had been his response.

The world is different outside your room. You'll find what you're looking for out here. Just give yourself time.

He'd made it sound simple. She had spent the past year convincing herself it was simple. But it wasn't.

20

Kirit
Present day

Kirit stared at his phone. The one laying on his teakwood table. The one in his pocket he would not place anywhere someone walking into his office could see it. Only one person used that phone, and not one day went by that Kirit did not curse the day he had taken the phone from Asif Khan. Except, his Kimaya was alive today because he had. But then that was life for those who fought it instead of lying down and taking its punches as they came. Warriors didn't get mired in guilt and regret, they focused on the goal.

The situation with Asif Khan had become serious enough that he should call his wife. Rupa, of course, was on one of her pilgrimages to Kashi. She had gone there straight from Dharamsala without even bothering to come home. It was one of the five holy

251

pilgrimages she went on every year. Most people strove to complete the five pilgrimages once in a lifetime, but Rupa was not most people. Usually, he would not disturb her spiritual journeying for anything. Communing with your gods was a solitary business, and Rupa made no bones about how seriously she took her communions.

Would she want to know about the threat to Kimi? Kirit hadn't paid heed to what Rupa wanted for so long that he no longer knew.

The real question he was currently pondering was if he needed to call her.

Many years ago, before he had lost her to her god, his wife had possessed great instincts. The word she preferred was *intuition*. It had been a huge asset in the movie business. She could take one look at a script and tell him if a project was going to be successful or not. She could take one look at his heroines and tell if they were making passes at him or not. He had been unwaveringly faithful, of course, no matter how hard and fast the temptations came. She had given up her own career to be his wife, and she had borne more pain than he could comprehend to give them a family.

How he'd loved her for it. It had felt unbearable sometimes, the volume of his love. So, yes, he'd been faithful. He'd been her slave. Not only for as long as she had been the woman he had married, but for a long time after she stopped. He had stubbornly clung on to his fidelity like a beacon of hope that someday she'd return.

After Kimaya got sick, her instincts weren't all Rupa lost. For a long time he didn't blame Rupa for losing interest in everything other than her god. Back then he shared her belief that their only hope of seeing their daughter reach adulthood lay in the hands of that all-knowing, all-controlling entity.

It had started with Rupa spending more and more time in front of the small altar in the kitchen with its inch-high silver idols of Ganesha, Lakshmi, and Krishna, which were part of every woman's trousseau. Slowly, the altar had moved to a room upstairs. Then as Kimi got sicker, that room had turned into a full-fledged temple. The small home-sized idols that had been in her family for generations had been replaced with human-sized marble statues that were bathed and clothed every day in addition to being meditated upon for hours and fasted in honor of in increasingly severe ways. Prayers were performed on a schedule to exacting standards and rules for which *strotra* was acceptable for chanting at which precise hour. Nothing could be out of place, because any error could throw all the hours of prayers out of alignment and incur the wrath of the gods who had so obviously decided to test them.

That too Kirit had understood. He shared Rupa's desperation to see their daughter live and thrive. But then she had abandoned Kimi. For a long time he had made excuses for her, seeing her actions as a mother's love, as her sacrifice for her child's health. It's what he had always done too. But one day Kimi had been so sick she'd been gasping for breath. Despite that, she had still managed to call for her mother. Rupa had refused to leave her meditation position in front of her idols in the middle of prayer. That's when Kirit had understood that it wasn't a mother's love that motivated Rupa, it was a selfish woman's inability to deal with the hand she'd been dealt. His own abandonment he could forgive, but the removal of a mother's loving hand from Kimaya's head he could never forgive.

He put down the phone he'd been holding. He was being fanciful. Even if Rupa cared, her only response would be to pray some more. No, she didn't deserve to know. He would handle Asif Khan himself. Just like he had done thus far. Because his love was real, unconditional. And because he was not a coward.

Love was supposed to be courageous and selfless.

It was the only reason he had let the Rahul problem continue. Rupa hated him for it. It had further fueled her mass punitive treatment of everyone and everything.

The boy lives in a chawl, *she had said. You might as well let your only daughter consort with the slum kids too.*

Truth was, her intuition might not be entirely dead because she had seen it, the danger that was Rahul. But again, she saw only what scared her, not what her child needed. It was obvious to any bystander that Kimaya was not the same after Rahul came into her life. Kirit had considered replacing him, but two things had stopped him. One, his Kimaya was too bright to be friends with any child who wasn't as intellectually superior as her. And two, Rahul would never cross the chasm between himself and Kimi. Kirit had made sure of that. Rahul would never forget the burden of debt Kirit had piled upon him. The kind of debt that repayment could never cancel out, because with debt timeliness was everything.

More crucially, Rahul would never forget

that Kimi came with a guarantee of loss. And no matter what Kimaya believed, Rahul didn't have the kind of courage it took to bear another loss. Not after what he'd been through. Kirit had seen it in his eyes the night of his sister's death.

Which is why Kirit could not decide if he was proud of Rahul or furious at him for not disclosing where Kimi and he were hiding out.

The good news was that if Kirit didn't know, Asif wouldn't know either.

The phone in Kirit's pocket buzzed. No wonder the bastard had survived all those bullets. The moment you thought about him, he turned up, like the immortal death god. Kirit sprang up and locked the door to his office.

He didn't greet the bastard when he answered. Not because he hated him with an obsessive virulence, but because someone else could have found Asif's phone and might be trying to trap Kirit.

"It's me. Sorry, not dead yet," Asif Khan said in that horridly rough diction.

"Pity."

"The pity is that you think you could send your daughter off to the police safe house and I wouldn't find out. Do you have any idea how easy it is to get your police force to sing like mynah birds? Turn on the TV."

Kirit hated taking orders from the bastard, but he turned on the small flat screen he'd had installed in his office mainly because so much of politics and public opinion was traded through the media these days. These television pimps had suddenly become the keepers of the vote bank.

Asif Khan chuckled on the phone when he heard the TV come on.

Kirit pushed off his desk, terror coursing through his body. Someone had shot three people outside a building in Colaba. Two of the bodies were identified as male police officers, and the third one was an unidentified woman.

Kirit's heart pounded so hard he could no longer hear Asif on the phone. He hung up, refusing to panic.

He called Rahul.

But Rahul didn't answer.

21

Rahul
A long time ago

"Have we not lost enough men to the police force in this family that Rahul suddenly wants to become a police officer too!" his grandmother said to Aie.

The two women were discussing him in the kitchen, and Rahul changed his mind about going in there. Nothing could drag him anywhere near that conversation, no matter how hungry he was. And he was starving. Trying to study for his engineering finals and his Civil Services Exam wasn't quite as easy for him as Kimi seemed to believe it was.

But then, that was Kimi. She romanticized everything. She certainly saw him as someone he wasn't. He still couldn't believe he was trying to get into the IPS. If he passed the exam, based on his score he could choose between the administrative service, the diplomatic core, or the police service. There was no doubt in his mind which he was going to pick. The idea of being an IPS officer, from the moment Kimi had planted that seed, had started a fire inside him. Not only did IPS officers lead law enforcement across the country, but they also commanded the national intelligence agencies. The weight of Baba's body had never eased off his lap, but the idea that he could be a part of ridding his country of criminal scum suddenly made it matter.

Plus, it wasn't anywhere near as easy as any exam he'd ever taken, and strangely enough, he couldn't walk away from something that challenged him this much. There was also his job at the kitchen appliances company, where he had worked all through engineering college. Sitting behind a desk for hours in a row had almost driven him out of his mind. Just the thought of going to work there made him break into a sweat.

Then there was the fact that Kimi had said those stupid words.

The next time I see him he will have decided to take the Civil Services Exam.

He wanted her to see him again.

It had been two years since she had left for Switzerland. Kirit had informed him that his services were no longer required and that the debt had been paid off in full. Every once in a while they got a new consignment of books and Rahul went in to help with cataloging the new arrivals. Or they got new computers and he went in to set them up. Those were the only times when he got actual medical updates on Kimi. Albeit after having to finagle them from the staff.

Rafiq was generally his best bet. Sarika was the one he had to keep his guard up with. Kimi's nanny made no bones about the fact that a servant boy had no business aspiring to a friendship with Kimi. He didn't disagree with her, but he still needed to know what was going on, and Kimi's e-mails were frustratingly lacking in medical details.

In the first two months that she was gone, he had heard nothing from her and it had felt a bit too much like panic. So much so that he'd been summoned to the dean's office for leaving classes early too many times because he'd been leaving to go to the lab to check his e-mails between classes. Finally, after two months, he had received a call from Kirit telling him that Kimi was fine and that she would e-mail as soon as she could.

She had reacted badly to this last breakthrough she had been so excited about, and it had taken a few months for them to stabilize her. Then they had decided to try another experimental treatment, which involved blood transfusions every few weeks. That had taken another six months. By this time Rahul had relived, over and over again, all the times her health had taken a terrible downturn after he had gotten carried away and done something he wasn't supposed to do. When he forgot his place and stepped over lines, Kimi tended to pay the price.

Then her incessant e-mails had started. Sorely lacking in details about her treatment, but effusively detailed about all the nurses and doctors and technicians: how each one looked, who she thought was "crushing" on whom. "It's exactly like *Grey's Anatomy,* Rahul. There's a Mc-Dreamy and McSteamy and then there's Meredith and Cristina. Only McDreamy is a nurse and Cristina is a social worker. And they all speak with European accents instead of American."

He had only watched a few episodes of the American show with her because she had talked about it so much that he'd had to promise to watch a few episodes on the condition that she stop talking about it. Which was all he could take because there had been far too much drama for him to keep track of all the medical cases.

"The show isn't about the medical cases, Mr. Goose!" She had unleashed her pout-frown at him.

"But the medical cases are what's fun." There was a man whose skin had grown so many warts he resembled a tree. They even called him Tree Man and a spider had crawled out of one of the gigantic bark-like warts that encased him. It had been almost good enough to put up with all the film-y drama.

Kimi had almost thrown up. How some-one who had been through those many medical procedures was this queasy he would never know. Just when the bizarre medical cases had become interesting, some people had started blathering on about lov-ing someone so much they couldn't breathe, and he had laughed, and Kimi had been sobbing and after that she refused to watch any more episodes with him. Which was a gigantic relief. Not that he'd tell her, because, God help him, he wasn't stupid!

As it was, she watched far too much American TV. Maybe that's why she was so optimistic all the time. The fact that she had never walked down a street in Mumbai, except that time he had taken her to his rock, completely astounded him when he thought about it. What would she think if she ever came to his home? With a thousand people living in a little more space than The Mansion, with its common bathrooms in the back, with a drain in the corner of the kitchen where Aie squatted down to wash the dishes, with the *paath* stools that they put down in a circle on the cement kitchen floor when they sat down to eat their meals.

Not that his family had eaten together in years. After he started working at the Patil mansion, Rahul had rarely ever been home for dinner. Even though Aie had known that he usually ate at The Mansion, she had continued to put dinner aside for him on a plate. When he started college, she had done it no matter how late he stayed at the kitchen appliance factory. Usually, he came home, took his plate to the outside room, and ate sitting on Baba's easy chair.

This was exactly what he wanted to do right now. But Aie was explaining to his grandmother that it only made sense that Rahul was taking the exams because his *baba* would have been so proud. There was no reason for him to go into the kitchen and add to that explanation. It was a good thing his grandmother only visited from Pune once every few years, because she enjoyed talking about her dead son and granddaughter a bit too much, and Rahul wasn't a fan of digging up ancient history. He knew both Aie and Aji were working to balance their pride with their worry about his future, and he didn't want to tip that over in any one direction.

No, he wasn't hungry enough to go into the kitchen. Instead of going back to his text book, he reached for the book he had picked up at Bandra station yesterday — a love story set in World War II that Kimi had gone on about in her last e-mail. He hadn't wanted to read it, but he'd seen it at the bookstall on the platform, sitting there like one of those things that you suddenly started to notice everywhere right after someone mentioned it, and he hadn't been able to stop himself from picking it up.

He sank into Baba's easy chair just as Mohit walked in, a battered-looking cricket bat tucked under his arm and his face streaked with dirt. A whiff of sweat hit Rahul and he almost coughed. Mohit at ten years old was a skinny thing. Rahul had taken after his mother's side of the family where the men tended to be thicker and broader. Unlike Mohit, Rahul had always looked older than his years. Mohit looked exactly like their father. Sometimes when he looked at Mohit, Rahul felt as though Baba had aged in reverse since his death and here he was.

"It's still bright outside. What are you doing back home so early?" Rahul asked as Mohit walked by.

His brother jerked to a stop, his expression so blank, Rahul wasn't quite sure what was going through his head. Then without answering he headed for the inner room.

"Mohit, I asked you a question." Why his tone was so stern, Rahul didn't know. He hadn't meant for it to be.

Mohit turned around, blinking up at Rahul in surprise as though he couldn't believe Rahul was actually speaking to him. "The game's over."

Something about the way his mouth drooped and his eyes lost their sparkle made Rahul get up and go out to the front veranda. A pack of very noisy boys was playing cricket on the playground.

He turned to find that Mohit's despondent face had turned defiant. "I'm too good for them," he said. "I was bored playing with them."

"You want to go down and practice with me?"

For a moment Mohit's eyes flashed bright with excitement. Then he stepped back, sullen again. "I can't. I have too much home-work."

"Tomorrow is Sunday. You can do your homework then. Let's go down and prac-tice." He almost added, "Like we used to," but Mohit had been so little the last time Rahul had played cricket with him — played anything with him — Rahul doubted he remembered it.

"Really?" Mohit asked when Rahul con-tinued to look at him.

Rahul held out his hand for the bat and Mohit shook his head. "It's broken."

"Is that why the boys won't let you play?"

"Who cares. They really play like girls."

Rahul flinched. Unsurprisingly, he thought about Kimi. "I'm sure the Indian Women's Cricket Team would not like to hear you say that."

"There's a women's cricket team?" Mohit asked, as though Rahul had told him their neighbors were from Mars.

"Yes, I think they are world champions too."

Mohit looked impressed and pointed his chin at the veranda. "Well, those losers sure don't play like world champions."

Rahul took the bat from Mohit. "Why didn't you tell me you needed a new bat?"

Mohit shrugged. He hadn't told Rahul he

needed anything for the past six years.

The bat looked like it had seen better days. A really, really long time ago. Lots of rope and duct tape held it together. A really impressive patch-up job. Even through all the repair jobs Rahul recognized it. "Is this my bat?"

Mohit got defiant again. His brother had a temper. Rahul wondered if he got in trouble with that temper and being a skinny guy. "Aie gave it to me a few years ago. She said you hadn't played with it for years. It was just lying there behind the cupboard."

Rahul hadn't played for years. Cricket was too slow for him. He needed the constant motion of football, the running until you were out of breath and the falling and feeling your knees and elbows as they scraped and bled. But this was Baba's bat and he had given it to Rahul, hoping he would follow in his footsteps and fall in love with his favorite sport.

Looked like his younger son was fulfilling their father's dream.

"No, it's completely fine. It was never really mine. It was Baba's. I think he would have wanted you to have it." Mohit's body sagged with relief. Had he thought Rahul would be angry with him for using his bat? "Did you patch this up?" He peeled the duct tape off and found a few small nails hammered into the broken wood. His little brother could fix things with so much finesse at ten years old? "This is impressive," he said.

Mohit beamed, then realized he was beaming and went back to scowling. "It's just a broken bat. And it won't work anymore anyway."

"Well, I think we could fix it one more time. Then I'll show you how to really break a bat and get you a new one from Linking Road tomorrow."

"Really?" Mohit said for the nth time that day and Rahul felt like a giant shit.

"Go get me the nail box and hammer." Rahul started peeling off the tape and tried to pry the nails out with his fingers.

Mohit nudged him with pliers. "You'll need these."

Together they pulled out the nails and then secured the broken wood with a couple long screws. They wouldn't hold for more than a few good strokes, but no harm in trying. Once the wood was secured, Rahul pulled out good duct tape from his backpack. He'd bought it for a college project. Mohit held the bat up while Rahul wrapped it up.

When they were done, Rahul handed it to

Mohit and asked him to swing. Mohit did.

"Wow, your form is fantastic."

Mohit whooped, and Rahul heard a giggle behind him and turned to find Aie and his grandmother watching and dabbing their eyes. How long had they been watching?

"He's the primary-school team captain," Aie said, her wet eyes glistening with pride. How did Rahul not know this?

"Well, then he's going to have to teach me some moves. Let's go down and break that thing the right way," Rahul said.

Mohit was really good. Rahul wasn't exactly great but he had a decent long arm and off spin. Yet Mohit swung his balls to the far reaches of the field as though they were full-toss balls. They kept going, Mohit turning his balls into sixers and fours, and finally on one lofty ball the bat split with a harsh crack, and all the boys who had joined them burst into cheers.

"In the garbage dump that goes," Rahul said.

But Mohit hugged both pieces to his chest. He didn't say more, but he looked somehow happier than Rahul had seen him look in a very long time. Rahul tried not to think about that.

"Thank you, Dada," Mohit said as they walked into their block and threw his arms around Rahul.

"Ugh, you smell," Rahul said and ruffled his sweaty hair, making him laugh as though it were a compliment. "Off to a bath."

Mohit disappeared through the back doors into the common corridor that led to the bathrooms. The silly boy had forgotten his towel. Rahul pulled a towel from the hook behind the door and took it out to the bathroom.

"Where's your towel, Captain-saheb?" he asked, knocking on the door.

The door opened a crack and a skinny arm stuck out. "Thank you, Dada," he said one more time as Rahul pushed the towel into his hand and went back into the block, smiling.

He heard a sniff from the kitchen.

"He used to be like this with Mona," he heard his mother say, and Rahul stopped in his tracks, his heart starting to beat faster. "She used to idolize him. Her *dada* was everything to her."

"But that's our Rahul," his grandmother said. "Everyone should have a big brother like him."

"If Mona hadn't died, Mohit would have known him. He would have been home more. He would have had a brother. My beautiful girl." Aie broke into tears.

Rahul wanted to go in there and comfort her. But he couldn't move.

Mona. Hearing her name scraped at that part of him where she lived. Constantly. Untouched. Because he needed it to be that way. It was a part that couldn't bear touching, the skin over it too easily torn, irreparable.

He squeezed his eyes shut and the hopeful, trusting eyes with which Mohit had followed him around today bored into him. He felt sick.

"I'm going out," he said to his mother but didn't wait to hear her response. He walked that path he always seemed to find when he had nowhere to go. On his way he found the sporting goods store open. He bought a bat. Shiny and new.

He found the rock on which he had always sat when he needed a rock to sit on, with water soaking up the hem of his jeans. He thought about the only time someone else had stood on the rock with him and wondered if she was okay. Wondered if he'd ever have a chance to bring her here again.

It was past midnight when he got home. Mohit sat up when Rahul opened the front door and let himself in. He had been waiting up for him. He rubbed his sleep-filled eyes. He had Baba's eyes. Mona's smile.

271

"Where did you go, Dada?" he asked.

"I had work to do."

"Will you still buy me a new bat?"

"Of course." He kept the bat behind his back. He had no idea why.

"Will you help me practice again tomorrow?" Why had he told Mohit he would help him practice? He didn't have time. He shouldn't have given the boy false hope.

"I can't. I'm busy, Mohit, I have to study for my finals and for my entrance exams. I have to start working to support Aie. You understand that, right?" He tried to sound gentle, but even to his own ears he sounded distant and harsh.

"Yes, Dada." Mohit's voice was small when he lay down and turned away. Then in a much stronger voice he threw over his shoulder, "I'm busy too. I probably won't have time to play tomorrow anyway."

Rahul didn't answer. He laid out his pallet on the floor, lay down, and pulled his cotton sheet over himself. The next morning he was gone before the sun rose. But he left the bat on the divan where Mohit could find it when he woke up.

22

Kimi
A long time ago
This was the third time in her life that Kimi
was returning to her own home after a long
absence. She remembered each time vividly.
Remembered how each of her homecom-
ings was characterized by some sort of
exuberant hope.

Exuberant. Rahul loved to call her that.
And yes, she had this weird, expandable
thing in her chest that had always been
there, the strangest combination of the
stretchiness of hope and the tautness of
determination. Like the minuscule bubbles
inside a soufflé that held it up, that made it
exist. The hardest thing to explain to people
about her life was that she had this sense of
permanency deep inside. Like you felt in
your home, like you belonged here and that
you weren't going anywhere, because that
sense of belonging had to mean that you

weren't going anywhere. Which wasn't at all what people expected from her.

Social workers, therapists, doctors were always trying to talk to her as though they were trying to assuage her fear of death. It made her wonder if she should be more afraid than she was.

When she came home from one of her "breakthrough" treatments, everyone around her seemed to wear hope as though they were dressed up for a wedding. The only wedding she'd ever attended was Rafiq *kaka*'s, when she was ten years old. It was supposedly a small enough affair that Mamma deemed it suitable for her to go. The Diagnosis had not come knocking yet, and Papa had insisted on taking her along. Mamma had put her in the heaviest, most embellished *anarkali salwar kameez,* which fell in a full skirt all the way to her ankles. It had felt fantastic when she first put it on. She had felt all grown up and almost as beautiful as Mamma, almost regal. But by the end of the evening she had started to feel the weight of the thick silk, the itchiness of the embroidery, the strain from having to stand up tall, and she had craved the relief of taking it off. The hope the household wore every time she returned from a new treatment seemed to fit everyone a bit like that.

This particular stint had been longer. More than three years in Switzerland this time. They'd given her another drug, used another method to replace her marrow, and they'd watched her body reject and accept their ministrations until it all stuck and she, like Frankenstein's monster, was ready to be unleashed into the world. Well, not quite into the world, but more like into her natural habitat.

Papa, naturally, had wrestled God knows how many more outrageously exorbitant medical equipment companies to ready her room for her return. Creating an environment to their specifications was the only condition under which her doctors had allowed her to go back home. But there was good news. She was no longer someone who had a "severely compromised" immune system. She was someone who had an "unusually underperforming" immune system.

This meant that only roughly thirty percent of the viruses and bacteria that infiltrated the air could kill her. The other seventy percent she could mostly fend off. And if they did make her sick, the good news was that there were drugs that could help her fight them off. As she had found out in Switzerland by contracting and communing with the three-odd infectious parasites that dared to infiltrate the atmosphere in all that sparkly Swiss pristineness.

Back home in Mumbai, things were, well, a little bit different in the pristineness department.

The doctors had even created a Power-Point presentation, complete with angry-germ-blob animation, to show them how many more pathogens she would be exposed to in the city of her birth. The city her mother wanted to keep her away from, but that her father could never leave and therefore she would never leave.

"Our recommendation is that you continue to live in Switzerland until we can find a way to get your body to make more normal levels of antibodies," Dr. Vaughn had said.

Which basically meant: "No going home unless you want to die, or unless you want to continue to live inside your bubble."

It was not even a question. She wanted to go home. It wasn't like she could be out and about in Switzerland. She could take walks in the countryside, but she couldn't go to malls or college or anywhere there were a lot of people. She probably could, but her mother would never let her.

If she had to continue to live an isolated existence, she'd rather do it in her own house, where her mother's prayer bells rang and the food tasted familiar and her father stopped by to discuss his work and where she had friends. Well, one friend. But it was Rahul, so he counted for at least a few. She had missed him so very terribly this time, one could even say that he counted for ten.

She had to come home. Promising to stay indoors was nothing new. And if an irrepressible urge to walk around the countryside suddenly struck, she could always go back to Switzerland for a few days as Papa had suggested. But if she let herself roll down the hill of honesty, the idea of another space-suit-wrapped plane ride into another pristine foreign hospital made her chest tighten the way it did when her oxygen levels fell fast and furious and a straitjacket wrapped and pulled against her lungs. The thought terrified her enough to never want to touch it.

The plastic curtain was gone. Replaced by an air curtain. She could walk around the house but with a face mask, at least until her body adjusted. The most incredible part, however, was that she could be touched. No plastic gloves as long as people washed their hands and scrubbed them with disinfectant.

She could shake hands. Shake hands! She loved it. She loved everything about touching people's hands. Which sounded a bit creepier than it was.

The first time the social worker had shaken her hand, she had refused to let it go for an embarrassingly long time. Papa had taken her hand from the social worker's and held it. But they kept warning her that it wasn't a good idea to take this for granted. It was always best to be careful and so forth. Another promise she'd had to make was to be extra, extra careful in India. Yes, because what was she going to do? Run around her empty room holding the hands of all the people there? It's not like her friends were lolling around the room the way Cher and Dionne lolled in *Clueless*.

Speaking of friends, where was Rahul?

Seriously, dude, how are you not here yet? she texted him. She loved text messaging. It was the most amazing thing, like being with someone all the time, but condensing your thoughts into only those words that were absolutely necessary.

Which, come to think of it, was how Rahul communicated anyway. Mr. Monosyllables. Papa had told her that text messages cost a lot to both send and receive, so she had to be judicious and considerate.

Then, just in case she didn't understand his mild suggestion, Papa had asked her pointedly to not send Rahul every thought that popped into her head.

That wasn't a very nice thing to say. She had no idea why Papa would accuse her of such a thing. It's not like he was privy to the e-mails she sent Rahul.

Definitely thought vomit.

She could bet anyone willing to lose money that Rahul barely skimmed her e-mails. Not that she could blame him. She did tend to go on. But then he would reference something from nine e-mails ago, and she was tempted to think that he actually did read them all very carefully. Well, truth be told, her e-mails were very well written and filled with all these great insights, things that suddenly struck her in the middle of a transfusion, like are "This too shall pass" and "Live every moment" opposing edicts?

"I had to look up the word *edict,*" had been his only response.

Which was a lie, of course, because he had the best vocabulary of anyone. Thanks to the word lists for the SAT she made him help her with. He had told her he could only get here in the evening, because Mister had a fancy job now. Assistant Superintendent of Police.

Assistant *Superintendent* of Police!

She kept saying the words out loud.

She'd asked him over and over again to scan and send her a picture of himself. But of course she hadn't actually expected him to do it.

Please don't call me "dude" his text message buzzed through. *That sounded like a text to the milkman.*

Lame, she typed. *Cross language jokes are so elementary school.* But even as she had typed the word *dude,* she had imagined him saying it so it sounded like the Marathi word for milk. Yes, it was lame, but who was she kidding? Rahul was making juvenile jokes. So, naturally, she couldn't stop smiling.

She heard the doorbell and jumped into bed. She had a new one now. The plan was to only switch it out with her old spaceship-style hospital bed when she got sick. Until then it stayed in a storeroom somewhere in the house, thank God! She hated that thing! (Only a little bit. She totally got how invaluable it was to her, etc.). Her new bed she loved. It had a bacteria-resistant polyurethane headboard that was thick and luxuriant and best of all *normal.* She pulled the sheets all the way up to her chin and waited.

The knock on the door came as soon as she had settled in and donned her I'm-sick expression. Watching *Grey's* had its advantages because she had no idea how she actually looked when she was sick.

"It's the look in your eyes that changes," Rahul had told her once when she had pestered him to tell her how it looked from the other side.

"Come in," she said as weakly as she could manage and tried not to giggle.

He let himself into the waiting area that led to her room.

Rahul.

It had to be her imagination because the smell in the room changed. His clean, soapy smell.

"Kimi?" he said tentatively, and something rippled inside her belly. A tiny little spark. Okay, it wasn't tiny.

"In here." How she managed to keep up the soft, sick-voiced pretense, she would never know.

And there he was, filling up the waiting room doorway where he had pulled a chair and taught her so many things. Algebra and chemistry and the stories of Premchand, but really just what it meant to be alive and have a friend. Where he had sat as they watched movies and fought about books.

He was in uniform.

Khaki stretched across his chest, which

was rising and falling in a labored way. The way he always breathed when he was anxious.

"What's wrong?" he said in that gentle, worried voice, and she knew she couldn't pretend to be sick the way she had been meaning to. "Should I call Sarika?"

"Ah, so you are capable of calling people then," she said, sitting up and throwing her legs over the side of the bed, watching him watch her and go from worried to relieved to irritated to amused so fast that each one of those emotions zinged in tiny sparks from her belly to her heart.

Finally, he settled on a smile. Not helping the sparks at all.

"You're late," she said, trying to frown but failing rather spectacularly.

"Not true. You can only be late if you postulated a time."

"Don't use big words to impress me."

"Come on, *time* isn't that impressive."

She jumped out of bed, laughter spilling from her. Because how on earth could she not let out the joy that was filling her up?

"There's no plastic curtain," he said with wonder in his voice, but he had not moved from the doorway.

"So there isn't."

"Does that mean I can come in?"

She laughed again and nodded and for no reason at all her eyes filled with tears. "But you have to wash up first."

He leaned his body back and peered at the sink that had been installed in the waiting room. The movement made his thick hair flop across his forehead, turning him for an instant into the boy who had jumped up onto her balcony every day to help with her homework. He walked to the sink, his eyes smiling his disbelief at her, and then he scrubbed and scrubbed and went on scrubbing his hands for so long she had a good mind to turn off the faucet herself.

She stood in the doorway where the plastic curtain had always separated them (she was still a bit terrified of crossing it) and watched him. Then he was standing in front of her.

He held up his hands. "Clean enough?"

She nodded again. It seemed all the words she had wanted to say to him were elbowing one another so hard to get outside that they were causing a traffic jam inside her. "There's only an eight percent chance that you'll kill me if you touch me."

He frowned.

What on earth? Really, that was the first thing she said to him?

"The disinfectant hand wash is effective

against . . ." He said the rest of the words with her. "Ninety-two percent of germs." They both smiled.

He reached over and wiped her cheek and she started. A quick stuttering jerk that made him withdraw his hand too fast.

"Was that not okay?" he asked, stepping away from her even before she answered.

She grabbed his hands in both of hers and tugged him back, her heart thudding. For so many, many reasons. This was Rahul. She was touching him, and his hand was rough and warm and heavy in hers and it felt like nothing she could describe. But it also terrified her. She wanted to pull it to her face, nuzzle it like a beloved toy, which basically made her sound like a psycho.

Truth was she really was terrified. When everything was a danger, and everything could spell loss, even something that felt so good had a way of filling you up with all the things it could take away from you. And she didn't know what to do with any of it.

"Hey," he said, in his gruff, gentle Rahul voice.

She had dreamed of his voice every day.

She threaded their fingers together and pressed their palms together, the way he had done through those gloves. But this, this was different. And yet it was the same.

Touching him was not like touching anyone else. Not that her experience was
particularly varied. Touching him was, it
was . . . "Does it always feel like this?"

"What?"

"Touching people?"

He swallowed. "No. But then not everyone goes nine years without touching anyone." He was trying to ruin the moment.
Trying to wrap it in Rahul logic. But that
made it worse. "It will stop feeling this
intense."

It seemed impossible. "It's not getting less
intense."

"Give it maybe more than seventy seconds?"

Gladly. She'd gladly give it all her time in
this world. "You remember what I told you
the last time we met?"

"It was too long ago." But that slight flush
told her he remembered.

"One part of it came true. You're Assistant
Superintendent of Police. Asst. SP Rahul
Surajrao Savant! Oh, Rahul, I'm so proud
of you!"

His only reaction was the darkening of his
eyes.

"What about the second part?"

"I don't know what you're talking about."
He had always been a bad liar. She loosened

her grip, just to make sure what she was feeling wasn't just her. He didn't let her hand go.

"Don't lie." She studied him study their intertwined hands. "And you're safe. Don't worry. Because I don't think I can." She was the one who finally pulled away.

"Phew," he said and swept a finger across his forehead. But his eyes shone. They shone so brightly she couldn't look away from them.

"Don't be too relieved. I'm researching it. Once I figure it out you have no choice. You have to kiss me."

He didn't say anything, and it made her angry. "I thought boys liked kissing girls."

"Not girls who are their friends."

"Why?"

"Because this is us, Kimi. We're not like that."

"Yes, Rahul, this is us. Who else could I ask?"

"Tell me what the situation is. You never did. You still can't leave the room?"

"No. Not until this drug they're working on is ready."

"Then why did you come back here? It's dangerous for you to be here and to not have the curtain." He stepped back.

"No. As long as I stay here I'll be fine.

There's an air filter and what-not. And how could I not come back? I had no friends there, no one to talk to. You're here, Rahul."

When that made him look like she had said something painful, her heart sped up for a whole different reason. "You'll come to see me every day, won't you?"

But she knew something was wrong before he even spoke.

"My transfer papers came in. I'm being transferred to Pune."

"They can't do that! Why can't you work in Mumbai? Papa will take care of it."

"What the hell, Kimi!" He was furious. "I did this myself. I made it into the IPS on my own. This was not something Kirit-sir did for me. My career is not his to direct."

She knew she shouldn't have said that. But she had an odd desperation rising inside her. If he wasn't here and she was stuck here, how would she survive it? Not after how long she had waited. "No one's directing anything. You can't go. And that's that."

"It's a job, Kimi. Regular people need those. It's not your little kingdom to direct."

Kingdom? Regular people? He, of all people, thought she ran a kingdom? He, who she had always been able to ask things of, the only person who cared what she wanted, not just what she needed. And now here they were, and he thought she was a spoiled child. And he felt the need to point out that she wasn't a regular person?

"You think I'm spoiled? You think this is me ruling my kingdom?" She looked around her room with its medicinal smell and the endless buzz of machines.

"Kimi . . ." He dared to sound as though he was warning her. The way he sounded when he thought she was manipulating him into something. It was their game. A game that was only fun if he was a willing participant. He wanted the same things she did. Didn't he? Or did he really think she was spoiled? Was the way she was really not regular? Outside of her illness she had always felt normal. Was that not true? Was she really so sick that she wasn't even a regular person?

Anger beat in her heart so hard she found it hard to breathe.

"I want you to leave. Go."

"Kimi . . ." He sounded bereft now. She knew the feeling. How was she going to get through this without him? She had gladly, even excitedly, agreed to come home because somehow stupidly she had thought he would be here to help her through it. The way he'd always been. But he didn't understand anything. And he had a life. In Pune.

Which was a four-hour drive away.

"When do you have to leave?"

"Actually, I'm already living there."

He had come to see her from Pune? That's why he had been late?

Maybe he could come see her every few days. She opened her mouth to ask him. But suddenly, she couldn't. He had called her spoiled. He had ruined everything.

"Go, Rahul. Leave me to rule my kingdom." And for the first time in her life she slammed the door in his face.

23

Rahul
Present day

It was a good thing Mohit had dragged himself out of bed and out the back door to the community bathrooms. A few years ago, Rahul had had a bathroom installed inside the block so they didn't have to use the communal one. But Mohit refused to use it.

Good. Because there was no way Rahul was letting Kimi even see the communal bathrooms. As it was, the crash course she had gotten in his idiot brother's antics was enough introduction to the chasms between their lives for one day. Rahul lived in fear of coming home one of these days and seeing Mohit with more than just a black eye. The local police *chowki* kept an eye on him, but going up against the gangs in the area wasn't exactly what Rahul had hoped for when he wrote those checks for Mohit's engineering college.

Kimi had giggled. Actually giggled when Mohit had introduced himself. And now she was off chatting away with Aie in the kitchen. When they first got here, Rahul had felt like he should say something. Somehow show her how to navigate his family, but he hadn't known where to start, and now she was doing a better job of it than he ever had. And damn if that didn't mess with his head.

He started throwing a few things into an overnight bag and threw a glance at Kimi's purple suitcase, and it made him smile. Which in turn made him angry. This wasn't a time for amusement. He called his travel agent to make a booking. They couldn't get on that plane soon enough.

He couldn't get out of here fast enough.

I want you to show me where you go when you run away.

He could have taken her anywhere that day. And she had been stupid enough to trust him.

That single day might have flipped his life like a coin, but it had flipped her life too. Even though she would never admit to his role in it. Maybe if she hadn't gotten soaked to the bone and run down a crowded beach with him, she would never have become sick. And maybe if she had never taken his hand and dragged him there, his hand would never have been able to suppress a memory that still woke him up at night sometimes. If not for that day, maybe they'd both have headed down altogether different paths that didn't lead them here. To his three-room home, where all their differences danced in the light.

Her laughter mixed with Aie's and filled the block. What could they possibly have found to laugh about? The usually familiar sound of her laughter felt alien here. Like it was shaking up sleeping ghosts and twisting together memories he wanted and didn't want with equal hunger. He felt as unbalanced as he had standing on the rock with the tide too high and the waves trying to dislodge them off its wet back. A bucking camel ride they had only survived by holding on to each other so they didn't topple headfirst into the ocean.

Dropping her off at the compound wall of the building adjoining The Mansion, dripping wet, was a moment he had carried with him ever since. She had climbed the wall and jumped onto the gatehouse with the deftness of a squirrel. For the second time that day she had looked down at him from the roof of the gatehouse with those humongous doe eyes and thanked him as though he'd been some big hero. When he had been the one who had needed it more than her. He had never before or since taken anyone else there.

His clothes had dried in the afternoon sun on his walk home. When he climbed up the dark *chawl* stairwell and emerged onto the veranda, the first thing he'd seen was Mona and Mohit playing cricket across the china-mosaic floor that led to their block.

As soon as they saw him they ran to him, both of them reaching up their arms until he picked them up and settled them on each hip.

Aie, Dada's home! Mona shouted in his ear, and he rubbed his stinging ear into her shoulder and wiped his still-damp hair into her neck, making her squeal.

Aie lives in our block, not on the moon, he said, and Mona giggled and wrapped her legs around him tighter.

Where have you been all day? Aie had asked as he put his siblings on the divan. His grandparents had gone back to Pune and the constant stream of mourners was finally gone too. It had taken just one month after he had given fire to Baba's cremation pyre for people to start laughing around them again, and to start behaving like themselves instead of doleful, whisper-voiced versions of themselves.

Aie, I'm hungry, he had said for the first time since Baba had stopped coming home.

Aie had responded with nothing more than a quick swipe of her sari across her eyes. *Food's ready, but first you have to get cleaned up. No filthy boys in my kitchen.*

Mona had screwed up her button nose. *Dada smells like football.*

Mohit had pinched his nose and nodded in wholehearted agreement.

Rahul had raised his elbows, threatening to shove the two of them under his armpits, and they had rolled back on the divan shrieking with laughter before wrestling him down and climbing all over him.

"What are you staring at?" Aie asked, coming out of the kitchen and catching him looking at the empty divan where the memories had been so alive moments ago, he half expected them to have messed up the sheets.

The sheets were pristinely tucked. And brand-new. At least Aie loved to shop for things for the block now, even though she refused to move out of the *chawl* and into his police housing. And he couldn't leave her and Mohit behind and move by himself. Especially not when he couldn't get through to Mohit, who had turned into someone Rahul couldn't even recognize. How had his life come to this? Him unable to get through to anyone he cared about.

Except Aie, who was easier than he deserved. Easy on him, easy on Mohit. He knew it was unfair to take her kindness as his due and expect her to be different with Mohit. But kindness wasn't what Mohit needed. Not when those kids he called friends could get him killed.

"Come in and eat something," Aie said, tugging him back to earth with her trademark gentleness and pushing him into the kitchen where Kimi was laying down the *paath* stools around serving bowls of food on the floor.

How did she even know to do that?

"We used to eat on the kitchen floor at my grandmothers' house when I was very little," she said, even though he had not asked the question.

She laid down Mona's stool and no one else seemed to notice.

"Our flight isn't until early tomorrow morning. We have to find a safe place to stay until then."

Aie's hand pressed against her mouth again. Why did the mention of the word *safe* always elicit fear? "Eat first. All decisions are easier on a full stomach," she said. "Where are you planning on flying off to?"

"Off to save the world again, I see." Mohit walked into the room, a wet towel slung over his shoulders and wetting his T-shirt. He looked more and more like Baba every day.

Mohit picked up Mona's *paath* and put it away, switching it with another one, and then plonked down on it. Then pulled Kimi down on the one next to him with far too much familiarity. "Will you bring Aie another medal for bravery to add to her collection?"

"Mohit," Aie said with absolutely no heat in her voice and watched Rahul with her patient Aie eyes. Stuck with her two boys who "did as they pleased" — her standard reaction to the entire Mohit mess.

"I'm sorry, I should stay home like you and make trouble with the roadside gangs instead of doing honest work to put a roof over your head."

"Well, it's the roadside gangs that keep your medals coming, so you should show some gratitude," Mohit said, and started serving food onto the steel plates in front of each stool. "Actually, given your mentor, you'd get the medals even without the gangs, wouldn't you?"

"Mohit!" Aie raised her voice this time.

She had heard Mohit say some version of this countless number of times, but she was horrified anew each time. Plus, Kimi was here. "Apologize to your *dada* right now."

"I'm sorry," Mohit said breezily, *"Dada,"* he added, making the term of respect for an elder brother sound anything but respectful.

"Did Rahul's *mentor* take those bullets for him in the line of duty too then?" Kimi said just as breezily, and Rahul's temples started to pound.

"Ah, she does have a point! Beauty and brains," Mohit said, leering at Kimi. But instead of looking uncomfortable, she smiled at him as though the ass was somehow amusing.

"Well, everything comes with a price, or haven't you heard my *dada* say that yet? It's his life's motto."

Before Rahul could react, Kimi pointed at Mohit's bruised face. "What was the price of having your face pounded?"

"It's a gory story. I don't want to offend your sensibilities."

Kimi laughed. Like, actually laughed out aloud.

Rahul shook his head. Mohit was such an idiot.

"What?" Mohit looked a few notches less cocky.

Kimi gave him a patronizing pat on his arm, and rubbed her chest in that barely skimming way.

"Sit down, *beta,* everyone's waiting to start," Aie said to Rahul. Mohit was already halfway through his first roti, but Aie and Kimi hadn't started yet. They were waiting for him.

There was no way he could eat right now. Fortunately, his cell phone buzzed. "You go ahead," he said. "I have to take this."

When he looked up, Mohit was grinning in a way that pressed every one of Rahul's buttons. He was doing his job, for shit's sake! Mohit could shove his attitude. As soon as Mohit saw his irritation, his smile widened. "Duty calls," he mumbled as Rahul left the room to talk to Maney.

"Asif's men attacked the Colaba safe house, boss," Maney said, his voice entirely exhausted.

Bloody hell! "Damage?" Rahul hissed into the phone, taking it into the inner room.

"We lost two constables. Sad thing is, they just happened to be passing by. They didn't even know anything about the safe house. We already knew about the leak, so we didn't have any men there. Also, a young

298

woman, she too just happened to be standing outside the building."

Asif's people had to have thought that was
Kimi. He was going to kill the bastard dead
this time. Kill him.

"You were right, boss, there's definitely a
mole in the department. It's the only way
the location of the safe house could have
leaked," Maney said.

Of course there was a mole. And there was
no way to find out who it was. At least not
until this mess was over.

"Boss, make sure you don't reveal your
location to anyone, not even to me. Also, we
caught another one of Asif's men. Seems
like a lower gang member. But the man's
not talking. Not even after some pretty
strong 'interrogation.' Doesn't seem like the
guy knows anything. Asif could have even
let us capture him to throw us off. With this
wily bastard, you never know."

"Keep the interrogation going and don't
ease up the search. I want every one of his
men in custody." The fewer men Asif had
around him when Rahul caught up with
him, the better.

Next he called Kirit.

"What the hell, Rahul, I've been trying to
call you! Where have you been?" Evidently,
the minister had already heard about the

shooting.

"We're safe, sir," he said with more calm than he felt. "I've disconnected both our phones. We're using a ghost right now and I can't give you this number. Kimi's safe, but I'm not taking any chances."

"I'm her father," Kirit said with more heat than he'd let slip until now. "Have her call me. I need to make sure she doesn't get any wild ideas."

"Yes, sir." Good luck with that.

"And, Rahul, use your discretion. You do not have to give in to everything she asks for. She's really messed up in her head over this Asif thing. Be a man, okay, son?"

Rahul would not dignify that with a response.

"That's a direct order, Rahul," Kirit said, when he didn't get a "yes, sir." "You do not indulge her wanting to chase after something a psycho said."

"Yes, sir." He was going to have to appease Kirit if he didn't want the minister putting a tail on him and ruining everything.

"Wow! That's a lot of 'yes, sirs' for one phone conversation," Mohit said, and Rahul almost pulled the little shit up by his collar. "Don't you get tired of your dog leash?"

"Letting your wastrel friends yank your

leash is a better option then?" Rahul slipped the phone into his pocket.

Mohit didn't like that. "You wouldn't understand my friends. Given that your friends carry Gucci bags," he said, pointing to Kimi's bag.

"I thought you were adorable, but you're really getting on my nerves with all your judgment, you know that?" Kimi held out a plateful of food to Rahul just as he started to fold up his sleeves. The damn pre-monsoon humidity was getting oppressive. If the rains didn't come soon, this humidity was going to squeeze the breath out of them all. She waited until he was done, her eyes hitching the slightest bit on his forearms before she met his gaze.

"Thanks," he said, accepting the plate, unable to look away from her eyes.

Mohit cleared his throat. "Really? You think I'm adorable?" He did that lecherous-grinning thing again, and Rahul saw that Kimi was about to set him straight and he had a completely untimely urge to smile.

"Okay, stop with the creepiness. I'm not your brother's girlfriend, he has no interest in me whatsoever, so your effort to piss him off, at least in this, is wasted."

Rahul's urge to smile died a quick death.

Mohit opened his mouth, but she raised a

hand in his face and picked up her bag. "First, it's not Gucci, it's Chanel. Don't worry, common mistake." She dug out a tube of something from her bag. "Put some of this on. You'll stop looking like a punching bag in a few hours."

Mohit studied the label. Rahul studied Kimi, his mind stuck on her earlier words.

Rahul has no interest in me whatsoever. He needed to remember that. No matter how much her presence in his home knocked everything inside him off balance.

"It's from a clinic in Switzerland. A mix of witch hazel, aloe, lavender, and some nuclear-strength anti-inflammatory drugs. Money has its advantages." She took the tube back, opened the golden cap, grabbed Mohit's finger, and squeezed some on it. "Not that you're ever going to find out, given that you dropped out of engineering school. Yes, Aie just filled me in. After topping your class for the first three years. A bit pathetic, don't you think?"

Mohit rubbed the clear gel into his banged-up eye and cheek, wincing. "What was pathetic was using blood money to get an education. I'll make my own way. Without selling myself. Thank you very much."

"Mohit!" Great. Now Aie was here. The inside room was too small for so many

302

people. Too small for everything erupting inside it. Rahul shoved the curtain aside and went to the outside room.

"Right, walk away. Naturally."

"Mohit *beta,* is this the time for all this?" Aie said in her most reasonable voice. "Go, go help Shanta *kaku.* All day they've needed help and you've been passed out. Go help take the mortar and pestle down to the storeroom. Go."

"Fine. But she should know what he is. She seems like a nice-enough girl." And with that he sauntered past Rahul and slammed the front door behind him.

24

Kimi
Present day

"I'm sorry," Rahul said after his brother had stormed off and his *aie* had followed because, as she'd told Kimi earlier, if she didn't join the spice-grinding mission soon she would lose her share of the spices she had paid good money for. Plus, it would start a storm of gossip in the *chawl*.

"What exactly are you sorry about?" she asked him, because his apologies were always such complicated beings.

He responded by looking like she had boxed him in his belly. Then went to the kitchen and put his untouched plate of food on the black Kadappa-stone counter next to a shiny stainless-steel sink — one his *aie* had told her Rahul had installed with his first IPS salary. The kitchen was dark and cool with no windows, and so clean everything gleamed under the single tube light —

the cement floor, the steel utensils lining the shelves, the bright white fridge that hummed.

He turned to her and leaned back into the counter. It was a gesture of fatigue. So, naturally, on him all it did was make him look more vibrant, those forearms alone strong enough to tear through any problem, his entire body emanating that restless energy that defined him. It reminded her of the first day she'd seen him, and that first day he'd climbed onto her balcony, his body glistening with sweat, the stained armpits of his shirt, the dirt under his nails, all of it proclaiming his labors like proud badges while his eyes sparkled with energy, fueled by purpose.

"The first available flight into Hong Kong is early tomorrow morning," he said. "I've booked it."

This time she did throw her arms around him. A quick hug before she could think about it.

He froze, but she didn't care. "Thank you, Rahul! You won't regret it. I swear." She pulled away, relief spreading across her face in a smile. She had known he would do it. And yet the fact that he had done it made this entire disaster turn on its head.

Through all his stiffness she saw a shadow

cross his eyes. He was scared. Unless she had lost her ability to read him, he was terrified. "We can't tell your father."

"Of course not." She didn't need him to tell her that. Papa would have an aneurism if she left the country right now. But Rahul was with her, so she'd be as safe as it was possible to be.

"He wants to talk to you. Use this phone."

She took the phone from him. It was still warm from his hands. "I mean it, Kimi, you can't breathe a word of where we are going to Kirit-sir. You can't tell him where we are right now either. His phone could be bugged."

She dialed her father's number.

"Where are you?" Papa snapped the moment she identified herself.

"I'm fine, Papa, how are you?"

He ignored her snark and her question. "You promised me you would keep me posted. You promised to stay safe."

"I am keeping you posted. And I am safe; I'm with Rahul." Who stiffened just a tiny bit, so she knew she had used a tone that had emotionally slashed him.

But her tone of trust was lost on Papa. "That's not good enough for me. I need to know where you are."

"I can't tell you that over the phone and

still be safe," she said much more coldly, because Stonewall Savant for all his stoicism looked like he needed a break, and the dismissive distrust for Rahul in Papa's voice made all sorts of discomfort collect in her gut.

"Kimi *beta,* please don't do anything rash. Asif Khan is a lunatic. Don't let him mess with your head." She had been so focused on Rahul, she hadn't noticed the raw panic in Papa's voice. She knew all the signs of panic in her parents. She could map exactly how much worry, hope, and disappointment every vibration of their breath held, but she had never heard her father sound quite like this.

Rahul's eyes filled with warning. Another thing she had an intimate relationship with — the degree of warning in his eyes. The warning was unnecessary. It wasn't like she would ever tell Papa that she planned to hunt down her donor. It was something he would never, ever let her do. Her donor's rights were sacrosanct to Papa. He had made that more than clear. "I won't let anyone mess with my head, Papa." She threw Rahul a pointed look. That phase of her life was over. "I love you." And with that she hung up.

"Thank you." Rahul had the gall to look

relieved. Finally, an emotion he could share.

"I didn't not tell him because you told me not to."

Naturally, he didn't respond.

"He doesn't understand that this is the only way to get rid of Asif once and for all," she added.

Rahul looked like he didn't either. But for him her word had been enough.

She looked around the kitchen. The idea of a shootout in the *chawl* was unacceptable. All those people, his *aie*, his Angry Young Man brother. "We're not staying here. Let's go wait at the airport."

"We can't be at the airport for that long. It's too public a place," he said in his DCP Savant tone.

"Well, I don't want to stay here. And that's that."

He winced and that awful shame flashed in his eyes again.

"The reason I don't want to stay here is that I don't want to put so many people in danger."

He rubbed his eyes, all his worry and exhaustion dragging at the gesture. "I know."

No, he didn't. And she'd had enough.

"Did you know that my family's sugarcane farms were mortgaged to the hilt before papa took them over? That the family debt was so large we were bankrupt? Did you know my grandmother had to sell her wedding jewelry when my grandfather was studying medicine so they could feed the family?"

"Why are you telling me all this?" his eyes said, because he was too proud to say the words.

"Wealth comes and goes, Rahul. Coming from adversity and overcoming it makes you better not worse than those who never have to." Who he was made her burn with pride and she'd be damned if she let him subject her to even one more of those flashes of shame. "Now, are we or are we not putting your family in danger by being here? And don't lie to me."

His flinch at the word *lie* was so minimal she almost missed it. "I don't lie to you, Kimi. I never have."

Not too long ago she would have believed him without a single doubt. Now all they seemed to do was wade through lies.

He took a breath as though trying to drag this runaway conversation back on track. "It's only dangerous if Asif finds out you're here."

"What's going on, Rahul?" His *aie* walked in, the alert focus in her eyes exactly like her son's.

"There's some trouble and Kimi and I need a safe place to stay."

"What kind of trouble are we talking about?"

"A gangster is after me," Kimi said. His *aie* had a right to know, had a right to ask them to leave.

Rahul's *aie* dabbed her forehead with her sari. Her fingers were yellow and some of the turmeric rubbed off on the white cotton and turned it yellow too. "Is there any chance he will look for you here?"

Kimi thought about the number of people she had seen as they'd walked down the veranda to get here. She turned to Rahul for an answer.

He studied her in that hooded way that she'd always thought of as him taking her temperature with his eyes. "I don't think so. Unless he finds out I'm the one watching her. And he doesn't know that. Plus, officially, I'm supposed to be living in the police housing quarters."

Aie started to rummage through some shelves. "Well, then, just stay here. There's the *mangalagaur* feast at the Ranes' on the ground floor, so everyone will be too occupied to snoop around too much. If anyone asks, we'll tell them that you're my cousin's daughter from America. You don't look like you're from around here anyway."

Kimi looked down at herself. Had she known she was going to meet Rahul's *aie,* she would have dressed with a little more care. But she was wearing a *kurti* and capris. It's what everyone wore.

"I'm from the other side of Bandra," she almost said, but his *aie* didn't seem to have meant it as a criticism.

Rahul's eyes got even more somber. "We can't stay here," he said.

Naturally, she said, "Thank you, that sounds perfect," at the exact same time.

Aie scowled at them, and then brightened when she opened a steel box and found what she had been looking for. She fished out a cloth bag from inside the box and extracted a bundle of plastic bags from inside that. "Decide what you want to do," she said so calmly they could've been discussing what to eat for dinner. "If you're staying, come and help pack up the spices. Everyone's gone off to prepare for the feast and left me to the task." She tucked the bundle of plastic bags under her arm and hurried off.

"I can change if this makes me stand out too much," Kimi said when Rahul didn't follow his *aie* and stood there like a tortured wall of silence. Maybe she shouldn't have bitten his head off earlier, because her words seemed to have slashed him. "I packed some T-shirts. They have silly stuff written across them, but nothing terribly inappropriate."

Something like heat flashed in his gaze as it swept her. Naturally, he blanketed it instantly. "I don't think it's what you're wearing, Kimi."

"You have an alternate plan?" she snapped. Granted that she'd had very little practice with knowing how to behave in public before The Great Escape, but he wasn't the only one who was a quick study. "Listen, I've worked as a journalist for a year now. I won't embarrass you. I swear."

This time a slash of pain cracked through that armor of his. He took a step closer. "Kimi —"

"Aie wants to know if you're coming to help with the spices." This time Mohit was back, and Rahul stiffened so much it was like watching a lake freeze over in those time-lapse videos.

The stiffening seemed to fan a deep (and very obvious) satisfaction in Mohit. He grinned like a three-year-old who had been handed an ice-cream cone. How did these men not see what was going on here?

"You should come. You'll get to see how the other half lives."

Kimi frowned at him even though she knew the jibes weren't aimed at her. "Why thanks! How can I refuse such an opportunity?" she said and made to follow him without bothering to check with Rahul.

Mohit threw her another one of those rascal grins and touched the deep purple bruise around his eye. "By the way, thank you. That witch hazel thing you gave me is magic. It totally stopped the throbbing." And then, entirely unnecessarily, he added, "Apparently, if you have enough money you don't have to feel pain!"

Kimi couldn't help it. She laughed. It was adorable how people patronized her. Money could do a lot of things. But pain, well, that came in enough shapes and sizes to be heard, no matter what you slathered on it. She would know. She'd had nine heart biopsies in the past two years.

"If I were you I would tread carefully. Kimi isn't what she looks like," Rahul said, rising to his full height and inserting himself between Mohit and her.

"And what do I look like?" she wanted to ask him. Instead she glared at him. She could fight her own battles, thank you very much. He could slink back behind his walls

313

and stop looking at her like that, his eyes filling with heat one minute, pain the next.

He rolled his eyes heavenward. For a moment he looked like he couldn't do this anymore, like he wanted nothing more than to break through those walls.

"Is she a gangster then? Someone you've captured to be your witness and are guarding, like in the movies?" Mohit snapped his fingers and tapped his head. The boy literally would do anything to annoy Rahul. "No, wait. Don't tell me. She's a cop! She takes bullets for medals, like you!"

Kimi ruffled his hair. "It's cute that the only pain you can perceive is a few punches and bullet wounds. And you think you're so tough."

He patted his hair back in place. But one look at her and he had the good sense not to look so cocky anymore.

"Have you ever had your ribs broken so someone could cut out your heart and replace it? Oh, and do you know what a heart biopsy is? Look it up. It's when they pluck out little pieces of your heart through a tube inserted into your neck. Oh, and I once had a cut infected for six months. They drained it twenty-eight times. From the same spot."

Rahul moved closer, but she couldn't look at him.

Mohit opened his mouth. She cut him off. "Now, I believe you were going to show me how the other half lives?"

He shut his mouth, and Rahul led them out onto the veranda, stopping only when they came to another green door. He held up his phone. "I need to check in with Maney." His eyes swept their surroundings in that special-ops sort of way that despite herself did funny things to her. "I'll be a moment." He started growling instructions into the phone. Those growls didn't help with the funny things happening inside her, and she turned away from him and caught Mohit watching her.

He looked over her shoulder to check that Rahul wasn't listening. For once he looked sincere. "Listen, I'm sorry for before. But really, your heart came from someone else?"

She was used to that incredulous expression. It must be pretty wild to run into someone who was a walking, talking medical marvel.

She shrugged, and Mohit walked straight through the front door of someone's home without even pausing to think about it. She glanced at Rahul again, checking to see if it was okay to follow Mohit. His eyes seemed to lose focus when they met hers. He'd been watching her, and hadn't expected her to turn around. Color suffused his face, or maybe she was projecting again. Very slowly he tipped his chin, telling her to go on.

Her stomach did another tiny flip, and she forced herself to turn away.

Mohit was waiting for her inside the door and watching her again, that cockiness returning fast.

She put all her irritability into her frown. "I thought you were sorry for being obnoxious before."

"I am and I like you so I'm going to let you in on a secret. You're wasting your time. My brother is already married."

She almost groaned out loud.

And there it was, back in all its glory, the cocky Savant grin. "He's married to his job. To his advancement. Don't buy into the tortured act. You don't know him."

She couldn't help it — she laughed again and took in the room. The air was suffused with the smell of turmeric and chili powder piled in yellow and red mounds on white sheets across the floor. "I'm not the one who doesn't know him. And if you stopped performing for him for one moment, you might actually get to know him too."

He didn't like that. His eyes got angry

exactly the way Rahul's did, and she knew how to gauge that look better than anyone. "I don't perform for anyone," he said.

Before she could respond, Rahul's *aie* came out of the kitchen with the lady Rahul had called Shanta *kaku* and handed Mohit a stack of plastic bags. "Here, fill these up. We're sealing them with a candle in the kitchen."

Mohit sat down next to the mound of turmeric powder and picked up the scoop poking out of it.

Kimi sat down cross-legged next to Mohit, and Shanta *kaku* giggled.

Aie gave Shanta *kaku* a look and she stopped giggling, but she didn't stop smiling behind her hand as the two women went back into the kitchen.

Kimi picked up a plastic bag and held it open so Mohit could scoop a measure into it. "Stop being so judgmental," she said when he looked impressed, "I am capable of holding bags open."

They filled the bags in silence for a few moments. "So what do you do? Other than torture your brother for a reaction?"

He didn't answer. He would be mortified to hear it, but he was so much like Rahul.

"I mean, since you dropped out of engineering college." She shook another bag

317

open and held it up.

He scooped turmeric into it and she put it on a tray. "I work for a grass roots community organization that trains people."

"Sounds impressive. What kind of training?" She blew at the next bag to open it.

He studied her again, with that Rahul-like frown folded between his brows. "We help people become employable. People from other states come here and take our jobs, so we make sure local businesses hire our people."

"So you bully people into hiring underqualified people?"

"They're not underqualified. They're good, honest people who refuse to brownnose and sell out." He dumped turmeric into the bag with such force most of it missed.

She shook it off her hands. "So, you don't need a degree, you don't need to be nice, but you're supposed to have jobs because you're from around here?"

"We don't compromise our principles."

"Right, your principles are why you dropped out of college when your brother has worked his butt off since he was sixteen to pay for your education?"

"Oh, but he wasn't the one paying for it, see?"

"Do you have any idea who I am?"

He studied her with mock interest, spinning the scoop in a circle around her face. "We've already struck off gangster and cop from the list of possibilities. Hmm, I know! You're a Bollywood starlet who's supposed to take India by storm anytime now."

"Funny. I'm Kirit Patil's daughter."

She let that sink in. He silently stabbed the turmeric mound with the scoop a few times.

"Do you know what your brother was doing the first time I saw him fourteen years ago? He was perched on top of a fifteen-foot-ladder scrubbing bird shit off the windows of The Mansion you seem to think he somehow went to and lolled about in for all those years."

He looked up at her. "I'm sure your father is very generous. But you really want me to believe that Kirit Patil paid my brother hundreds of thousands of rupees for cleaning bird shit?"

Kimi tapped his scoop with her plastic bag and looked at the door over her shoulder to make sure Rahul was still on the phone outside. "No, your brother also tutored me and cataloged our library and set up computers and fixed things that broke and worked in the garden. And although he had already worked so much of it off, he paid my father back every penny my father had ever spent on your education in just two years after he got his commission. There isn't a paisa of debt left."

"Maybe my brother just made that up to impress you." But he looked anything but sure.

"Oh, he doesn't know that I know. I only know because I'm really good at listening at doors and at hacking into my father's computer." She lined up the filled bag of turmeric next to the others.

Mohit's jaw was still set in stubbornness, but in his eyes she could see that she had just upended his life. When she'd first met him barely a few hours ago, she had been amused by how obvious his attention-seeking obnoxiousness was. But maybe it wasn't so much obvious as it was familiar. If she understood anything, she understood how daunting Rahul's distantness could be and how damn much it hurt.

"Listen, Mohit, I'm sure your friends do good work, but you can be so much more helpful to them with an education, don't you think? If your brain is anything like your brother's, you can employ more people yourself someday than you can bully reluctant employers into hiring for pathetic wages. I'm just a stupid rich girl, but that seems pretty clear to me."

Rahul walked in and his eyes found her, amusement lighting them up for the barest second as he registered her sitting cross-legged on the floor amid all those yellow packets. In a flash he was serious again and went off to survey the block for threats. Although, if someone had been hiding in an inner room and hadn't done anything by now, they weren't that much of a threat in the first place, now, were they? But he was Rahul and he would make sure.

Mohit lowered his voice to a whisper. "So how long has this been going on?" His eyes danced with playfulness again. He glanced between the door Rahul had gone through and Kimi. "How long have you been in love with my brother?"

Kimi looked down at her hands. She didn't remember touching the turmeric, but her fingers were yellow. "It doesn't matter," she said absently, picking up another bag.

"Come on, don't tell me you don't see that *the fire burns equally on both sides*," he said, using the oldest Bollywood line in the book and clutched his heart dramatically.

She shook the plastic bag at him and tipped her chin at the scoop in his hand. "You misunderstand me, young one," she said just as dramatically. "I'm not the one who can't see it."

25

Rahul
A long time ago

Nothing could make Rahul step inside a hospital. It had been years since he had been inside one. Nothing good could ever come of it. Now Kirit was asking him to visit Kimi in the hospital. Begging him.

"I can't, sir," he said, trying to ignore the desperation in Kirit's voice on the phone.

Desperation that was completely uncharacteristic and spotlighted how hard Kirit was fighting to keep his despair in check. He sounded at once determined and angry and afraid to acknowledge any of it, because the second he acknowledged it, it would become reality. Rahul knew exactly how he felt.

Rahul had felt that way once. But it had lasted a day. His determination had held up for less than twenty-four hours, forever taking away any faith in his being able to get into a fight with fate and win.

Kirit still believed he had control. He had, in fact, been able to transform his faith into reality for so long, Rahul, if he were another person, would have believed that money was the one thing that could make you build reality out of your desires. But Rahul was who he was, and so, he tried every day to change what he could change with his hands — with his gun and his pen and his fists. As an officer of the cadre he could combine those three things. He had never expected to love anything again as much as he loved his job. But he loved it. And right now he had work to do.

"I'll come see her when she comes home."

There was a long pause. Kirit trying to work out what Rahul wanted to hear, and Rahul willing him not to say what he wanted to say. Because even if there was the slightest chance that the saying of words could turn them into reality, then Rahul didn't want Kirit to tell him that Kimi might not come home. They were two chorus dancers in fate's chaotic dance drama, thinking they had control, knowing they had none, but following the cues they were given and begging for the outcome they wanted.

Kirit adjusted his tone, trying a different tack. "She is very attached to you. I don't know if I should have allowed her to get so attached to you. But she is."

Rahul said nothing. There was no response to that.

"She used to be such a bright child. Not just in the sense of being clever. But in the sense of spreading brightness around her. I used to call her my early-morning sunshine. Always gentle, always caring, always spreading happiness. One generally loves one's child simply because that child is theirs, but Kimi — how could she not be loved by anyone who met her? It was the brightness; it was contagious."

Yes, Rahul was aware. If Kirit meant to change Rahul's mind, he wasn't succeeding.

"Even after she got sick she remained bright for a while. She held on to it. But then it started to fade. It was no longer her being bright, but her trying to be bright. An attempt made for the benefit of her mother and me. My morning sunshine through a muslin curtain. But it returned, her brightness returned when you started to become her friend. Her mother thought it was dangerous, for many reasons, to allow a friendship like that to grow. I'm being honest with you today, so I'll tell you that your young anger made Rupa uncomfortable. But Kimi was a different child after she had a friend. So, even though we were afraid for her, we both knew that leaving your friendship intact was part of helping her stay healthy. Somehow you two had a connection. It was almost as though she had found a brother."

Rahul felt sick.

I want a boy to kiss me.

It was the nausea that kept him from responding. What Kimi was to him wasn't something he ever thought about. She was the one who did the analyzing in their friendship. All he knew was that she was a part of his life that never touched any other part of his life. She sat apart from everything else, an entire section of his life all her own. That's all he knew and that's all that mattered.

This was probably the time to assure Kirit that he would never abuse the trust Kirit had put in him by letting Kimi and him be friends. But the fact that Kirit was telling him all this now, when Kimi was sick, was something that would make him angry if he allowed himself to feel anger. But he didn't. He understood everything Kirit was saying to him. Kirit and he had a secret language born of a shared awareness of a bullet that had exploded in the wrong chest and now a

326

common love for a girl neither could bear to lose.

"Please, Rahul. She won't stop asking for you."

"I know."

"Then how can you refuse to come see her?"

Because he would not go and say good-bye. He would not step into a hospital. "I can't, sir, I have far too much work to do. I can't leave this assignment in New Delhi right now."

He thought he heard a sob. But it was so strange to think of Kirit as allowing his will to weaken that it had to be his imagination.

"I need you to listen to what I'm saying, sir. I'll see her when she comes home."

This time Kirit did not hesitate. "It might be too —"

"I'll speak to her on the phone, if that will make you feel better. But I really can't leave this case right now."

Suddenly, he wanted her on the phone. Wanted to hear her tell him that he was being an idiot. He knew he was. But he knew what he knew and he was not going to visit her in a hospital.

"What is wrong with you, Rahul?" Kirit snapped. "She can't talk on the phone. They have a bloody tube shoved down her throat.

She's barely breathing, but she says your name."

"Then tell her what I've already told you, tell her that she can see me when she comes home."

Kirit disconnected the phone without answering.

A week later, Kimi came home. For a week after that she refused to see Rahul. He visited The Mansion every day and waited in the kitchen with Cook for Kimi to send word that it was okay for him to go up. Usually, he ran up the back stairs as soon as Cook let him in. But now, Cook asked him to wait in the kitchen, stiff bodied, as though she didn't even know who Rahul was. For the first time since he had started working at The Mansion, none of the servants would let him into the main house.

Kirit refused to meet him.

"Come on, Sarika *tai,* just five minutes," he wasn't beyond begging. "If she's too sick I'll just see her and leave, I won't wake her up."

Sarika had always been the most stern of all the staff, making no bones about her disapproval when he stayed late or if she caught Kimi laughing too hard in his presence. And unlike with the other staff, her

328

attitude toward him hadn't changed after he'd become an IPS officer. "Kirit-sir has been very clear — Kimi-baby gets to decide who visits her. And I already told you Kimi-baby said she never wants to see you again. Stop wasting everyone's time."

Finally, after four days of sitting in the kitchen waiting for Kimi to calm down with no success, he made his way to the back of the house and used the pipes to climb onto her balcony.

He wasn't angry with her for being angry, but he refused to apologize. Maybe what he'd done was wrong, but he did not regret his actions. He knew without a doubt that if he had walked into that hospital that day something horrible would have happened. What he hadn't known was how hard it would be to wait for the buzz of his phone to finally tell him that she was home, followed by the seemingly endless flight from New Delhi to Mumbai to get to her. And then being shut out like this.

Her drapes were open and she was reading in her wing chair. He knocked on the glass, startling her. She met his eyes across the glass and it was like losing his footing on a ladder and flying off it.

She took her own sweet time to walk to him, but instead of pulling the curtain closed, she opened the French doors. "I thought you were my friend," she said, looking up at him with none of the anger he had expected and far more sadness than he ever wanted to see.

"Is that why you wanted to say bye to me?"

She thrust her chin forward, but her eyes softened. "I just wanted someone to hold my hand and to tell me everything was going to be okay."

He lifted his hand to touch her cheek, but then lowered it again and walked across her room to the sink to scrub his hands. "You had a lot of people there to do that."

She made a frustrated sound and followed him into the room. "How can you not understand that it's not the same thing? I have one friend. You are my one friend. Is it that hard to understand what it is to have only one friend?"

He understood. He had only one too.

"You're thinking you understand, don't you? That I'm your only friend too. I wish there was a word for what you're doing. I wish there was a word for being blind to someone's situation because you think you know how it feels and you use some tiny part of your own experience and extrapolate it to theirs without realizing that you have a choice and that they have none." She walked away from him again, deflated this time, her shoulders drooping, and sat down on the bed.

He sat down next to her. "I couldn't do it. Don't you see? I can't do this. Whatever it is you want from me. I can't. I'm not the person you think I am."

She turned to him then and grabbed his hand, looking so frightened he knew what she was going to say even before she said it. "Don't you want to be my friend, Rahul?"

Twenty-two years old and sometimes she sounded like such a child, able to boil her needs down to the simplest things. And yet she was the wisest, oldest soul he knew.

He pushed a wisp of hair off her forehead. "I will always be your friend, Kimi."

And because she started to cry, and because he knew that no matter what he told himself, he wasn't her friend only because she needed it, he said what he had never said aloud before. "I've never left a hospital with good news."

She squeezed his fingers and lifted them to her cheek. He still couldn't believe she could do that. Couldn't believe how long and hard she had struggled to be able to do it. Then she leaned over and kissed his cheek. He wanted to stiffen, to pull away, but he pressed into her kiss. An incredibly soft sensation that softened everything inside him. That somehow made all the hard places loosen. And the loose places harden.

"You are the bravest boy I know, Rahul."

"Yes, so brave I can't even go into a big, scary hospital."

Her lips smiled against his cheek, and he was oddly glad that he could feel the smile instead of see it. Had he really thought of her as childish? She saw everything. That was the thing about Kimi, trapped in a world more limited than imaginable, she constantly used her mind to roam beyond the confines of all the limits she had no control over. She had a mind and a heart that saw more than most well-traveled people would ever see.

She had always known why he hadn't come.

"It was not your fault then, and it will not be your fault when it happens to me."

He interlaced his fingers in hers. There were no words. Nothing he could ever say could be a response to her words. But suddenly he understood why she was so patient about her mother's superstitions. She understood her own role as an instrument of pain, and she wanted those she loved to have help, any which way they could get it.

Not only had she decided to be patient with his beliefs too, but she'd given him the seeds to heal his guilt, in case the thing they both did not want to happen happened. It was more than anything anyone had ever done for him.

That softest kiss consumed him, swallowed him whole, overwhelmed him. He was trapped between the need to run before he was lost and the desire to stay here forever and be soothed by her lips on his cheek.

What the hell, her lips were on his cheek. Panic rushed through him. He pulled away. "Kimi, what are you doing?"

She smiled her too-wide smile. "I told you that you would be the first boy I kissed."

"It's not funny, Kimi. You just gave everyone a scare and now you're —"

"What? I can now. Didn't you hear?"

She was the only one who told him about her health anymore. Who would have told him? "Hear what?"

"That I'm almost like a normal girl now. I can even go walk around outside and everything."

He leaned back and studied her. "You're serious?"

"Have I ever lied to you about my health? This new medication they gave me with the transfusion basically makes my heart create normal levels of platelets. So, I can actually fight off infection now." She made kung fu moves with her arms. "I can, in fact, do much more than just kiss you." She scooted closer but stopped when he backed up. "One would think you find me unpleasant, Rahul."

"So this medication it . . . it cured you?"

She laughed, got off the bed, and went back to the balcony and leaned into the carved marble railing.

He followed her, a weird discomfort churning in the pit of his stomach.

"Yes. I'm cured," she said without taking her eyes off the ocean. "For now. It's an *interim* cure."

"In the interim between what?"

"Between being cured and having my heart give out."

He grabbed her arm and turned her to him, but he couldn't form the question.

"There is this breakthrough," she said with a mirthless laugh. "A drug that can fix the immunity problem. But that could potentially destroy my heart."

"Kimi, no!" What had she let them do to her?

"It was the only way I could come back home from the hospital." She hugged her arms around herself and looked up at him, her eyes tired in a way so familiar there were no words for it. "No, really, this is good news. Apparently, hearts can be replaced but immunity is nowhere to be found for a body like mine."

He went down on his knees in front of her. She lifted her arm, but instead of reaching for him she wrapped her arms back around herself. It was a reflex, the fear of touching him, touching anyone. She had kissed his cheek. He had soaked it up and then berated her for it because it had scared him. It had been an act of bravery. But now that he had punished her for it with not understanding, she was terrified again.

He stood back up and cupped her face, and brought his lips close to hers. For a moment he could feel her warm breath and her racing heart with every part of his being. Then she froze. It was the slightest movement, but he felt her withdraw. He let her go and stepped back, furious.

Furious with himself because of what he had been about to do. Furious with her for the price she had chosen to pay for his stubbornness. Furious because what choice did she have? Furious because she wouldn't stop testing him. Everything she stood for, it felt like a constant test of courage.

"Have you been outside then?" he asked, needing to put all that fury somewhere.

Her chin dropped a fraction of an inch. Her arms wrapped tighter around herself. The ocean breeze had pulled strands of hair from her always tidy ponytail and they swished a little around her cheek — it was the only way he knew she had shaken her head.

It had been years since he had thought about her delighted, hiccoughing laughter when her toes had touched the warm ocean foam as she stood on his rock. Mere meters from them that very same ocean churned on and on for as far as the eye could see. What kind of girl watched the ocean from her room every day but had never touched it with her toes? He remembered thinking that. Cruel in his judgment and unaware of the decade ahead.

He almost reached for her hand, overwhelmed by the urge to sneak out over the wall the way they had done that day. He wanted to be on the rock with her again.

"I'm still not supposed to push it and get infections because the harder my system has to work to fight things off, the faster things could deteriorate."

"So what, the doctors have given you a green light to go out, but you can't?" Or her parents wouldn't let her.

"It's not a green light exactly. It's more like a greenish light for now. I'm supposed to be careful. And Mamma says —"

"And, you're going to be careful by not leaving this room until what? How long?" He was being a bastard by not understanding her fear. But he did understand it, and he hated how it sat on her. Her illness had sunk into her soul. It had told her all the things she could never do so many times that it had erased what she wanted. Altered how she saw herself.

"Why are you being like this, Rahul? I thought you would be happy for me. For us." Again she lifted her hand, but she couldn't touch him. All she had ever wanted was in front of her, and all those years of fighting dragged at her, paralyzed her.

He went back into the room. "Come with me." He held out his hand.

"Where?"

"To the rock, you remember the rock? Come on . . ."

She didn't move. "You showed up weeks after I was sick enough to die, and now you're upset with me because I won't traipse off with you to the filthy oceanside?"

"I came as soon as you came home. You

made me wait in the kitchen for four days."

"You waited in the kitchen?"

What did it matter where he had waited? But she looked so angry he knew she hadn't done that to him. He had always known. It wasn't just anger, she looked humiliated, the way he should have been but hadn't been because wanting to see her had over-ridden every other emotion. Everyone in the house, all the staff, hated that she had chosen to befriend someone so beneath her. He didn't care. No one else needed to understand them. He would wait in an animal pen if that meant they'd let him see her.

"You're here now. Come with me." All he wanted was to get her out of here.

She pressed back into the railing. "I can't. I'm not ready to go anywhere yet."

He knew Kirit and Rupa would never let her come home unless she was well enough. But he also knew that she wasn't leaving here today. Truth was, no matter how much he wanted it, no matter how much she wanted it too, he could not imagine her ever leaving this place. Too much time had gone by for her to ever reclaim what she had lost. The sadness of it felt an awful lot like anger.

He went back to her, looming over her. "So you're planning to continue on here.

Inside this room? You just made this bargain with your life and nothing's changed?"

"Everything's changed." She placed her hands on his chest with a tentative tremble that he hated. "Don't you see? I can touch you now, Rahul. We can do things now. We can be together."

He stepped back. It was the last thing he wanted her to say.

"Now we can be more than just friends." She was about to say "finally," but the expression on his face stopped her.

What could be more than being friends? What could be more than what it felt like to wait by the phone to hear that she was okay? More than waiting to discuss every case with her? More than waiting to run his whole damn day by her? More than knowing that what she was thinking was not possible? Kirit had warned him repeatedly. Her mother would never leave the *puja* room if Kimi chose to be with him, a *hawaldar*'s son from a *chawl.* Plus he didn't think of her that way. She was a friend, that was all.

A friend whose heart was going to last only a few more years. If that.

"What about your life, Kimi? What do you want to do now that you have a chance?"

"I told you what I want to do."

He waved her words away. "That's not

what I mean and you know it. The Kimi I know would want to leap walls, she'd want to go into a classroom, she'd want to solve all the world's problems. And when fear paralyzed her, she'd fight it."

She stepped around him and went back into the room. She sank into the huge, engulfing wing chair that seemed to swallow her up. If he didn't know her so well, he'd think she was hurt because he had rejected her, but he knew the things that hurt her most, and he knew she was looking like he had just put a knife in her back because he had pointed out what was hurting her the most.

Stepping out into the world after being locked up and afraid for so long wasn't as easy as he had just made it sound. He wanted to apologize. But he couldn't.

She looked up at him. "I'm tired, Rahul. I need to rest."

He swallowed all the things he wanted to say. Because they were futile. The best thing he could do for her was to step out of her way.

As he turned to leave, she reached for him and he placed his hand in her outstretched one, the time he had reached into the plastic glove flashing between their joined hands as though it were still there. Her hands were cool and soft except the tip of her forefinger where the clamp of a machine had made a permanent callus. The delicate beauty of her fingers in his made him conscious of his own bruised knuckles, his roughened calluses — the stark contrast between their hands giving form to all the things that separated them once they left this room, the way she now could.

The intensity of the connection only added to all the reasons why he would do well not to forget all that separated them.

"Will you come back and see me before you go back to New Delhi?"

That would be a terrible idea. "Yes," he said, and then he crossed the doorway where a plastic curtain had hung like the unbridgeable distance between them given physical form, and he left.

26

Kimi
A long time ago
Kimi had it on good authority that she could not live without Rahul. She had tried. She'd been so angry with him when he hadn't come to the hospital, when he had turned all combative when she refused to leave her room. But she knew that wasn't the real him. The real him wanted the same things she wanted. The real him wanted to be with her. She knew that and she would bring him around. How could she not? Sometimes the people you loved didn't know what was best for them and you had to be their good sense. Wasn't that what Mamma used to say to her?

Some days she missed her mother's aphorisms so terribly she wanted to storm into the temple room and steal her away from her gods. Not for too long, because Mamma needed what she needed, but only until she could give Kimi a few more stories, a few more of her lines to live by. The ones Kimi had collected years ago — before her vibrant, loving mother had disappeared behind her meditative shell — didn't feel like they were enough anymore.

But Kimi couldn't bring herself to enter the temple room. She didn't know why. Maybe because it belonged so definitively to Mamma. Maybe because the one time she had peeked in there, Mamma had seemed so far away that Kimi hadn't recognized her and it had been terrifying.

"She needs her Krishna," Papa used to tell her years ago.

Kimi understood. Mamma needed to hold Krishna accountable for this one child he had left her with after taking away seven. Krishna himself had been the eighth child of his parents and the only one to survive after his evil uncle Kamsa murdered the first seven to reverse the prophecy of his own death. The fact that Kimi, her eighth child, had lived was a sign. So, yes, Kimi understood her wanting to make sure that he did not rescind that sign and withdraw his gift even though it only left the tinkling of prayer bells as her daughter's share of her.

Kimi realized what a selfish thought this

was. The fact that she was judging her mother's love was wrong. She knew that.

Especially since she wasn't blameless in what had happened to her parents.

Papa was no different. His days were spent maintaining his power, multiplying his money, so he could do the monetary part of her parents' joint life's work: Project KAKA. There was a time when Papa used to endlessly explain Mamma's actions — she is doing all this for you, for the babies she lost. But somewhere along the way it had stopped. Her parents hadn't just stopped referring to themselves as a single unit, but they had stopped referring to each other at all. They had become individuals isolated in their obsession with their vastly different methods toward achieving a joint cause.

Truly, she was grateful for their love, but sometimes the weight of their fears piled on top of her own isolation became unbearable.

How easily Rahul had said, "Just leave the house and come with me to the beach."

Over the years, she'd seen the hordes at the beach grow from her bedroom window. All those people, all those germs. She saw the pathogens in the air the way the doctors had drawn them in their PowerPoint presentations. She saw them in her nightmares where they bit pieces out of her until she was mutilated beyond recognition.

Even so, Rahul had been right to push her. What was the point of losing your heart to your freedom — she chuckled at her cleverness — if you didn't have the courage to claim that freedom?

It was time to claim it.

She checked her watch as she paced her room. Rahul was coming over today. He had been on some super-secret mission in some remote part of the country for the past few months. The idea of him running around with a gun trying to hunt down criminals who also had guns made her stomach cramp, but the last thing she wanted him to see when he got here was worry or fear. Especially after he had found it so repulsive.

She checked her watch again. He should be here in five minutes. Rahul had always been punctual, but now he was never, ever late. Ever since he'd become a cop, he'd taken on this new avatar. As though he'd taken all the extra-virtuous things about him and honed them into this near-robotic person in terms of precision.

He'd always talked minimally, which worked well for her because he was a great listener, but now he was precise to a point of monosyllables. He'd always taken himself rather too seriously, but now he was downright severe in his worry about the world and all that was wrong with it. He'd always been punctual and dependable, never agreeing to do something if he wasn't one hundred percent sure he could deliver. Now, well, right now it was seven fourteen and he'd told her he'd be here by seven fifteen, and she could count down the seconds . . . and there it was, the doorbell.

She steeled herself to execute her plan. First, she would be all breezy and friendly and not obsessed and desperate the way she sometimes felt around him these days when he went all distant. Ever since she had seen him in that uniform, he made her go all gooey inside. How did one deal with that when it was your best friend? Okay, truthfully, it had been long before the uniform.

She would deal with it. If all he wanted right now was to be friends, that's all she would demand. Because sooner or later he was going to come around and see that she was the one — because she was, she just knew she was. Second, she would prove to him that she was brave, that she was done being locked inside the house. She could just see his face when he found out what she had done, how very ready she was to "blow this joint," as they said in Hollywood movies.

It had been a tough decision, but she had to do the hard thing and go away for two years. God alone knew how she was going to convince her parents, but Rahul would help with that.

She stepped outside her room and watched him run up the stairs. The main stairs. She couldn't believe they had made him take the servants' stairs all these years. She had put a stop to that, and she didn't care that Sarika *tai* had given her the silent treatment for a good month for it.

His vitality was a living force. His eyes smiled when he saw her, although he didn't yet give her the pleasure of a full-blown smile. It was his way. He made you work for that smile.

He stopped short, his eyes turning a strange kind of intense for just a second. She was standing at the railing, outside the door to the waiting area of her room. It was a first for them, her greeting him this way. She walked around the house and the grounds now. Another thing she had to be grateful to him for. If he hadn't goaded her to use her freedom, it would have taken her much longer to leave the confines of her room. Sometimes she didn't understand

347

herself. Why was the one thing she had wanted so badly so hard to claim?

"Exactly on time," she said, leaning into the railing and watching him. He was still in uniform. Which meant he had gotten off the plane and come straight here. He hadn't had a chance to go home and change as he'd like to have done. But he'd committed to a time and he wouldn't be late. If there weren't these things, these parts where he understood that she waited, understood what waiting meant to her in a way no one else understood. If there weren't these parts where she saw so clearly how much he cared, she would have let him go, would have believed what he wanted her to believe.

"Always." He walked up to her, and she held out her hand feeling like Emma greeting Mr. Knightley, when she wanted to be Lydia and throw herself at Mr. Wickham, giggling madly.

He smiled and took her hand, and she got the full-faced smile she'd been hungering for. "You're thinking of literary comparisons to how we're greeting each other, aren't you?"

Did she need to prove her "he loves me" theory anymore?

Ah, but all in good time, right?

She tugged him into the room. "Certainly

not Cathy and Heathcliff, not even Mercedes and the Count," he said, his eyes doing
that searching thing.

Thank God for that. Those were not love
stories to aspire to.

"You didn't stiff-curtsy, so it isn't your
usual Elizabeth and Darcy."

Getting warmer.

"Ah, Emma and Knightley, of course." He
looked jubilant at having solved it. But it
was she who felt all the jubilation, all the
way down her arms to her fingertips.

He looked away from her face, suddenly
not as jubilant. She couldn't let tension
creep between them today.

"Okay, so guess what's happening today?"
she asked, trying not to bounce on her toes.

He relaxed and smiled again. "You're going to let me take you to the beach?"

She balked — tongue-hanging-out-all-
agog, eyeballs-popping-out-like-a-cartoon-
film balked, making him laugh out loud like
the Rahul he was inside.

"Seriously? Because I was being sarcastic."

Did he really believe her such a coward?
She must've pouted, because he said, "Okay,
okay, sorry, I should not have said that."

Good, he was in a let's-not-fight mood.
Which meant they were on the same page.
She picked up his hand again and dragged

349

him toward the stairs.

"What, we're leaving right now?"

If she thought about it she would chicken out. "Let's at least leave the house. That much I've been doing."

He gave her his "I'm so proud of you" look, and she took it without telling him about the knee-shaking, clammy-palm reaction she had every time the front door opened. At first it had happened every time she stepped out of her bedroom. While that had slowly reduced in intensity, the front door was still a little nerve-racking. But the very thought of the gate made all of her nerves turn into twanging rubber bands at once.

But not today.

Rahul and she headed down the corridor. The prayer room was silent. So, Mamma was still at the temple. Sarika *tai* stepped out of the kitchen. She still worked at the house part-time, just in case Kimi got sick and needed a hand. "Baby, everything okay?" she asked, her concern turning to alarm when she saw Rahul next to Kimi.

"Yes, thanks, Sarika *tai,* just going to walk around the back lawn with Rahul." The last thing she needed was another conversation in which Sarika dropped as many references to all the work Rahul had done in the house.

Kimi had long stopped kidding herself that any of that had been praise for Rahul's hard work, and she was getting tired of having to point to all of Rahul's achievements without provoking any real admiration.

If Rahul thought it was strange she had lied about where they were going, his face didn't give anything away.

Then Mahesh the doorman jumped up when he saw her and studied his watch, even though there was a floor-to-ceiling teakwood grandfather clock salvaged from the palace of Kolhapur sitting right across the entrance lobby from him. "It's a little late for Baby's walk?" he said without moving to open the door.

"Yes, a little late today, *kaka,*" she said. "But it's still light outside."

Rahul watched silently as Mahesh did a quick bow and nod and opened the door. "I lighted all the mosquito lamps earlier, so Baby should be safe from bites."

"Thank you, *kaka,*" she said, and Rahul followed her out, where they were stopped by *mali kaka,* the gardener, who also started when he saw her out at this time of day. Unless it was because she was with Rahul. But no, that wasn't it this time, because pride shone in Mali *kaka*'s rheumy eyes when they fell on Rahul's uniform, and he

351

straightened and saluted him. Instead of smiling at him or being embarrassed, Rahul saluted back, a quick, smart flick of hand against forehead that flashed a whole different Rahul at her.

For a minute her absolute belief that she knew him, all of him, inside and out, teetered. But he walked to the gate and she followed him, her heart hammering at the thought of what lay beyond those high wood-and-brass gates. This was where she had first seen him, standing right by the gate, the storm inside him too large to be dwarfed by her vantage point on top of the gatehouse.

"Wait a minute, Rahul," she said, breathing hard. "Why don't we walk for a bit on the back lawn?"

He came back to her, leaned into her ear, and pointed at the gatehouse. "Remember that girl, Kimi? You know what struck me most about her that day?"

"That she had freakishly large eyes. I know, you've told me a million times."

He smiled like that boy he'd been. Storm Boy.

"She still has freakishly large eyes. But back then her eyes held adventure."

She swallowed. Then took the hand he proffered and her feet began to move.

It had been exactly what she needed to hear. Adventure — she had craved it with a mad, childish wanting. It used to make her want to skip. It used to make her feel like she was bursting out of her skin.

Twelve years and it was gone without a trace, and she couldn't backtrack to the moment when it had disappeared.

She ran past him and stopped when Bhola smiled widely at her. "Hello, Kimi-baby," he said, pulling the gate open. "Saying bye-bye to Rahul? Very good," he said in careful English. And it made her smile even wider.

"Baby's not just here to say bye-bye, Bhola-ji," Rahul said, his tone weirdly light and excited, as though by running past him she had let something loose inside him too.

Bhola didn't look happy, but before he could say more, Rahul dragged Kimi out the gate, letting Bhola's protestations fall on deaf ears. As they stepped out onto the street, the street took a dive down a slope. She stumbled and clutched Rahul's hand tighter.

He stopped and let her steady herself. This was her home — she had lived here all her life, and she had forgotten that stepping out of the gate led to a street that resembled a slide and that it was lined on both sides by stone walls overflowing with bougainvillea.

She looked around her, taking it all in, and laughter bubbled out of her. It was beautiful, and she would never forget again.

Rahul let her go and straddled something that looked an awful lot like something the gang in *Dhoom* had driven. "Is that a motorcycle?" she asked incredulously.

He beamed — and Rahul never beamed these days. "Let me introduce you. Kimi, this is Tina. Tina, meet Kimi. And she's a Bullet. She doesn't like to be called a —" He lowered his voice to a whisper in Kimi's ear. "Motorcycle."

That made her laugh even more, which made him beam even more. He touched Tina almost carefully, as though he were petting a precious but temperamental pet, and handed Kimi a helmet.

"What about you?" she asked, but she took it and put it on her head.

"There's only one and it's your first time, so you get it."

"You're protecting my virginity, how gallant!" she said, and his beaming smile tipped over into a laugh. "Now I know why they call a condom a helmet."

He snapped the clasp under her chin, his fingers against her skin making gooseflesh skitter down her arms. "Your first ride and you're already making phallic biker jokes.

I'm impressed." Best part was he looked impressed, and she already felt like she was flying on a motorcycle — or rather, on Tina!

Of course she was wrong. Because flying down the street on Tina was like nothing she could have imagined. For one, they started out on a slope. Which basically meant that no matter how gingerly she placed her hands on his shoulders (she had no idea why she suddenly felt shy straddling the seat behind him), gravity made it impossible not to press down hard on them. And hello-wow! Was this how all shoulders felt beneath your hands? Because omergadabove! His were firm and undulating and filled her hands in a way she felt everywhere.

Then he started the bike, and as he twisted around those shoulder muscles did even more bulgy business under her palms, sending an unholy buzz zinging through her.

"Ready?" he asked, and as soon as she nodded, they started moving. Which meant the bike went from a twenty-degree incline to a sixty-degree incline, and every curve of her body went flush with his. The *V* of her legs clamped around the *V* of his legs, her nether regions settled into his butt, and her entire front basically splattered against his back like a jacket.

Her physical being that had orbited him

for so long, too afraid to touch, in one instant was transposed on his, like a second skin. And it was so much sensation, despite the sum total of inertia and gravity acting on her near-horizontal body, she wiggled back, using those shoulders of his to find her balance, to reclaim her senses. But all those novels she'd read, all those things that were supposed to warm between your legs and tingle across your breasts, they weren't an exaggeration. She was feeling every one of those things pulsing inside her.

What a stroke of luck that he couldn't see her face, that they couldn't talk, that she didn't have to let him go.

Within minutes the steep slope was gone and the street flattened out. Reluctantly, she put just a hair of distance between them. Thankfully, momentum didn't make it easy to pull away. When she could think again over all those buzzing body parts, she realized that the ocean was at most a minute from her home and it had been more than a few minutes. They weren't headed for the Carter Road beach.

She leaned into him again. Doing it consciously was even better than being accidentally slammed into him (which, she wouldn't lie, was rather amazing too). Those beating parts warmed again, but this time they didn't embarrass her. He slowed, and she automatically reached up and shouted into his ear, "I thought we were going to the beach."

She had no idea how he heard her but he did. Because he leaned back into her and said, "We are."

She felt something then, something she had only ever felt with Rahul. It had taken her all these years to be able to name it. It was trust. For whatever reason, she had never once in her life doubted that she would get what she needed from him. Not always what she wanted, but what she really needed. It was why she was able to tell him to leave, to never darken her door again. It was why she could push him away and pull him to her whenever the fancy struck, because she trusted that he would always come back, and as long as he was there, everything always turned out okay.

She settled into him. Feeling not just warm between her legs but warm in her heart. Feeling oddly powerful with the purring bike beneath her. Feeling those shoulders and absorbing every dip and flex that commanded motion and surrendered to it. Somehow it all gathered together inside her like a force, like harmony, like movement that took her out of herself and placed her

357

into herself all at once. She could ride like this for hours, being speed, being an amalgam of particles flying in the wind. Flying with a force that righted everything as though it had never been wrong.

"Where are we?" she asked, when they slowed to a stop after what had to have been an hour but felt like a heartbeat.

"You feeling okay?" he asked, twisting around.

She nodded and let him examine her with eyes she couldn't see because of the reflective Ray-Bans she had given him for his twenty-first birthday. She had sent them to him from London, which was probably why he had accepted them, because it was too much of a bother to send them back. The fact that he actually wore them made her already too-full heart wobble like a water-filled balloon. She struggled between removing them so she could see his eyes and leaving them on his face because she loved that he was wearing them so much.

His thick hair was slicked back from the ride, making him look like a cross between a film star on the red carpet and a mobster out on a hit. But he was wearing his uniform with golden stars shining on his epaulets. It was the oddest combination and it reflected everything she was feeling perfectly.

As they made their way down the lane toward the beach, he reached into his pocket and pulled out something. Even without seeing his eyes her heart sped up. It was a face mask. One of those white fabric ones that hooked over your ears.

Wordlessly, she took it from him, realizing suddenly that she was out in the open with people. It was terrifying, but she only let it be for a moment. Her body was supposedly doing its job with this new drug, so Rahul was right, she had to trust it.

She tucked the mask into the pocket of her jeans. "Do you carry it around just in case you run into a sick girl?"

"I carry it around in case my friend needs it." He took her hand as they came upon the ocean, which was in full-frothing churn. There was barely a soul around. How far out had he driven? The tide was coming in. She knew it well. She had watched it from her window almost every day of her life. Up close the swelling was different. More violent yet still somehow smaller in scale.

They walked, her ponytail flapping in the wind and slapping her cheeks. They talked, their words soaking up the sunshine and dancing in the ocean breeze.

He told her about the cases he was working on.

He was beautiful when he talked about his work. His eyes got a little darker, his mouth just a little more animated, the timbre of his voice just a little deeper. She was entirely lost in him when suddenly he stopped and pointed at the ocean. She turned away from him and faced it. The sky and sea had gone a brilliant pink, like the bougainvillea that spilled from the walls around her home seen through the yellow lenses of her childhood sunglasses. A sunrise and a sunset were the only time you could stare the sun in the face as though it were nothing more powerful than a vibrantly painted ball.

It was impossible to look away. They stood there rooted, fingers interlaced, as it descended before their eyes from its brilliant perch and sank smoothly into the fast-darkening water.

"Thanks," she said when only an orange cap remained at the edge of a pink tinged ocean.

"For?"

"For forcing me to come out."

He didn't answer, just sank down into the sand taking her with him.

After they had stared at the darkening waves for a while longer, he removed the

Ray-Bans and turned to her again. "I'm sorry."

"For?"

"For what I said about you not leaving home being cowardly. That's not true."

"It was true. I'm glad you shook me out of my cowardice." And then quickly, before she lost her nerve, "I got into a university in America."

His entire body went still. "America?"

"I've always wanted to be a journalist, remember?" She wrapped her arms around her knees and pressed her cheek against them, watching him.

His eyes crinkled with amusement.

"What?" she asked.

"So you went straight from not wanting to come to the beach with me to applying to a college in America?"

"The point is that I did come to the beach with you. And now you have to go with me to Columbia." But she was smiling, so he knew she wasn't serious. He wouldn't leave his job if someone held a gun to his head. Well, someone did all the time and still he didn't. "And if you can't, will you at least help me talk to Papa?"

Rahul laughed. "Why would he listen to me?"

"Because, haven't you noticed, he listens

361

to you about me. You're the only one he listens to, because he knows."

He didn't ask what it was exactly that Papa knew. It was the thing she wasn't allowed to mention no matter how much the setting sun made her want to mention it. Because she knew he wasn't ready to admit he felt that way too. But it kept growing bigger and bigger inside her and harder and harder to hold in.

"I don't think he'll let you go — your mother most certainly won't. But I'll try to convince him only on one condition — you have to come back."

It wasn't an admission exactly, but she would take it.

She sat up. "Of course I'll come back. You're here, Rahul." She leaned in and gave him a kiss on his cheek.

He didn't stiffen, so she put her head on his shoulder and he wrapped his arm around her. Naturally, it wasn't to hold on to her, it was to pull her away. "Come on, college girl, time to get home before they send out a search party."

But when she didn't move he stayed there with his arm around her, watching the waves until she was ready to go back.

27

Kirit
Present day

Kirit had spent half the day fielding questions from the press about Asif Khan's escape. How had the press even found out? When Kirit discovered who had leaked the story, he was going to make sure that the person never worked again.

As usual Rahul was taking his duty seriously. So much so that he wouldn't tell Kirit where he was and Kirit hated that he had to put his trust in Rahul so completely when he no longer had any control over his actions. But it was his only choice right now and so he refused to waste anger on it.

There was too much to be managed. The press was demanding someone's head on a stake. Given how high profile the Asif Khan capture had been a few months ago, the public would only be soothed by sound bites from their "Hero Cop." Especially since the villain he had defeated had not only risen from a coma but also had already been responsible for killing three innocent people.

Thanks to the media, gory pictures of the Colaba Killings, as they had already nick-named the tragedy, had been witnessed by every child in Mumbai. No wonder it had become so hard to make a hit movie these days. Who cared about fictional drama and mayhem when real life in all its deranged glory played perpetually on TV screens.

The car ground to a halt as soon as they turned into the steep lane that led up to his home. The driver turned around and looked at him for instructions. Press vans lined the road and the crush of bodies mobbing his gate made it impossible to get near it. What more did they want? He'd recorded his statement and had it distributed to all the major TV channels.

"Sit on the horn," he told the driver, and the driver went for it. Even so, the hundred-foot distance took them half an hour.

As soon as Kirit walked into his empty house, his peon took his briefcase from him and his cook handed him a cup of tea. And then all the servants discreetly disappeared. He walked through the house. Not a sound. He had never thought he'd miss the tinkling of the prayer bells. He peeped into Kimi's room on his way to his office. It was bright now. She had painted the entire room a turquoise blue and had the wall between the sitting room and the bed area removed. It was one big room now with bright yellow and black furniture with a million cushions in every shade of yellow strewn across the couch and bed. "No white and no plastic." Those had been her instructions to the designer. She had even covered the white marble floor with a black rug with huge turquoise-and-yellow flowers she called "daisies on steroids."

He smiled for the first time that day. His Kimaya had always known exactly what she wanted.

He took himself to his study, locked himself in, and dialed.

"Fame's a beautiful thing, isn't it, Karan Kumar?" Asif Khan said by way of greeting. "When was the last time you were mobbed by the press outside your house?"

"You killed three innocent people, you bastard," Kirit said into the phone, turning on the three TVs in the room like an idiot-box-addicted child.

Even as he said it he knew how idiotic he was being. Asif was a gangster who killed just to spread terror and to get thrills out of it. The lives of three people meant nothing in his deranged head.

"You are hilarious, Kirit!" Asif said predictably breaking into villainous laughter so stereotypical it couldn't possibly be real life. "I'm going to miss you so much. I mean, you had an innocent person killed to get your precious daughter a heart and now you're pretending to have the sobs for some dead people on the road?"

That laughter was sick. Like a really bad film. Like the most horrible nightmare. Kirit didn't have nightmares. Kirit slept soundly every night. Jennifer Joshi's death was not on his hands. It was on this bastard's hands alone. Kirit's conscience was clear.

"Come now, admit it. You danced, didn't you? When you found out that dead woman was not your daughter? You can tell me. We're practically friends now, we understand each other so well. You got a boner, didn't you, when you realized she was someone else's dead daughter. Tell me, which temple did you go to and feed beggars?"

He couldn't let him get to him this way. He was Kirit Patil. The longest-serving chief minister of the richest state in India. Calm, he was always calm and in control. That's why people elected him. Because this kind of shit that intimidated other politicians didn't touch him.

On all three TV screens uniformed policemen pulled a girl's body on a stretcher out of an ambulance. Kirit knew the girl on the stretcher wasn't Kimi. But he couldn't stop seeing her face on the girl's corpse.

"What, no words from the glib minister today? Maybe I need to call Nikita Sinha. Does she know it was you who sent her to America to cheat the good doctor? No, of course she doesn't. If she did, the police would know too. Oh, wait. Maybe that's the way to go. I'll tell Nikita Sinha and Jen Joshi's husband who did that to them. They'll report it. And then not only will the public know, your daughter will know too. Because all I want is for her to know. Actually, all I want is for her to be dead. But only after she knows how her daddy cut out someone's heart for her."

Kirit refused to react. He turned off the television sets and tossed the remote control across the table. He wasn't the one who had cut out Jennifer Joshi's heart. Asif Khan had done that.

"Okay, enough silent games, Kirit. I know you're listening. I can hear your breathing. It stinks of guilt. Be a man and at least own what you did. Stop whimpering. It's making

367

me sick. Tell me where your daughter is and maybe I won't kill her. Mother promise." His uncouth voice scraped against Kirit's spine, and he'd had enough.

"First, you're the one whimpering and making me sick. And second, I'll find you before you find her. And that's the real promise. Not one of your empty threats."

He shouldn't have let his anger show because the bastard just sounded more amused. "I'm curious — how did you pull off that entire thing with Nikita Sinha without her knowing it was you?"

"Because I use my brain."

"Right. Your grand brain. But it doesn't compensate for brawn, does it? When you can't even control a tiny woman enough to stop her from double crossing you. I've heard your wife doesn't even want you anymore. She doesn't think your *brain* isn't big enough, does she?"

"Don't you get tired of your own filth, Asif? It's got to be tiring to be you."

"Not really. It's great to be king."

This time Kirit laughed.

"Laugh at this, *chutiya:* How's your day dealing with the *presswalas* been?"

Of course. Asif was the one who had leaked the news of his own escape to the press to make life miserable for Kirit. This meant he was desperate and entirely un-hinged. Not a great combination.

"You're on TV right now, by the way. You're so boring on camera. Are you sure you were a superstar? You look like some-one's old tired grandfather. No wonder the press is calling for that Hero Cop of theirs. Now, *he's* one-hundred-percent superstar hot. Where is he anyway?"

Something must have changed in Kirit's silence because Asif's tone got all alert. "I was going to wait until I found your princess and use her to bring the cop to me. Since he seems to enjoy rescuing distressed dam-sels. But maybe I'll get him out of the way first."

"Asif, did the coma kill your brain? He's the pride of the Mumbai Police right now. He's already emptied half a magazine of bullets into you once. If I were you, I'd run as far away from him as possible."

"Very protective of him, you are. And you're usually ready to throw anyone who isn't of use to you into the fire. Interesting. Why the soft spot? I wonder."

"The coma did kill your brain cells. Go after him for all I care."

"Right. For once I think I'll listen to you. Let's save your hero some time. I'll just go

after him myself. I never thought I'd say
this again, but thanks!"

28

Kimi
Present day

One question — that's all it took to ruin what could have been a really nice day with Rahul's lovely *aie* and his surprisingly adorable brother. For a while there, it had even felt like Stonewall Savant was done with his walls. But Kimi should've known better. Letting her guard down with Rahul was no longer an option. She had to stop being idiotic enough to let hope unfurl inside her again and again.

All she had done was ask him a simple question. They had left his home in the most awkward good-bye in the history of good-byes. She had hugged his mother and Mohit. While all Rahul managed by way of good-bye was a look at his watch as though it were his salvation from her "exuberance."

"Your *aie* is beautiful. I love her," she had said as he started the car, her heart full of

371

something. Okay, not something. It had been joy. The joy of having been within feet of him all day. The joy of being in the home where he had been a boy. The joy of knowing the people who saw him at his worst but whom he lived for.

Instead of thanking her for the compliment he had stiffened. How had she ever thought she understood the man?

"Mohit isn't half bad either," she had said, because leaving things alone was a skill she was still working on.

He had almost smiled at that.

And then she had asked him about Mona. "How come you never told me about Mona?"

He had hit the brakes so hard, she'd blessed the great soul who invented seat belts. After that he'd been driving like a madman, cold anger emanating from him in waves.

She tried to wait it out. Watched the bright city lights zoom by. It was still dark, but you wouldn't know from the steady flow of traffic. He looked like he was focused on the road, but she knew better, and before she could stop herself, she touched his arm, because she couldn't just sit there with him so distraught.

He yanked his arm away. "What the hell,

Kimi! What do you think you're doing talking to Aie about me behind my back?" He had never used that tone with her.

"Behind your back? You were in the bathroom, and we had a conversation. What was I supposed to do, stand around like a statue without a tongue? They get enough of that from you, don't you think?" Great. So much for trying to make him less distraught. Why couldn't she learn to leave things alone?

That made him race through traffic some more with even less concern for little things like other cars. "Stop trying to fix my family. This isn't one of your American TV dramas with characters struggling with their neat little demons. We're just regular people. Just butt out of my life, okay?"

He screeched to another halt when a rickshaw attempted a suicidal maneuver in front of them and then went back to racing along.

"Gladly," she said, mostly because it would be too ironic for her to die in a bloody car crash. "I didn't ask you to take me to your home, you know."

"I didn't ask for this either," he snapped. "It's not like I had a choice."

This was a side of him she had never seen. This was Storm Boy turned mean. And all she wanted was to not be here with him right now.

Naturally, a second after that thought passed through her head, they hit traffic — at two-bloody-thirty in the morning! And he became so doggedly focused on staking out their surroundings, she might as well have been a package he was in charge of delivering. Which was just as well. Because she'd heard all she needed to hear.

When they reached the airport and checked in, he got on the phone and stayed on it, growling instructions until their plane took off.

As soon as they had taken off, Kimi locked herself in the bathroom and shoved her medications down her throat. It was a handful of pills, and usually once they went down and she clamped down on her gag reflex and her body worked around its need to throw off the blast of immunosuppressants, things settled down fast enough. Just her luck that the stupid churning and gagging was particularly bad today and it wouldn't stop.

She could never predict the days when it would be worse than usual. It was one of those things she had to live with as a transplant recipient. When she returned to her seat next to Rahul, he sat up all alert. Great, now he cared.

"Kimi, what's wrong?" he asked as though the past few hours hadn't happened. As though the past bloody year hadn't happened.

She was too nauseated to answer. Then, as soon as her butt sank into the seat, the shakes started, and she pulled her knees close and turned away from him.

He had never seen her after she took her immunosuppressants. Her preference was that no one ever saw her right after. Especially when it was this bad. All she wanted to do was curl up into a ball to stop the plane from spinning. All she wanted from him was that he not break his damn silence. When the flight attendant handed her the eye mask, she slipped it around her eyes and fell into a shaky, queasy, fitful sleep. When she had a reaction to her medication the only way she could get through it was by waiting it out.

A blanket was wrapped around her when she woke up, and finding it made her shaking worse so she pretended to continue to be asleep until they landed.

Kimi had no memory of flying into Chek Lap Kok airport. None at all. Usually, she remembered each airport she had flown into in great detail. She remembered the color of the uniforms of the people who worked there. She remembered how kind the immigration staff was to her. She remembered the pity in all the eyes that fell on her. Something about a dying person stripped everyone of their ability to hide their fear of mortality and their relief and guilt at being alive.

"What are you thinking about?" Rahul asked when the person in the immigration line in front of them moved and she didn't notice. Or she thought he asked the question. He might not actually have said the words. And knowing his questions whether or not he had said the words was really starting to annoy her.

She took a step forward because his hand was hovering at the small of her back, and she couldn't bear to be touched by him right now. Not after what he had said to her last night. "I was just thinking how flying upright is completely different from flying horizontal on a gurney, plugged into machines and drugged out of my mind."

She had meant to push him away. And that sort of answer usually did the trick. But instead of giving her one of his finely honed distant looks, he moved a step closer. "Tell me what it was like to travel like that."

Now he wanted to get chatty — really?

He might be done with the brooding portion of the trip, but for once she didn't care. Not after he had asked her to butt out of his life in that tone, as though she were some sort of hateful, nosy stranger. And now he wanted to talk about how traveling on a plane on your own two feet was different from doing it on your deathbed?

"Well, for one, it's interesting to see how *regular people* are treated." So, yes, she stretched out the words *regular people* because she was done with his labels. "As opposed to someone hanging from the cliff of death."

As expected, he looked so guilty one might think he had personally caused her to hang from the cliff of death for twelve years, instead of being the person who had made it bearable.

Of course she knew why he was being nice to her again, why his anger had cooled so fast on the plane. But she didn't want him being nice for that reason. If he was only nice to her when she became sick, then she had to question everything their friendship was. Had it always been only sympathy? It made their entire friendship teeter beneath her feet. And she didn't know what lay underneath if that crumbled.

"Kimi, are you sure you're okay?" he

asked as they got closer to the immigration desk.

She gave a quick nod. He looked miserable, and it made her feel like she was stuck in an ugly farcical play. His guilt somehow cheapened something she struggled with every day. She didn't want her health to be a currency between them, didn't want it to be the thing that brought him back. Until he found a way to pull away again.

Moments of clarity always came from the most unpredictable quarters. After seeing him with his family, she knew that his angst, his distance, it had nothing to do with her. All the hope that one day he would see what he was turning away from, it was gone now. It wasn't her. It was him. He couldn't let anyone near. At least not out here in the real world.

In her bubble, somehow he had been able to lock everything else out too. That's why he had told her that the world outside her room was an ugly place. For him it was. It's why he had kept her separate from everything. He had never spoken about his family. He had kept their relationship pristine, so when she was gone, the damage would touch nothing else.

She was two years into her transplant. She hadn't had a single episode of rejection —

which was rare and encouraging news, and something she worked toward with everything she had. She had never missed a single dose of medication, never disobeyed a single doctor's instruction and she never would. Truth was, despite all her effort, she came with a big warning label of "Impending Loss." When he looked at her, that's what he saw. It wasn't what he wanted to see. Even in her anger she knew that. But he had lost too much for him to see past it.

The Great Escape was going to have a tragic ending again after all.

They reached the immigration officer and he had no questions for them. He slammed a rubber stamp into their passports and welcomed them to Hong Kong without a smile. All these years she had dreamed of roaming the world with Rahul, of running off on adventures with him — not for the adventure itself but because their time together would not be limited. It had always felt like their friendship had been a prisoner to time, confined by good-byes. She would have given anything to not have every meeting hurtle too fast toward an inevitable good-bye. She had always had too many things to tell him, too many things to watch with him, to show him.

We'll do it tomorrow, he always said.

And she waited.

Their tomorrow had come and gone and now here they were, stuck together on a plane, at an airport, in a foreign land, and all she wanted was to not be near him.

"Do you want to go to a hotel first and rest?" he asked when they finally got through customs and were waiting for a taxi.

"I just want to get this over with." A bed of tulips, bright red and vibrant, stretched out behind him, and suddenly, she remembered being at this exact spot almost two years ago and waiting to go home to him. She had wanted to show him those tulips so badly she had almost tasted his reaction. This moment felt like something she had forced into existence by the sheer stubborn will with which she had wished for it. And now here the moment was, and he didn't even look at the tulips. What a waste dreaming was sometimes.

"At least tell me what's happening to you." For a moment he sounded like her Rahul. "Listen, I'm sorry. I shouldn't have said what I said in the car. But if you aren't feeling well, please let's just rest for a bit. Please, Kimi."

"I'm fine. Nothing is wrong with me." Apart from the nuclear-level anger that came with her epiphany. Having off days like this was just part of being a transplant recipient. Even if she had the energy to explain that to him, what was the point of it?

He had never asked her what it was like to live with a foreign heart in her body. She had shared every bit of her illness, her wait and recovery with him, but now that she was living The Great Escape, there were so many things every day that were unique to her existence, just letting someone know would have been such a relief. And of course, by someone, she meant him.

Butt out of my life.

"Mount Elizabeth Hospital," she said to the driver and settled into the cab. Rahul slid in next to her. His body was tight with worry, his eyes dimmed with concern. Truth was, she felt like shit and all she wanted was to squeeze into him and to have him hold her. He was all of two feet away, for heaven's sake. Two feet of distance that seemed today to trap within it miles and miles worth of barriers. Where was the girl who had dragged a boy to a rock in the middle of the ocean?

Where was the boy who had shown up at her door despite being told to go away? Nine times, no less. Yes, he wasn't the only one who kept count of things. How could two adults have such a hard time navigating an emotional landscape that they had skated around with such ease as children?

"I hate being an adult," she said. And he laughed, and she looked at him because that laugh was a giant spike shoved into all the pressure trapped within them. His eyes met hers, and for one instant they burned with the truth in his heart and the world felt right.

Then his phone buzzed and there was another update from Maney. Apparently, Papa had been on Maney's case about finding out where Rahul and she were.

"I'll call him," Rahul said. "Don't worry about it. No, you will not lose your job. I promise you that."

"Let me talk to Papa," she said when Rahul hung up.

"He can't know where we are."

"Really? Because you haven't already told me that a hundred times."

He dialed. "Sir, it's Rahul."

"Where the hell are you?" Her father was so loud she heard him across the two feet separating her from Rahul.

Rahul didn't flinch. "In a safe location, sir."

"I need to know where."

"I can't take the chance that someone isn't

listening in. And I haven't told Maney or anyone else. Please let them do their job."

"But you aren't doing your job. None of you. That bastard is still at large."

The muscle in Rahul's jaw worked. "I realize that. But Kimi is safe and Dr. Joshi and Nikki Sinha are safe. And we will catch the bastard. Have you heard anything more from Khan?"

"No. But I think it's too dangerous for you to watch Kimi. He knows you. You shot him. What if he comes after you? I want another officer assigned to her."

Kimi snatched the phone from Rahul. "No other officer is watching me, Papa. It's Rahul or no one."

"Don't be an idiot, *beta.* This isn't the time for emotion."

"It's not about emotion. It's about ability." Rahul's gaze locked with hers. She turned away. Today was not a good day for her immunosuppressants to be acting up. Her stomach had stopped feeling like it was too small in her abdomen, but she felt too tired to fight the only two men in her life who mattered. "Please stop threatening Rahul's team. You have to promise me no one is going to lose their job over this."

"Fine. Now let me speak with Rahul."

She handed Rahul the phone. "I'm not

383

happy, Rahul. I'm disappointed in how you're handling this." Papa had lowered his voice, but she could still hear him. "Call me when you're alone."

"You can say what you want in front of Kimi, sir. I will share whatever information you give me with her."

Kimi had the strangest urge to cry.

"Why do you think he's this insistent on you not finding the donor?" Rahul asked after Papa had called him unprofessional in his most disappointed-Bollywood-dad voice and hung up.

"You know he's just worried about us, right?" she said, sounding a little bit like a pathetic Bollywood daughter. "He takes my donor's rights very seriously. You know how he is about ethics and not doing anything morally wrong."

The fact that Papa and Rahul respected each other meant everything. This couldn't ruin that. They were the two most honorable men she knew. Mamma had once told her long ago, when her mother still told her these things, that our ancestors' good karma filtered down through generations as good fortune. Papa's goodness was probably why Kimi was alive today.

"Is what we're doing wrong?" she asked.

"You said you felt sure that the reason

Khan targeted you has to do with your heart. Do you still feel that way?"

She thought about Khan's bloodshot eyes when he had run the back of his fingers along her scar and asked her where her heart had come from.

"Yes." She had to follow this to the end.

"Then it isn't wrong. What do you have planned?"

"We're going to see my surgeon. We became friends when he treated me in postoperative care. I had a meeting scheduled with him today, we're going to be a little late, but he'll understand." She had made the appointment last week, and fortunately postponing her flight by a day hadn't messed things up too much.

Rahul's discomfort at entering the hospital was palpable. He did it all the same. She wanted to hold his hand and assure him that nothing bad was going to happen. But all she could manage was meeting his eyes. As always, an entire tangle of memories matched up in their gazes and it eased some things and made others worse.

Dr. Gokhale gave Kimi a long, warm hug. "How is it that you're even more beautiful than before, Kimaya?" he said, and she smiled. She had forgotten what a handsome man he was with those gray eyes, so rare for someone who was Indian.

He had told her his eyes were a freak genetic incident. Both his parents had dark eyes. They'd had to live through a lot of mailman jokes, since his parents had lived in America when he was born.

"How do you feel? Although if you feel anything like you look, I'm going to call it a grand success."

She had to be the vainest person on earth, because for the first time that day she didn't feel utterly shitty. "It's been great, thanks to you and Dr. Girija. Not a single rejection episode yet."

She loved the smile he gave her — pride mixed with a genuinely invested caring so rare in doctors. Even Dr. Girija, who had been like a surrogate aunt through her life, worked hard to maintain a healthy doctor-patient distance. But Dr. Gokhale had the kind of bedside manner where he let you in. Or at least he had always let her in.

"I know," he said. "Girija's been keeping me posted about your progress. You know how rare it is to not have any rejection episodes. It seems to have been a really good match, and add to that what a great patient you are, and I just know we are going to beat the odds."

"Yes we are," she said and hugged him again and met Rahul's eyes over his shoulder. "This is my friend, Rahul Savant."

The two men shook hands. "Ah, so this is Rahul. Pleasure meeting you. I've heard so much about you."

Rahul said nothing. Which was fine because Dr. Gokhale was obviously more interested in what Kimi had to say. He led them into his private office. It was filled with pictures of him hiking up every major peak in the world. He had loved to talk about his hiking trips, and his stories were what had inspired Kimi to give it a try, and now she loved it so much she had sworn to make it up every one of these peaks.

"You already know I'm planning to do Everest Base Camp next year," he said. "The offer to come along is still open."

He had asked her to go with him to Nepal earlier this year. She was already running and doing longer and longer hikes by herself, and Base Camp was definitely on her list of things to do. The only reason she hadn't said yes was that she didn't want to give him the impression that she returned his interest in any way. Of course he was interested. He had all but put it out there before she went back to Mumbai after three months of postoperative care under him.

When her future had seemed so set in her mind.

Now that it hadn't turned out that way, she had to find a way to go on around it. She was going to find a way. "Everest Base Camp sounds lovely. Let me think about it again."

"You'll have your own personal doctor with you. So there's nothing to worry about," he said in that soothing physician's voice.

Rahul had taken a seat by a sunny window so the fact that he pulled his sunglasses on again seemed normal enough.

She sank into the leather couch next to the doctor, which was great because sitting across from a doctor's desk wasn't her favorite thing, and she was immensely grateful to Dr. Gokhale for knowing it.

"So how can I help you, beautiful girl?"

She wasn't a fan of the constant references to her looks, but the fact that Rahul made the effort to deliberately relax into his chair made her hang on to her smile. "I'm thinking about writing a book about the transplant experience."

Again, the enthusiasm in Dr. Gokhale's face was warm and genuine. "I think that's a great idea. Each experience is so unique. It would be great for people to know what your journey was like." It was so easy to talk to him. He always said the right thing.

She slid Rahul a glance. He stood and started studying the photographs on the walls, but his entire attention was focused on their conversation. He was on the case.

"So you'll help me?" she asked.

"Of course!"

"I was hoping to speak with the donor family. Do you think you could introduce me?"

She had thrown that out without warning, but instead of getting defensive his expression stayed calm. "You would have to talk to the transplant surgeon about that."

Rahul turned to him with an alertness that had DCP Savant written all over it in block capitals. "Do you do only postoperative care then? I thought you also did surgeries." He finally broke his silence. Good thing he spoke because she was speechless.

Everything was fuzzy surrounding her surgery, but she could have sworn that Papa and Dr. Girija had both told her that Dr. Gokhale was her surgeon.

"Of course I do surgeries," Dr. Gokhale said with a little more arrogance than was strictly necessary. "I've done thirty open-heart surgeries and two transplants. But Kimi's transplant was done in Mumbai. She was only brought here postop."

Kimi stood. "That can't —"

"Is that common?" Rahul cut Kimi off and removed his sunglasses. One look at his eyes and she controlled her shock.

"Not common. But we are one of the best postoperative and rehabilitation facilities in the world. So, complicated cases coming to us post-surgery isn't uncommon either."

Kimi's mind was racing. She had no memory of going into surgery, of coming out of it. But she had always thought that was normal because of all those drugs, and the fact that she was on a heart-lung machine and mostly comatose.

"You definitely did an excellent job with her treatment," Rahul said. "Thank you. How does that work, though? You must have to consult very closely with the surgeon, at least initially."

Dr. Gokhale shrugged. "I spoke with Dr. Bhansal a few times. But Dr. Girija and I were the real team." He smiled at Kimi. "And our star patient, of course. Without her hard work and willpower, we'd never have seen the success we've seen."

Kimi tried to return the doctor's smile, but all she could think was: Who the hell was Dr. Bhansal?

Dr. Gokhale was about to say more when

his phone buzzed and he pulled it out of his shirt pocket, his expression turning quizzical as he looked at it and then at Kimi as Rahul watched.

Before he could answer the phone, Rahul tripped over something, falling on the doctor and knocking him off his feet and his phone out of his hands.

"What on earth!" The doctor landed on his butt on the carpet.

"Sorry, my foot caught the edge of the rug." Rahul helped the doctor up and bent down to pick up his phone, which had stopped buzzing in all the commotion. He threw Kimi a loaded look, and she went to Dr. Gokhale, holding his hands, dusting him off needlessly while Rahul quickly studied the phone behind him.

"You aren't hurt, are you?" Kimi tried to hold the doctor's gaze away from Rahul.

He blushed and seemed to forget all about Rahul. "I'm fine," he said with a shaky laugh and rubbed his thumbs across Kimi's hands.

"Rahul can be really clumsy sometimes." She pulled her hands away gently. "I'm so sorry."

"It's not your fault." He took the phone Rahul handed him.

"Thank you," Rahul said. "You've been a great help."

Kimi thanked the doctor too as he hugged her good-bye and reminded her of Everest Base Camp. But her mind was miles away, pulled between the place and time where there were no memories and so many lies, and that look Rahul had just thrown her.

Rahul took her hand as they left. She knew she should yank it away. But she needed it. To feel anchored in this moment, where truth floated just out of reach. His hand in hers was truth. The fact that it was the only hand that she had ever wanted to hold was truth. The fact that she didn't even have to tell him the questions running rampant in her head was truth.

He was already on the phone with one of his intelligence guys to track down Dr. Bhansal before they were inside a cab, his focus on his job again, his hand back on the other side of those two feet of distance they couldn't seem to bridge.

"What did you see on his phone?" she asked when he ended the call and turned all the considerable focus of those eyes on her once more.

He reached across that buzzing distance and took her hand again, sending awareness flaring through her body, making warmth set her heart to rights even though she knew what was about to spill from his lips would set everything off-kilter again.

"That call Dr. Gokhale received was from Kirit-sir."

29

Rahul
Present day

Things that tested you were supposed to make you stronger, weren't they? Rahul didn't feel strong. He felt as powerless as he had as a teenager, wanting to put his fist through a brick wall. Dr. Gokhale seemed like the perfect match for Kimi. He understood her illness. It wouldn't throw him off. Wouldn't make him want to pick her up in his arms and tuck her in bed until whatever was leeching her of color passed. If it passed. Would a doctor have this ball of fear inside every time she looked like her knees were going to buckle?

And when she looked that stoic, a doctor would know how to respond to that. Wouldn't he? She had been in the bathroom for far too long. She'd disappeared in there the moment she made it up to their hotel room on shaky legs. He wasn't sure if it was because she was sick again the way she had been on the plane or if it was the shock of her father constructing such a complicated lie.

He paced their hotel room, back and forth from the wall of windows to the bathroom door. There was no way he was leaving her by herself, so they had just one room and it was where they were going to stay until it was time to catch a flight home later tonight. He could only hope that Kirit had been careful when he'd called Dr. Gokhale and that he wouldn't inadvertently give away their location.

He tracked the sounds in the bathroom with desperation, wondering if it made him a total psycho to knock on the door and ask how she was. His patience could only bear so much.

Why had he said those things to her in the car on the way to the airport? Why had he let his anger take over so completely? The mess that was his family — it wasn't her fault. Aie should never have spoken to her about things. Kimi had enough to deal with without having to soak up everyone else's shit.

Because she did. She was a damn sponge that soaked up her environment, dissolved into it. She had no fear of losing herself to anything. For someone who had so much to fear, how did she have no fear? That moment when she had bitten his head off for being ashamed of his own home brought on a rush of regret. Her eyes had burned with pride in him. Pride he'd seen in her eyes from the first time he'd met her. Pride that had stayed steadfast no matter what he'd done. Seeing it in his home, in his mother's kitchen had changed everything. It had conflated the pressure of being this close to her and not being able to be with her, be hers.

She had laughed with Aie over dinner. She had ruffled Mohit's hair. Ruffled his hair, for heaven's sake! Mohit, who snapped Rahul's head off for even looking at him, had practically been eating out of her hands by the time they left. Making fun of the red and yellow spice stains on her white pants, in her hair. All that color had made her look like she had just played *holi.*

Rahul had tried to wipe some yellow off her cheek, but each stroke of his thumb had painted a rising blush in its place. And heated his blood. He'd had the insane urge to touch the blush with his lips. Mohit had walked in on them and laughed and Kimi had glared. But then she had laughed too as though she and Mohit already had inside jokes to share.

Fifteen minutes, he had left her alone with Aie for all of fifteen minutes, just to quickly wash up and change for the flight, and that had ruined everything. He had known from the way she looked at him when he came out that something had changed in how she saw him. A sense of foreboding had enveloped him, as though he had climbed on a runaway handcart going downhill with no way to avoid a crash.

Then she had said the name he had never wanted her to say, never wanted her to know. And his anger had killed everything. He had pushed her away again. Harder than he ever had. Because she'd dared to reach for that piece of him that had turned him into a coward.

So long as she'd been angry too, things had been fine. But one moment she was her vibrant self and the next moment she looked like she was shaking on the inside and he couldn't remember why he had been angry. He would have done anything to pull her into his lap and hold her until it passed, but the one time he tried to reach for her she withdrew into herself, rolled into a ball, and fell into a fitful sleep. Thank God for that ridiculous eye mask she had pulled on because he hadn't been able to stop watching her sleep, mapping every frown that creased her forehead, every wave of discomfort that pursed her lips.

By the time they reached Dr. Gokhale's office, he thought she was feeling better. But after he'd told her about Kirit's phone call, she had collapsed into herself again.

"Did you know?" she asked, storming out of the bathroom. Finally. "Did you know that my transplant happened in India?"

"How exactly would I have known?" He turned away from the view of the city and studied her across the hotel room.

She was in a rage, her hair out of her ponytail and cascading down her back, her face freshly washed. Her red T-shirt with a towel-wrapped Minnie Mouse, barely containing her anger. But it wasn't just anger, it was anger darkened by betrayal and heartbreak. The way she had looked on their way back from Kalsubai Peak.

The fact that Kirit had called Dr. Gokhale meant Kirit knew. Of course he knew. He was the one who had orchestrated the entire deception about where the surgery happened. But why?

Kirit had told Rahul that they were taking her to Hong Kong for the transplant when they'd put her on a heart-lung machine. Then he'd sent Rahul away after blaming him for her condition. Except, he hadn't

398

taken her to Hong Kong until after the surgery. And everything about that felt like having stepped on the tip of a gigantic anthill of killer ants.

"Seriously, how would I know, Kimi? You had a cardiac arrest and they took you away. I didn't even get to say good-bye." And the most important case of his career had been imploding around him.

"Oh, I'm sorry, I shouldn't have had that cardiac arrest. How bloody insensitive of me." She let out a grunt of frustration. "And you wanted to say good-bye? Really? Is that why you left me without a word? Right after . . . right after . . ."

He knew what she wanted to call it. But he could not hear those words from her right now. "I'm sorry I left. It was . . . I couldn't . . . You were sick, Kimi, and I was scared of what I had done."

Another grunt. "You were scared? So that made it okay for you to run into another woman's arms?"

"What are you talking about?"

"Great, are we going to do this right now? Are we going to pretend?"

"I'm not pretending. Whose arms did I run into?"

She looked like she was going to kill him. "Jennifer Joshi. That's who. When did you become such a good liar, Rahul?"

What the hell? He'd only lied to her about one thing. And this was certainly not it.

"Jen was working with me on a case. Yes, we became friends. But that was all." Jen, amazingly enough, had reminded him so much of Kimi. Which is probably why he had been drawn to her in the first place. "All we were doing was working on a case." The idea of him and Jen was entirely laughable.

"Right. You were *working* your case, all right. I came to see you, Rahul, because I couldn't bear that you had left like that. I saw you with her. Was being with me so awful that you had to go kiss another woman?"

"I never even touched Jen, let alone kissed her, I swear. I have no idea what you saw, but it wasn't me."

"So carrying her up to her flat in your arms while kissing her is not touching her? It hadn't even been two hours since we'd made lo—"

That's when it struck him — "How did you have that heart attack, Kimi? Where were you when you collapsed?"

She didn't answer. But he knew. He had gone back to see her again, because he had realized what a coward he'd been leaving her like that. It had been too late. She was already in the hospital unable to keep her heart beating on its own.

For the past two years he had thought it was because of what they had done, but she had followed him and seen him with Jen. "You walked home through the streets of Dharavi? When you knew that your heart couldn't take it?"

"I didn't know that. I didn't think about that. I saw you kissing another woman hours after we'd made love." She rubbed her scar again. "It hurt, Rahul."

She has an unhealthy obsession with you. I trusted you. You made a promise. You need to keep it and stop this madness. No good can come of it, Kirit had said before sending him away from the hospital.

She wasn't the one with the unhealthy obsession. His own obsession was what had put her on a ventilator. He had sworn he'd give her up if she came back home alive.

And he had.

Over and over again.

But she'd come after him with her preposterous idea and her newly healthy body.

I can't live without you, Rahul. And I know you can't either. Now we don't have to.

It had been beautiful, the hope in her eyes. She had sparkled with it on top of that mountain. She always saw things so clearly.

To her everything was in its simplest, purest form. He would have given anything to not see them as the mess they were.

I don't feel the same way about you, Kimi. I've only ever thought of you as a friend.

It had been that easy to get her to believe him.

"Sorry," he said. Not because she had misunderstood something she'd seen him do, but because he'd lost count of all the times he'd hurt her.

She sat down on the bed in front of him without accepting his apology.

"Are you feeling better now?" he asked, because she looked better than she had on the plane, but there was exhaustion in her eyes.

"Don't," she said, looking up at him. "Don't make everything about my health. Is that all I am to you? A sick friend? Has it always been only sympathy? Is that all I am, your charity case?"

You're my heart. He wanted to tell her. *My heart.*

He was so tired of not saying it. Of pushing her away. Of being terrified of losing her. Of causing her pain over and over again.

But all he could do was shake his head. She was hungering for a fight right now. She was feeling pushed into a corner, and she needed to push back at something.

"What are we, Rahul?"

"What do you want from me, Kimi?" He couldn't bear to look at her when she was hurting this much. He turned away and looked back at the city — giant spikes of glass shooting up from a thick bed of greenery. A lifeless thing anchored in a life-giving thing.

"I don't want there to be lies between us," she said from behind him.

"Not this again, Kimi, please. I didn't kiss Jen and I didn't know anything about the transplant. But whatever this is, I'm going to get to the bottom of it. I'll get you your answers. I swear."

"Thanks," she said, coming to stand beside him. "I need this, Rahul. I need to know. I need . . ." She trailed off, and he knew he should let it go. But he turned to her.

"What do you need, Kimi?"

Those huge, soft eyes blinked up at him, gauging how much to risk again. "I need you to not shut me out."

He thought about the Post-it note she'd left on Tina. "I'm not the one who shut you out." She had told him she wanted nothing more to do with him. Over and over again.

"Do you really want me to butt out of

403

your life?"

God, no. He had been so lost without her for the past year.

"Can you please not shut me out today? Just for one day. Please?"

He touched her cheek, her skin butter-soft against his fingers. How did she not know that he couldn't shut her out? That there would be nothing left of him if she removed herself from him?

"I didn't ask your mother questions about you, I swear. I think she was just trying to warn me off." She leaned into his hand, the afternoon sun catching all those blond highlights that she loved so much. That he loved so much. Because she did. Because they made her happy.

He couldn't not touch them, couldn't not trace the golden lines radiating from her worry-creased forehead. "Everyone keeps warning you. Why don't you listen?"

"Because you're you, Rahul."

"I'm not who you think I am, Kimi." And yet he wanted to be everything she thought he was.

Those soft lips parted in a smile. "Haven't we had this conversation before?"

That would be all their conversations. They were in a loop, bonded atoms, the positive and negative forces inside them perfectly balanced between attraction and repulsion to hold them in each other's orbit.

Her hand went to her scar again, rubbing it in those light strokes she seemed to crave when she was in turmoil. "Why do you do that?" he asked, touching the lightest finger to her hand on her chest. "Does it hurt?"

"No," she whispered. "Actually, the scar itself is numb. It's like touching something with no nerve endings. When I touch it, I feel it on my fingers but not on the scar itself. Here, give me your hand." She took his hand. "Stick out your index finger." She did the same with her hand and lined up her index finger flush with his. "Now use your other hand to stroke our two fingers together."

He did as she asked. It was the oddest sensation. Like feeling only half a touch.

"Strange, huh?"

He stroked their joint fingers again, unable to stop touching her. Unable to fight that fight anymore. "I can't feel things either," he said. "Not the way people do. Not the way you do." She was looking up at him, one side of her face lit up by the sun. "It's just like this. Like a part of me is numb. Whatever Aie was warning you about, it's true."

She turned her hand and intertwined their

fingers, touching palm to palm, transforming one touch into another, transforming everything inside him. "Now that I think about it, maybe your *aie* wasn't warning me away from you. I think she just wanted me to understand."

He couldn't look away from their clasped hands, alive with a connection he felt all through his body. "Understand what?"

She pulled his hand to her lips. "How deeply you hurt. So I wouldn't hurt you."

He pulled his hand away and sat down on the bed. She followed him, looking down at him until he looked up at her. Her eyes were equal parts soft and fierce. "Will you tell me about her?"

For the longest time he couldn't speak, couldn't feel anything. Then all at once, his throat constricted around his silence. The pain growing unbearable until he let it out.

"Her name was Mona," he said, and the sob that escaped him was the last thing he'd expected.

She cupped his face, taking everything he was feeling into her hands. He couldn't remember the last time he had cried, but trying to hold back the tears made his chest burn. "Just don't stop touching me," he wanted to say. Instead, he said, "Aie shouldn't have told you."

Kimi sat down next to him without letting his face go, then she wrapped her arms around him and pressed her cheek against his chest. His heartbeat raced beneath her ear.

It had been so long since he'd felt her arms around him like this. Since he'd thought about Mona, her sticky-sweet breath. Her chatterbox voice. It was terrifying to let it out like this, to feel it again. What if he lost it? What if he forgot?

He didn't know if he said those words out loud. But if Kimi heard them, there would be two people who would remember. And he knew Kimi would remember. "She was eight years old. And just so . . ." His voice scraped out of his tight, raw throat. "So beautiful and smart. And she never stopped talking. You would have been best friends, the two of you. If one of you ever stopped talking, that is."

She smiled through the rivers that were wetting his shirt. Why couldn't he do that? Why couldn't he cry like that. Because that's exactly how he felt.

She stroked his face, his chest. "It had been only two years since your *baba* died," she said, looking up at him with those wet doe eyes.

"Don't, Kimi. Don't pity me. Please."

She stood. For a moment he thought she was angry again, because her eyes blazed. If she walked away from him now, he was going after her. But she didn't walk away. She climbed into his lap and took his face in both hands again. "Is that what you think I'm feeling for you right now, Rahul. Pity?"

Her breath was sweet and warm, and too close to his lips. He should pull away.

"You're not?" he said into her lips. Fuck pulling away. Fuck ever letting her go. She was everything. Everything and he was nothing without her.

"Not even close."

And then she did it. She bent down and he reached up and their lips met. Something electric sparked through his chest, through the room, through the entire bloody universe. Hot and bright. Bright and hot.

She inhaled. A tiny gasp. And everything but her and her lips went up in flames.

His hands cupped her head, her scalp warm and perfect in his hands, her hair silk between his fingers. He took her lips, her breath, sucking on the soft, lush sweetness, nudging for entrance. Pushing as she pushed back. Groaning as she groaned. Sounds, taste, breath, all of it becoming one thing. One huge, pulsing inferno. Fast, so fast. Head spinning, blood surging places, hands everywhere. Her fists in his hair, the pain of that pull everywhere, in his chest, his belly, his dick. All of him thrown wide open in hunger and need. Teeth against teeth, tongue against tongue. Breath, running short, until he had to pull away to suck one in, panting, unable to pull away even as he pulled away.

"Why haven't we ever done that before?" she said, just as breathless, just as tightly pressed into him. Pressure against pressure.

A laugh escaped him, easing the inferno, coloring it in with joy. "Because —"

"It was a rhetorical question," she said, pressing a finger to his lips. Then she slid off his lap without removing her finger and straddled him. And then she kissed him again and again.

When his hands had dug under her shirt and his brain didn't have a single thought left in it except: Please don't pull away from me, don't ever pull away from me again, she pulled away. Just a little bit. Then in her most coquettish American movie accent she said, "Officer Savant, I think you should know that I'm not a virgin."

30

Kimi
A long time ago
Kimi had never expected it to be easy, convincing Rahul to help her lose her virginity. But she hadn't expected to hit a wall of such dogged determination either. One would think she had asked him to run his fingers (or even other long, tubular body parts) through a sugarcane juicer machine.

"I'm not going to 'do it' with you, Kimi." If his words weren't brutal enough, his utterly stern look finished the job spectacularly.

"Why?" Thankfully, being unfazed in the face of extreme hopelessness was her special skill.

"Because I can't."

"You can't?" Her eyes must have reflected her shock because he gave her one of those arrogant looks she shouldn't love so much but did. "You mean you won't."

"I mean I'm not having this conversation with you." He looked around her room as though it were a cage and he'd forgotten how he got here.

"Why?" She wondered if she needed to lock the door.

He narrowed his eyes at the door she was staring at. "Because it doesn't work like that."

"By 'it' you mean making love?"

He cringed.

"So, you don't like making love?"

"God, Kimi, can you stop calling it that?"

She looked at him, utterly confused. Although, in a perverse way, this was turning out to be more fun than she had expected. Rahul was never flustered by anything.

Maybe there was something else wrong. Maybe he thought she should be entirely unaware of these things and it bothered him that she wasn't. She actually had a really good idea of the mechanics of the thing. She had read all the books, watched all the porn. She had read the entire Kama Sutra online. It was weirdly acrobatic, even bordering on unsavory, unless you were double-jointed. Thank the heavens above that romance novels didn't bring horses and elephants into the thing!

He started pacing, as he was prone to do when faced with a challenge. She felt oddly comfortable talking to him about this, which pretty much summed up why she was doing it in the first place. She shot a quick glance at his, y'know, nether regions. Okay, so in this at least the novels were wrong. There wasn't much movement. But she couldn't be sure because it was a quick glance. It wasn't like she could stare. Plus his shirt was covering things a bit. Evidently, not all men "became instantly hard as stone" when the woman of their dreams mentioned making love, which apparently wasn't his favorite term. Good to know. She'd better find another term ASAP.

"Then tell me how it works?" she asked because he was sliding fast into his broody, silent space from his problem-solving, pacing space, which truth be told she should have been better prepared for. Well, no matter, she was prepared now. She could call it "fucking." But yuck. Maybe "having sex." Yes, that should fix the cringing.

"I don't know," he mumbled. Mumbling was a step away from silence. A step in the right direction. Good.

"You don't know how it works?"

Again that arrogant expression, laced with that look he got when he knew exactly what she was up to, and when he didn't know how to say no to her, didn't know how not to give her what she wanted. It was the hottest bloody thing in the world.

She felt a warming in her own nether regions — very much like in the novels. And just like that she knew she would get her way.

But first he would try all he could to steer her away from her goal. The one she knew she was going to reach.

She played her ace. "I don't want to die a virgin, Rahul."

He groaned. Who would have thought making him blush would be so much fun? It was terrible of her, but she loved it. Like anything that was near impossible to do, doing it made her feel like a goddess.

She didn't intend to die. Even so, the odds made it impossible to not give the option its due. The success rate for heart transplants was seventy-five percent.

"Are you not feeling well?" he asked, tenderness dilating his eyes, even though he usually was spot-on about how she was feeling. Even better than Mamma and Papa. He always saw. Maybe because it was so easy to let him see.

"Never better," she said. This wasn't exactly true, but her medications were doing their job. And her surgery seemed like it was going to happen. The donor was hooked up to machines in Hong Kong, and she was flying there next week to wait. Hence the need for speed.

"You're my friend, Kimi."

"Then you should care. You should care that I don't die a virgin. Why can't you help me? It's even a thing — friends with benefits."

"You watch far too many Hollywood movies."

"And you don't watch nearly enough, officer," she said in her best American accent, trying to look petulant, but the tenderness in his eyes made it hard.

He sat down on the bed next to her. He smelled of industrial-strength antibacterial soap — the smell of her life. But under that sharp medicinal tang she could smell him, the real him. His scent was surprisingly soft. Like sweet spices. Totally at odds with how he looked, like an outlaw who galloped on his stallion across mountains and ravines, meting out justice to peasants, rough-edged and vibrating with restless energy. His smell and his eyes were all that was soft in all that rugged armor. The combination had made her so breathless for so long, she had never had trouble believing those novels.

Those tender, melting-tar eyes searched her. "Tell me what's happened."

She didn't want to talk about the surgery. It made all the heat gathering inside her freeze up.

"It's me, Kimi." He touched the edge of her sleeve, caressing it the way she wanted him to caress the rest of her.

"We found a donor match."

His eyes widened before he closed them. Good thing because she couldn't bear to see the fear that flared bright there. Then he was shaking. Again, just for an instant. She caught all his responses even though they flashed by in fractions of moments, like intense cloudbursts that condensed time. It was their dance. Him blanketing his reactions and her registering them before he did, and both of them not acknowledging the thin ice she stood on as the temperature continued to rise.

Yet again, he put it all away the way he always did with anything concerning her health. He was the only person in her life who made such a valiant effort to not burden her with her own brokenness, and she loved him for it.

"I'm going to Hong Kong next week. This person is in a coma and unresponsive to treatment. The doctors aren't hopeful for a recovery. Once it happens, things will go fast, so I have to be there when the family makes the call to pull the plug."

He reached out and plucked her fingers out of her lap where they fidgeted of their own accord. She grabbed his hand and placed it on her chest just below her collarbone. Her nipples peaked and pressed against her blouse at the touch. But what was hotter than the spark that zinged down her belly was the way his eyes darkened at the touch.

"They're going to cut it out and replace it," she said. "Dr. Girija says my chances are —"

"One hundred percent." He cut her off. "You're here for a reason, remember?"

It's what she always said to him. *I'm here for a reason.*

"Yes, I'm here for a reason, and you are here for one too — so that your best friend does not die a virgin."

"You are not going to die."

"We don't know that. All I know is that I'm not going anywhere until we do this." She poked him in his chest. Anger surged through her. Because really, enough was enough!

He grabbed her finger off his chest. "Fine. Lay down and take off your clothes."

"I beg your pardon?"

"Well, you want to do this. Let's do this."

"Really?"

"Less talk, more action, Ms. Patil." He stood, stepping back, as though making space for her to get on with the undressing.

"Why do I have to take off my clothes first?"

"Because you're the one who wants this."

She scowled and he tucked an errant lock of hair behind her ear, his eyes softening again. "How will things ever be the same if we do this, Kimi?"

She grabbed his hand off her cheek and squeezed it. "I promise nothing will change." How could things between them ever change? He was all that connected her to the world. What made the world outside exist. He was her constant.

And she was all that was unstable in his world.

Maybe it was unfair of her to ask this of him when there was a chance that she'd leave him with a lifetime of memories to haunt him.

She sagged into her disappointment. "It's okay if you don't want to. It's okay if this is too much to ask."

He laughed. One breath of a laugh whooshing out of him against her ear,

417

because he had moved so close to her.

He wrapped both arms around her. "You always ask for too much, Kimi."

She melted into him. Not in the hot, melty sort of way but in the way that was all theirs. Their world.

"You are too much."

"Thank you." She looked up at him. Her cheek rubbing against the denim of his shirt. His smell, his feel, the texture of the air around him so familiar it was home.

"For what?" Even his clove-scented breath was home.

"I know you don't mean it as a compliment when you say I'm too much. But I love it."

"Why?"

She couldn't answer. She knew he was only asking because he wanted her to verbalize it. So he could refute her words and tell her that she was wrong, that she was all the things she wanted to be. That she was not less. That she was too much.

The best part was that he believed it. He had given her that. The belief in her wholeness. And because Rahul never lied and Rahul had more integrity than anyone she knew, that made it true.

"So you'll do it?"

He stroked her back and in his eyes was

the answer before he spoke it. "I have a few conditions."

"Oh, Rahul, thank you!" She squeezed her arms around him. Like a little girl. Definitely not sexy. Naturally, he pushed her away.

"But not right now. I need to talk to the doctor first and make sure it's okay."

She laughed. "Quite full of ourselves, aren't we? I already talked to Girija Auntie. I'm stable, my medications are working, I'm good to go. We can't get too acrobatic, that's all."

His cheeks took on that incredibly hot deep red again. Who would have thought just talking about it would make her always stoic IPS officer blush? "You told her you were going to ask me to have sex with you?"

"No, I asked her if I could have sex. Period."

"So she basically knows. Because who else would you ask?"

She smacked him. "That is not true. I could actually ask any number of people!"

More of that smugness oozed from his smile. "Okay." He split the word in two the way he always did when he meant the opposite of it.

"I could! I could call someone. There are escort services and stuff, y'know. You aren't

419

my only option."

"I'm honored. I think."

She giggled.

"And now I'm totally turned on. Because who can resist a girl who picked him over — did you say escort services?"

"If you keep making me laugh, how are we going to do it?"

"You actually mean right now, don't you?"

"I leave next week."

He pulled her close. "Wow, you really know how to seduce a guy." But he was holding her very tightly.

She looked up at him, the back of her neck crinkling with the effort. The sight of his lips and eyes ignited that heat inside her again, pushing away all the other things that the fear in his embrace was bringing to the surface. She went up on her toes. Finally, she was going to kiss him.

He put a finger on her lips. She'd been so wrong — the heat from a minute ago was nothing. She felt his finger everywhere. "No kissing."

What?

He caressed her cheek. The rough pad of his thumb turning her soft. "No getting angry. My rules."

"How can we make love without kissing?"

"No calling it that either. You want to do

it. We're going to do it."

"You make it sound like a hardship. I thought making . . . doing it . . . was supposed to be enjoyable."

He smiled, but for an instant he let all the things inside him loose in his eyes. "I'll make it good for you, I promise. But, Kimi, I can't, I have to . . ."

"I know. Don't say anything more. Please." This might be their last memory together. He had to protect himself. He who had never forsaken the girl who came with the inevitability of loss.

He tipped her chin up until she met his eyes. "Hey, the other rule is to tell me if you don't like something." He kissed her forehead and something vagrantly sexy flared through her, opening her up so fast and fierce, she wanted to wrap herself around him. Wanted to touch him with her entire body.

"I like it. I'll like everything."

He smiled against her forehead. "Go slow, tigress. We haven't even started yet." He dropped kisses on her lids, his breath turning her brows so erogenous she moaned.

"I thought we weren't kissing."

"Oh, there will be kissing. Just not on the mouth."

He got right to it. Her ears, her throat.

Slow at first, tentative, then his breathing sped up, gathering up a storm. His lips dragged over her shirt, leaving wet heat on her skin. She was dying. She snuck a look at him. His eyes were closed, his face tight with something. Control? She didn't care. This was Rahul, her Rahul, and that's all that mattered. The only damn thing in the world that had any meaning at all.

His fingers grasped her buttons, then pulled away. "Also, we're going to leave our clothes on."

Wait, what?

But his mouth touched her breasts and she lost her ability to think, to talk, to breathe. He could do this through metal armor and she wouldn't care. "Just don't stop," she tried to say, but it came out gibberish and he smiled into her nipple. Seriously, like smiled around a part of her body that wanted to shove itself down his throat, and there was so much sensation, she might pass out from it. She grabbed his hair with both hands.

He tried to pull away. "Kimi, you have to calm down. Breathe."

She panted. Nodded. Pulled him back.

"I'm trying to go slow here."

Slow?

He'd just tried to ingest her nipple whole.

That was going slow on which planet?

She climbed onto him, straddling his lap, and pushed him back on the bed.

"That's not going slow, Kimi."

"It's slow, it's slow," she tried to say, but she was kissing his jaw so it basically came out as "Mphh miplmph."

A laugh started in his chest, but her teeth found a tendon in his neck and a shudder went through him. He rolled her over on her back and reached for her jeans. So, change of plans. Change of speed.

"Breathe," he said, cupping her down there.

She bucked off the bed. Breathe? What was that?

He looked like he was in pain, but he didn't stop. His hands shook as he unbuttoned her jeans and slid them off.

"I thought we weren't removing clothing." She lifted her hips for him.

"I'm not a magician, Kimi."

"Oh, yes you are," she wanted to tell him, but her jeans were off and his tongue was inside her — omurgodabove — navel. And things were exploding between her legs. Where he went next.

As in really went.

Okay, her heart definitely could not survive this.

Could. Not.

He licked her. One long, lapping lick. Then he went to work until she was thrashing her head like a crazed person and pulling out his hair. And making half-sobbing half-screaming sounds she couldn't recognize as her own. A pulse was beating — with the force her stupid heart could never seem to muster — right between her legs. Where all her being had gathered and lit up like a bonfire. Her clitoris, her vagina, her entire darned reproductive system was saying hello to her. *Hello! Here we are. Right here! Where were you all our lives?*

When she looked down at him he was smiling against her underwear. He looked almost as happy as her vagina, which kept on beating like wedding drums.

"Who wears underwear with lollipops on it?"

How could he talk?

"Don't be rude to that underwear. I'm framing it and putting it on my nightstand."

His smile widened. But by the time he had brought himself up to eye level, the laughter was gone from his eyes, intensity and arousal rising in its place. He stared at her lips. She'd never seen him like this before. So much hunger, so much pleasure and pain. Not the kind of pain she'd put him through

424

so many times. This pain was new. This pleasure was new. The beating body parts, definitely new.

I'll make it up to you, she wanted to say. If she came home she would make it up to him every day of her life. For putting him through this. For giving her this.

She sat up, her nether regions so aware and awake they clenched. He sat up too and she grabbed his face in her hands. She had never wanted anything as badly as she wanted to kiss him, and she had a rather spectacular list of things she wanted really badly. Like wanting to live. Right now wanting to kiss him was giving the wanting to live a run for its money. But she had promised.

He pushed away from her. She grabbed his sleeve. His sleeve! She seriously needed to start acting like a grown-up.

"Where are you going?"

"We're done, aren't we?"

"No, we're not. You promised."

"You enjoyed that, didn't you?"

"You did not promise me enjoyment. You promised to have sex with me."

"That was definitely sex, Kimi."

She stuck her finger in his face. "Don't patronize me, Rahul. I had an orgasm. It was spectacular. Better than anything I've ever given myself. But we are not done here."

He sank back into the bed, his eyes suddenly hot again. "You give yourself orgasms?"

All by itself her voice dropped to a whisper. "Yes. Do you want me to tell you how?"

He groaned, and she reached for his belt. Something about the way he groaned gave her the courage to unhook it.

She expected him to pull away, but he just swallowed.

"Stop being old-fashioned, Rahul. We're both adults. You're not taking my honor. My honor is not buried in my crotch. And if it were, you just made it explode out of there. It's probably splattered across the ceiling." She started unzipping his pants. "I want this and you promised."

He smiled. "Keep talking." He removed her hands from his pants and kissed them. "But keep these up here." He put her hands on his shoulders.

"Are you saying my talking doesn't turn you on?"

"Most definitely." He removed his jeans, then pulled off her underwear. His breathing changed.

They lay back down on the bed, side by side.

"That's you not turned on?" she asked, looking down at him, and he dropped a kiss on her forehead and smiled again.

"Say something about women's rights or art or science." He reached down and cupped her again, his fingers warm against her bare skin, and she would've given him anything.

"The longest recorded male orgasm went on for ten seconds. The longest female orgasm lasted forty-five seconds."

"Thank you," he said, and there it was again, that smile in his voice.

"Only forty-five percent of women who are virgins experience pain during their first intercourse."

"This might hurt." He rubbed a finger against her opening and she gasped. "I'm sorry."

"Just don't stop," she said, pressing into his hand. "I don't think I'm in the forty-five percent."

He kissed her cheek, that smile nudging at her as his finger nudged elsewhere. She clenched without meaning to and his jaw worked. "You're one of a kind, Kimi."

Pleasure was coursing through her, and joy. Seconds ago she had wanted to laugh. Now she wanted to cry, and then he touched his thumb to her clitoris and it all turned to sensation. Dear lord above! Another orgasm danced beneath his fingers. Two strokes and it exploded through her, completely without her permission.

"Relax, sweetheart. Shh." He removed his finger, leaving her bereft. "Please tell me you have condoms."

She leapt at the side table, almost knocking him off the bed. The bed started to shake. He was laughing. Right now he could guffaw like a hyena and she'd grab on to him and never let him go. She extracted a box. Her fingers were shaking so much she couldn't get the blasted things to work. He took the box from her, heat and laughter dancing in his eyes. He extracted one and slid it on in a matter of seconds.

She hadn't seen too many penises that weren't on a computer screen (okay she had seen none), but his was beautiful. Like, seriously beautiful. She reached for it. But he caught her hand. "You have to relax, Kimi. Please."

Relax? How could he use that word? She was panting. He pushed her back on the bed, and she grabbed him and wrapped her legs around him in a death grip as he slid into her. The fit so tight and slick and so bloody hot she couldn't breathe.

"Tell me what to do," she said. "Tell me

what you need."

But he had no instructions to give. His entire face was flushed, the furrow between his brows deeper than she'd ever seen it.

"God, Kimi," he said and then he was pumping into her. And she had no idea what pain was or pleasure. She had no bloody idea what anything was. Because everything inside her was soft and wet and clenching around him. She held on to his arms, his back, her fingers digging into rock-hard muscle and keeping her in place.

Every inch of her turned to exhilarating, maddening tightness. Filled-up. Whole. Engulfed. She fell into herself, fell into him in another gush of pleasure. Not the hot blast from before but sparkling echoes of that explosion, reaching every cell that held her together as she held on and watched him come apart in long uncontrolled thrusts.

He threw back his head and the sound that escaped him unraveled him entirely. A sob, a moan, a wild scream of release. His buttocks clenched and unclenched beneath her ankles, over and over until he sagged into her with such relief she pulled him to her, stroking him, his hair, his back, as sore, consuming pleasure throbbed where they joined.

She wanted to go on holding him as though forever existed. In all the times that she had believed she didn't care if she went on living there had been defeat and frustration. In this moment there was a belief that she was alive and, no matter what happened to her, this mattered. She mattered.

He lifted his face off the crook of her neck where she knew she would find skin marked by his mouth. Where even as he pulled away, he left behind the pinpricks of razor burn. He didn't meet her eyes, just extracted himself from her and moved away so fast it made her glad to have the cover of her blouse. He sat at the edge of the bed, his back to her, his head in his hands, his breathing labored. Despite his still buttoned shirt, he looked entirely naked, exposed to his bones.

The silence between them labored to breathe too. She reached for her underwear and pulled it on. He reached for the tissue box and held it out to her, still not looking at her. "You okay?" he said finally, his voice hollow and full at once.

She made a sound, envying him his ability to not look at her. She couldn't take her eyes off him, couldn't move again without throwing herself back in his arms, couldn't speak without telling him everything in her heart.

This heart had better be the real thing. Because she could not leave him this way. Could not let all the precious feelings inside her go unsaid. She could not give him up.

"I have to go," he said, pulling on his jeans as though the effort took everything he had left. "I'll see you at the airport."

And with that he walked away from her.

31

Rahul
A long time ago

"Where the hell have you been?" The last thing Rahul needed was to deal with Jen's wrath right now. But it was valid; all her damn anger was valid. She had been trying to call him for the past hour, but he had been too busy. "The bastard showed up! He pressed a gun to my belly. Do you know I'm pregnant? Are you aware?" Jen pointed at her protruding belly.

Yes, he was aware. Of all the fucked-up things about this case, the fact that Jen was carrying a child was somehow the worst part. He had once tried to tell her to go slow when she'd been badgering him relentlessly to try and find two of her patients who had gone missing. She'd dragged him through the narrow lanes of Dharavi where the two sisters had lived, questioning all their neighbors about their whereabouts.

"Should you really be racing around in the heat in your state?" he had asked her.

She'd bitten his head off, lecturing him at such considerable length about how pregnancy doesn't impede one's ability for locomotion that he had learned his lesson and never referred to her pregnancy again.

She wasn't the kind of person you could try to be overprotective of. In fact, all attempts to get her to back off chasing these thugs who were stealing organs from undocumented slum dwellers and leaving them untraceable met with a: "You have a better plan, officer?"

That had reminded him so much of Kimi.

Suddenly, it was clear to him how everything reminded him of Kimi. He had refused to admit it, and now he had gone and made the biggest mistake of his life. The way her arms and legs had clutched him as he pumped into her, unable to stop. Blood rushed to his face.

Here he was, on duty, with a pregnant woman telling him a psychopath they'd been trying to track down had pressed a gun to her belly, and he couldn't stop thinking about the violent satisfaction of releasing inside his best friend. And the raging need to go back to her right now. He had left her, possibly lost and embarrassed and needing him. He imagined her now, her arms wrapped around her knees, wondering what she had done wrong to make him flee.

Truth was, he wasn't as worldly as she saw him. Sex had never been an enjoyable experience for him. It had always been a purely physical release, something that came tinged with self-loathing and the memory from long ago of his fourteen-year-old hand forcefully pressed against a khaki-clad dick. But he hadn't thought about that once today. He hadn't even remembered it until he had tried to sit up and she had tried to hold him and he'd seen a wash of pleasure in her eyes so pure and untainted, all the self-loathing had descended on him like a wave that took you down too fast to outrun.

"Hello, Rahul, are you even here?" Jen snapped her fingers in his face.

"I came as soon as I got your message." He just hadn't seen it because he'd been too busy. "Tell me everything."

"First, I think my friend in Qatar might be able to get us the records for all the transplants performed across the Gulf in the past six months. He did say that there's been an unusually rapid rise in numbers. For years there were no organs and now people are moving up the list as though it's the Costco line on the day before Thanksgiving."

"Excuse me?" Usually, he got a lot of Jen's American references because Kimi made him watch so much American TV and movies.

"Never mind. I'm absolutely sure the organs are being pulled off our donor registry database." Jen had worked like a madwoman over the past six months to compile a donor registry in Dharavi because the rate of organ failure was so high.

One day, she had noticed two of her patients disappear suspiciously, and she hadn't been able to let it go. She'd made his life hell until he had listened to her and finally found a few desecrated body parts buried in sewage. Then five more people had disappeared, and he had realized that she wasn't a mad American charity junkie desperate to find the meaning of life in the slums of Mumbai. She was just a doctor who wanted to save lives.

They had become friends and watched as the tally of people on her registry who disappeared rose and rose. Unfortunately, no more bodies ever showed up. This made the case impossibly hard because the victims were undocumented. And those who didn't exist couldn't disappear.

Now the bastards who were wreaking this havoc had broken into Jen's clinic. The place was completely trashed. Broken glass and papers strewn everywhere. A picture of Jen with her husband, Nikhil, slashed up. Rahul was careful not to touch anything until his forensics team arrived.

"The thug and all his cronies wore masks, but I could tell they were desperate. I swear I don't even know what stopped him from emptying that gun into me. He knows something. I can smell fear, and he was scared enough to explode. Maybe he knows how close we are to busting him."

Rahul kicked himself again for not having picked up her text sooner. But his phone had been on Kimi's desk, and his ears, and all the rest of him, otherwise occupied. Not that he would have made it here before the bastards left, even if he'd had the good sense to show more control.

"He took my laptop. But of course he underestimated this brain." Jen tapped her head. "What kind of idiot leaves important information on a local drive?" She called her assistant on the phone. "Can you bring me your laptop? I keep all my records on a remote server. He'll never find them."

"You should have been a cop," Rahul said, as the forensics team arrived and started to comb through the room.

"So why are you hurtling between total distraction and looking like your best friend died?"

The question was so unexpected, Kimi's pleasure-dilated pupils flashed in his mind, harsh and bright. Her breath had been sweet. How could anyone's breath be sweet? Her moans had seeped under his skin. And he had left her behind. When he knew that might be the last time he'd ever smell that breath, hear those moans.

"Rahul, seriously, what's wrong?"

"It's weird that we're working on this case. My friend, she's been waiting for a heart donor for a few years now. She just found out that they might have a match for her in Hong Kong." He still couldn't believe that the drug that was supposed to give her a new lease on life had started to destroy her heart within months, and also destroyed her dreams along the way. *I guess Columbia's going to have to wait,* had been her only reaction. Even though it had taken all her wily powers of persuasion to convince her parents to let her go.

"Is the donor on a ventilator?"

"Yes."

"Medicine is magic, isn't it? Nikhil loves to say that."

"Actually, she's magic all by herself."

"Ooh! DCP Savant's in love."

Rahul stood so fast Jen stumbled back. "Shit," she said, losing her footing and landing on her bum. "Calm down, tiger!"

"I'm sorry." Rahul went down on his knees next to her. "Are you okay?" He tried to pull her up and she stumbled again. Her bare foot was bleeding.

"Hell! I think I stepped on broken glass." She stared down at her foot. "Just my luck. My stupid feet are so swollen, I had to take off my shoes."

It was bleeding pretty badly. She tried to reach it, but it wasn't easy to do over her pregnant belly and that made her laugh. She shoved her foot toward him. "Do you see anything?"

He picked up her foot. The shiny edge of broken glass was peeking out of the bleeding cut. "I think I see it. Do you have some tweezers in here?"

She pointed to a turned-over cabinet that they couldn't touch because he couldn't contaminate the crime scene.

"See if you can get it with your fingers."

He poked around but couldn't.

"I have some tweezers upstairs in the flat."

"I'll go get them."

"Or I could walk up there. No point waiting down here. We have to get out of the forensics team's way anyway."

"You're not walking on that foot." He found some gauze and pressed it lightly on the wound.

"Well, then, Romeo, why don't you carry me up there and tell me all about your lady love."

"She's not my lady love," he said, and still all he could think about was how her skin had felt under his lips, around his damn cock. Had he always known?

He had never let himself think about it. About wanting to touch her, to kiss that mouth, that upturned nose, those deeply set eyelids and long arched brows. He had never let himself think about it because he knew it should never happen. And now it had and he would never, ever be able to stop reliving it.

"Well, chop-chop," Jen said. "Unless you want to daydream while I limp up on my torn-up foot."

He shook his head and scooped her up, setting off another spurt of laughter. Apparently, his misery was incredibly amusing to Dr. Joshi. For a pregnant woman she was really light. He stepped into the street and the line of street vendors turned to stare at them.

"We're going to get the rumor mills to go completely wild, aren't we?" she said through her laughter.

"As long as your husband doesn't show up and decide to shoot me." Rahul hadn't met Nikhil Joshi, but he knew that he was visiting from Africa this week.

That made her laugh even more. "Nic and guns mix like you and a tutu. Plus, he's one of those guys who doesn't feel jealousy. To him, it would be such a sign of weakness and distrust in me that he'd be mortified if he let himself feel it."

"Sounds like a great guy." Especially since the idea of seeing another man carry Kimi anywhere made him feel crazed right now.

"He is. And so are you, officer," she said and wrapped her arms around his neck and kissed his cheek.

That took him so much by surprise he stopped in the middle of bounding up the stairs. "What was that for?"

"For carrying me up the stairs as though I don't weigh as much as a whale. And for being you. Your Kimi is a very lucky girl."

Those would be the last words he would ever hear her say before the day spun into disaster so fast, the wreck would be impossible to salvage.

■ ■ ■ ■

Getting Forensics to record the scene and then debrief took another hour. He tried to text Kimi a few times. Typed and deleted his apology over and over. Finally, it made sense to wait and speak with her in person. Not that he knew what to say to make things right.

Was that as good for you? Too cheesy.

Can we do that again? Too needy.

I love you.

Tina jerked under him as he revved the accelerator too hard.

Well, at least he knew what he could not say to her. Because, what the hell!

He needed to get a hold of himself. One roll in the hay and he was starting to turn into an idiot and forget himself.

Kimi was his best friend and the most beautiful girl he knew. Why was he surprised that she had made his head explode? Among other things.

By the time he reached The Mansion, his damn heart was singing, like a fucking lunatic. He hadn't felt this light in as long as he could remember. He kept feeling all sorts of feelings and sensations squeezing and tingling through him. A tiny part of him kept warning him that this sort of joy could never end well. But this time he didn't believe it.

Yes, he'd been an idiot and had run because what he was feeling had become unbearable. But surely, Kimi would understand. She had looked ecstatic enough that she couldn't turn him away now. He parked Tina by the bougainvillea pouring down the stone wall of The Mansion and broke into a run. This time toward her, instead of away from her. Because, he couldn't not. All those times she'd thrown him out and he'd run back should've been a sign. He couldn't run from her.

They were going to find a way to work this out. No matter their differences.

Bhola usually saw him from the gatehouse and hurried to open the gates. Today he glared at him and waved his hands as if to shoo him away.

"Open the gate, Bholaji."

Instead of letting him in, Bhola stepped out of the gate and came at him. If Rahul hadn't known what a softie Bhola was, he would have backed up at the menace on his face.

"What did you do?" he growled, shoving Rahul in the chest.

"What? Where's Kimi?"

442

Bhola grabbed his collar, but he couldn't hold on because tears started streaming down his face, and Rahul's heart started to pound.

"Which hospital?" Rahul shouted over his shoulder, running back to Tina.

"Lilavati," Bhola said through sobs. "But she may not be there by the time you get there."

At first they wouldn't let him in. "Family only in the ICCU," they said.

He flashed his badge, ready to fight anyone who stood in his way. But the badge did the job.

He ran through the hospital until Kirit Patil grabbed his arm and stopped him.

"She doesn't want to see you. Whatever you did, you almost killed her."

They were the sweetest words he'd ever heard. She was alive. He wouldn't ask for anything more. Nothing more. "Just tell me how she is."

Kirit gave him a look of disgust. "She's had a massive cardiac arrest. They're trying to stabilize her. If she stays stable we're flying her to Hong Kong in a few hours."

A few hours. Good. That was a good thing. She was going to be okay.

A nurse came out of her room. "Are you

Rahul?"

Kirit tried to hold him back, but Rahul pushed his hand off his chest.

"She wants to see me?" he said directly to the nurse, who nodded.

He was inside her room so fast he didn't hear what Kirit said behind him.

"Kimi?"

She looked shrunken in the huge machine-like bed, her eyes sunken, her lips blue, her skin almost gray. Had it been just a few hours since he'd seen her so vibrant she had shaken his world?

He took her hand and she moved those huge eyes to him. "You came back for me." She had barely whispered the words when a siren went off and all the instruments in her room seemed to blink and blow up as her hand fell limp in his.

Someone yanked him away from her and pushed him out of the room that filled with doctors and nurses so fast his answer stayed trapped in his throat.

I'll always come back. But she already knew that. She had to know that.

"I want him out of here," a woman's voice said behind him, and anger swelled inside Rahul. Anger at her, anger at all the truth in why she wanted him to stay away from her daughter.

444

"Rahul, I think you should leave," Kirit said behind him.

He nodded without looking back. He couldn't look away from the door to Kimi's room. Couldn't step away from the sounds of physicians fighting to revive her.

One, two, three . . . and the electric thump.

They were fibrillating her. Kirit stood beside him in silence. Their breathing loud despite the sounds.

One, two, three . . . another thump.

"She's back."

How did he not collapse with relief?

Dr. Girija came out of her room and told Kirit that they were putting her on a heart-and-lung machine.

Kirit turned to him again as soon as the doctor was gone. "Leave now, Rahul." There was a finality in his voice this time. "This heart is her last chance. I'm not sure if she'll make it home because we won't keep her on the heart-lung machine if the transplant doesn't work. She didn't want us to."

Rahul turned on him. "She's coming back. How can you talk about her not coming back?" The last time he'd felt this kind of rage at Kirit, he'd just lost Baba. He pulled back his anger. He wasn't going to lose anyone this time.

"How could you do what you did? She

would not be on that machine if not for you."

A painting on the wall tilted to one side as Rahul backed up into it.

"Whatever you're thinking, it's madness," Kirit continued, not backing down. "Kimi is not a normal girl. She hasn't had a normal life. How could you take advantage of that? She has an unhealthy obsession with you. I trusted you. You made a promise. You need to keep it and stop this madness. No good can come of it."

He was right. No good had ever come out of Rahul getting anywhere near her. And he'd hurt her enough.

"Just bring her back. Please."

With that he left her behind. Because he'd do anything. He'd leave her alone forever, if it meant she'd be okay.

He made that promise over and over again as he sat on their rock, until the restless waves had soaked through his pants all the way to his knees, until the sun had drowned into the ocean, leaving nothing but darkness. All these years and it felt like he'd never left this spot.

The next day, when he heard his emergency ringtone go off, he thought everything was over. And in a way it was, because some bastards attacked Jen and her husband in an alley near their flat.

By the time he reached the crime scene, Jen and her baby were already gone. Her husband had been moved to the hospital with a head injury and her registry database was wiped clean. Not a trace of the evidence she had been collecting was anywhere to be found.

32

Kimi
Present day
Our dreams are often too large for reality to ever match up.

A transplant counselor had said that to Kimi after her surgery.

It was a lie.

Life was more spectacular than Kimi could ever have imagined.

Lying in Rahul's arms was so much more than all the dreaming she'd done about it. It was like being inside an explosion of him. She was lost, drenched in the intensity of his scent and heat and sound. The memories of him flooding her on the inside, the reality of him wrapped around her on the outside. His hands. Everywhere. They could be everywhere. Everything. Strong and tender and hot and resourceful.

And the talking.

Rahul, making words, real ones. No decoding grunts. No deciphering the look in his eyes, the tightness of his jaw. It was like coming home after years of being lost.

"Why are you grinning?" he asked, tracing a callused thumb up and down her spine. Her (ahem) bare spine. "And now you're grinning more."

"How do you know?"

"You smile with your entire body," he said.

She snuggled into him. Drunk. She was drunk on him.

He pulled her close. "How do you do it?" he whispered into her hair. "How are you not afraid that the joy will disappear?"

She breathed him in. "Because of you. I'm never afraid that you will disappear. Because you always come back." She had been a fool to forget, over and over. She wouldn't again. If anything went wrong, she would remember this, relive this moment, and use it as a beacon to find her way back to it.

He stiffened the tiniest bit. "Those were the last words you said to me before your cardiac arrest in the hospital."

"You came back for me," she said, remembering.

Without pulling away from her he turned on his side. She found herself facing the wall of his chest, lean and cut with tight, perfectly round nipples she wanted to touch. He pressed his lips to her forehead. "I'm sorry I left you that way that day. Not my proudest moment."

She didn't want him apologizing. She wanted no apologies between them. Not when they were fitted together like this. Two halves of a whole falling into place. Yes, it had hurt when he had left, but she understood now. "I sprung that on you. It still amazes me that you gave me that." She still couldn't believe she had just gone to him and asked him to have sex with her.

"I didn't give you anything, Kimi. Nothing that wasn't yours all along."

He tipped her chin up, his dark, dark eyes drinking her in. His hand fitted around her butt and pulled her in tighter. Her fingers reached up and tangled in his hair. Yes, he was hers. *Hers.*

She stretched up until their lips touched.

They kissed lazily. Taking their time, soaking up each other's admissions, spoken and unspoken, picking them from each other's lips, turning them into reality, and stashing them away as memories. He had this sound he made when he kissed, like he couldn't get close enough. It was a sound she wanted to tease out of him over and over. She wanted to rub it into her soul.

She had felt this same desperation when

she had gone looking for him that day. This needing.

"I remember now what happened." He pulled away and stroked her lower lip with his thumb. "Jen hurt herself, and I carried her up her stairs because she had glass in her foot. I had to pluck it out with tweezers. We were talking about you when she kissed my cheek. But it was just her way, it wasn't —"

"I know. I wasn't thinking clearly. I was so afraid of losing you, and when you left it felt like I had lost you. And I was so tired of being afraid and of having no control over what slipped through my fingers. I had to do something about it. I couldn't just sit there and wait for you to come back to me. So I came after you. I went to your *chowki* and they told me you were at the clinic."

He stroked her hair. He seemed to love to touch her hair, seemed a bit obsessed with it, and she was totally okay with that. "I'm sorry. But it really wasn't what it looked like."

She knew that. A part of her had known it then too. But between being sick, and having made love to him, and knowing the surgery might not work, everything had been tangled into snarls inside her.

"You thought I had done that to you, left

451

you and run into another woman's arms, and you were still happy to have me back. Why?"

"I don't know why. But right then, it was all I wanted. To see you once before I left." She nuzzled deeper into him. "Sometimes I don't know exactly how to navigate what I'm feeling. I don't know if what I'm feeling is real or right or how to go on around it. I feel several things about one thing and it's a vortex and I get stuck in it."

"Kimi," he said, although she wasn't done. "You know I think there's no one else like you, right? But that's not just you. Most people have no idea what to do with their feelings. Most don't even know that they don't know."

"So what you're saying is that I really am like everyone else!" She bit the finger he was tracing her lips with. "Seriously, though, I knew even when I was angry that my anger was misguided, and then I was angry about that, and all of it hurt more and more and I started walking home, because I needed to get away. After that all I remember is feeling lightheaded and then it was like a truck had driven over my chest and parked there."

His hand stilled on her lips. "I'm sorry," he said again, and this time he pushed away from her and sat up, and a prickle of panic ran down her spine.

She sat up and pressed her forehead into his back. "But see, I knew. Even when I woke up in the hospital I knew you'd be there. Through all the feeling lost and being too tired to know how to go on, you've always been my compass, Rahul."

He took her hand and tugged her up to standing. "And currently the compass is pointing toward the airport. Now that we know we were looking for your donor in the wrong place, we've got to go look in the right place." She knew that expression. Nothing would stop DCP Savant from getting to the bottom of the case.

They had a few hours before they had to head back to the airport. She had to get something straight first. She sat back on the bed and looked up at him with all the fierceness in her heart. "The heart attack would have happened anyway. It had nothing to do with me following you or with us making love. My heart was basically done. I'd been in congestive heart failure for two years. It wasn't your fault."

He didn't respond to that, but he bent down and kissed her again, with a touch more desperation than before.

"Maybe we don't need to know where my heart came from," she said, completely

surprising herself. "Maybe Papa is right —
if my donor wanted anonymity, maybe we
should respect their rights. Maybe that's
why he was calling Dr. Gokhale — because
he knew I'd drag you here after he went
through all this to protect the donor's
rights." Because Papa would never have lied
without good reason. Without a right reason.

"What about Asif Khan?" Rahul said so
gently that she knew he didn't agree with
her. "What about the person who aided
him? What about the person who put Nikhil
and Nikki through hell? What about Jen and
her baby?"

But what could that possibly have to do
with Papa lying to her about her transplant?
"Maybe I was wrong. What if Asif was only
messing with my head the way Papa said he
was? What if my heart has nothing to do
with Asif Khan?"

If Kimi knew anything she knew that she
could sense when something terrible was
coming. She pushed it away, this feeling that
rose inside her out of nowhere. The past
few hours had been idyllic. The idea of going back into the world where these secrets
waited to destroy everything made her want
to burrow back under the sheets. A madman's gun was pointed at her. Worse yet,
pointed at Rahul, because he was standing

in wait to get between that gun and her. She jumped out of bed, dragging the sheets with her, and wrapped her arms around him.

"Hey, it's going to be okay." He held her tight. "I'm here."

"Are you?" she wanted to ask. Suddenly, everything was shaky again. He had told her they weren't possible the last time she had laid herself bare in front of him.

I don't feel the same way about you.

She wanted to ask him how he felt now. But she couldn't. Her need to hold on was too strong, even if it was lies she was holding on to. Suddenly, that's how she felt about her heart too. She wasn't sure she wanted to know where it had come from. The truth didn't feel as important anymore. There's this desperation that takes over when you taste joy after waiting a lifetime for it, and it's a very powerful thing.

The last time Kimi had been on a plane going to Mumbai from Hong Kong, she had thought she was going home to Rahul. Unlike her flight into Hong Kong, she remembered everything about her flight back to Mumbai. She hadn't had a single doubt in her mind that he would be waiting for her with open arms.

Not quite how things had turned out.

Now here he was reaching across the armrest from the seat next to her, unable to stop touching her, fingers interlaced, his breath on her cheek as he spoke in her ear. It was all so normal that her entire being felt right with it. She kept wanting to kiss him. But they were in public. Still, when the flight attendant turned the lights down, Kimi reached out and touched his lips. He grabbed her and kissed her and kissed her as though he'd been waiting too.

"Is this normal?" she asked him, wanting to climb into his lap and keep on kissing him. "Is this healthy? This feeling of being obsessed with you. Like if I close my eyes you'll disappear."

He stiffened, all the heat in his eyes disappearing in a flash. He pulled away and sank back in his seat.

What? What had she said?

She placed a hand on his chest. It was the slightest movement, but he flinched. How could someone who had kissed her like that moments ago flinch at her touch? She was about to ask him what was wrong when his eyes softened again. He dropped a quick kiss on her lips — as much a peace offering as a plea for understanding. Their feelings and their silences had tangled up inside them for so long it was going to take time to sort through them, to learn to navigate them.

"A movie?" he asked, which translated to him not wanting to have that conversation. But he didn't withdraw from her, and that was everything.

A movie was exactly what they needed. It was such a part of *them.* They had watched a total of fifty-eight movies together over the years, some across a plastic curtain, some not. And that was not counting the fact that they had watched *The Great Escape* eight times. This was no mean feat, because for a long time Rahul hadn't wanted her to watch it.

But that title was so perfect, she had pushed and pushed. Prison escape movies were their favorite, naturally. And prisoner of war movies she especially loved, because the prisoners had done nothing to deserve being imprisoned, except be brave.

It is the sworn duty of all officers to try to escape.

It was her favorite line from the movie. It was her sworn duty to get out of her room, and she was perpetually digging tunnels and shoring them up. And when one tunnel didn't work she used another. The metaphors were delicious and she loved them.

"The escape ends in disaster," Rahul had warned her, ruining it for her before she'd ever watched it. She had still sobbed through that ending, as he'd known she would. Which is why he'd told her — to soften the blow. He'd been right. Somehow, knowing beforehand had made it less painful when the moment of truth came.

"But three escaped," she loved to say. Those felt exactly like her odds. Three in sixty-five.

"Let's watch *Tangled,*" she said as they went through the list of movies on the plane's entertainment system.

"A cartoon film?" he asked, incredulous.

"It's Rapunzel," she said. "But this Rapunzel is all happy and chirpy and her prince is a thief."

So they watched a magical princess take on the world after being locked up for an eternity, as a starry-eyed boy followed her around. Then it was time to take on reality again.

The huge teakwood Ganesh carved into Dr. Girija's front door beamed a welcome at them. For all the years Dr. Girija had been Kimi's doctor, she had never visited the doctor's home. Amazingly enough, this was exactly the kind of front door she would have expected to find.

"Kimaya, Rahul, how nice to see you!" Dr. Girija said, letting them in and looking only mildly surprised. If Kimi didn't know better she would have thought her doctor had been expecting them.

Dr. Girija had one of those doctor personalities that instantly put you at ease but never let you forget that you were sick. She seemed eager enough to answer questions, and yet you felt like you had no questions when you were around her.

Kimi had considered calling Papa and questioning him directly. Even after she'd had time to process the fact that he had lied, she couldn't go to him with an accusation. What would she even accuse him of? Each time she tried to think about why he might have lied, her mind hit a wall.

"We'll get to the bottom of it," Rahul had said on their drive to Dr. Girija's home. He had insisted that they not call Dr. Girija before they showed up at her door.

Naturally, he had made sure she was home by having someone stake out her location.

Kimi had pulled on one of Rahul's shirts before getting off the plane and tucked her hair into a baseball hat they bought at the airport. "Do you also want me to wear a fake mustache?" she had asked, making him smile. She was already so used to him smiling at her like that again, it was as if he had never stopped.

As soon as she settled into the sofa, Kimi pulled off the hat and untucked her ponytail so it swung down her back. She hated wearing hats or anything on her head. Something about the pressure made her head hurt.

"Girija Auntie, please don't bother with tea," she said because the doctor had rushed into the kitchen as soon as they arrived and she was supposedly making tea — although a maidservant was pottering about with her inside the kitchen.

Rahul held up his phone and tapped it.

Kimi glared at him. "What did you do?" she mouthed.

"Is your phone working, Kimi?" Girija asked, coming out of the kitchen. "I can't seem to get a signal on my cell phone and my landline is also dead." She picked up the remote and turned on the flat screen covering an entire wall. "At least the TV is working."

"I forgot my cell phone at home, sorry," Kimi said as an image of some bodies being carried into an ambulance flashed on the screen with the headline: "Still no arrests in Colaba Killings."

"All this violence in the city is terrible,"

Girija said directly to Rahul. "Did you know the two cops who died?"

"No." Rahul took a cup of tea from the tray a maid brought in and handed it to Kimi.

Wasn't Colaba where the safe house they were supposed to go to was located? Kimi tried to catch Rahul's eye, but he avoided her gaze and turned off the TV. Which probably meant these Colaba Killings had something to do with the safe house and he hadn't bothered to mention it to her.

He held up his cell phone. "Mine's working fine. Let me take a look." He took the phone from Girija's hands and pressed a few buttons and handed it back. "Don't know what's wrong with it. Try powering it off."

Girija gave him a tight smile and turned to Kimi. "Everything okay with you two?" She gave Kimi a wink. "Did you need a contraceptive prescription, then? Are congratulations in order?"

She had always been so nice to Kimi. She felt horrible being here. "Actually, I wanted to talk to you about something. I've been thinking about writing a book on my transplant experience. I was wondering if you would help me."

Girija's smile faltered for a second.

461

"That's a great idea, Kimaya. I'm happy to help."

She was about to sit down when Kimi said, "Thank you. Do you think the transplant surgeon would speak with me as well?"

Girija stood back up before her bottom touched the sofa. "Sure. Why not? I'll put a call in to Dr. Gokhale tomorrow. I'm sure he won't mind."

The cup of tea shook in Kimi's saucer and she put it down.

"So Dr. Gokhale was Kimi's transplant surgeon in Hong Kong?" Rahul said with impressive calm.

Girija looked from Kimi to Rahul and then at her watch. "Kimi knows Dr. Gokhale treated her. Listen, I'm late to pick up my daughter. Come to the office tomorrow and we can talk then."

"Sure," Rahul said, and Kimi stood. "Thanks so much for your help."

Then just as Girija was walking them to her front door he added, "Does Dr. Bhansal still fly in from New York to do surgeries at Lilavati?"

"What?" Girija stopped in her tracks.

"Dr. Bhansal — I've heard he's one of the best transplant surgeons in the world and that he consulted on Kimi's case."

"Who told you that?" A sheen of sweat

broke out across Girija's upper lip. "Listen," she said a little more aggressively. "As far as I know, Kimaya was taken to Hong Kong for her surgery and recovery. I'm just her cardiologist. You're going to have to call Dr. Gokhale for details. But I really have to go."

With that she pushed them out the door and pulled it shut.

33

Rahul
Present day

Rahul watched Kimi as she twisted her ponytail into a knot and turned her back to him. He put the hat on her head and tucked the stray strands into it, wanting to stroke the back of her neck, wanting to kiss that petal-soft skin.

She waited for his touch. But he couldn't. Not now, not when he knew what he knew. Not when she was struggling so hard to avoid what she wouldn't let herself see. Not when a killer was on the loose and he wasn't the only dangerous one.

He had to keep his focus.

He walked past her to the stairs and checked his phone.

"Did you jam Dr. Girija's cellular signal?" she asked.

He shrugged. He needed the doctor to not be able to use her phone for a little bit

464

longer, until he had made a phone call. But he couldn't do it in front of Kimi.

"We need to find Dr. Bhansal," she said.

"No point." He had no doubt Dr. Bhansal had performed the surgery here in Mumbai. There was only one person who would have all the answers, but Kimi wasn't ready to ask those questions, and he wasn't ready to pull the rug from beneath her feet yet.

He dialed Maney and took Kimi's hand, leading her down the stairs.

"They got into your flat in the police housing," Maney said as soon as he heard Rahul's voice. "But we captured two of his men. Alive. One of them's close to singing. And, boss, you can't go back to your mother's place."

"I know. I'll find something. Make sure they don't get anywhere near the *chawl*." Rage shook inside him. "And cover The Mansion. No one leaves or enters. I mean absolutely no one."

"Got it, boss. The bastard has pulled out all the stops. He's hardly got any men left, but he's lost his head. Shooting at the police housing means he doesn't care what happens anymore. He just wants you and Kimi Ma'am. Although I don't think he knows you're together. Don't trust anyone."

"Got it. And, Shankar, thank you."

They got into the car. They needed to find somewhere safe where he could decide how to confirm what he suspected.

Kimi had been watching him in silence, her color high. She pulled the hat off her head. "Tell me everyone in your building is okay."

"They're fine."

"Call your *aie* and make sure." It was an order. All the softness was gone from her.

"That will only worry her."

"You can't hide information from people to protect them, Rahul."

There it was. He'd known this was coming since those images had flashed across Dr. Girija's TV screen.

"Are you going to tell me or do I have to ask?"

When he didn't respond, she stopped trying to rein in her temper. "Those deaths in Colaba — were they at the safe house? And you knew, didn't you?"

"Listen, Kimi, I didn't get a chance to tell you, that's all." It wasn't like he had purposely hidden it from her. It wasn't like her knowing would have helped anything.

Naturally, that's not how she saw it. "Someone got killed because Asif's men thought they were shooting at me, and you thought I didn't need to know? You promised not to lie to me, Rahul!"

"And I didn't."

"Withholding information is the same as lying."

No, it wasn't. Things were seldom that simple. "We don't have time for this, Kimi. Do you know anybody who lives around here that we can go to?"

"We're in Juhu, right? Didn't Nikhil say we could get into his cousin's flat if we needed to?"

Bingo. He could kiss her.

Well, duh — as she would say. He called Nikhil, and Nikhil sent him instructions for how to get into his cousin's apartment.

This cousin was apparently a big film star, and the apartment was even more white and pristine than Kimi's bedroom had been when she was isolated. Except there were huge painted canvases all over the place that Kimi couldn't stop staring at.

"They're a bit dark," he said.

"It's no secret that I find dark and broody irresistible. God help me," she said and then, "I'm going to go freshen up." She looked so angry at herself, so frustrated with him, he went to her.

"Kimi."

She turned on him. "What?"

"Nothing."

She walked away from him, no sign of fatigue in her step, and he knew she was having a good day, health-wise. The rest was just courage. Everything she believed about her heart had changed overnight. Everything she believed about the person she loved most in the world was about to change too. It was happening again. He had reached for what he wanted. And disaster was about to follow.

He went out onto the balcony and shut the French doors behind him.

"You asked me to call you when I was alone. I am now. Kimi isn't here."

"You have to tell me where you are, son."

He flinched at the word he had heard come out of Kirit Patil's mouth so many times. The way he said the word *son* mapped their relationship. A burden, a lifeline. A master, a mentor.

And now, a cop and a criminal.

"We're safe. Why did you tell everyone that Kimi's transplant surgery took place in Hong Kong? Why did you lie about it?"

There was no more than a single beat of silence. The minister was good. Very good.

"What are you talking about? Of course her surgery happened in Hong Kong. Why would you accuse me of such a thing?"

"We went to Hong Kong." But Kirit

already knew that. He had called Dr. Gokhale. Called Dr. Girija. It was obvious from Dr. Girija's behavior today that Kirit had called her and warned her they were coming and asked her to stick with the lies.

"You had direct orders not to leave the country. You are forgetting your place, Rahul."

"No, sir, I think I'm finally remembering my place."

Another beat of silence. Kirit used it to completely alter his tone. "Listen, son, we aren't on different sides here. You have to know that."

"It's a pretty elaborate lie to tell. All the records have been falsified." And that was the least of it. How was Kimi going to get through this?

"Listen to me. There's no foul play. All I was doing was trying to keep this out of the media. The plan really was to take her to Hong Kong. We had a brain-dead donor there. But then the donor heart collapsed and we were back where we started. And Kimi had no time left.

"Then a donor became available here. But if we had made that public, the media would've camped outside the hospital. On top of everything we were going through I couldn't handle the media scrutiny. Do you remember how that *Times* journalist was on my case about how much money I was spending on Kimi's treatment? I was a Bollywood star, for hell's sake; did they think I'm a pauper? Not to mention the fact that my ancestors left behind a thousand acres of sugarcane plantations. Just because every politician in this country fucks his motherland to be paid like a whore doesn't mean I do it too. I've never stolen a penny that wasn't mine."

"Money isn't the only thing one can steal." Kirit was good, but suddenly Rahul could see every nuance of every lie. It was like turning on a light and having it flood the darkest corners.

"Listen, Rahul, you don't know anything about this. This isn't something we should be discussing over the phone. I'll come and see you. Tell me where you are."

"You know that's not possible. You'll lead him straight to her."

"I know you'll do anything for Kimi. I know she pushed you into this wild-goose chase. Just wait until we've talked. Don't do anything foolish. She's been through enough."

"She has a right to know."

"No!" For the first time there was a note of panic in Kirit's voice. "You can't tell her.

Not now. Not when she has a chance. She's alive. She can walk down the street. Isn't that enough for you? What are you trying to do, impress her? Why? You're leading her on. You know what you're thinking is never going to work. You can never be more than friends."

"What is more than being friends?"

"Don't play games with me, Rahul. You gave me your word."

"I was nineteen years old, and you had no right to extract that promise." That promise had cost Rahul too much already. "And I think you should know that I broke my word a long time ago."

You will never touch her as anything more than a friend.

Instead of getting angrier, Kirit's voice got calmer. "You're right. I was wrong to extract that promise. Forget everything I said about the differences between us. I know she won't marry anyone else anyway. You two deserve to be together. I was wrong. You don't have to worry about a thing. I'll convince her mother. Just don't say anything to her until we've talked."

Was the man mad? Kimi would never forgive him if he lied about this. But how was he ever going to tell her? All he knew was that he was done lying to her. Lying about his feelings, lying about what she had to know, what she already suspected but couldn't wrap her head around. Even when she didn't know the half of it.

"You can't leave The Mansion. The officers posted outside will arrest you if you try. And, sir, that's an order."

After hanging up he checked on Kimi. She was still not out of the shower, so he went back out to the balcony and called Maney and recorded his voice. Then he dialed Nikki's number. It was time.

He had already texted Nikhil and Nikki, and they were waiting for his call even though it was barely morning in America. "Nikki, you remember how you said you would recognize the voice of the person who sent you after Nic?"

"Of course I'd recognize him. I'd recognize him in my sleep."

"I need a favor. Is Nikhil close by?"

"I'm here," Nikhil said. "You're on speaker. What's up?"

"I have a couple recordings I need you to hear. Do you think you could tell me if one of those voices is his?"

"Do you need to even ask? Of course," Nikki said.

"Nikhil?"

"It's her call, man."

Rahul needed to be completely certain about this. So, he had recorded Maney and also another constable.

He played Maney's recording first. "Tell me where you are," Maney said.

"Not him," Nikki said, sounding disappointed enough that Rahul didn't need to ask again.

He did it anyway. "You sure?"

"She's not dignifying that with an answer," Nikhil said with a smile in his voice, of all things. Nikhil was a handsy guy. Rahul could only imagine all the rubbing and soothing going on.

"Okay, next one." He played Kirit's recording.

"Tell me where you are," Kirit said. It was an order. Not a shred of doubt in his voice that Rahul would do his bidding.

Doesn't the dog leash get too tight? Mohit had asked him.

There was a gasp on the phone. Then silence.

"That's him," Nikhil said.

"Nikki?" Rahul had to be sure.

"Yes," she said with a tremor in her voice that he felt crawl up his spine. How could it be that Kirit could inspire such terror in a woman this strong? What had he done to her?

"I'm sorry, but I have to ask. Can you listen to it one more time?"

"I'll listen to it as many times as you want. It's him."

"It's him," she repeated three times after that, and then Rahul stopped replaying it.

"I'm sorry," he said. "And thank you."

"Who is it?" she asked with the tone of someone gathering up all her reserves.

"Can't tell you yet. But I will very soon. Stay where you are. You're safe there."

"Thanks," Nikki said. "How's Kimi?"

"Fine," he said, knowing what a gigantic lie that was about to become.

He heard the gentlest knock on the glass behind him and turned. Her hair was wet, her cheeks pink from the heat of the shower. She was wearing a T-shirt that said MAD IN MUMBAI and shorts that showed off her spectacular legs. Legs he shouldn't notice right now. She slid the door open and stepped outside, the ocean breeze flooding with her smell. She sat down next to him and sidled into him until he wrapped an arm around her and pulled her close. As soon as he did it, she swung her legs over his, so he lifted her up into his lap and she placed her head on his shoulder.

She filled him up. Always had. It didn't matter how he labeled it. Love, friendship

— with her it had never been two different things. Him and her — they had never been different either. If they had, all the destruction around them would have separated them. But it hadn't.

He had thought giving in to his feelings and reaching for her somehow had the power to create disaster. But their feelings, their oneness, that's what had the power to shield them through the disasters. Kimi was right — the disasters would have happened anyway. But without each other, they would never have been able to get through them.

Kirit had recognized the connection. He had used it, used Rahul's own misinterpretation of it. That promise he'd extracted from Rahul had been manipulation of the worst kind. He had fanned Rahul's belief that anyone he allowed himself to love too much was destined for destruction. And Rahul had bought into it completely.

Now here they were again, at the threshold of Kimi's life being destroyed again. It didn't feel uncanny anymore. Instead of blaming himself and wanting to leave so she might be safe, he knew the only way they could get through it was together.

Her eyes were closed. Her breath was steady against his chest. If he didn't know her better he'd have thought she had fallen asleep. But her body was awake, alert with possessiveness and loose with trust.

He felt a rush of protectiveness so violent, he would've done anything to shield her from the truth. Her pride in her father's strength, his integrity, was the cornerstone of her existence. But she was more than just that. She could swallow pain and digest it until it disappeared like it never existed.

"I don't want any more lies between us," she said without opening her eyes.

"I've only told you one lie," he said. "And you never believed it anyway."

She looked up at him, and his phone buzzed.

"Yes, Maney?"

"Who's Maney?" a guttural voice said, and Kimi jumped off Rahul's lap as he stood. "Is that the bastard I had to shoot to get this phone from him?"

"Where's Maney? If you've hurt him —"

"Right now I would worry about your brother, not about some cop."

Rahul thought he was going to be sick. "Where's Mohit?"

"He's your brother, DCP Savant. You tell me where he is."

Kimi was already out the front door with Rahul following close, the phone squeezed to his ear. "He's done nothing to you, Asif.

Your grudge is with me. Tell me where to meet you." He held Kimi's arm. She wasn't going anywhere.

"*Arrey wah,* a smart police officer. Are we in a Hindi film or what?"

"Where do you want me to meet you?" He shook his head at Kimi. She needed to stay right here where it was safe.

"I'm in your home. You have twenty minutes to get here. Oh, and bring the esteemed chief minister's daughter with you or you won't see your brother or anyone else who lives in this shithole alive. At twenty-one minutes, if I don't see her, I start shooting." One click and the line went silent.

"You're not going," Rahul said as she slammed the elevator button.

"I heard him. I am. We don't have time to figure this out." She stepped into the elevator.

He didn't move. He was not taking her with him.

She grabbed him and pulled him in. "Making it from Juhu to Bandra in this traffic in twenty minutes is going to be near impossible. We don't have time for this. We'll figure it out in the car."

They ran to the car. Rahul sat on the horn and drove like he had never driven before.

He called for backup. Not hearing Maney's voice at the other end of the line turned his rage nuclear. But Maney's second in command sounded calm and in control. "Maney-sir is in surgery. He should be fine. The bullet hit his stomach."

"Stay in the outer perimeter of the *chawl* compound. And wait for my signal." They screeched into the playground he'd grown up on with exactly two minutes to spare. If Asif Khan spilled a single drop of blood here, Rahul would never forgive himself.

Groups of children were playing on the ground. A smattering of the regulars was hanging around on the upper and lower verandas looking unconcerned. How had Asif made it into his block without anyone knowing? Kimi pointed her chin at his block, and he caught a man in a white kurta he'd never seen before leaning on the railing outside his front door. The man gave him a little wave and lifted the scarf over his hand to flash a handgun. He pointed at Kimi inside the car, tapped his watch, and beckoned them up.

No. He was not taking Kimi into a shootout with him. "Drive to the police chowki and wait for me there."

"Don't be crazy, Rahul. Mohit is in there.

Your aie might be in there. I'm coming with you."

That was not going to happen. "We don't have time for this, Kimi, you're not —"

A man tapped on Kimi's window and repeated the move. Flashing a pistol under a scarf wrapped around his arm, he directed Kimi to get out.

"We have no choice," Kimi whispered and unlocked her door.

Rahul ran around to her side. God, if it turned out fine, he was never letting her go. And he'd be the best bloody brother in the world to Mohit. Just let him be unharmed. Please.

The man pushed the scarf covered gun into Kimi's back and held out his hand for Rahul's pistol, grinning at them with tobacco stained teeth. Rahul slipped him his gun, and the bastard tucked both guns into his jeans and followed them up the stairs.

Rahul swept the area. There seemed to be only two men out here. If Asif was the only one inside the block with Mohit, he could do this.

The grandpa on the corner block asked how Rahul was, and Rahul stopped and answered him, keeping his tone normal. This was the time when the *kakus* and his *aie* usually collected in one of the blocks to

479

make sweets and savories for their catering orders. This meant that his *aie* wasn't at home. Thank God.

Kimi smiled at the grandpa, completely calm and composed. No sign of panic. He wanted to push her into one of the blocks where she'd be safe, but Asif's goon was following close. He led them into Rahul's home, shut the door behind him, and frisked Rahul for any more weapons.

The madman he had shot only a few months ago sat in Baba's chair. His baby brother was kneeling at his feet, his hands bound up behind him with duct tape. But his eyes shone with calm, with that arrogance that had brightened his eyes even as a baby and as a toddler every time he leapt into Rahul's arms.

"Perfect timing," Asif said and tapped his gun on Mohit's forehead.

Rahul met the bastard's eyes. "I'm here. Let him go."

Mohit looked at him. Rahul couldn't remember the last time they had looked at each other eye-to-eye, as though the other were precious. Loved.

I got you.

I know.

"Do you know who told me where to find him?" Asif asked through a mouth full of

480

tobacco.

Rahul didn't care. "What do you want?"

"Do you know I can't move my right arm? I can't take a piss?" He patted his right side with his left arm. "I pee into a fucking bag!" He shouted that last part.

Neither Kimi nor Mohit flinched, and Rahul felt such raw pride he knew he was going to tear this bastard limb from limb to get them out of here.

"So let them go and you can blow my bladder out."

"*Arrey wah,* what a big hero you are, huh?"

Mohit caught Rahul's eye, threw a glance at Kimi, then at their *baba*'s chair — the one Asif was sitting on.

It was three against three. Two men behind Kimi and him, and Asif next to Mohit.

"So what, your plan is to shoot the three of us in my home and walk out of here? What will that get you?"

"Revenge."

"True. But the *chawl* is surrounded by officers, and unlike you they are armed with automatics. You're not leaving here alive, unless you let these two go."

"There are no officers outside." But Asif threw a look over Rahul's shoulder at the same time Mohit threw a look at Baba's chair and made a quick flipping motion with his chin.

"If you don't believe me, go ahead and shoot. Otherwise send these two out and you can walk out of here with your gun held to my head. I'll call off the officers."

"I said, there are no officers," Asif repeated, and his gun shook in his hand as his agitation rose. Leaving the hospital hadn't been the fucker's brightest idea.

Kimi let out a pained gasp, and Rahul turned to see her clutch her heart and collapse right there in the middle of the doorway between the outside room and the kitchen.

It threw the two men off for two seconds, which was enough time for Rahul to lunge at them, turn their guns on them and fire, just as Mohit rammed his body into Baba's chair and flipped it over. Rahul emptied what was left of the bullets into the psycho's head as Mohit rolled away into a ball.

34

Kimi
Present day

"You're bleeding," Kimi said, looking at Rahul's shoulder.

He ignored her and looked at her monitor. "Your numbers still normal?"

She hated being in a hospital bed with electrodes stuck to her chest, especially since she really was fine and all of this was just a precaution. She had only pretended to collapse. It had been the only thing she could think of to cause a distraction. Rahul and Mohit had used it perfectly, moving with the precision of machines. That cop DNA had to be a real thing.

Naturally, Rahul had insisted she come to the hospital and have everything checked out. They had to bring Mohit in anyway. He had flipped Asif's chair with such force he had dislocated his shoulder and hit his head badly enough to need stitches. They were fitting him for a sling in the next room. Rahul had been going back and forth, switching off between the two rooms with his *aie,* who had been so calm and loving in the face of all the madness that Kimi wanted to beg her to sit by her so she could snuggle into her. The thought made her crave her own mother. Something that she hadn't done in nearly a decade.

She had tried to call her mother as soon as Rahul reconnected her phone. But neither of her parents was answering their phone.

Rahul looked as guilty as ever. As though he and not Asif Khan were responsible for everything. But he was here, still reaching for her hand every few minutes, leaving her only to go look in on Mohit. He had held Mohit so long and hard after he emptied the contents of that gun into Asif that he might have done even more damage to that dislocated shoulder.

"That was fantastic. Really stupid, but fantastic," he kept saying. And then, "I'm proud of you. So proud of you." And "I'm sorry. So sorry." It was that last part that had made Mohit break down.

It had been Rahul the way he used to be with her, the way he had only been recently when he forgot to be distant. The way he was being now, his heart in his eyes as he watched her. Mohit had obviously never seen him that way, and he had sobbed like a little boy and forgotten to say nasty things. He had, in fact, been entirely speechless in the face of Rahul's big, burly affection.

"Rahul, can we have someone look at that shoulder, please?" Kimi said.

"It's not my blood. It's Asif's." Rahul had shot the man at close range. No chances this time. No pieces of his head left intact.

She stood, dragging all the tubes and wires with her, and yanked his arm.

He winced.

"I can tell when you're hurt, okay?" she said.

He looked down at his shoulder, plucked a few tissues out of a box, and pressed them into the cut. "It doesn't matter. It's just a scratch. One of the ricocheting bullets must have nicked me." He pushed her back into the bed and sat down next to her. "I have something to tell you."

"I don't want to hear anything until a doctor looks at your shoulder."

"Kimi, please. It's time to listen. We have to talk now before I go and take care of it." His dark as tar eyes were soft with understanding, and she knew things were even worse than she could imagine.

He studied her, trying to decide what to say. How much to say. Trying to manage this for her. She'd had enough of people managing things for her. No more.

It was time for her to stop acting like she was made of glass. Papa had lied about her surgery. Asif Khan had run a black-market organ ring. She wasn't stupid. "How bad is it?"

He looked like she felt, as though someone were squeezing him between plates of glass that were about to shatter. "I'm going to have to make an arrest in Jen's murder case."

"But you killed Asif Khan. You got her murderer. Who else is there to arrest?"

He took her hand. Suddenly, she didn't want to be touched. Didn't want him looking at her this way. Didn't want to hear what he had to say.

"Your heart — you were right to think that your heart had something to do with why Asif was after you."

She tried to pull her hand away. He didn't let it go. Every single time she'd had a bad diagnosis, somewhere in her heart she'd known what was coming. It was that gauge inside that signaled impending disaster. It was going mad right now. And Rahul's face reflecting all the panic she was feeling only

486

made it worse.

"You already know that Asif was stealing organs from people on Jen's registry," he said gently.

She didn't look away, but she could barely stay upright.

"This is what I've put together. We'll have to confirm the details."

"Just tell me, Rahul." If he'd put it together, there was no chance in hell that he'd gotten it wrong.

"When they couldn't find you a donor, Kirit-sir somehow found out about Asif and went to him to procure a heart for you. Jen was on the organ registry too. Asif had access to the registry and found out that Jen was a match for you. He had her killed so you could have her heart."

She felt numb. Tears started streaming down her face, but her eyes felt dry.

The image of Jen in Rahul's arms kissing him filled her head and squeezed the breath from her lungs. She had felt such choking anger and hate.

"I'm sorry," he said uselessly, as though all his bloody apologies ever fixed anything.

This time she yanked her hand away with enough force that he let it go. "Why is everything your fault, Rahul? Are you God? Do you make people pay for organs, do you make them kill people for you?"

"Kimi." He reached for her again, but she got off the bed. She wanted to rip off the wires and tubes, but she couldn't make herself do it. She never disobeyed doctor's orders. She had sworn never to. And now that she knew Jen had died so she could keep on living, how could she do anything to put it at risk? This heart that was snatched in the middle of a vibrant life, this heart that was a symbol of the cruelty in her genes.

"Have they arrested him yet?" Suddenly, she was scared. "Do you know where he is?"

"He's at home. He can't leave."

"Will you be the one to take him in? Please."

He didn't move. He sat there as though he understood what she was feeling, as though he knew he could never understand. "There's more," he said.

What more could there possibly be?

"The person who threatened Nikki and sent her after Nikhil. That was him too."

No.

He tried to take her in his arms. She pushed him away with all the violence gathering inside. "Don't touch me, please."

"Kimi, please. None of this is your fault."

How could she not laugh at that? "Really?"

she wanted to say. "Would any of this have happened if it weren't for me?" But she could barely breathe, let alone make words.

"Let me help you," he said again, trying to hold her, but she pushed him away again.

"Help me how? Will you let him go? Will you let him get away with it?"

"Is that what you want me to do?"

She couldn't look at him, couldn't see if he would do that for her. More mayhem in her name.

"Of course not," she said, when what she wanted to say was, "What about me? I'm a criminal too. I took the heart."

For the rest of their lives, she would be a constant reminder to him of a dead friend, of a heinous crime. He was right in thinking that love wasn't worth it. That it always ended in loss and pain. That the price of getting what you wanted was always too high.

"I want you to go," she said. "I want you to be the one to arrest him. Will you make sure no one hurts him?"

He nodded. "I owe him that much," he said before he walked out of her room.

She ran to the door and called after him, making him turn around. "You owe him nothing, Rahul."

He didn't respond.

"But you will make sure he's safe? Please."
"I promise." And then he was gone.

35

Rahul would be here soon. Kirit took the gun out of the drawer and called his wife.

As expected, he got her voice mail. A mechanical voice telling him she was not available. Even now at the very end, she remained unavailable. "Attachment is the heart of all suffering," she loved to say. Every conversation with her was a reminder of that little ditty of hers.

"This isn't an apology," he said into the phone. "But I did want to tell you that I loved you once and thank you for giving me the most beautiful thing in my life. My regret is that I have to leave her in the hands of the parent who doesn't know how to be a parent anymore. If she ever needs you, try to be there for her. I doubt she will. We've both learned how to live without you. She loves that boy, and I'm giving them my blessings. As long as you don't stand in their way, I have left you well taken care of. Use the money how you will. Go on and spend all of it on your gurus, who tell you to choke your ability to live until it is all gone, if you must. But let Kimi give life a chance."

He hadn't expected saying good-bye to her to hurt like this. But life was full of surprises. He hadn't expected any of this. Amazingly enough, the biggest problem with sugarcane farming was the husk waste. Sugarcane, like life, made you pay in tons of unsavory, unusable husk for a bowlful of sugar. Once that husk started to decay, the smell of that thing could burn your nose hairs.

And yet, the bowlful of sugar was worth it. Just like his Kimi. His only regret was that he wouldn't be able to say good-bye to her.

As expected there was a knock on the door. Kirit picked up the gun and held it to his head. "On time as usual, DCP Savant," he said as Rahul walked in and froze, his tall, proud form taking in the situation with deadly calm. It was a strange time to feel pride in this boy who had never really been a boy. He'd been more of a man than most men, even when he was a boy.

"Please put the gun down, sir," he said in

that even negotiator's voice.

"Have you told Kimi?"

"You can tell her yourself. Please put the gun down."

Kirit couldn't help it, he laughed. "You want me to tell her? I thought you loved the girl. How are you okay with what it will do to her?"

To his credit, the boy looked utterly destroyed.

"She's capable of handling more than we give her credit for," he said. "But you can't do this to her. You can't leave her with a dead father on top of everything else she has to handle." He took a step closer, and Kirit released the safety.

"Don't come any closer or I won't get to say what I need to say. What I need you to understand and explain to Kimi."

"Fine. I'm listening. But please take your finger off the trigger."

Kirit left his finger where it was. "Did you know I was an orphan?"

Rahul shook his head.

"My parents died when I was two. My uncle was forced to take me in. But I barely ever saw him. My nanny was my only source of affection, and I decided that she was my mother. At eight, I insisted that she take me to her home. It took one trip to the servants' quarters for me to know definitively that she was not my mother. That I had been lying to myself. Her three children argued constantly. They made no effort to be nice. She smacked them when they misbehaved but there was nothing hateful about it. What I saw in their home that day, it was like nothing I had ever seen before. I spent my entire childhood seeking it out — this thing that made families families. The ownership and the ability to be filterless and your very worst and best at the same time. I wanted it more than anything else.

"What attracted me to Rupa was that she shared my yearning. We were on a film set with some children, and she wanted to play with the children all day. She was such a mother even before being a mother. Her first movie was a super hit. She was set to be a star. But when I offered her a family, she jumped at it. I told her then that my wife would not work. That our children would have to come before everything else. She agreed. No hesitation. It's what she wanted too. When she got pregnant that first time, I thought the sheer volume of my happiness would kill me. But we couldn't keep the babies. Three boys and four girls we lost before my Kimaya stayed.

"Ten years — that's all we got. For ten

years I had a family. Because Rupa went through all that pain. I promised her that I would never let it be in vain. That our family would never break apart. Kimi turned us into a family. She became our life. I would have done anything. I would have cut out my own heart if it meant we got to keep Kimi."

"Jen was pregnant too. Did you know that?" Rahul said, as though everything Kirit had said meant nothing. "Her husband and she were also going to start a family."

"It doesn't matter, Rahul. It couldn't matter. How dare you not understand? You, who knows Kimi. Knows what she is. Could you let her go? Would you let her go if you had a choice to keep her?"

He was about to answer. But Kirit couldn't let him deny it. He swung the gun between them. "Don't lie. I've asked you to let her go. I've told you how dangerous this connection between you two is. You can never keep her happy. Not because she's a princess and you're barely a step above a beggar, but because you could never bear the pain of living with loss hanging over your head. Your cowardice would kill her spirit. If I had let her die when I was offered a solution, what would your life have been? And she *would* have died. We had come to the end of the road. I was offered a bridge and I took it."

"What you were offered was the chance to steal another human being's heart. You made the decision to let another person die, so someone you love could live."

"It wasn't like that. Asif tricked me so he could blackmail me. I thought I was paying to get to the top of a list of recipients. I didn't know he would kill someone."

"So it was okay to let other people on the list die?"

"Judge me all you will. But you know you would have done the same thing." Kirit's finger tightened on the trigger.

"I don't know, sir," Rahul said, not moving a muscle. "But Kimi has to live with the knowledge that her life comes from someone's death. And now you want her to live with the additional burden of knowing it made you take your own life. After how hard she's fought for you. You're the coward here." He took a step closer. "I lied earlier. Kimi already knows it was you. And her only response was that I don't let anyone hurt you. She won't be able to live with what you're about to do. You know that."

Kimi knew? The entire burden of the pain he had caused her descended upon him, making the gun feel too heavy in his hand.

"You said yourself I know her. I do know her. Kimi believes you always do the right thing. She understands your motivations better than anybody. All the things you just told me. When you tell her she'll understand. If you turn yourself in and take your punishment, she has only your crime to deal with. She might still forgive you. Don't take that choice away from her. Please. You've already taken too many choices away."

Rahul's form got blurry as Kirit's eyes filled with tears. His baby girl. He'd never asked her what she wanted. And she'd never complained.

"Her life has just started. Don't end any chance she has at happiness this way."

The gun trembled in Kirit's hand.

"Put the gun down."

He tried, but he couldn't pull the trigger. Kimi really was just starting out. He couldn't take her lease on life away from her.

It was the hardest thing he had ever done. Harder even than reading the last rites for seven babies. He put the gun down.

Rahul was on the gun in a second. He popped out the magazine, pulled out a pair of handcuffs, and called to the officers who were standing outside.

Five officers stormed into Kirit's office,

497

guns drawn. Rahul handed the handcuffs to another officer and left the room.

The officer turned Kirit around. "You are under arrest for abetment in a criminal offense and intentionally participating in a criminal activity." The click of the handcuffs was louder than he had expected.

"I release you from your promise," Kirit said to no one in particular.

Rahul was exactly the kind of man his Kimi deserved.

36

Kimi
Present day

Kimi used to think Rahul's apologies were complicated things. That showed how much more she had left to learn about life.

In the span of these past few weeks, she'd heard enough apologies to last her a lifetime, and they had all twisted and untwisted the braid of her life.

First, her mother had rushed back from Kashi. Her mother had never rushed back from anything, ever. No matter what. And she'd been in a panic. Mamma's worry had been such a part of Kimi's life once. Long ago before Kimi had lost her freedom to one room in her home, and her mother to another. But the worry had felt like an old friend, instantly worming its way into Kimi's heart again.

"I'm sorry, *beta,* so very sorry," she had said, rushing into Kimi's hospital room and wrapping Kimi in a hug that still smelled the same. "I was sitting on the banks of the Ganga when I saw your face in Mother Ganga. You were calling out to me. 'Mamma!' It was so clear. Like a mirror, like you were right there, but not you now, you at every age as one. And I saw my *baba*. Smiling at me after all these years of anger.

"Your grandfather had been so angry at Kirit and me. He thought we had lost our balance in our quest to become parents. He wanted us to listen to the universe. His belief was that if we pushed the universe too hard, it would push back. He died three months after you were conceived. He was perfectly healthy. Then one day he didn't wake up. No doctor could explain why his healthy heart stopped. But the week before that he had told me that if God took him so Kirit and I could end our penance, he'd gladly go.

"I saw him on Mother Ganga and he smiled at you, and I knew, just knew, that we had finished paying the price now. And then your father called, and it was a miracle. Here I had my vision, and there I heard his voice on my phone telling me you needed me."

Were you a prisoner of your parents' thinking?

Kimi sure hoped not.

She wanted to care for her mother's great epiphany. But everything was blurry and slow. Even more than it had been after her surgeries and transfusions and treatments. She was glad Mamma was back, because seeing Papa handcuffed and behind bars was not something she could have done by herself no matter how numb she was.

Rahul had been by her side, incessantly, every step of the way, but she couldn't bear his presence. It made the heaviness worse. With her parents, with the bail and bonds and lawyers and paperwork, she could distract herself by doing things. One look at Rahul, and she wanted to collapse into herself.

"Don't do this, Kimi," his lips kept saying. "Let me in," his eyes kept saying.

Ironic? Yes.

But that's the way it was.

She resigned from her job, gave Rambo to Rumi, then plucked all her dream stories from her cubicle wall, and brought them back home and tucked them away.

Then there was her father's apology. Her father apologized and apologized. She heard every one of his excuses from across a table in a jail visiting room. Everything from how his uncle had locked him up in his nursery

501

for crying, to his vow to her mother that she would not lose another child. But she could see them as no more than excuses.

Would she have done the same? It was a question that was asked over and over again by the press to panels of experts. Apparently, the public wasn't quite as judgmental about a father going to the black market to save his daughter as one would have expected. The TV was rife with arguments about moral-ethical dilemmas, but it wasn't quite the one-sided stoning one would expect either.

All she knew was that if this is what love was, an excuse to justify murder, she didn't want any part of it. Not from her parents and not from Rahul, no matter the pain that flashed in his eyes every time he looked at her.

"None of this is your fault," Nikki said to Kimi, handing her a cup of chai.

Kimi still couldn't believe she was sitting in Nikki and Nikhil's living room, drinking chai with Nikki.

How Kimi had made her way to Nikki and Nikhil's flat after they returned from Chicago, she would never know. But it had been her turn to apologize, and she had to.

They hadn't turned her away. Hadn't turned her apology away. Hadn't turned her gift to Joy away.

She had found the perfect little Lhasa Apso for Joy, and Joy was very much in love.

"Why don't you hate me?" she asked Nikki, because Nikki was the kind of person of whom you could ask something like that. Nikhil had taken a little more time to adjust to the fact that his dead wife's heart actually beat inside Kimi and that he had lost Jen because of Kimi. He hadn't been mean, just shaken. But then he had come around with his signature kindness.

"Because you weren't responsible. You didn't even know. You have to stop punishing yourself. Maybe even stop punishing Rahul?"

She ignored the mention of Rahul the way she always did these days. "Can I ask you a horribly personal question? You don't have to answer."

Nikki nodded.

"Is that how being a parent feels? Would you do that for Joy? Kill for him?"

Nikki put her chai down and threw a glance at Joy and Nikhil playing with the puppy. "I did some pretty horrible things when Joy was under threat. I thought I would have done anything to keep him safe. But in the end I couldn't go through with it. I had to find a way to not destroy Nikhil's life again."

Kimi watched Joy. Nikhil was trying to teach him how to get Lucky to fetch a ball. The puppy would not let the ball go, no matter how much Nikhil begged. But the moment Joy put out his hand, Lucky dropped the ball into it. It made Joy roll over with laughter and that made Nikhil double over too, and try over and over again.

There was so much love there, so much life. Maybe love wasn't what had turned her father into a monster. Maybe it was his choices. Maybe it was his inability to accept loss as her grandfather had known all those years ago. That wasn't love, that was just who Papa was, who he had allowed himself to become.

Nikki looked away from Nikhil and Joy and met Kimi's gaze. "To answer your question, no, I don't think I would cause the death of another human being so Joy could live."

"Thank you," she said and hugged Nikki. For the first time in a month, she felt like she could breathe, think, feel.

"And thank you," Nikki said.

Kimi had donated ungodly sums of her father's money to help Nikki set up a network of safe houses for victims of sexual abuse and human trafficking that Nikki had dreamed of opening. Kimi had introduced her to a hotshot Bollywood director's wife who had also been working on a similar project.

Kimi was doing a story on the project. Her first real story. Until this moment, she hadn't cared if it ever got published. But now she knew she would find a way to get someone to publish it. It was a hopeful thought, and it felt surprisingly good inside her. Even more surprising was the need to share the hope the moment it returned. And there was only one person she wanted to share it with.

37

Rahul
Present day
Rahul was going to miss the ocean. He was going to miss Mumbai, Bandra, the *chawl,* The Mansion, this rock. All of it was home. Well, all of it used to be home.

Without Kimi none of it was.

It had been a week since he'd seen her.

He had tried to help her with the paperwork for Kirit Patil's arrest. She'd been composed, but there was no peace in her calmness. She had been numb and distraught and distant. Inside herself.

She had shut him out. This time for real.

"Why don't you tell her how you feel?" Mohit had asked him that morning. They had taken to going for a run every morning. Physical exertion was something they both enjoyed. He had learned that his brother had stopped playing cricket in elementary school. Around the time he had bought him

506

the bat and then forgotten that he needed a big brother. He couldn't turn back time, but he could give Mohit an explanation, and he had tried.

Amazingly enough, Mohit still remembered so much about Mona although not too much about Baba. Aie had made her boys take a box of old things down from the loft and the three of them had gone through the dust-covered memories. Mona's school workbooks with doodles in the margins, birthday cards she had colored in, her doctor set, her science medal, the doll Rahul had pressed into her hand when the fever had developed. They had started in silence and then found their way into old unforgotten stories, one word at a time, holding Aie as she finally spilled the tears she had held in for too long.

Someone from Mohit's gang of friends had led Asif to him, and Mohit had rethought his loyalties and decided to go back and finish his engineering degree. Unlike Rahul, he enjoyed designing machines and tinkering with them all day.

"Kimi knows how I feel," Rahul had told Mohit, and Mohit had rolled his eyes. Kimi, naturally, was suddenly best friends with his brother. It was probably why he was back in college. Rahul had felt like a teenager asking, but he had asked anyway. "Has she said anything to you? About me, I mean."

Having his baby brother laugh at him had been a bit humiliating but also nice, in a strange way. "She'll kill me if I get in the middle of this. She's been through some solid shit, so I would be patient, give her time." He had patted Rahul's shoulder. "You know how she is. She'll find a way to put it behind her."

"And you know this from knowing her a month?"

"Am I wrong?"

Truthfully, Rahul didn't know. Everything about her felt different now. And it didn't matter, because he was leaving. He had accepted a posting in New Delhi. He left next week. He had a ton to do, but he couldn't get off this damn rock. The tide was rising, and if he didn't leave soon the path of rocks leading back to the beach would get submerged and he'd be a soaking-wet mess. Well, even more of a soaking-wet mess than he already was.

"You're leaving Mumbai?" she said from behind him.

He twisted around and caught her swaying precariously on the rock. He grabbed her arm before she toppled into the ocean and she maneuvered herself down next to him, squeezing in tight because there was no space for distance here on their rock.

"You weren't even going to say good-bye?" she said before he could answer the previous question.

"You asked me to leave you alone."

But she had come for him.

In all the times that she had asked him to go away and leave her alone, he'd been the one who had gone to her, unable to stay away. Now here she was.

She had come for him. And for the first time since he had told her about Kirit's crime, she looked like herself. A slightly dimmed version, but the brightness was there, shimmering under that beautiful skin, shining behind those beautiful eyes, waiting to find its way back again.

"I came because there are a few things I have to get off my chest," she said in a tone that attempted to dump ice on the warmth rising fast inside him. "I need you to hear me out. And then you can decide what you want to do."

He already knew what he wanted to do. But he raised a hand, asking her to go on.

She didn't, not for a long while.

So he waited, watching her watch the waves.

Finally, she spoke, not to him but to the

waves, her chin resting on the knees she was hugging close. "What Papa did. It's heinous. Every time I think about it, it makes everything I've lived through worthless. I hate it. I hate everything about it. I hate myself for it."

"I know." His words made her squeeze herself tighter.

"Do you know what the worst part of it is? It was love that made him do it. It was love that made my mother disappear into temples for all those years." She went silent again for several long moments and then finally faced him, her cheek pressed against her knees. "You know I've always loved you. Always. For as long as I can remember. Even over the past year when I tried so badly not to, I did." She straightened and rubbed her hand across her chest, where that puckered scar sliced her in half and gave her life.

He had dragged his lips up and down that scar. He wanted to do it again now, forever.

"You make me feel this, this thing inside that makes me *me.* And I think I might be addicted to that feeling. I crave it. All the time. You know how I crawled into your lap that day? You remember that?"

All he could manage was the barest nod.

"I want to be able to do that whenever I

want. It makes me whole, Rahul. It makes everything all right. Maybe just for a few moments, but when you hold me, everything falls into place, here." She flattened her hand and pressed it into her scar.

Thus far he hadn't heard anything he couldn't live with. But he knew she was working up to a "but." A big one.

"Kimi," he said, loving how her eyes glowed at her name on his lips. "You know how I'm always telling you I never lied to you? Well, I did. But only one time."

"I know," she said.

He had to say it anyway. "When I told you I don't feel the same way. When I told you I didn't want you. I was telling the biggest lie of my life."

He reached to wipe the tears that rolled down her cheeks.

She shook her head, and he withdrew his hand. "Let me finish. I know how you feel. I always have. But don't you see? That's the problem. It doesn't matter that we love each other. Because look at what love does. It makes us cowards. What's the difference between my father and you? You're both terrified of the pain of losing those you love, specifically me. You deal with it by keeping me at a distance. He deals with it by doing whatever it takes to keep from losing me."

Distance? She thought he kept her at a distance? Was she insane? She was so deep inside him, he could barely breathe from it.

"See, look at your face. I know how you feel, and I know how it makes you act. It sends you off behind your walls, terrifies you, makes you lie and push me away. But you know what, Rahul, I'm sick of it. I just found out my father loved me enough to let innocents die. This isn't love. Not his, not yours. It's fear. And I can't live with it. I don't want to." With that she stood.

But she had to be out of her mind if she thought he was letting her go after that.

He held her hand. "That's it? You come here, you have your say, and then you walk away?"

She didn't move.

"How can it not be love, Kimi? How can it be the same thing?"

She looked down at him. "Tell me how it's different."

Where did he start? When there was no beginning, no end to this thing in his heart. "I don't think I can, Kimi. I don't think there are words to explain how I feel. It's like you're inside me, all the time. And still when you aren't near me, it feels like I'm missing myself. How can I not be afraid?"

For a moment she went all soft — eyes,

lips, body. But then she steeled herself and sank down next to him again. "You think I don't understand? That monster shot at you." Her voice hitched. "You're a cop, Rahul. Every day you leave the house with a gun holstered to your chest. I've seen you wearing a bulletproof vest. Do you know what I thought the first time I saw you in a vest?" She swallowed, but she didn't break eye contact. "I thought, your head is exposed. They cover your chest, but your brain can still be blown away. Every day for the rest of my life you will go out that way and chase down psychopaths. I'm not the only one who comes with a high probability of loss."

He had never considered that. Never considered that she had pushed him to do something he loved, even though it meant she lived in fear of losing him.

He let her hand go and cupped her cheek, cradling her softness in his roughness.

She leaned into his touch. The way she always did. "I'm scared too, Rahul. But my fear of losing you I can handle. What I can't handle is being afraid of how far you'll go to not lose me. I won't live forever. You won't either. But the truth is, I was born with a shit ton of problems with my body. If you can't deal with that, we have no chance."

He smiled. Only she could call them a shit ton of problems as though she were talking about pesky bird droppings on a window.

She stroked his smile, her touch soft. But her eyes were fierce. "I can't constantly be afraid of you not being able to deal with the pain of losing me. I can't be afraid that you will push me away because you can't handle that I can get sick again. Or worse, that you might do something horrible to keep me alive. I want you to love me for me, for now, for as much time as we have. I swear I'll do all I can to take care of myself. I already do. But that's it. If that's enough, I'm yours. If you can only love me if you have a guarantee that I'll be around forever, then find someone else to be terrified of losing and let me go."

He wrapped his arm around her and pulled her tight against him. The way his arm fit around her, her waist in his hand, her side flush into his. The rightness of it. The inevitability of it. How had he ever considered letting that go because he was too much of a coward? How had he ever believed it even possible?

She looked up at him, about to say more, but he dropped a kiss on her lips. The current that buzzed from her lips to his lit up his entire body. Above them, thunder rumbled through the monsoon sky. For weeks now, it had been swollen with possibility, stubbornly refusing to give the earth what it craved. They looked up, a joint expectation gathering in their eyes, and caught the first drops of the first rain on their faces.

She grinned like a bloody two-year-old and he had the crazy urge to do the same. Then she got somber as a yogi again as she faced him. "I can't see my death in your eyes every day, Rahul."

He pulled her close until their lips were touching again. "Will you talk so much the entire time we have together?" he said against her lips. "Because we're going to be together." Because they already were and always had been. "Forever. And with so much talk that could be a very" — he stretched out that word, rubbed it against her lips — "very long time."

Her smile against his mouth was the sweetest sensation he knew. "Why, yes, officer," she said, doing her best American accent from the movies, "unless you find a way to shut me up."

Oh, he knew exactly how to shut her up. In fact, he knew nothing he enjoyed more. And so he did. For a nice, long time. With the ocean churning around them and the long-awaited rain drizzling down on them.

When the ocean rose to their ankles, he pulled away. "You want to go home?" he asked. Not that he had any idea where their home would be.

She nodded. Didn't even ask where.

"It's where we're together, you goose," she said. "But New Delhi sounds nice for a bit."

He took her hand, and they hopped the rocks back to the beach, tracing a path as ancient and familiar as the thing that tied them together. The rain made a racket as it pitter-pattered against the already noisy ocean. The heady scent of parched earth as it drank up the raindrops rose around them.

"I feel like I should make some sort of grand declaration," he said, stradling Tina and starting her up. "This moment calls for it."

Kimi hopped on and wrapped herself against his back. "I don't need promises, Rahul. I don't want to be loved to the point of madness."

He twisted around and fitted his helmet on her head. "Kimaya Patil," he said, "I, Rahul Savant, promise to love you just short of the point of madness." And with that they were off.

■ ■ ■ ■

READING GROUP GUIDE: A DISTANT HEART

SONALI DEV

■ ■ ■ ■

ABOUT THIS GUIDE

The following questions are included to enhance your group's reading of Sonali Dev's *A Distant Heart*.

DISCUSSION QUESTIONS

1. Kimi often pushes Rahul to do things she wants him to do because she thinks they are good for him, like becoming a police officer. On the other hand, Kimi's parents push her to do things they think are good for her. Do you think this is love or crossing boundaries? Why?

2. Rahul is thrust too early into adulthood, and Kimi is trapped in an extended childhood. How do you think this influences their choices and their story?

3. If you were in Kimi's place, would you be able to forgive Kirit? How about Rahul's brother, Mohit? Would you be able to forgive Rahul if you were in Mohit's place?

4. Rahul doesn't visit Kimi in the hospital because he's sure it would lead to bad

things. Have you ever felt ruled by superstition? How does this story explore superstition?

5. Kirit starts off thinking he was paying to move Kimi to the top of the heart transplant list. He believes this is somehow less evil than purchasing a heart outright on the black market. Do you think one is different from the other? How and why?

6. How did the twin timelines work for you in terms of storytelling?

7. Kimi and Rahul come from vastly different financial backgrounds. Kimi feels like that is only an issue because she's the one with the money. Do you think society's perception of significant financial inequities between couples is biased based on gender?

8. Kimi tests Rahul's friendship repeatedly by pushing him away. How did you feel about the way they both navigate this aspect of their relationship?

9. As a parent, can you identify with Kimi's parents' obsession with keeping Kimi alive at any cost? How far would you go for a

loved one? How far is too far?

10. What are the lessons Kimi and Rahul are taught about love by their parents, their community, each other? What are the similarities and differences?

11. Grief is a natural response to loss. It is the emotional suffering when a beloved thing is taken away. The grief associated with death is familiar to most people, but individuals grieve in connection with a variety of losses throughout their lives. All of the characters have multiple things to grieve over. What other losses aside from death have any of the characters been affected by and how does that affect their grieving process.

12. The stages of grief are: denial, anger, bargaining, depression, and acceptance (in any order). Were these evident in any of the characters during specific times of their lives? Did you see them transition from one stage to another or reach acceptance?

ABOUT THE AUTHOR

Award winning author **Sonali Dev** writes Bollywood-style love stories that let her explore issues faded by women around the world while still indulging her faith in a happily ever after. Sonali's novels have been on *Library Journal,* NPR, *Washington Post,* and *Kirkus* Best Books lists. She won the American Library Association's award for best romance in 2014, is a RITA Finalist and *RT* Reviewer Choice Award Nominee, and is a winner of the *RT* Seal of Excellence. Sonali lives in the Chicago suburbs with her very patient and often amused husband, two teens who demand both patience and humor, and the world's most perfect dog. Find out more at sonalidev.com.

The employees of Thorndike Press hope you have enjoyed this Large Print book. All our Thorndike, Wheeler, and Kennebec Large Print titles are designed for easy reading, and all our books are made to last. Other Thorndike Press Large Print books are available at your library, through selected bookstores, or directly from us.

For information about titles, please call:
  (800) 223-1244

or visit our website at:
  gale.com/thorndike

To share your comments, please write:
  Publisher
  Thorndike Press
  10 Water St., Suite 310
  Waterville, ME 04901